# STONES
## OF
# JERUSALEM

**Other Books by Bodie and Brock Thoene**

*Jerusalem Vigil*

*Thunder from Jerusalem*

*Jerusalem's Heart*

*The Jerusalem Scrolls*

*Shiloh Autumn*

*The Twilight of Courage*

*The Zion Covenant Series*

*The Zion Chronicles Series*

*The Shiloh Legacy Series*

*The Saga of the Sierras*

*The Galway Chronicles*

*The Wayward Wind Series*

# BODIE AND BROCK THOENE

# STONES
## OF
# JERUSALEM

## THE ZION LEGACY

*Book V*

VIKING

VIKING
Published by the Penguin Group
Penguin Putnam Inc., 375 Hudson Street, New York, New York 10014, U.S.A.
Penguin Books Ltd, 80 Strand, London WC2R 0RL, England
Penguin Books Australia Ltd, 250 Camberwell Road, Camberwell, Victoria 3124, Australia
Penguin Books Canada Ltd, 10 Alcorn Avenue, Toronto, Ontario, Canada M4V 3B2
Penguin Books India (P) Ltd, 11 Community Centre, Panchsheel Park,
New Delhi–110 017, India
Penguin Books (N.Z.) Ltd, Cnr Rosedale and Airborne Roads, Albany,
Auckland, New Zealand
Penguin Books (South Africa) (Pty) Ltd, 24 Sturdee Avenue,
Rosebank, Johannesburg 2196, South Africa

Penguin Books Ltd, Registered Offices:
Harmondsworth, Middlesex, England

First published in 2002 by Viking Penguin,
a member of Penguin Putnam Inc.

1   3   5   7   9   10   8   6   4   2

Map illustration by James Sinclair

Excerpts from *The Poems* by Propertius, translated by W. G. Shepherd (Penguin Classics, 1985). Copyright © W. G. Shepherd, 1985. Reprinted by permission of Penguin Books Ltd.
     Excerpts from *The Holy Bible, New International Version.* Copyright © 1973, 1978, 1984 by International Bible Society. Used by permission of Zondervan Publishing House. All rights reserved.
     Excerpts from *Complete Jewish Bible,* translated by David H. Stern. Copyright © 1998 by David H. Stern. Used by permission of Jewish New Testament Publications, Inc., Clarksville, Maryland.

*Publisher's Note*
This is a work of fiction. Names, characters, places, and incidents either are the product of the author's imagination or used fictitiously, and any resemblance to actual persons, living or dead, business establishments, events, or locales is entirely coincidental.

LIBRARY OF CONGRESS CATALOGING-IN-PUBLICATION DATA

Thoene, Bodie, 1951–
Stones of Jerusalem / Bodie and Brock Thoene.
p.   cm.—(The Zion legacy ; bk. 5)
ISBN 0-670-03051-1
1. Israel-Arab War, 1948–1949—Fiction.  2. Jews—Palestine—Fiction.
I. Thoene, Brock, 1952–   II. Title.
PS3570.H46 S76 2002
813'.54—dc21          2001046560

This book is printed on acid-free paper. ∞
Printed in the United States of America
Set in Minion

This story is for our grandchildren:
Connor, Titan, Ian, Jessie, and Chance—
*you are loved!*

"Let the little children come to me. . . ."
—Matthew 19:14

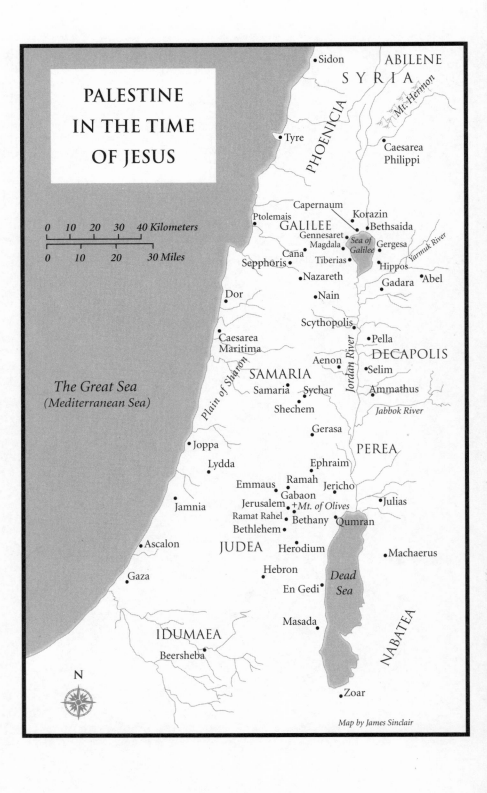

**PALESTINE IN THE TIME OF JESUS**

0    10    20    30    40 Kilometers

0    10    20    30 Miles

The Great Sea
(Mediterranean Sea)

Sidon

ABILENE

SYRIA

PHOENICIA

Mt. Hermon

Tyre

Caesarea Philippi

Capernaum
Ptolemais        Korazin
GALILEE        Bethsaida
Gennesaret        Gergesa
Magdala   Sea of   Yarmuk River
Cana        Galilee
Sepphoris     Tiberias   Hippos
Nazareth        Gadara   Abel

Dor

Nain

Scythopolis

Caesarea        Pella
Maritima        DECAPOLIS
Aenon
Plain of Sharon   SAMARIA   Selim
Samaria   Sychar   Ammathus
Shechem        Jabbok River

Jordan River

Gerasa

Joppa        PEREA

Lydda   Ephraim

Emmaus   Ramah   Jericho
Gabaon
Jamnia   Jerusalem   +Mt. of Olives   Julias
Ramat Rahel   Bethany   Qumran
Bethlehem

Ascalon   JUDEA   Herodium   Machaerus

Gaza   Hebron   Dead
En Gedi   Sea

IDUMAEA   Masada

Beersheba

N

Zoar

Map by James Sinclair

# PROLOGUE

*The Russian Compound*
*New City Jerusalem*
*May 28, 1948*

The underbelly of spiraling smoke glowed red from the inferno that raged in Old City Jerusalem.

Tonight the conquered Jewish Quarter was totally engulfed by flame. Captured synagogues, homes, and shops collapsed upon themselves with a rumble like thunder. It was a scene reminiscent of Kristallnacht in Nazi Germany.

Tens of thousands of sacred Torah scrolls from Jewish schools and houses of worship were heaped in the streets by the conquering warriors of the Jihad.

Hebrew writings were doused with kerosene and ignited as the Jihad Moquades danced in celebration of their great victory. Tongues of flame devoured the ancient writings. Fragments of parchment drifted over the walls on the breeze. The Jewish-held New City was blanketed in gray residue. Jews who survived the battle for their existence grieved for what was lost.

Among the mourners was eleven-year-old Yacov Lubetkin. The boy was one of twelve hundred Jewish refugees expelled from the Old City that afternoon. He sat on the steps outside the hospital in the Russian Compound to watch as flames consumed the dome of the Great Hurva synagogue. At his side was his Arab friend, Daoud ben Baruch. Two urchins roaming the souks of the Old City before the Islamic Jihad against the Jews had been declared, they were brothers of the heart.

The body of Yacov's grandfather, Rabbi Shlomo Lebowitz, had just been buried in the garden beside the chapel, with twenty-two others.

Yacov was stunned and exhausted. His face was monochrome, the color of ashes. Solemn brown eyes were tearless as he sat in speechless misery.

His world had come crashing to an end. How many dead had the Old City Jews left behind in their exodus? Who would find those trapped in the rubble of bombed-out buildings? Who would say kaddish over the graves of those buried in the rose garden of Gal'ed? No one was left. Not one.

The despair was palpable.

"Why?" Yacov whispered. "Why do they hate us so, Daoud?"

Daoud grasped Yacov's hand and said nothing. It would be hard to imagine the Old City without a single Jew. Had there ever been such a time? Daoud wondered, searching the profile of his friend.

The old underground synagogue of Ben Zakkai had existed for two thousand years, since the time the Roman Legions burned the Great Temple to the ground.

Eight hundred years ago, Maimonides had come to Jerusalem and found Jews praying at the Western Wall.

There were Jews in the Old City when the first Moslem Seljuks conquered it.

And in the Crusades.

Then when the Turks came.

And when the English entered Jerusalem after the First World War.

Now life as they had known it had come to an end.

Inside the makeshift hospital, teams of doctors performed surgery on the wounded with anesthetics secretly carried to besieged Jewish Jerusalem from Tel Aviv on the backs of men and mules. At least it was something, wasn't it? Some glimmer of hope for Jewish survival, Daoud thought.

And there were other things to be glad about, weren't there? Like the baby. Yes. Daoud would tell Yacov about the baby. He inhaled, then coughed. The acrid scent of smoke only partially masked the smell of death that permeated the city. Choosing his words carefully, Daoud said, "Something good has happened inside hospital as you were burying Rabbi Lebowitz."

Yacov did not acknowledge his friend, and yet he did not stop him from speaking.

Daoud continued, "A baby girl was born to a woman whose husband is missing. She said she would not name the baby until her husband came back to her."

Yacov blinked at the conflagration and remarked bitterly, "No one is coming out of that alive. My sister Rachel's husband . . . Moshe? He stayed behind . . . and so many others. I told my sister . . . there's no one left."

Daoud reckoned that this was probably true. "Maybe you are right, my friend. But all the same . . . when you were beside your grandfather's grave, this is what happened: the baby was born. I heard it cry with my own ears. And when the doctor showed the mother her little girl, he said to her, 'If you will not name her, then I will.' So, you know what he called this new baby?"

Yacov, reflecting a moment, replied, "They should call her Mourner . . . because she will never see her father."

Daoud shook his head vigorously. "No, Yacov! Listen to this! The doctor said to the mother, 'Dear lady . . . until you see your husband again, we will call this little girl Hope. Because . . . you know . . . it is written . . . every new baby born into such a world as this is proof that God still has hope for us. . . .'"

Yacov only stared at the crimson-tinged clouds billowing up from what had been his home.

Daoud was sorry he had told his friend the story. Maybe it was not a good thing to speak of something good to someone in mourning like Yacov.

At last Yacov dipped his chin in acknowledgment. "Grandfather used to say that very thing." The boy smiled at a memory. "He would have said it again if only he had lived. To hear that a baby was born tonight of all nights . . . now that we've lost everything but our lives. I remember him saying, every time a new baby was born . . . God is an optimist. . . . So, that's all we have left, Daoud. Hope. Maybe it's enough. Now it's everything, isn't it?"

■ ■ ■ ■

Bathed and dressed in full-length white linen tunics, Moshe Sachar and Alfie Halder returned to the main hall of Jerusalem's hidden library, far beneath the Temple Mount.

The candle flame wavered, then slowly extinguished to a glowing speck on the end of the wick. A finger of smoke pointed upwards. Light collapsed upon itself; yet, within the immense chamber, it was not dark.

Golden planets, stars, constellations, and galaxies glistened realistically above the heads of Moshe and Alfie as they sat together at the table.

Hebrew letters written on the open scroll sparkled, distinct and readable.

Alfie, slow-witted but somehow wise, looked up into the night sky and whispered in awe, "He spoke and there was 'light.'"

Moshe stared in wonder at the ceiling as the Great Nebula of Orion emerged in a mist of blues and muted shades of lavender. For an instant the four stars of the trapezium seemed to separate into eight double stars spinning in perfect orbit around one another. Galactic details discovered only in the recent past were faithfully reproduced on the domed ceiling of the main hall.

Tiers of balconies and shelves packed with clay manuscript jars climbed the walls like roses on a trellis. On the exterior of every container phosphorescent letters gleamed gold, identifying the precious contents.

Moshe gazed up at the depicted universe and traced the spidery thread of Hebrew text connecting pinpoints of light with the words "The heavens declare the glory of God."

After a moment Moshe remarked, "The first time I was here with Rabbi Lebowitz he lit a lantern. I read for hours, never suspecting what was hidden by the glare of it."

Alfie nodded his big head. "*Ja.* Sure. I seen a rabbit once in the road. Blinded in motorcar headlamps. You know. The rabbit stayed put. Didn't hop away. So, the old rabbi pinned you like a rabbit in the light, eh?"

"And the next time as well," Moshe said wryly. "I didn't see the stars. I thought the vaults were unadorned stone."

Alfie grinned at the sky. "I didn't have a torch. The ceilings of the side rooms. Food storage. Places for sleeping. The bath. The cistern. The skies are like this, *ja?* Each one different. Like camping on a mountain in the summer and looking up, you know? Stars. Too many to count. A candle ruins it."

Often Moshe had walked through the desert wilderness at night with merely a lantern to guide him. While the beam lit the ground under his feet, it obscured the wonders of a star-frosted sky. It was the same here. True illumination had been prevented by the lamp he carried. A tiny flame had blinded him to the glory all around. Wax and wicks and matches were a hindrance, not a help, in comprehending the mystery of the chamber.

Clearly this was a place of wonders, waiting to be discovered. Everything meant something, the old rabbi had told him. Moshe tried to think through the instructions Rebbe Lebowitz had given.

"Rebbe Lebowitz said I would have to learn to tell time if I had to stay here." Moshe glanced at his wristwatch. The second hand swept faithfully around the dial. Would the timepiece last? If there was light so far beneath the ground, then there must be some method to measure the passage of hours and days, months and years.

*Years!* Could they stay here for years?

"There's no time here. See?" Alfie said, unconcerned. "The stars don't move. Just everybody's story . . . waiting. Over there." He gestured expansively at the tiered shelves. "All around. They're waiting to be opened. To tell what happened. See? This is where you and me wait too. You read. I listen."

Moshe glared unhappily at the watch face. Another sweep of the second hand, yet the minute did not advance. "What's this? Broken?"

"Throw away your watch, Moshe. It'll make you unhappy when you think of Rachel. Time is . . . you know . . . a tree saying it owns the wind. You can't keep time here. Not here. Not inside the books. Stars don't move here."

Moshe sighed. Alfie clearly did not understand that the painted universe above his head was not real. Or that time continued on as usual in the world above their heads. It was a period of great sadness. The sun had set for the last time on the Jewish Quarter. Soon it would rise upon an Old City completely emptied of Jews and under strict Muslim rule. Muslim religious leaders would claim the heaps of Jewish rubble were proof that Allah had no mercy for anyone in El Kuds who did not follow the ways of the Prophet.

Moshe held the watch to his ear. It ticked comfortingly. "It's five in the morning. Saturday. Shabbat." He thought about his wife of three months, Rachel, and their last good-bye. Was she well? Had the mortally wounded Rabbi Lebowitz lived long enough to explain where Moshe had gone? Or was she left to wonder?

Upon the rebbe's urging Moshe and Alfie had descended into the secret tunnel beneath Jerusalem and entered the chamber exactly twelve hours earlier. Could it be? Moshe shook his head in disbelief. Only yesterday the Jewish Quarter of the Old City had fallen to the Arab Legion. By now everyone had been taken away. Fifteen hundred Jewish civilians, including Moshe's wife, Rachel, were escorted to the Jewish-held New City and mercifully released. As for the handful of surviving Jewish Haganah defenders, they were now on their way to an Arab prison camp in Jordan. British officers serving in Jordan's Arab Legion had saved them all from being massacred by an enraged mob of Muslim mercenaries who came from Iraq, Iran, Syria, and Egypt to exterminate the Jews and the nation of Israel.

Moshe and Alfie had escaped through the underground passageway. Even now the mighty Jewish synagogues, Torah schools, and homes of the Quarter were being looted and burned to rubble. Sacred Torah scrolls, manuscripts, and Jewish religious artifacts were piled in heaps in the street, then torched. Yet as the smoke from three thousand years of Jewish presence in Jerusalem blotted out the dawn, Moshe Sachar and Alfie Halder guarded the most precious treasures of Jewish antiquity: the Jerusalem Scrolls.

The warren of passageways beneath the Temple Mount might still be discovered by the Muslim mobs and traced to the chamber containing the manuscripts. If that happened, Moshe and Alfie would seal off the entry to prevent its desecration and destruction. And yet, in so doing, they would also block their own way of escape forever.

From the moment Rabbi Lebowitz had shown him the library, Moshe had understood the risk and the importance of their charge. Alfie had simply accepted the task cheerfully and without question. Storage rooms were stacked with food cisterns filled with water, enough to last for years. Each guardian had a place to sleep, clothes to wear. More important for Moshe, an archaeologist and professor of ancient languages at Hebrew University, there were thousands of manuscripts to study and translate. Enough to pass a lifetime happily, if not for the fact that he had to leave Rachel behind. Rebbe Lebowitz had given him the order in which the first documents should be studied. There was also a sheaf of instructions, written in code, as to what must follow.

"Only twelve hours." Moshe rolled up the first scroll of Miryam Magdalen and Marcus Longinus and returned it carefully to its storage container.

Then Alfie's eyes widened in amazement. He stared over Moshe's shoulder at nothing. "You'll see her again," he declared with certainty. "She's well. And the children. All of them. Jerusalem will be fed and washed. Yes. I see."

Moshe turned to look behind him. There was no one there. What vision had the big man seen? "Where have you gone?"

Alfie grinned, suddenly returned. He seemed not to hear the question. "The bath is nice, huh?" he blurted cheerfully. "The Hitler Youth kids in Berlin used to call me *Dummkopf, ja?* And hurt the other ragged kids . . . Blind. Deaf. Kill them first, they did. Like shooting sparrows out of the trees in the park. Then chase me home, throwing dog *Scheiss* at me. . . . 'Alfie! Alfie! *Dummkopf! Dummkopf!*'" He nodded at the painful memory. "So when I was sad because of it, my mama put me in a bath. I had this blue boat. The water helped. Good to play in water when you're sad. Put a kid in water when it's sad, she would say. Water works wonders, you know? No boat here though. No razor neither. Just water. The old rabbi had a beard. I guess I don't mind a beard. No mirrors here to look at my own face. It would be nice to have a boat, though."

"Alfie . . ." Moshe was certain the big man had heard some distant voice, seen someone from far away. "I need you to tell me."

Alfie closed his eyes and frowned. He shook his head sadly from side to side. "It's the same as it ever was. Truth can't speak. Light can't shine. *Sekel. Torah. Kever. Hayyim. Keter. Sod.*" He whispered, "Our ears have heard about him. Soon our eyes will see him face-to-face."

"When?"

"Soon."

"How?"

"It's written." Alfie's eyes snapped open. Tears brimmed.

Moshe recognized the six Hebrew words Alfie had spoken. Reb Lebowitz had recorded them as a part of the code he left for Moshe in a letter of instruction.

Had Moshe, in turn, read those words aloud to Alfie? Was Alfie simply parroting back what he had heard Moshe say?

Moshe scanned through the rabbi's letter until he found the list.

> *SEKEL*—Understanding
> *TORAH*—The Word
> *KEVER*—grave
> *HAYYIM*—life
> *KETER*—crown
> *SOD*—secrets

"What about now?" Moshe questioned Alfie.

Amusement crept across Alfie's broad face. "Read. I like stories."

"That's all?"

"It's everything."

Moshe accepted the statement as a sort of command. The old rabbi had left a detailed list of seventy scrolls to be studied first and the order in which they must be read. Scroll one, the first scroll of Marcus Longinus and Miryam Magdalen, had been returned to its place on the shelf.

What was next?

The second document on the list was identified simply as HAVER BAR YESHUA. The number of the shelf and scroll container was listed. Tier One. Scroll Three.

Moshe found it with ease. It was unique from the rest. Of higher quality. The jar was a first-century amphora with an exceptionally beautiful vine leaf pattern around the neck. Its purpose was to hold the best wine at a banquet. Moshe guessed that whoever had written this document must have been quite wealthy.

Alfie leaned forward eagerly but said nothing as Moshe opened it. The scroll was wrapped in a strip of multicolored woolen fabric. Homespun. Tightly woven material. Perhaps Galilean. A tiny brown feather was secured by the knot. Moshe carefully worked to open the parcel.

An instant later a fine lambskin scroll lay before them. The creamy discoloration of antiquity was slight. Like the first document, this appeared to be in perfect condition.

The title was written in square, neat Hebrew letters.

BLESSED ARE YOU WHO MOURN

# ADONAI

The name of the boy was Lo-Ahavah, which meant "Not Loved." The unwanted child of a prostitute, he had been abandoned at the quarry two years ago. The last thing his mother shouted at him as she walked away was, "Lo-Ruhamah! You are not pitied! Lo-Ahavah! You are not loved! Lo-Ammi! You are not my people! Don't follow me!"

His one friend, Hayyim, called him *Avel*. This meant, "Mourner," because it was a long time before the deserted boy had stopped weeping in the night for his lost mother.

Seven or maybe eight years old at the time known as the seventeenth year of the emperor Tiberius, Avel had no proper surname. He could have been the son of a stonemason from Gaul, or perhaps of a Roman soldier, a Greek philosopher, or even a rich Jewish merchant whom he passed daily on the street. Some said he had the look of the northern boundaries of the Roman empire about him. He was thin, but that was from lack of food. If properly cared for, he would have been a husky lad. His hands were square like those of a stone carver, his feet large like a soldier's. His eyes were blue as the sky on a summer day, nose straight, and cheekbones high. His hair was fair and straight.

"I'm too cold to sleep," Avel whispered to Hayyim.

Hayyim, who was nine, was as dark and scrawny as Avel was fair. "You wake me for that?" Hayyim replied drowsily. "You're always too cold unless you're too hot. I was dreaming of bread and pennies. A good dream."

Avel scolded, "Dream on, and we'll miss the real thing! It's Purim! Today is the day of *mattanot le-evyonim!* Presents to the poor, remember? The bread and pennies of Herod Antipas. Remember? You can't eat dreams. You can't spend dreams in the souks."

"Why'd you wake me? It's still dark."

"We'll be late. The fire's almost out." Avel stretched his hand toward the embers.

"Hmmm. Yes. The sun'll be up soon." Hayyim squinted toward the opening of the chamber.

"Shouldn't we go? Maybe they'll toss the bread and the pennies, and we'll miss it."

"A few more minutes." Hayyim snuggled further beneath the heap of filthy straw that served as bed and blanket.

Avel nudged him hard. "I smell bread in the ovens! Get up! Look there! Nearly everyone's gone already!"

Hayyim scanned the places around the fire where other boys slept. Even in the darkness he could see most of the straw nests were deserted. The others had snuck off, hoping to get the best positions for the handout. "Sure. All right." He sat up in the chill air and shuddered.

Dawn had not yet penetrated the chalky caverns of the rock quarry outside the walls of Jerusalem. It was here, in the hollow places of the earth, that enormous blocks of stone had been chiseled away to build the glorious structures of the city.

Beneath all this glory and all but ignored by its keepers, the poorest inhabitants of Yerushalayim lived in the empty stone womb where the Temple of the Almighty had been conceived and born.

Yochanan the Baptizer had once angered the rulers of the Sanhedrin by proclaiming that *Adonai,* the Lord, preferred the company of the Jerusalem quarry Sparrows over the companionship of those who strode the corridors of power above them. But neither Hayyim nor Avel had ever seen nor heard *Adonai* walking among them.

Abandoned by God and the temple masons long ago, the quarry served another purpose. Within the hewn chambers of Jerusalem's skeleton lived garbage sifters, bone pickers, madmen, idiots, and blind, deaf, or lame beggars.

Lastly there was a large contingent of orphan boys, known officially as *link boys.* Unofficially, however, they were called *Jerusalem Sparrows,* because they were plentiful and of such trifling value.

By day the Sparrows slept in the caves or stole food from the merchants in the souks. By night they worked for bread by bearing torches through Jerusalem's lightless and treacherous streets. This service of linking one part of the city with another by light was approved of by the Jewish religious leaders. Temple charity funds provided torches for the link boys, just as another part of the sacred treasury, called the *Korban,* bought sacrificial animals. Each night flocks of hopeful Sparrows waited outside the Temple gates and public buildings to guide travelers. They worked in pairs. Light to any part of Jerusalem, no matter how distant, could be purchased, two Sparrows for a penny. A half-penny each: this was the value of a Jerusalem Sparrow, whether boy or bird.

On this morning one hundred and forty-five link boys found sanctuary in the quarry. Destitute and without kin, they were from five years old to thirteen. Any child younger than five never survived long enough to be counted. Any healthy male older than thirteen was no longer qualified to receive Temple charity and so joined the ranks of bandits and cutpurses. The age of maturity was judged to have arrived when a boy sprouted a beard. Thus it was decreed: no beards among the Sparrows.

Neither were there females in the caverns. A girl-child would not live one night.

The Jerusalem Sparrows shared the common goal of enduring on the fringe of a world that barely acknowledged their existence.

But today Purim and the birthday of the son of Herod the Great had dawned, and the Sparrows would be fed! The poor would be remembered! Charity and mercy would reign for one brief hour in the Holy City. From the balcony of the Hasmonaean Palace Herod Antipas would bow to the cheers of the people and offer them bread to eat today and money to buy a meal tomorrow!

Avel did not remember such an event in all his lifetime. "Come on, Hayyim! If we're going to be partners, we have to make a pact, eh? If I get a loaf of bread, I'll share it with you! If you get a penny, we'll share it. Half and half."

"This isn't a link," Hayyim said doubtfully. "We're not bearing torches. Why should I share what I get?"

"Because maybe I'll catch something, and you'll come up empty. Then you'd want to share. Wouldn't you? And if we don't stick together, Kittim will cause trouble. He'll take whatever we get, and we'll never see it again."

Kittim was the chief of Sparrows. He had a beard. It was scraggly, but a beard nonetheless. Kittim had sprouted his beard three years ago, yet he managed to dodge the authorities and remain in the caverns. He was at least sixteen. He took half of the earnings of the younger boys, saying they did not need as much to eat. From the older Sparrows he gleaned one-fourth of their take. He wore real sandals on his feet and had a cloak. He ate when he wanted and walked through the souks like a person instead of a Sparrow. No boy in the quarry was brave enough to resist him.

"Kittim. Someday the Temple Guard will catch up with him. Throw him out of here." Hayyim rubbed sleep from his eyes and picked straw from his matted hair. "Or he will insult one Roman too many, and they'll crucify him."

"Happy day. But until then we have to stick together." Avel extended his hand to Hayyim. "What do you say?"

"All right, then. A pact. Partners." The two clasped hands on the bargain.

Then, using the burnt end of a stick, they drew beards on one another's chins and darkened their eyebrows. The children of Jerusalem's wealthy would dress in Persian silk costumes today.

"What's our disguise for the play of Queen Esther?" Avel queried when the makeup was finished.

Hayyim frowned. "We are poor Jews. That's it! The poor Jews the evil Haman wants to destroy."

Avel considered the answer with satisfaction. It was good that even a Jerusalem Sparrow had a part to play on such a day as this.

■ ■ ■ ■

Breaking the wave of darkness, the billowed moon sailed west over the rim of the world. Stars followed after, fleeing the approach of dawn. Tattered clouds, like scarlet banners, drifted on the east wind.

"Red sky at morning," Centurion Marcus Longinus remarked to Tesserarius Quintus as the two men stood on the ramparts of the Antonia Fortress overlooking Jerusalem.

"A stormy day for certain," replied Quintus. The grim-faced, square-jawed Roman veteran was old enough to be father to the thirty-two-year-old centurion.

Marcus clasped his battle-scarred hands together and leaned against the parapet to gaze down on the courtyard of the Jewish Temple. "We don't need a bloody sky to prophesy what the day holds for Jerusalem, do we, Quintus?"

"No, we do not," the guard sergeant replied testily. "Another Jewish festival! Purim! And the birthday of Herod Antipas on top of it! Two years ago I was here for the celebration. They'll be drunk. Half the Jews over the age of thirteen. And some younger besides. Today is rife for stampedes and riots."

The Jewish festival of Purim fell on the fourteenth day of Adar, the same day Herod Antipas celebrated his birthday. For the authorities it was a dismal combination. Purim commemorated the victory of the Jewish queen, Esther, over the wicked Haman, who planned to kill all the Jews of Persia. The rejoicing of the Jewish people was, according to some, a Talmudic command. Some rabbis taught that it was important to drink wine until it was impossible to recite a complicated rhyme. Others believed enough alcohol must be imbibed to put a person to sleep. Regardless of the official interpretation, water was for washing. Wine was the beverage of choice. Sobriety and sacredness had no part in the celebration of Purim.

"Today is proof of a divine sense of humor," Marcus mused. "Herod Antipas was born on Purim."

Quintus elaborated, "Why not? Day of the drunks. Everybody's happy. Antipas was born drunk and has been drunk ever since. Perfect fit if you ask me."

Herod Antipas and his court had come up to Jerusalem six days earlier. Heralds had been sent out into the streets to announce his intention to fulfill the mitzvah of *mattanot le-evyonim,* the giving of food and money to Jerusalem's poor.

Marcus replied, "The Jews will be swarming after Herod's free bread like honeybees in the comb. The sicarii will buzz like hornets among them, stinging where they can. And that's the tune Jerusalem will hear on this birthday of Herod Antipas. Honeybees and hornets. It's up to us to figure out which is which."

Quintus patted the hilt of his short sword. "We have the very thing to swat a few if they get too fierce.

"That's why Governor Pilate called us back to Jerusalem."

Quintus shrugged and grinned. "About time. Half a year of chasing bandits in the wilderness. The troopers are growing restless. Edgy, if you know what I mean. They need a trip to the house of the Samaritan women. Too long without a woman will spoil any man's disposition."

Marcus scratched the beard he had grown while on desert patrol, but did not reply. Quintus' observation was aimed at him.

It hit the target.

It had been a long time since Marcus had been with a woman. Six months since he had known for certain that Miryam of Magdala was the one woman he wanted. Yet with that certainty had come the knowledge that he could never admit his love to her. For her to be seen with a Roman officer again would surely destroy her attempt at a new life.

Now that Miryam was a follower of the teacher Yeshua of Nazareth, Marcus had given up his home in Capernaum, withdrawn from Galilee, and requested that Commander Felix return him to active duty. Certain he would get his wish, he had welcomed the least desirable assignment in the Roman army. He and his century of one hundred men patrolled the barren wilderness east of the Jordan river that led to the Dead Sea.

But as the Spring cycle of Jewish festivals approached they were required in Jerusalem.

The smell of baking bread wafted through the air.

Herod Antipas planned to distribute free bread and freshly minted coins to the masses. This was also a common practice by the rulers of Rome to win popularity with the people. But such fetes never turned out well. Marcus had witnessed several such gatherings dissolve into tragedy and violence. He hoped that Antipas had ordered loaves enough for everyone and that tiny brass coins would fall like rain.

Nothing, however, could make Herod Antipas popular. He was hated by everyone, including his half-brother, whose wife now shared his bed.

It was a delicate and complicated situation. Antipas had other siblings. He was also loathed by his half-brother Philip, tetrarch in Golan, on the other side of the Galilee. Rome had quite a job of keeping the Herod brothers from tearing one another apart. Each ruled a piece of Palestine. Each wanted the other piece. Ah, well. There was never enough to satisfy everyone. Not land. Not bread. Inevitably, it would turn ugly. It always did. Marcus winced at the thought of what this day would bring.

Marcus muttered, "Happy birthday, Herod Antipas. Lecherous bag of guts."

Quintus guffawed in agreement.

Jerusalem had hated Antipas' father, Herod the Great, with a legendary vehemence. And yet consider what Great Herod had given them in his effort to win their love!

The Temple. The glory of Jerusalem spread out beneath Marcus' view. Another Purim custom, called the *mahatzit ha-shekel*, required that each adult male Israelite donate a half-shekel toward the maintenance of the Temple in Jerusalem.

"Strange creatures, these Jews," Quintus remarked. "They camp in squalor in the fields during their autumn holiday, while the temple they've built for their god is the most glorious in the world. I'd like to tuck a single golden pomegranate into my pack, let alone the clusters of golden grapes as big as a man."

Marble walls and enormous gates overlaid with gold, silver, and Corinthian bronze testified to the glory of the exterior. Marcus had glimpsed the beauty of the inside through the open portals. "Such a palace built for their god will eventually provoke the jealousy of emperors, I think."

"Enough gold and silver to sink the Roman fleet," Quintus said. "There's no other reason for Rome to be interested in this place. Easy enough to conquer an army of peasants camped in huts and waving palm branches. Attack them when they're collected here praying and dancing. It'll come to that one autumn."

Marcus knew Quintus was remembering the Fall festival when Miryam was dragged before Yeshua of Nazareth in the courtyard of the Temple and condemned to be stoned.

From where Marcus stood he could clearly see the pavement where she had cowered before her accusers, where the enigmatic Yeshua had stooped to write in the dust with his finger; where the religious rulers had backed away in shame at what they read.

That moment had freed Miryam's soul.

It had also changed Marcus forever. He knew then that he had lost her and yet, somehow, his love for her was greater than his own desire.

Now he was here again.

The walls of the Antonia fortress soared over the Temple Mount. The stronghold was an ever-present reminder that while the Jews might keep their worship of a never-named deity, it was Rome that ruled.

Three of the guard towers at the Antonia's corners were equal in height, but the fourth . . . the one nearest the Jews' sanctuary . . . was taller than the others. From its peak a man could survey the entirety of the Jews' holy mountain. Marcus could clearly see the unfinished frame of Pilate's aqueduct. Rumors were thick that the Roman governor had run out of money before the project was complete. It was a pity. If Jerusalem needed anything, it needed water.

The Temple Mount was enclosed by the three-quarter-mile circuit of the double colonnade. The expanse displayed a patchwork of paving stones: rich browns, like Marcus's eyes, somber, glistening blacks, warm ambers, and mottled grays flecked with crystal.

It was on this, the loftiest vantage point in Jerusalem, that Marcus and Quintus stood as the sun cracked open the horizon. A beam of blinding light struck the gold gilt cornice of the Temple and pierced Marcus' eye. He squinted and shielded his face with his hand. He noted, "I've heard that this is the year the Jews will say their blessing on the sun."

"There's a kind of worship I can understand. The sun will appreciate their gratitude! Especially after such a winter!" Quintus said enthusiastically.

"Only every twenty-eight years. They say on that day the sun returns to the same position it held in the sky on the fourth day of creation. It shines through that corridor of east-facing gates and directly into the Jews' sanctuary. The light striking the gold inside is blinding, they say." Marcus pointed to the T-shaped roof that identified the holiest part of the Temple.

"So the Jews are secretly sun-worshippers?" Quintus inquired derisively. "Like your relatives in Britannia, eh?"

Marcus laughed at the jibe. After years of duty in Palestine, he knew that the guard sergeant was not serious. Marcus was half-British but raised wholly Roman. His ruddy complexion, russet hair, and stocky build concealed a man educated in the equestrian class of Rome. "Mother once told me my Druid kin worship in the stone circles at Winter solstice. Shortest day of the year. Freezing cold. Wind howling. Blowing snow and rain sideways. Miserable. The priests offer their daughters to the sun in hopes it will come back. A long way from all this . . ." He gestured toward the gleaming edifice.

"One sun-worshipper is like another. Solstice. Equinox. Jews blessing the sun every twenty-eight years. What's the difference?"

"Jews are scholars. Mathematicians. The equinox. A way of calculating time. The sun is halfway through its journey north and south. Day and night are equal in length. I've heard the rabbis teach that equinox is a day to remember that their one God created the heavens and the earth and divided light from darkness."

Quintus snorted. "They might as well worship the sun! Or *anything*, for that matter. One god! They say when the Roman conqueror, the magnificent Pompey, entered their shrine a hundred years ago, he found nothing inside . . . nothing! What's the purpose of keeping secret an empty room? What use is a god who has no form you can recognize and whose name you can't speak? It's pointless!"

Quintus, like most legionaries, despised the Jews. Perhaps, Marcus thought, one day the battle-worn guard sergeant would hear the words of Yeshua and feel differently. Until then there was no use in Marcus' trying to explain what he had seen and heard.

Marcus swung his arm westward from the gleaming expanse of white marble and traced the ramp of the causeway connecting the Temple Mount to the city. Beyond the foot of the incline rose the honey-colored stone structure of the Hasmonaean Palace, the site of Herod Antipas' Purim birthday celebration. Crowds were already gathering in the plaza near the building. Masses of people flowed down the slope to fight for the expected largesse.

"Bread and circuses," Marcus mused, changing the subject. "Antipas will give them bread, but it's up to us to see that the entertainment doesn't get out of hand."

Passover would follow in about a month. After three years as Prefect, Pontius Pilate had learned the hard way that Jews were a troublesome bunch and public celebrations often excuses to riot.

At any rate, no bandit, brigand, thief, or murderer turned down a chance to blend into the Jerusalem mobs. The sicarii rebels Marcus had been chasing in the wilderness would doubtless walk openly in the streets of the city for these coming days. Perhaps they also required a visit to the house of the Samaritan prostitutes.

# ADONAI EL

Daybreak.

With the sharp staccato notes of the shofar the first sacrifice of morning was offered. The courtyard of the Temple reverberated with the clamor of prayers, hymns, bleating sheep, bellowing cattle, and the cooing of doves.

The business of worshipping the Most High was a gigantic machine. Thousands of men from the tribe of Levi served as supervisors, police, musicians, and doorkeepers. Hundreds more *cohanim*, priests, conducted the ritual slaughtering. Workmen hauling stones and scaffolding, and artisans working in gold leaf and bronze carried out their assignments. The present expansion of the holy site had already lasted more than thirty years. Two hundred chief priests oversaw every aspect of devotion from tithe collecting to charity dispersing.

Caiaphas, *cohen hagadol*, High Priest of Israel, raised his razor-sharp knife and recited the prayer of blessing as he slit the throat of a lamb. The creature did not make a sound as it lay before him. It fell instantly limp as its life drained into a bowl. An assistant took the container from Caiaphas. The blood was splashed onto the four horned corners of the seventy-five-foot square altar as Caiaphas called out in supplication.

The air, already redolent with wood smoke, became thick with the aroma of charred animal fat and incense. The meat of later sacrifices would be eaten by the temple workers and their families. But the first and last lambs of each day's worship cycle were dedicated to *Adonai Elohim* alone . . . an appeal of propitiation for the whole community of Israel.

Today's unusually plentiful offerings purchased by Tetrach Herod Antipas would also be divided. Some would be returned to Antipas for his birthday banquet. The rest would be shared among those on duty at the Temple that day.

The skins of all sacrificial animals belonged to the *cohanim*. Needless to say, the priests and their relatives had a thriving business in leather goods.

It was easy for the common folk to spot the *cohanim* and their kin. Portly and soft, they were shod in the best leather sandals. In the winter they wore warm coats lined with sheep fleece.

Antipas, whose lust for his brother's wife was hotter than the flames of the altar, was providing a veritable fortune in hides to those who tended the fires.

This was on the mind of a Pharisee named Nakdimon ben Gurion as he completed his prayers, then lingered to watch the proceedings with his uncle, Gamaliel.

Both men were members of the Sanhedrin, a council of seventy religious leaders headed by the high priest who ruled over Jewish affairs in Jerusalem. Nakdimon was in his early-thirties—young to be on the council. He had inherited the position when his father died the year before.

Secretly called *The Bull* by his servants, Nakdimon was head and shoulders taller than any of his compatriots. His brown eyes were heavy lidded, his mouth turned up in perpetual amusement behind a thick brown beard. The Bull was a pleasant, easygoing man, and so the secret name had nothing to do with stature or a hot temper. Rather, Nakdimon had sired a herd of seven children: six girls and one boy. His wife of thirteen years had died bearing his son a year and a half ago. Since that day Nakdimon had dedicated himself to his children and the study of Torah. He resisted the urgings of friends and relatives to remarry. Like an eagle or a swan, Nakdimon embraced only one mate for his lifetime, and now Hadassah was gone. He was not interested in starting over in matters of love.

"Herod Antipas hopes to appease the Almighty with blood from bulls and sheep," Nakdimon observed. "And he appeases the people with bread and pennies. But where are the worshippers? Everyone in Judea is gathered at his gates. The Almighty is a jealous Lord. No one, not in heaven or earth, will be satisfied when the day's over, I think."

His uncle, Gamaliel, a man short of stature but long on wisdom, was a respected rabbi of forty-nine. He stroked his grizzled beard and noted, "As to the reaction of the Almighty to Herod Antipas' offerings, that's no business of Caiaphas or others of the *cohanim*."

Nakdimon replied, "The guilt of Herod Antipas will provide leather enough for every pilgrim's sandal to get a new sole."

"Sacrifice of the guilty has always been a matter of the soul," Gamaliel countered in mock seriousness.

Nakdimon answered, "His is a soul that has trod too long in the gutter, I think."

"The steps of a good man are ordered by *Adonai*, but as for the soul of the wicked?"

Nakdimon chewed his lip and gazed thoughtfully upward at the gold-faced cornice of the sanctuary as he considered his response.

Too long the hesitation. Gamaliel's sharp mind moved to other matters. Nudging Nakdimon, Gamaliel inclined his head toward the altar. "Look. He grows tired already."

Caiaphas and his assistants finished their prescribed course of sacrifice. Hard work, this daily offering of blood to cover the offenses of the guilty. So much guilt. So much blood. Other *cohanim* stepped up to take their place while a shift of a hundred moved silently to spell wood carriers, animal tenders, and those who butchered and divided the meat.

For the next eight and a half hours the seamless ritual would continue with rotating teams of men descended from the priestly tribe of Levi.

The last, true, hereditary high priest of Israel, however, had been the renowned and beloved Onias. He had been assassinated over one hundred fifty years before. Since the murder of Onias, the high priests of Israel had been political appointees; the office for sale to the highest bidder.

Caiaphas, friend of Rome, was no exception. Two decades earlier his father-in-law, Annas, had been high priest. Annas had been succeeded by each of his sons, then later by Caiaphas.

One family holding onto power because of their intimacy with Rome, Nakdimon thought.

Now Caiaphas was heir to the mantle of religious authority. A ruthless and corrupt man, he practiced the twin religions of power and pretense.

Nakdimon noted that Caiaphas was as adept at butchery as he was at politics. His white tunic was not marked with a drop of blood. Merely his hands were stained. Caiaphas turned and dipped his fingers in a bronze basin of water.

Since childhood Nakdimon had watched his own father swaying on the fence between his faith and the power of Rome. These days Nakdimon often wondered if it mattered to the Almighty what sort of man stood in the shoes of Aaron. Of legendary Zadok. Of the martyred Onias.

This was useless speculation, he knew. There was no righteous man in all this broken nation with the authority to step up to this altar. What man could offer the blood of the lamb for the sin of another with pure heart and clean hands?

Like the ignorant peasants of the provinces, Nakdimon often found himself wishing for the Deliverer to come to Jerusalem. A dangerous hope since Rome stationed its troops so close . . . on the battlements of the Antonia.

The smooth stone face of the looming fortress was more than merely a symbol of Roman rule. The gleaming facade was designed not solely for beauty but to repel any attempt to scale it. The boastful arrogance of its watchtowers looked down . . . in both senses . . . on the Jewish worshippers. Colonnades and courtyards, fountains and baths, made the Antonia as much palace as stronghold, capable of housing five hundred of the occupying forces of Rome in comfort. From there they could descend to violate the sanctity of the Temple Mount in less than two minutes' time.

Just as the Temple Mount dominated the skyline of the Holy City, the Antonia lorded it over the Mount . . . and the Roman occupiers over all!

And still the humiliation was not complete.

Within the Antonia the Romans kept the sacred garments worn by the *cohen hagadol* when he interceded for the forgiveness of Israel. Thus, the high priest of *Adonai Elohim* had to ask permission to dress for the once-a-year atonement ceremony.

Nakdimon turned his face away from the Roman soldiers watching from the ramparts of the fortress. His perpetual smile had faded. His pleasant expression hardened. *Oh, for a leader of courage to rouse the people! To sound the shofar in a call back to righteousness and then on to battle. How many Roman soldiers in Palestine? Fewer than five thousand altogether!*

Gamaliel whispered as though he heard Nakdimon's thoughts. "A dangerous vision, nephew. A vision your father had as well. We spoke of it privately in our younger days. He and I counted the years until Dani'el's prophecy would be fulfilled, you see, starting from the decree to rebuild the sanctuary. Seven sevens rebuilding the Second Temple, then sixty-two sevens until the Holy One of Israel will be cut off . . . whoever he is and whatever that may mean!"

Nakdimon did a quick multiplication in his head. "So about ten years remain until the fulfillment."

"Not quite," Gamaliel explained. "You must subtract the years of Jubilee from the total, one for each fifty years . . . which reduces the count by nine."

"But that means the time predicted by Dani'el will arrive within the year!"

"Close enough," Gamaliel agreed. "And don't think High Priest Caiaphas doesn't know these things . . . and fret about them! But what's from God won't be stopped by man. Nor will it be born before its hour." And then, linking arms with Nakdimon, the rabbi escorted him away from the front of the altar. "Come. I'll show you something."

Glancing aloft to judge the direction of the breeze, Gamaliel led his nephew to a vantage point from which the black smoke of the sacrifices did not obscure their view of the front of the sanctuary. The Temple appeared to be a perfect cube, one hundred fifty feet wide and the same measurement in height.

Sunlight streaming over their shoulders from behind flooded the Temple entrance. This archway was 105 feet tall and 37½ feet wide. The opening had no doors, but the surface around the entry was of hammered and polished gold, shimmering like a mirror.

The arch of precious metal perfectly framed Nakdimon's view into the first chamber of the Temple. The beam of light illuminated a tapestry that screened the further recesses of the Holy Place. Concealed by the curtain, Nakdimon knew, were a pair of golden doors, 82½ feet high and 24 feet wide. It was said that the outer curtain and golden doors symbolically separated earth from heaven. Through these doors the *cohanim* passed in their daily service to *Adonai Elohim.*

Inside the sixty-foot chamber were the seven-branched menorah, the table of holy bread, and the altar of incense, where a mixture of thirteen pleasant spices continuously ascended to the honor of the Almighty.

Behind the swirl of aromatic smoke, an inner curtain embroidered with vigilant cherubim sheltered the Holy of Holies. There the Ark of the Covenant rested; the place where the presence of *Adonai* came down to use Jerusalem as His footstool.

Only the *cohen hagadol* passed through the inner curtain, and he only once a year.

But any worshipper standing in the court of the Israelites could view the magnificent tapestry at the entry to the sanctuary and marvel at the mysteries that lay within.

It was to this outer curtain that Gamaliel directed Nakdimon's attention. "Tell me what you see."

Nakdimon studied the blue, purple, white, and scarlet embroidery. Since he had seen it many times before, he considered what the question truly meant before he replied.

Displayed on the eighty-foot-high panel were stars and planets . . . the heavens as seen from Jerusalem. The shimmering archway made it appear like a window into heaven on a star-studded night. The background color of the fabric was the deepest, richest purple. It was possible to imagine that the tapestry really was the sky. There were puzzling elements, though. Nakdimon could not remember seeing a night exactly like it.

"Something for you to ponder, Nephew," Gamaliel instructed. "The night pictured on this map of the stars and planets is the one Caiaphas fears most."

"He fears it?"

"As Herod the Great quaked in terror when the wise men explained the meaning of a different sky."

"Do you know the meaning of it, Uncle?"

Gamaliel smiled enigmatically. "Perhaps."

"Will you tell me then?"

"It is a puzzle. And when you have found the right questions to ask, I may be able to help you with a handful of the answers. Though no one knows them fully. This I can tell you: *Adonai* is watching over the shoulder of our *cohen hagadol* as the blood of the innocent is poured out on this altar each day. Yes. Caiaphas may think the Lord is not at home in Jerusalem, but *Adonai* is watching."

Nakdimon knew there was no use pressing Gamaliel for more information about the enormous tapestry. The renowned rabbi was known for requiring his pupils to work through the most tangled enigmas without aid. Curiosity was like the headwaters of a river, he often said. Left to run the course, it would, in time, wind its way to the sea.

A flight of brass trumpet calls soaring upward from the city caught their attention. "Enough for now. Come along," Gamaliel said. "Let's see how Herod Antipas wins Jerusalem's heart if he can't have its crown."

■ ■ ■ ■

At the first blare of the trumpets Marcus gathered his cohort and set off from the Antonia down the causeway toward the Hasmonaean Palace.

Latecomers anxious to reach the distribution of bread and pennies scowled as the legionaries forced them to move aside.

"Keep your eyes open for bandits," he urged his men. "We don't want any trouble today, but we'll be ready if it comes."

Marcus hoped the allocation of Purim gifts would go smoothly. Herod Antipas had been urged to withhold the handouts until the troopers were in position. The tetrarch had also been warned to let no more than four files of supplicants pass the palace gates from east to west, so that order could be maintained.

The people assembled in the plaza already numbered in the thousands.

Purim was supposed to be an occasion of joy and celebration. Marcus clung to the notion that this day would remain exactly that.

Yet at the same time he remembered that Herod Antipas was notorious for doing only what seemed best to him . . . without regard to the consequences.

■ ■ ■ ■

A vulture, soaring on an updraft, floated lazily overhead.

Opposite the plaza of the Hasmonaean Palace was a vendor of earthenware vessels, everything from palm-sized clay lamps to mammoth red-lacquered amphoras. Two pair of olive oil containers, taller than either Hayyim or Avel, were permanently mortared into the stonework beside the merchant's doorway. There was barely sufficient space behind the display of jars for two Jerusalem Sparrows to find refuge from the press of the crowd.

The sun was not high enough above the gleaming marble edifice of the Temple for its rays to dispel the morning chill in the valley below. Yet on this fourteenth day of Adar, Avel was sweating. The size of the crowd awaiting the distribution of money and bread was already enormous. Avel would never admit it to his friend, but the tightly packed, jostling throng made him nervous.

Nor was he the sole anxious one in the mob.

From his hiding place, Avel studied a man whose movements were not in keeping with the holiday spirit. Unlike the other laughing, eager Purim celebrators, this lone, cloaked figure never raised his eyes toward the palace. His movements were furtive and restless.

A pickpocket, perhaps?

Or a fugitive with a price on his head?

When the man jerked the rough sleeve of his robe across his forehead, the tip of a dagger concealed beneath his clothing caught in the fabric and rode up.

A murderer! A sicarius! But who was his target?

Avel raised his hand to point, but Hayyim slapped it down. "Are you trying to get us killed?" he hissed. "Don't you know who that is?"

Avel shook his head.

"That's bar Abba, leader of the Galilean rebels."

Had anyone else detected bar Abba's presence? Was the alarm even now being delivered to the Roman soldiers that there were murderous assassins in the waiting throng?

Avel knew that sicarii threatened with capture would slash their way to freedom without regard to anyone unfortunate enough to be in the way. The alternative was an agonizing death on a cross.

"What's he doing here?" Avel whispered back.

"Don't you ever listen?" Hayyim scolded. "Kittim bragged he would go to the arena today, right? Herod Antipas is bringing rebels from his prison in the desert. He'll make them fight to the death or feed them to the lions. Bar Abba must be here to try to release them."

Bar Abba was a folk hero to the common people. It had only been two years since the man, then an upright citizen, had spoken out in favor of restraint and passive resistance to Roman sacrilege. He had once offered his throat to be cut to protect the honor of his nation's religious practices.

Bar Abba and his supporters had won that confrontation, but at a cost to Governor Pilate's pride.

Since that day bar Abba and others were branded as brigands and hunted like animals. The Romans had captured two young brothers and crucified them. And their crime? Disrespect for the majesty of Rome! As a leader of the rebellion, bar Abba could expect no less severe a punishment than crucifixion, especially since it was said he had personally killed three collaborators and two Roman soldiers.

"It's none of our business," Hayyim instructed. "We're here for our share of the *mattanot le-evyonim*. Other than that, we stay out of the way. Got it?"

Avel nodded, relieved his friend was again taking charge.

The shade cast by the square guard tower on the western edge of the Hasmonaean Palace shortened, as if drawing back into the wall to avoid something about to be unleashed.

The shadow of the vulture drifted over the heads of the crowd. It was joined by another and another.

Suddenly apprehensive about what the day would bring, Avel hoped they would not have to wait much longer and that the lines for the charity offerings would move quickly. His neck hurt from craning it around the curve of the amphora, and his stomach rumbled. "Nothing's happening," he protested to Hayyim. "Can't we get out of here?"

"Wait!" Hayyim corrected sharply. "Bar Abba isn't alone in the plaza. Look!"

By peering through the narrow slit, Avel could see the Gennath Gate, no more than a hundred paces away. Beside the portal was a beggar clad in filthy robes. A clumsily wound headscarf stained with blood drooped across his face.

"That blind man?" Avel queried.

Hayyim laughed at his friend's simplicity. "That's Asher, one of bar Abba's spies," he corrected. "The stain over his eyes is pigeon blood. He smears his robes with fish guts and rancid fat. It keeps the space around him clear."

In every corner of the plaza except that near Asher, the still-swelling throng was packed ever tighter. From all directions more people converged on the Hasmonaean Palace.

Over the murmur and laughter of the mob, Avel heard the rattle as the counterfeit beggar violently knocked his walking stick against a begging bowl. Shouting, "Help me, brothers!" Asher's high whine pleaded, "You who have eyes to see the pennies, spare a coin for a blind man!"

Hayyim turned toward Avel and raised his eyebrows.

It had to be a sort of signal.

Hayyim nudged Avel in the ribs. He gestured toward a dark-complected, scar-faced man standing on a stone block directly below the palace's balcony.

"He's called Dan," Hayyim said. "The worst of the sicarii. Likes killing."

Dan the assassin leaned against a balustrade, posture and sneer reflecting haughty nonchalance. He displayed no concern about being a known murderer a dozen times over with a reward of a hundred denarii on his head.

Another blast of trumpets startled Avel.

The crowd hushed.

On the second story of the Hasmonaean Palace Kuza, Herod's steward, appeared. "Good people of Jerusalem," the round-faced little man shouted in his official seneschal's voice. "Herod Antipas, tetrarch of Galilee, and heir to the noble house of Herod the Great, thanks you for honoring his birth. He is pleased to offer you gifts for Purim to express his gratitude."

Cheers greeted these words, and the mob surged forward.

Soon! The distribution of bread and pennies would happen soon!

Avel stopped thinking about rebels and assassins and remembered he was hungry.

Any moment now the throng would be organized into columns to pass beside the gates. There the Purim *mattanot le-evyonim* would be given.

The tramp of hobnailed boots echoed under the archway of the Gennath. A mounted, black-uniformed Roman officer called harshly, "Make way, there! Make way!"

The squalling complaint of an oxcart's ungreased wooden wheels added to the confusion. The thud of the marching footsteps was so methodical and precise . . . Roman legionaries!

"Oh, no!" Hayyim groaned. "They're bringing the prisoners in now! Keep back! Something's going to happen."

At the same instant, six servants, bearing baskets, joined Steward Kuza on the balcony.

Avel heard the rebel Asher bleat from the gate, "Look out, brothers! Help me get out of the way of the Romans! Don't let me get trampled by the Romans!"

The pretend beggar's voice had a note of genuine entreaty and fear.

But Avel knew it was meant to be a warning in case bar Abba and his men were not already alerted to the oncoming legionaries.

And then Avel saw bar Abba flinch.

The brigand flung his hand up to his face as if something struck him on the nose.

From the balcony of the palace coins arced in gleaming sprays as if one of Herod the Great's fountains was spewing bronze droplets. It was one of these that had hit bar Abba.

No systematic dispersal of charity this. That would be too dull for Herod Antipas and his guests, too boring and too slow.

Instead the tetrarch purposefully unleashed a free-for-all in the streets.

Knots of people went down on their knees to scramble for the pennies wherever they landed.

The rest of the crowd shouted and waved for money to be thrown toward them.

The already carnival-like atmosphere was charged with voracity. Who would get a penny? How soon would they run out?

Despite his previous words of caution, Hayyim streaked out of their hiding place while Avel remained concealed.

Darting in and out, Hayyim raced toward the nearest clump of wrestling onlookers.

"Get out of the road!" Avel heard the mounted Roman officer bellow again. "Move aside, I say, or feel the lash!"

The whistle of a scourge and the resulting cries of pain were lost in the clamor of the crowd's zeal to snatch up the coins.

Where was Hayyim? Avel had lost sight of his friend in the wild gesticulations of the mob.

Coins pelted down as the servants tired of tossing them and began to fling whole handfuls.

Finally Avel saw Hayyim dive into the snarl of humans. The boy scuttled after a spinning penny.

■ ■ ■ ■

Still on the elevated portion of the viaduct Marcus witnessed the surge forward as the first handouts fell from the balcony.

This was no giving of charity to the poor; it was a recipe for a disaster.

Panic spread as onlookers tried to escape being crushed.

"Bring the squad along at the double," Marcus urged Guard Sergeant Quintus.

Marcus had a clear view to the Gennath Gate. Another squad of legionaries tramped into view, escorting a cartload of prisoners. Waving, shouting, and battling amongst themselves, the residents of Jerusalem paid no attention.

On a prancing pale horse at the head of the dismal procession was the man Marcus hated most: Praetorian officer Vara.

Vara was every foul, brutish thing Marcus could imagine. If others had not prevented it, Marcus would have killed the man with his own hands when he had had the chance.

Under guard by Vara's troops, seven chained prisoners were stuffed into the cage on the oxcart being trundled through the entry. All were half-naked wretches, with hair and beard in tattered tangles. Of these, six appeared either sullen or defiant.

But the seventh pressed his face against the bars and lifted his eyes toward the Temple, as if unaware of the tumult around him or the fate awaiting him. He stared eagerly toward the holy mountain, like a pilgrim whose arduous journey had just been completed.

Marcus was certain of the captive's identity: it was the Jewish preacher, Yochanan the Baptizer. For offending Herod Antipas Yochanan had been arrested and thrown into the dungeons of Machaerus, where he had languished since.

The tetrarch could not possibly mean to execute Yochanan in the arena! Such an event would ignite uproar and uprising like Judea had never seen. Though opposed by the religious leaders, Yochanan was believed by many of the common people to speak with the authority of the Almighty.

But Herod Antipas surely had a scheme in mind. By bundling the Baptizer into Jerusalem in the company of common criminals, Antipas was camouflaging Yochanan's arrival.

There was no time for Marcus to ponder this. The very real horror of a full-scale riot was unfolding. It had to be stopped immediately, or hundreds might be killed.

Compounding the terror and worsening the mayhem was Praetorian Vara's decision to order his men to use spears to clear the way. Vara drew his sword and flailed about him at hapless bystanders who had no escape.

■ ■ ■ ■

Two breaths in quick succession, and Avel dashed out of hiding.

Immediately he was buffeted on every side. The clamor was louder than ever. Was everyone in Jerusalem starving? What else could make them fight so? Or was it the idea that anyone gave them something for nothing? Was that all a leader had to do to be a king?

"Antipas! Antipas the Great!"

Avel ducked around the rotund man shouting these words. Surely the fellow had never gone even one full day without eating. Yet the man bellowed his support of the Galilean tetrarch as if Antipas were King David himself come again.

The frantic waving caught the attention of a servant on the balcony. An instant later a saucer-shaped loaf spiraled toward earth. The fat man plucked it deftly from the air.

Reaching up, Avel begged, "Please, sir. A bit of bread for . . ."

A meaty hand knocked Avel sprawling.

His fingers were stomped by leather sandals before he could get to his knees. Then he was hit from both sides. A woman fell across him as he struggled to rise.

He tasted warm blood in his mouth. He had bitten through his lip. His head ached from the pummeling.

Desire for food entirely forgotten, Avel wanted only to return to the safety of the pottery shop.

But how? Which way was back?

Around him, hemming him in on every side, was a wall of flesh.

Drums pounded. The tramp of soldiers and horse hooves made the ground vibrate.

Avel crouched, burying his face in his arms, fearing he would be crushed. Then he heard Hayyim's familiar voice calling his name.

"Avel! Get up! This way," Hayyim urged, grabbing Avel's tunic. "Come on, stupid! Not far! Follow me!"

Sniffing back blood and tears, Avel nodded and let Hayyim guide him back to shelter. "The Romans are coming," Hayyim observed. "They'll break it up. I don't want to be here when they do. . . ."

Hayyim halted, squatting behind the wine jars. He squinted and then his eyes got big.

"What?" Avel asked, staring in the same direction as Hayyim.

Hayyim extended a bony forearm in the direction of the street. From their crouched vantage point Avel saw the briefest glint of sunlight on metal.

A single penny, standing on its edge in a crevice between two cobblestones, remained undiscovered.

Avel shuddered at the thought about going back for it. He braced himself for the mission.

"My turn," Hayyim corrected. "Watch an expert at work." Hayyim made a comic face and dashed back into the melee.

■ ■ ■ ■

It was at that instant Marcus' eyes met the hate-filled gaze of the rebel bar Abba. There could be no mistake. Marcus had once held his sword at the man's throat. The revolutionary commander was no more than twenty yards away. But how many hundreds of terrified innocent citizens occupied the intervening space?

Bar Abba! Here in Jerusalem! What was his plot? It had to be drastic for him to risk his neck. Nor would he be alone.

"Draw swords!" Marcus ordered. "Sicarii!"

Screams of fear overcame the shouts of exuberance as, across the courtyard, Praetorian Vara forced his horse forward into the packed throng. Reining it up sharply, he made the snorting animal revolve slowly in a tight circle. As if in battle, it lashed out with its hooves as it spun.

A man stumbled past, clutching a lacerated face. Another potential recruit in the fight against Rome, Marcus thought. If the Jews had a decent leader the soldiers would be in big trouble. The rebels could take Jerusalem, today!

Marcus looked back.

Bar Abba had vanished.

Where was he? Would he exploit this rage?

A boy darted out of the crowd into the space between Vara and the oxcart.

A second child pursued, calling after him, "Hayyim!"

"Clear off!" Vara bellowed, spurring his mount toward Hayyim. The horse leapt forward, striking the child in the forehead with an iron-shod hoof.

At Vara's urging the crazed beast repeatedly stomped and pawed the body.

The boy flipped and tossed with each strike as if pieces would fly off. His companion cowered, wailing in helpless horror, "Hayyim! Hayyim!"

There was an infuriated roar from the mob. Marcus knew this spark was an instant away from the inferno of insurrection.

Vara bawled, "Keep away from the cart, or I'll kill the prisoners. Don't you know that Tetrarch Antipas intends to release them in honor of his birthday?"

It might have been a lie, but it made the mob hesitate.

Rebellion and massacre hung in the balance. "Beat the drums!" Marcus yelled. "Trumpets!"

The blare and thunder in the confined canyons of stonework was deafening. It sounded as if a legion . . . two legions . . . a whole army of Romans . . . were in Jerusalem.

A high, iron-studded gate in the Hasmonaean Palace swung open, and the prisoner cavalcade moved forward.

The moment for rebellion had passed.

"Disperse!" Marcus commanded after the echoes died away. "The ramp is open, as is the Gennath Gate. No one will harm you if you leave peacefully. Go now."

The crowd needed no further urging, but flowed away in both directions, leaving little knots of people clustered around motionless victims.

In the muddle bar Abba had escaped, but that fact was not as unpleasant to Marcus as the realization that he and his men were more hated than ever.

# RAHUM

It had all happened so fast.

Avel sobbed over the broken body of Hayyim. Around them the crowd swarmed, wailing, gathering the dead and injured. Hayyim's spindly arms and legs were shattered, rib cage crushed from the weight of the horse. Only his hands seemed uninjured. Avel raised Hayyim's left hand to kiss it. A bright bronze penny fell from the clenched fist. Avel picked up the coin in disbelief, moaned, and buried his face against the still-warm corpse. "Hayyim! Hayyim! My friend! My brother!" His keening was lost in the roar of grief rising from hundreds in the street.

Avel was covered in Hayyim's blood. Face and body, feet and hands. His blond hair was matted with Hayyim's gore. The comic beard drawn on Hayyim's face was a reminder of the hope they had carried with them that very morning.

"Are you injured, boy?" a Roman centurion asked.

Avel could not tear his eyes from Hayyim. "No! Not me! I'm not hurt! It's Hayyim! The soldier's horse trampled him! What can I do?"

"He's dead, boy. Are you his brother?" The officer put a hand on Avel's shoulder. It was meant to be a kind gesture, but Avel did not welcome the kindness of Romans.

The boy jerked away. "No. My friend . . . Hayyim is . . ."

"Go fetch his kin to take the body away." The officer straightened and backed up a step. His order was matter-of-fact. How could the man know Hayyim had no kin? No one to mourn him but Avel.

"It can't be! No! Hayyim! Wake up, Hayyim! Somebody help me! They killed Hayyim!" The centurion was gone. Avel raised his arms into the air, begging for help from the crowd and then imploring Hayyim's soul not to leave him!

The toe of a shoe nudged him. It was Kittim. "What did that Roman pig want with you?"

"I don't know. He told me to fetch Hayyim's family."

"Get up, Avel!" the leader of the Sparrows commanded. "Hayyim is dead. Stop your whimpering. There's nothing to be done. Get up, I say!"

Avel looked up. Kittim glowered at him, disgusted by his grief.

"They've killed Hayyim." Avel's words came in jerking sobs.

"Don't act like a woman. Filthy Romans. They'll kill us if they have an excuse." Kittim's teeth were gritted behind his beard. His dark eyes blazed hatred. "Romans. This is what they care for the life of a Jew. Even a very small one. Two Sparrows for a penny, they say. And they mean it. Get up then, Avel. Don't let them see you weep. We'll take Hayyim back to the quarry."

"Come on, Avel," urged one of the older boys, grasping the Mourner by the shoulders. "Come on! We've got to get him out of here."

Six on each side, the Sparrows made a litter with their arms to carry Hayyim. Avel, like one who had lost a brother, followed a pace behind the procession bearing the lifeless body.

Hayyim's broken arms and legs were askew. A perfect hoof print was carved in his brow. His head was thrown back. Blood dripped from his gaping mouth. Eyes surprised and wide in death fixed on Avel.

Avel stared at him in horror. He clutched the penny in his hand. For this Hayyim had died?

■ ■ ■ ■

Marcus turned his back on the dead boy and his friend. There was nothing more he could do. He withdrew his cohort to a side street away from the scene of the riot. The grief of the mob might yet turn to fury. No doubt they would somehow blame this chaos on the Roman presence at the palace. If the Jews rounded on his soldiers in their rage, the civilian body count would rise.

Quintus, sword drawn, stood beside Marcus as the Jews retrieved the bodies of their dead and wounded.

"We saw it coming, didn't we, sir?" Quintus asked.

"Being right gives me no satisfaction." Marcus watched as a troop of children carried off their fallen comrade. And there were many more dead and injured besides.

Quintus growled, "Herod Antipas is to blame for this. I'll swear to that, if there's an inquiry. It might have been handled differently. And bar Abba got away."

Marcus did not comment. If bar Abba had come to set his fellow brigands free, he had failed in his mission.

As the crowd dispersed, two ragged Jewish men came forward. Clearly shaken, they caught sight of Marcus and the cohort. Instead of turning away, however, one of the men raised his hand in a gesture of peace to Marcus. "*Shalom*, Centurion Marcus Longinus."

It was a minute before Marcus recognized them as followers of Yochanan the Baptizer. These were the same fellows Marcus had taken to the desert fortress to visit the Baptizer in his prison cell six months before. Philip of Bethsaida was tall, curly-haired, Grecian in his features, and thinly bearded for a Jew. The other, Avram, was stubby of build and unremarkable.

Quintus scowled as they approached. Marcus put his hand on the old soldier's arm in a signal that he should stay put.

"Peace to you," Marcus responded to Yochanan's talmidim as he went to meet them. They stood at arm's length from one another in the center of the street and did not offer their hands in greeting. To have done so would have been perceived as an impropriety by both Romans and Jews. They stood close enough to speak to one another in subdued conversation.

"And peace to Yerushalayim," said Philip. "A sad day for Zion."

Marcus glanced over their shoulders toward the litter of debris where the happy throng had gathered merely hours before. "Is there ever a happy day for this unhappy people?" Marcus countered. "I saw the Baptizer on a cart with other prisoners."

"We followed him here," Avram said. "They haven't let us visit his cell in many months. We brought a few things for him . . . a cloak from his family." Avram took the bundle from his pack.

Marcus wondered what physical condition the Baptizer must be in after so many months of confinement. "He'll be in a bad way."

"Yes. No news. No light," agreed Avram. "All his talmidim thought he would perish before this. But your soldiers brought him here. Do you know why, Centurion? We hoped he would be released. Yochanan is not a man to survive in a cage. You saw that for yourself. Can you tell us anything?"

Marcus shook his head. "I've been in the desert these past months chasing rebels. The politics of Rome and Herod Antipas escape me."

The two men exchanged uneasy looks. "And how is your servant boy? Carta. He lives? He's well?" Philip asked.

Marcus shrugged. "In Galilee last I saw him. Safe. With friends. Better off there than with me."

"He thrives," emphasized Philip. "We've seen him. He's a follower of the one who saved him."

They did not say Yeshua of Nazareth aloud. It was a dangerous name to speak openly in Jerusalem these days.

Marcus jerked his head downward in acknowledgment. "I'm glad for his life. Glad for . . . all of it. More than that. I'm grateful his life was spared. And you . . . you carried word about his injury to the great Teacher . . . Did I thank you?"

"No." Philip smiled. "But there's a way. . . ."

Marcus knew their request before it was asked. "You want to speak to the Baptizer? Is that it?" He considered the daunting task of getting these two past Vara and into Yochanan's cell.

"If you could help us."

"Did you recognize the Roman on the horse? That's Vara. The devil who nearly killed Carta. There's a reason he's escorting the prisoners. My guess is . . . whoever ordered the Baptizer brought here wanted him to arrive safely . . . for a reason. Not likely anyone will open the prison gates and let you in. And I'm not the man to try. I'm out of favor."

"We must try," pleaded Avram. "We need your help, Centurion."

Marcus owed them. They had intervened with Yeshua and because of their words, the Teacher had healed Carta, whom Marcus considered almost a son. But this?

Marcus stared past them to the palace gates, then nodded reluctantly. "I'll be at Herod's banquet tonight in the company of my commander, Dio Felix. I'll speak to him. He's a good man. A tolerant man. At least he can tell me what's going on, eh? And if he can help . . . well, I'll have a word with him. That's the best I can offer. Meet me over there," Marcus said, pointing, "at the wine merchant's shop. An hour before dawn tomorrow."

His reply evidently satisfied them. "We won't forget your kindness, Centurion," they promised. "*Shalom* to you."

"Peace to you and to your master. And safety." He bade them farewell, sensing there would be neither peace nor safety in Jerusalem tonight.

■ ■ ■ ■

Marcus had every intention of forcing his thoughts into the path of duty.

He steeled himself to remain on guard outside the Hasmonaean

Palace until relieved. Keeping the fragile peace was what mattered. He told himself he would give no further consideration to either the death of the child, or to Yochanan the Baptizer, until after his detail was replaced.

It was the sight of Vara's horse that changed his determination.

A Samaritan legionary, one of those in the prisoner detail with Vara, appeared at the gate to the palace courtyard. At the end of a lead rope was the Praetorian's dappled gray horse.

Bellowing for a water carrier, the soldier demanded two skins, double quick. Then in complete disregard of the dangerous tension lingering in the streets, the man proceeded to wash the legs of the skittish animal in full view of passersby.

Scrub the blood-spattered hocks.

Cleanse flanks and belly where crimson droplets clung after the frenzied assault on Hayyim.

Red tinted streams traced the outline of cobbles already stained with blood.

Marcus' resolve to remain rooted exploded. "Keep the men alert," he commanded Guard Sergeant Quintus and strode across the plaza.

Intently brushing the off-side flank of the stallion, the groom did not see the centurion's approach.

Marcus seized the horse's halter just under its chin.

The sudden movement startled the horse and he hopped sideways. A pointed hoof landed atop the Samaritan trooper's foot.

The soldier jerked up, shouting a wrathful oath.

Then his tone moderated slightly at the sight of Marcus' uniform.

"Get inside the walls at once!" Marcus barked through gritted teeth. "Get that animal inside! Are you trying to reignite the riot?"

Sullenly, with an exaggerated limp, the legionary complied.

Marcus knew his vehemence was really aimed at Vara, so he tried to tell himself to slow down. But he was shaking with fury.

What he saw in the courtyard increased the level of his rage.

The oxcart bearing the prisoners was parked in the center of the square . . . and the captives remained confined to their metal cage, exposed to the midday sun.

"Why are those men still there?" he demanded, rounding on the groom once more.

"Sir?" the trooper said dully. "Because no orders have come to move them."

"Here's one then: get them into their cells! At once! Leave the water!"

The legionary hesitated, as if he would cite Vara as a higher authority, but the menace on Marcus' face made the guard draw back. He mumbled something about fetching the jailer and took himself off.

Approaching the cart, Marcus noticed that the captives were prostrate with exposure and thirst, expressions dull, faces without much comprehension.

When he extended a skin of water through the bars, it was grasped eagerly. The contents were devoured noisily and quickly.

Yochanan the Baptizer was the last to drink. When he had taken a mouthful, he lifted his dark, brooding eyes toward Marcus in unspoken thanks. A flicker of recognition followed, a softening of the grim expression.

"I know you," he croaked hoarsely. "Yes? You came once to Machaerus . . . with Philip and Avram."

Marcus acknowledged the accuracy of the memory. He glanced over his shoulder before he replied, then lowered his voice. "They're nearby. Seeking permission to see you. They brought your cloak."

Yochanan nodded. "My mantle belongs to truth and mourning now. They'll find them traveling together on the road to Jericho. But I've been so long without word, without news," he rambled. Then another recollection struck him. "I asked you . . . about . . ."

Raising his hand, Marcus mutely requested Yochanan not to speak the name of Yeshua . . . not in front of men who would sell their souls to escape execution. "I've seen your cousin." Marcus chose his words carefully. "I don't know exactly who he is, but I've witnessed for myself what he can do. The blind see. Lame men walk. Lepers are cured. The deaf hear." Thinking of Miryam he concluded, "And he gives hope to the hopeless."

Yochanan almost smiled. "Then . . . I am content." Searching the hardness of Marcus' face, the Baptizer's eyes moved to the centurion's grip on his sword hilt. "Don't . . . friend. Go now and live . . . go quickly! And . . . I thank you for . . . the water."

A detail of Herod Antipas' guards marched around the corner of the stables. They were led by the legionary Marcus had dispatched, but Vara was not with them. "We're to move the prisoners into cells, Centurion," the trooper reported, "and turn over sentry duty to these men." He produced an iron key to unlock the cage.

After a last pointed stare at the legionary Marcus turned again to Yochanan. A sense of irrepressible sadness washed over Marcus at the sight of this fearless holy man caged like an animal. "Good-bye," Marcus said, wondering if this really was farewell. How often had he clasped the hand of a comrade before a battle and felt this same dread? "I'll do what I can to bring your followers to you."

Yochanan shook his head. "It doesn't matter now. You've brought me everything I need." Did the Baptizer share Marcus' sense that the battle was nearly over? "*Shalom.*" Yochanan raised his hand in blessing.

■ ■ ■

The dead Sparrow lay in a long niche carved into the quarry wall. Hayyim's broken body replaced the giant stone block that had been hewn out and hauled away to build the sanctuary of the Most High. Covered in palm branches the space made a fine funeral bier. It had been used many times for the beggars and link boys of Jerusalem.

It was normally the duty of women to keen for the dead, but there were no women in the cavern. All was silent except for the shuffling of feet. There was not even a scrap of linen for a shroud. Nor spices for embalming. No family to mourn. Just Avel, who crouched, red-eyed, in the dust at Hayyim's feet.

The link boys filed past and placed palm fronds over the body. Hayyim's hand protruded from this improvised shroud. His fingers gently curled, as though he were asking for a penny.

Avel stood, held Hayyim's hand a moment, then tucked it beneath the covering.

The beggar occupants of the quarry came last to pay their respects to Hayyim. Grown men, broken, dirty, and stinking as though they were also dead, gazed curiously at the diminutive form on the ledge, shook their heads, and went away.

Avel was left alone. He stared at the smoke-scarred roof of the cavern and tried to think. What would he do since Hayyim was gone? How would he stay warm in the straw at night without Hayyim beside him? With whom would he share his meager ration of bread? Who would carry a torch beside him through Jerusalem's narrow, twisting alleyways? Hayyim would be forgotten . . . as though he had never lived.

Kittim, chief of the Sparrows, swaggered to the niche and towered over Avel. Kittim's sandals were new. The hem of his cloak was not frayed.

Avel stared at Kittim's dusty toes. There was a rustling of palm fronds as Kittim lifted them briefly and studied Hayyim's gray face.

The sky was orange beyond the entrance to the cavern.

Kittim mused, "They say Romans lay the cornerstones of their cities on top of human skulls. So here's a little Jewish head for them. L'hayyim! To life, eh?" He laughed. "Too bad. This will cost me. Hayyim got a link almost every night."

Avel closed his eyes. He thought of his mother. Of the men who came to their room in the middle of the night. He remembered her screaming at him to get out. Then the walk to the quarry through a dozen unfamiliar lanes so he would be lost and not find his way back to her hovel. *"You are not pitied! You are not loved! You are not my people! Don't follow me!"* Hayyim had shared his bread with Avel that night. Showed him where to sleep. Taught him how to survive. Avel had no friend but Hayyim.

And now?

Kittim nudged Avel with his foot. This meant Avel must speak up or be kicked. Kittim asked, "So. Hayyim was after a coin when he was killed?"

"Yes."

"Did he get it?"

If Avel lied, Kittim would search him. "Yes."

Kittim responded by putting his grubby palm out. "It's mine. I've lost a Sparrow and lost income. Give it to me."

Avel decided he would keep Hayyim's last penny forever. Even if he were starving, Avel would never spend Hayyim's penny. It had cost too much.

Avel fished his own coin from the rag that served as his money pouch.

Kittim snatched it out of Avel's hand. "Any more?" Another harder nudge.

"No," Avel lied, then cowered as the blow landed.

"Stupid! You let your partner die for a penny, and you come up empty-handed?"

Avel hated Kittim fiercely but nodded meekly.

"Go get your torch," Kittim commanded. "Every Sparrow who failed to earn his keep today will work tonight. Jerusalem won't be dark just because Hayyim is dead! And you'd better come back with something for me!"

"But . . . what about Hayyim? The burying?" Avel protested.

Kittim shouted, "What about him? Hayyim's dead." All the Sparrows turned furtively to take in the confrontation. Would Avel be beaten? "Don't think you're going to get a night off! We'll bury him. So there's an end to Hayyim. You'll get another partner or go hungry! That's the rule! But for now, I said, go fetch your torch! You've got work to do tonight."

Avel knew better than to argue.

He knew better than to weep, but tears burned his eyes.

Grief and loneliness threatened to choke him.

He wanted to cry out and pound his fists against Kittim's sneering face! Why not? Why not let Kittim kill him? Then it would be over! Why did the horse fall on Hayyim instead of him? How could he be such a coward? How could he go on living when the one person who had been kind to him lay cold and smashed on the quarry stone?

*"You are not loved! You are not pitied!"*

Half-turning for a last look at Hayyim's bier, Avel joined the group of young link boys who waited beside the heap of torches.

■ ■ ■ ■

Tendrils of steam wreathed Marcus as he sat on the edge of the heated pool that evening. Twisting his back and rotating his head, Marcus stretched his muscles. He hoped the tightly knotted cords in his neck and shoulders would release, but so far nothing helped.

The underground chambers of the Antonia were fitted out as a gymnasium for the Roman legionaries, with separate accommodations for officers and enlisted men. Though modest in extent, the Antonia's facilities possessed rooms for exercising and massage, and pools of three different temperatures.

Since stripping off his armor and sweaty uniform, Marcus had endeavored to put the affairs of the day behind him. His helmet lay on the floor beneath a bench, and his soiled tunic was a rumpled mass atop his dagger.

No matter how easily he discarded his official apparel, he could not escape the scenes of the riot. Every time he closed his eyes and leaned back in the hot water, he saw the puny frame of the beggar boy being pulverized.

Nor was it solely the memory of a senseless tragedy that bothered him. Marcus was tormented by the thought that he might have prevented the boy's death. If he had moved quicker, if he had anticipated the disturbance and arrived earlier, could he have intervened?

Grasping the bone handle of a strigil, Marcus swept perspiration from his upper arm. Splashing oil from a jug onto his shoulder, he scraped vigorously at the spot without any conscious attention to his actions.

On the other side of the pool Tribune Felix, the military commander of the Galil and Marcus' superior officer, laughed. "Are you trying to cut off your own limbs, Marcus? You've been sawing away fiercely for at least a quarter-hour."

With a wry smile, Marcus tossed aside the scouring tool. Felix had spent the day in conference with Governor Pilate and had missed witnessing the violence. "I knew something appalling was bound to develop today," Marcus said, "and I couldn't stop it. Useless."

Twenty-five people had been trampled in the disturbance. Six of them, including the link boy ridden down by Vara, had been killed.

Combing his dark hair with his fingertips, Felix disagreed. "Could've been much worse, and you know it. Between the mob's frenzy and Vara's idea of crowd control, it was your arrival kept the death toll under a hundred. But shake it off, man. We are summoned to Herod Antipas' birthday celebration. From what I hear of Purim everyone drinks till your own name is banished from your thoughts. Besides, with your beard, you already appear the part of a Jewish nobleman."

Wrapping a towel around his waist, Marcus moved to the bench and sat. "But I hear you have another pleasant duty beforehand?" he joked, trying to join Felix's attempt at lightening his mood.

Felix grunted and made a sour face. "The Sanhedrin. Governor Pilate needs the assistance of the Jews . . . that is to say, their money . . . in order to complete an aqueduct scheme for Jerusalem. Their high priest has cooked something up, but I'm to lend an official Roman presence to the meeting."

Pantomiming a toast, Marcus saluted. "Better you than me, Commander. The politics between Romans and Jews are inscrutable at best. It's easier chasing outlaws."

The connection to capturing criminals reminded Marcus of the question his other grim thoughts had temporarily pushed aside. "Do you know why the Baptizer was brought to Jerusalem today?" he asked.

"The wild-man Jewish prophet? He's locked up in Machaerus."

Marcus shook his head. "Not anymore. I saw him in the cart with Antipas' other prisoners. You don't think Antipas intends to kill him in the arena?"

"Even Antipas isn't that stupid," Felix observed. "He could cause the whole province to explode. You must be mistaken."

"I know what I saw," Marcus replied. He made no mention of his conversations with Yochanan or the Baptizer's talmidim.

Snapping his fingers, Felix declared, "I know! Antipas intends to release the Baptizer. Think how that'll please the crowds . . . maybe more than bread and pennies."

When Marcus looked doubtful, Felix added, "Don't try to understand it. Who can get inside the mind of Herod Antipas?" Then shamming an elaborate shudder he added, "And who would want to!"

There was a clatter of steps in the hall outside the baths and the gabble of laughter.

"No," Marcus heard Praetorian Vara's grating voice argue. "I am *not* sorry to miss tonight's banquet. Pay mock homage to a mock ruler like Antipas who pretends to govern a dung heap like Galilee? No! The sooner I get back to Caesarea and out of this crawling nest of Jewish maggots, the happier I'll be."

Vara! Marcus should have killed him after he raped Miryam. He had wanted to do so after what Vara did to Carta. And now today's brutality.

Shouldn't mad dogs be destroyed before their rampages injured more innocents?

The tramping steps came nearer. "Lessons like today will teach the rabble to keep out of the way, eh?" Vara boasted to his cronies.

Marcus glanced down at his side. The hilt of his dagger was within easy reach. By the sounds of his approach Vara would pass by the vapor-shrouded entry to the bath. He would never see Marcus until the blade had already swept across his throat.

At a footfall nearby, Marcus' hand leapt to the weapon.

He peered up into the eyes of Tribune Felix.

"I read your intention on your face," Felix said. "And I won't let you throw your life away, not like that. I didn't post you to the desert so you could destroy yourself on almost your first day back. Nothing you can do will return that boy back to life . . . but *you* will end up crucified. And if your attempt fails, Vara will win . . . truly win . . . and laugh as he watches you die."

Marcus slumped back against the cool tile of the wall. "As you say, Commander."

The outline of Vara's bearlike form passed by the entrance to the bath. His harsh, braying laughter continued to echo until at last it faded down the hallway.

# VE-HANUN

That evening Nakdimon climbed the Temple Mount steps, pausing on the first landing to survey the expanse of the portico looming above. Built on top of the marble colonnade known as the *royal basilicon* was a row of offices. A gleaming dome stood over the exact center of the priests' chambers. Directly beneath the rotunda lay the cedar-paneled council house, meeting hall of the Sanhedrin.

It was a high honor and a significant responsibility to be one of the seventy elders of Israel. It was also an undeniable source of pride. Some men dwelt more on the honor and the responsibility. Others on the pride.

Nakdimon frowned at the thought. As a Pharisee and a strict observer of Jewish religious laws, he was in the minority on the council. Most of the members were Sadducees. That faction supported Temple ritual and Temple honor. They inclined more toward politics and personal gain than worship. The high priest and most of his ardent supporters fit this description precisely.

Nakdimon's uncle Gamaliel had urged his attendance at tonight's assembly. "Caiaphas is scheming again," Gamaliel suggested. "By calling a meeting when he knows most of the council will be at Purim celebrations, he hopes for an easy victory about something. You and I must find out his objective and delay it, if necessary."

The Sanhedrin chamber was less than half full when Nakdimon arrived. He was one of the last three to enter. He took his seat beside his uncle, at one end of the U-shaped arrangement of benches.

Several of the elders talked loudly of the holiday gatherings they had been forced to leave. Irritably they discussed how anxious they were to return to their guests. A few were clearly several goblets of wine ahead of the rest, intent on fully implementing the drinking tradition imported to Judea by the Jews from Babylon.

Seated alone against the far wall, in the area usually occupied by students and scribes, was a Gentile: a Roman officer in full dress uniform. Nakdimon recognized the young man as Tribune Dio Felix, military commander of the Galil.

Caiaphas swept into the chamber, surrounded by a bustling swarm of attendants. "Are we all present?" he demanded. Without pausing for a response, Caiaphas continued, "Let's begin. I'm certain other business calls us to be quick. As you know, Jerusalem is chronically short of water. This is also true of the level of water in the Temple cisterns. We must increase a reliable supply, or even the ritual baths will experience a shortage."

The council members nodded. It was no secret that having enough water for the Holy City was a continual worry. But if the need was universally agreed to, why make it the subject of a hasty, secretive meeting?

The high priest resumed, "Governor Pilate has proposed extending Herod the Great's aqueduct, connecting it to an adequate spring in the mountains to the south. Once completed, it will meet our needs for many years to come."

Expressions of approval echoed around the chamber before Gamaliel asked dryly, "And how does the governor propose paying for this construction?"

With polished assurance the high priest responded, "There's sufficient money in the Korban allotment alone."

Gamaliel was on his feet again before Caiaphas had finished his sentence. "Korban funds cannot be diverted to a building project," he said firmly, "no matter how worthy the undertaking. I'll never approve such a sacrilege."

Jewish law required that every adult male pay half a shekel to the maintenance of the Temple in Jerusalem. The annual remittance had recently come in. The collected money paid the priest's living expenses and subsidized Temple repairs.

But Korban was something else again. The Korban allotment, required by Jewish law, was used to purchase animals for sacrifice to the Almighty. Just as the chosen creatures were considered off-limits for any other use, so also was Korban money consecrated and untouchable.

Making a conciliatory gesture, Caiaphas said soothingly, "Perhaps the worthy Gamaliel didn't hear my earlier comment. The aqueduct will refill the temple cisterns. If there's no water for cleansing ceremonies, there'll be no sacrifices, Korban money or not. It's an entirely proper use of the resources."

Nakdimon stood. "If you think there was a disturbance in the city today," he said, "imagine the rampage that will follow the disclosure of such a misuse of the Temple tax."

The wealthy young Joseph of Arimathea also expressed reservations, but no one else raised any opposition.

Caiaphas thanked Tribune Felix for attending their gathering. "I know you are summoned to Herod Antipas' birthday banquet," he said. "So we won't detain you further. We'll bring the matter to a vote shortly and give Governor Pilate the result tomorrow."

The Roman departed.

Gamaliel, Nakdimon, and Joseph attempted to force postponement of the matter until a session of the full council, but they were overridden.

To no one's surprise the verdict favoring the aqueduct was twenty-seven to three.

■ ■ ■ ■

After the rigged outcome of the Korban vote, Nakdimon expected a speedy dismissal of the council. To his surprise Caiaphas moved the assembly to a second agenda item.

"There's another matter relating to tax collection," the high priest said. "There is a spirit of unrest in the land, as we saw today. Known rebels were observed in the crowd, provoking violence."

So the shifting of blame for the bloodshed had already begun. It would not do to openly censure Herod Antipas for his folly or the Romans for overreacting. The fault must lie elsewhere.

The change of topic was also a clever device to redirect the council's conscience away from what they had just condoned.

"We have been vigilant," Caiaphas continued, "in monitoring those who would encourage conflict. We're making every effort to bring them to justice. Here is an account."

By these phrases Nakdimon knew the high priest meant spying on and trying to trap those deemed threatening to the official position. The witnesses introduced confirmed Nakdimon's assessment. Eber and Caleb were the high priest's creatures. Common in speech, appearance, and dress, they could appear innocently curious while infiltrating any gathering.

Nakdimon knew they also manufactured evidence as needed.

"They just returned from the Galil to give testimony about the so-called rabbi, Yeshua of Nazareth."

Everyone present recognized the name. Nakdimon had been in Jerusalem the previous Succoth when the itinerant preacher from the north announced that he was the water of life.

The Temple authorities were certain Yeshua was undermining their authority. They had laid a trap for Yeshua on that occasion and it had failed. But Caiaphas never gave up easily. So it was not surprising the attempts continued.

"Most recently," Caiaphas elaborated, "Caleb and Eber were instructed to quiz him about paying taxes to Rome." This was an obvious ploy to ferret out rebel sympathizers, Nakdimon thought. Taxes paid to Rome supported the army of occupation. The taxes also rendered tribute to the divinity claimed for Roman emperors. To pious Jews this was distasteful; to radical Jews it was an abomination. "And what was the result?" Caiaphas demanded.

Eber and Caleb exchanged glances, as if neither was willing to speak first. Finally Caleb admitted, "It didn't go as expected, Lord."

As Caiaphas' face darkened, Eber explained. "We framed the question exactly as you instructed. We asked this Yeshua if it was permissible to pay the tax to Caesar."

"And what was his answer?" Caiaphas thundered.

Caleb scanned the council chamber, as if searching for a sympathetic face. Finding none he responded, "He asked us to show him a coin, and Eber produced a silver denarius. Then Yeshua inquired whose portrait and name were on it."

Nakdimon involuntarily reached toward his belt to touch the money pouch that hung there. Everyone knew Emperor Tiberius' face and inscription were on those coins. Nakdimon had four such in his possession. Where was this leading?

"Well?" Caiaphas insisted when the narrative paused.

"The rabbi evaded the question!" Eber explained. The spy made it sound as if Yeshua did not play fair.

"He said we should give to Caesar what was owed to Caesar, and to God what was God's," Caleb concluded.

Gamaliel's laugh rung throughout the dome. "What a glib debater this country preacher is," he declared. "Beaten you at your own game, did he?"

Nakdimon understood that while Gamaliel's words were addressed to the spies, they were intended for the devious high priest.

Caiaphas' face purpled with anger. "This man's dangerous," he hissed. "He's gaining in popularity, and he doesn't regard authority. He'll be the cause of more unrest if he isn't stopped."

Caleb spoke up hopefully, like a pet dog who had failed to retrieve a stick might offer a shoe instead. "Yeshua consorts with the worst elements. Prostitutes, tax collectors, other notorious sinners. There's no doubt he's a very suspicious character."

As Gamaliel laughed again, it was clear the elders recognized the sarcasm in his mirth. "Be warned," he said at last. "If Yeshua of Nazareth is a truly righteous man . . . and other reports maintain that he is and that he performs works of charity and divine blessing . . . then we should not oppose him. We should listen to what he preaches and judge it on its merits, not on hearsay and entrapment."

Caiaphas harrumphed. "How can he be righteous and yet friendly with the worst sort of sinners? What merit can there be in an uneducated charlatan? Especially one from the Galil? Look to your Scripture: no true prophet ever came from the Galil."

That was not correct. Nakdimon knew. The prophet Jonah, the lone Jewish seer recorded as successful with a message of repentance, was from the Galil.

Nakdimon did not speak his thoughts, however, as the disconcerted and fuming high priest dismissed the gathering. Gamaliel's words still rang in Nakdimon's ears: "If Yeshua is of God, his message will stand. We must not oppose it."

■ ■ ■ ■

Several rounds of toasts to Herod Antipas had been drunk by the time Felix slipped in to take his place beside Marcus at the table.

Marcus noted that his commander seemed pleased.

Felix drained his cup, wiped his lips on the back of his hand, then remarked with satisfaction, "So, Marcus! Governor Pilate will finish his aqueduct with Jewish funds."

"The Sanhedrin voted Pilate's proposal through?" Marcus asked, surprised.

"The high priest, Caiaphas, is a crafty fellow. Between the two of them, he and Pilate could rule the world effectively. Caiaphas calls the council meeting on a day when it's a religious duty for the Jews to drink themselves unconscious. Well done, I say. Two-thirds of the council didn't attend. By the time they recover from their Purim hangovers, it'll be too late. I wasn't invited to stay for the vote, of course, but I lingered outside their chamber long enough to overhear it. Then they went on to other business," Felix concluded with a trace of wary skepticism. He inclined his head toward the high table where Herod Antipas called for another cup of wine. "The way the Jewish high priest and his friends cling to power rivals anything I ever saw in Rome. They are more devious than Praetorian Prefect Sejanus. Pilate and Caiaphas managed to leave Antipas out of the equation. They'll get the credit when the aqueduct is completed."

This was indeed good news for Pilate. Thus far, his rule of Judea had been a miserable experience. He had failed in every attempt to win the affection of the people he governed and had offended Jewish religious sensibilities in every way imaginable. But Jerusalem needed water. A Roman aqueduct would be a monument to Pilate's governorship, and remembered for ages to come.

Marcus scanned the faces of Antipas' guests. Most were already well on their way past caring about what decrees had been voted by the Sanhedrin tonight.

The furnishings of the Hasmonaean banqueting hall benefited from the flickering torchlight. When seen clearly the floors were scuffed from a century of foot traffic and neglect, the wall hangings frayed and tired looking. Once the home of Israel's rulers before being replaced by Herod the Great's lavish courts, the Hasmonaean Palace was now a relic.

Roman governors like the austere Pontius Pilate made themselves at home in Jerusalem around Herod the Great's fountains and bathed in Herod's marble pools. Herod's sons, on the other hand, were permitted to use this old palace when visiting Jerusalem, but only at the express indulgence of Rome.

The sour look on Antipas' face suggested to Marcus that resentment over his diminished status was never banished from his thoughts. Antipas, that fat, sallow-complected offspring of Herod the Great, was doing his best to be a gracious host, but bitterness smoldered in his furtive, heavy-lidded eyes.

None of the other costumed party-goers appeared to notice. The room's conversation boiled with bawdy humor and intoxicated, raucous laughter.

In contrast to the deep spirituality and solemnity of most of the other Jewish holy days, Purim was, for some, a time of unalloyed debauchery. Antipas' guests, in particular, were eager to take their freedom to a bacchanalian extreme. Snatches of off-key singing rose up spontaneously from different tables, swelled enthusiastically, then died away dismally when no one could remember the words to more than one verse.

While those at the high table and the Roman officers present remained unmasked, the other attendees wore elaborate headgear. Chest-length false beards, blond wigs, feathered visors, and animal faces mingled with comically exaggerated human features.

With each passing minute the revelers grew louder and more drunken.

Marcus was not drinking. He could not shake the feeling that he might yet be called out to quell further unrest. Marcus was relieved to be partially hidden by the dancing shadows, like the faded tapestries and chipped serving dishes. This birthday gathering and Purim celebration was attended by enough dignitaries of higher rank that a centurion from the Galil was relegated to a third arc of tables, away from public scrutiny.

The humble position suited Marcus completely.

"You look more prepared for battle than celebration, Marcus," commented Felix from where he reclined on the couch at Marcus' right. "Your mouth couldn't be clamped tighter if you were facing a thousand Parthians with a single century of troopers." The tribune shrugged and waved his wineglass for a refill. "Enough of duty. Since we have this corner to ourselves, we can speak almost freely." He guffawed as the evening's theatrical performance began. "I can see there is no love lost between Antipas and the high priest, Caiaphas!"

Just then Kuza, Antipas' steward, entered. Made up to resemble Caiaphas, Kuza paraded pompously up and down the aisles. His nose and chin were grotesquely elongated, his fingers dripped with rings, and he carried a full wineskin. Striking a dramatic pose, he waved an admonitory forefinger and bellowed, "Listen to me! Hear the words of your *cohen hagadol:* you must only drink wine! Water is not kosher . . . not . . . not . . . not! Miserable sinners, drink up to atone for your sins!"

It was common at Purim gatherings to poke fun at teachers, religious leaders, and government officials. Even so, Marcus noted cynically, none of the revelers had the temerity to mimic Antipas, or his wife, Herodias.

Felix applauded, then shouted over the din, "The Jews would be better liked by the rest of the empire if they acted like this more often."

Two years before before, at their first meeting, Marcus had been reticent about speaking his mind to Felix. Since then his thinking had gone through several gyrations, from trusting the youthful officer to having misgivings and outright suspicion, and on to friendship again. Felix's family in Rome was wealthy and powerful in its own right. Felix did not fear either Governor Pilate or the machinations of Vara. The young commander moved effortlessly through the dangerous maze of political intrigues.

Marcus observed Antipas as the tetrarch shouted insults at the pseudo high priest. The charade may have been posed as a joke, but there was much truth to the insults, Marcus thought. It galled Antipas not to be the king of the Jews. Caiaphas and the Sanhedrin had more real power than Antipas.

When his father died, Antipas had expected to be crowned in his place. Instead Rome appointed a whole succession of governors for Judea, leaving Antipas to rule a territory of hicks and hayseeds and desert brigands.

The word *tetrarch* meant Antipas governed one-fourth of Herod the Great's estate. That quarter was occupied by unruly Galileans and the rest given over to the bandit-ridden wastes of Perea, east of the Jordan.

Felix consumed another goblet of wine. He urged Marcus to follow suit.

Marcus sipped uncomfortably as the counterfeit high priest paraded around the room, posing bogus religious questions. "And when the six days were finished, what did one angel ask another? Don't know!? The correct response is 'Who told *you* you were naked,'" he roared.

Kuza demanded kisses on the lips from the female guests for all their wrong answers but presented his sanctified backside toward the men. Marcus knew what Kuza was trying to accomplish. Kuza's wife, Joanna, was a follower of Yeshua of Nazareth in Galilee. Ever mindful of his precarious position in the court of Herod Antipas, Kuza played the role of the high priest with an exceptionally high degree of mockery. This pleased his master immensely. Antipas laughed until tears coursed down his cheeks.

Felix suddenly asked, "What do you know about the wife of Antipas?" He gestured with his chin toward the heavily rouged, angular cheekbones of the lady Herodias.

Marcus snorted. "Should you ever become governor here she'll be one of your biggest headaches," he asserted. "That harpy'll tear out your liver if you get in her way. Antipas wouldn't think of challenging Rome, but because of her prodding he'll try to get Pilate dismissed and himself crowned. They say the distribution of bread and pennies was her idea to win the support of the Jews of Jerusalem to their cause."

"Her bread and pennies are small change compared to Pilate's aqueduct, eh?" Felix shrugged.

Marcus knew Pilate and Herod Antipas hated one another. And the high priest ignored Antipas while courting Pilate's favor. But Antipas was not stupid. He could not afford to alienate Pilate entirely. After all, the woman he sent away in order to marry Herodias was the daughter of a neighboring king. Antipas might need Rome's protection before all was said and done.

With the arrival of a servant bearing a platter of triangular-shaped meat-filled dumplings the conversation was interrupted. The Roman officers continued to study the faces of the players in the deadly game of political intrigue: Antipas and Herodias.

■ ■ ■ ■

Gamaliel called Nakdimon as they exited the council chamber. Drawing Nakdimon aside, the older man lowered his voice. "You have an opinion?"

Grimacing, Nakdimon replied, "The rabbi of Nazareth has some powerful enemies . . . though I'm not sure why. Six months ago Caiaphas was satisfied with merely discrediting him. This clumsy business with the coin could have gotten Yeshua arrested and punished by the Romans. It's become dangerous nowadays to be a country preacher."

"You're thinking of Yochanan the Baptizer as well?" Gamaliel asked abruptly.

Nakdimon elaborated. "I went out to hear the Baptizer myself. Nothing seditious in his preaching. Harsh accusations against scribes and Pharisees. Myself included. But I stayed. Yochanan never attacked keeping the law . . . he condemned hypocrisy and pretense."

"He and Yeshua of Nazareth are cousins."

"A whole tribe of fire-breathing prophets?" Nakdimon said, laughing.

Gamaliel raised a finger in warning. "The connection explains everything. The Baptizer publicly acclaimed Yeshua as a righteous man while he was baptizing at the Jordan. If the masses rebel and make Yeshua king, then of course the Baptizer would be exalted to high position. Official prophet perhaps. Like Samuel to King David? Or a new high priest?"

"But how do you know such things? Never mind," Nakdimon concluded, lifting his palm to silence his uncle's protest. "Like the *cohen ha-*

*gadol,* you have your sources. This accounts for why Caiaphas is so anxious to discredit Yeshua. To silence him."

"He's afraid Yeshua is gaining a following that will end in open rebellion against Rome. Failure of such a revolt would give Rome an excuse to destroy us."

"And if Yeshua succeeded?"

"His kingdom would still mean the destruction of the high priesthood of Caiaphas. Possibly of us who rule the affairs of our people."

"The Baptizer called us a brood of vipers," Nakdimon interjected. "I heard that with my own ears. But what if Yeshua is . . . authentic?"

"My point exactly. Frankly, Caiaphas was relieved when Herod Antipas arrested Yochanan and saved him the trouble . . . and the blame." Gamaliel reasoned. "There's a rumor abroad that Herod Antipas intends to release Yochanan to please the crowds. If true, it explains why Caiaphas is agreeable to Pilate's aqueduct scheme. The enemies are choosing up sides. If Yeshua brings an army, Caiaphas will have the soldiers of Rome join the Temple guard to defend his authority. There's more," he said, "which I'll explain later. Right now I need to catch the young member from Arimathea before he leaves. Unlike the rest of Caiaphas' yeasayers, Joseph appears to think for himself. But I have a favor to ask you."

"Anything," Nakdimon replied staunchly. "Name it."

"A trip to the Galil? Caiaphas has his tribe of spies. Coached in exactly what they are to report to the Sanhedrin. Maybe, in the interest of fairness, we should see firsthand what's happening in Galilee. I can trust you for an unbiased account."

Nakdimon considered the nature of the request. "Of course," he said. "I've wanted to meet the fellow. Talk with him. Tales are thick about his miracles among the common folk. The ignorant will believe any delusion that gives them hope. As for the rest of us? We remain skeptics. But then . . . Simon of Capernaum says he witnessed Yeshua heal a paralytic in the home of Kuza, the steward."

"A staged performance or real?" Both men knew Simon the Pharisee was a hardheaded man, difficult to impress. For Simon to relate any such story was significant.

Nakdimon shrugged. "Question of the hour."

Gamaliel concurred. "It might be wise to interview witnesses. Warn them there will be consequences if they help perpetrate a hoax. You know what I'm saying? Discreetly. Get the details. Find the truth. If there is truth to be found."

"I've felt restless ever since Hadassah's . . . since she's been gone. Perhaps the travel will help."

Clapping his nephew on the shoulder, Gamaliel declared, "Good! I knew I could count on you. Enjoy Purim with your children, but go before next Sabbath if possible. I'd go myself, but I must keep close to this Korban issue. The aqueduct. It'll not get resolved as easily as Caiaphas thinks."

■ ■ ■ ■

Kuza, as the imitation Caiaphas, continued to harangue the crowd, urging them to drink and to practice for the soon-to-come *megillah*. The play would recount the story of how Queen Esther defeated Haman in his attempt to annihilate the Jews of Persia.

Salome, stepdaughter of Herod Antipas, would play the character of the beautiful Queen Esther, savior of all the Jews of the Persian empire.

Kuza, with a change of hats, would perform dual roles as both narrator of the story and Mordechai, Esther's uncle.

Marcus wondered if Herod Antipas had invited the crowd of non-Jews here to witness the spectacle for a purpose. Did the tale of Esther contain a message? A warning he wished to convey to the Roman overlords?

Herod Antipas, for all his dissipation, remained as clever as a fox. Every move contained a motive.

Every party-goer had received a noisemaker. Marcus was handed a clay jug full of dry beans as a rattle. Kuza explained that when the word *Haman* was spoken, the audience was to make so much noise the name would be drowned out.

The counterfeit high priest led the crowd in reciting its lines. "When I say 'A Jew of the tribe of Benjamin whose name was . . .'"

"Mordechai!" bellowed those in the audience who could still speak.

"And when I mention Haman?"

The hall erupted with buzzing, whirring, clattering, and booing, in accordance with the dictum *Yimah schmo*—"May his name be erased."

Pseudo-Caiaphas shook his head sadly. "You are still wallowing in your sin," he chided. "The rule is, you must drink *ad de lo yada*—until you cannot tell the difference between Mordechai . . ."

Cheers, shouts!

". . . and Haman!"

Hisses, catcalls, stomping, and scattered applause.

Kuza encouraged them, "Some of you are nearing repentance. But as for the rest: drink up!"

Kuza strolled cheerfully through the audience, stopping to encourage each guest to imbibe. When he neared Marcus and Felix, he greeted them enthusiastically, repeating his comedic routine. As laughter swelled around him, he stooped to whisper through a forced smile, "Marcus, keep grinning as if I am telling you a most obscene joke. Herodias is plotting. I overheard it. She says her Haman truly will be no more after tonight."

Marcus laughed loudly and forced himself not to look at Herodias.

With that the comic master of ceremonies straightened and announced, "Well done, Centurion! A fellow who grasps the true meaning of Purim! And now, honored guests, I depart to call forth the heroines, heroes, and villains of our most noble entertainment! The Purim *megillah* of Esther!"

Applause and boos followed Kuza from the banqueting hall. Marcus considered Kuza's information. Who in the room would Herodias consider her personal enemy? Roman officials or officers? Not likely. Only one man came to mind.

# EREKH

Nakdimon left the council house.

Waiting outside the Temple gates was a flock of Jerusalem Sparrows, their torches aloft. Dirty. Half-starved. Shoeless. Clothed in cast-off rags.

They implored him: "Me, sir! I'll take you where you want to go!"

"No! I know the way! You're the rabbi Nakdimon! I know your house!"

Nakdimon scanned their eager faces. Homeless boys. Hungry and without parents, they depended on the charity of men like Nakdimon to stay alive.

"Choose me, Teacher!"

"No! Choose me!"

"I can get you there quick! I know the way to your fine house, sir!"

Tonight there were just twelve boys with torches blazing and one more whose torch was unlit. They were fewer and much younger than the usual crowd. The average age of these Sparrows was seven or eight years old. Nakdimon reasoned that the larger, stronger boys had managed to get their hands on the free bread. By now they would have devoured their bread and be warming themselves by an open fire.

These thirteen scrawny birds were clearly not tough enough to wade through today's riot and capture either bread or penny. But at least they had survived. It was reported that among the dead was one of the Sparrows, trampled under a Roman horse.

Nakdimon examined the face of each child. Their pleading fell silent beneath his pained expression. How could he choose only one pair to guide him home?

He asked in a cheerful voice, "So, were you at the palace of Herod Antipas today? Did you get yourself some bread? Eh, boys?"

Sad, almost guilty looks passed between them.

A thin, pale fragment of a boy replied, "We were there. But us that you see here, we're not big enough to reach, sir. Such a crowd, sir. Like at Succoth. Everyone was drunk and screaming. Fighting for it, you know? Some of us got lucky. Some didn't."

The child did not mention his fallen comrade. But the memory of his death was plainly written on every face.

"Where are the other link boys tonight?" Nakdimon asked.

The spokesman responded after a long hesitation. "A Sparrow died today, sir, whilst he was getting a penny 'neath a horse. So the other boys, they're burying him at the quarry. They sent us younger boys out to link."

Another piped up. "We're all there is. The older boys sent us out to link, lest Antipas think giving us free bread has made us lazy. If such a thought came to his honor, sir, I'm sure there'd never be no more free bread nor pennies neither. The olders sent us young ones out to work whilst they mourn a while and bury Hayyim down by the quarry."

Nakdimon stared at the youngster, trying to discern if such a thing could be true! *Hayyim?* The name meant "Life." How could it be that children were left to bury life? If Hadassah ever heard such a story! If she had been there with him to see these faces! Nakdimon knew she would have taken them home for Purim supper with her! Fed them stewed chicken and found businesses to apprentice them to! Impractical Hadassah would have gathered the torches and led these little ones home by their own light! And Nakdimon would have been commanded by his beloved to pay the bills.

But Hadassah was gone, too good a soul to stay in such a grim and desperate world. And Nakdimon was left alone, without her light, to find his way.

Silence was accompanied by the soft lapping of torch flames. Then, from down the road, came the sound of music from the banquet of Antipas. Joy seemed an intrusion, an insult to their grief.

They exchanged glances and shifted uneasily as they waited for Nakdimon to choose.

He said aloud, "I can't do everything you want, Hadassah."

Their expressions confirmed it was an odd comment, since there was no woman to be seen. Was he speaking to the first Hadassah? The ancient Queen Esther? After all, her Purim festival decreed that the poor should be cared for on this day.

They could not know that Nakdimon often spoke to his own dear Hadassah, though she had been gone these eighteen months. It helped him think through what he should do.

The boys looked to see where Hadassah might be. Was she in the shadows?

"Who will link for you, sir?" asked the spokesman.

Nakdimon pretended to count them. He pointed to the pale, blue-eyed youngster whose torch was burned out. "You and your partner will guide me."

A chorus of protest arose. "But he hasn't got light!"

Nakdimon asked the lightless Sparrow, "Where's your partner, boy?"

"He hasn't got a partner," scowled the leader.

Nakdimon demanded, "Every Sparrow has a partner. It's decreed." Then again to the lightless boy, "Where's your partner?"

"Hayyim is dead, sir," replied the child solemnly. "I sit *Shiva* for him. And I won't light my torch for seven days."

"Then how will you earn money for bread?" Nakdimon queried.

"My heart's in Hayyim's grave. How can I eat?"

Nakdimon nodded. "You observe *Shiva* for your friend, Hayyim. Commendable to show such respect for the dead."

The boy's blue eyes flashed. "Even the poor know how to mourn. Hayyim was my friend."

"I would say the poor know best how to mourn the death of life. You could give the rest of us lessons, eh?" Nakdimon motioned for him to come forward. "What's your name?"

"Avel Lo-Ahavah."

*Mourner. He who is not loved. Avel, who had no light to carry in this darkness.*

Nakdimon put a hand on the boy's brow. *I know you well, Avel. We are old friends, but you don't know it.* "So, Avel. You'll guide me home tonight."

The others shouted their objections. Would Avel get an entire penny for himself?

"It's black as pitch!"

"You'll fall!"

"He'll lead you into a ditch."

"Pick me!"

Nakdimon shrugged. "In Jerusalem these days one torch is as bright as another." He turned his face to the sky. "What do you say, Avel?"

The grieving Sparrow answered, "They're right. It's a very black night."

"Then all of you will guide me," Nakdimon said.

"You mean all of us, sir?"

Nakdimon nodded absently, looking at no one as he imagined Hadassah's stern expression. She would say it wasn't enough. And she would be right. He spoke to her as though she was there. "It's a trifling thing, I know. But I can't manage more tonight. You can't expect me to go down to the quarry and say *kaddish*. But at least it's something."

The spokesman questioned, "But sir, there are a dozen of us. You just need one team to light you."

Nakdimon stooped to look Avel in the eye. "This once, Mourner. Come on, then. Yes. You and your friends. Thirteen of you. My wife would enjoy watching me coming home in a blaze of light. So, Avel will take the lead. Like a flock. One penny each."

■ ■ ■ ■

The house of Nakdimon ben Gurion occupied a broad stretch of the western hill of the city. It stood on a corner where two roads intersected. One led toward the Gate of the Essenes, where the city wall perched above the Valley of the Hinnom. The other lane curved in a graceful arc toward the Temple Mount. An extensive garden of figs, grapes, and pomegranates stretched behind the house, the whole enclosed by a high wall. Many wealthy citizens resided in this favored part of Jerusalem. In fact, Caiaphas' imposing palace was not far away.

In honor of the festival of Purim, all the walls surrounding the homes of the affluent were ablaze with oil lamps. The link boys' flickering torches had added nothing to the illumination for the last three blocks.

Twelve of the Jerusalem Sparrows exclaimed openly and repeatedly about the splendor of the neighborhood, though they could not see into the interior of any of the dwellings. The windows of the rich only overlooked their own courtyards. Despite the blazing lights, the poor could never glimpse the rich at their tables. Nor were the wealthy obliged to view the less fortunate passing by outside.

Avel, carrying his unlit torch, neither saw, heard, nor cared. When the procession arrived at Nakdimon's gate, he was sunk in gloom.

Avel had mourned for his mother, yet she had never loved him. She had never cared about him, so his grief was for what should have been.

The loss of Hayyim was much, much worse.

Hayyim had been his friend, his teacher, his protector. They had divided scanty food, inadequate covering, and momentary pleasures, all somehow multiplied by the sharing.

Now he was gone.

The rest of the link boys bubbled and laughed with pleasure as Nakdimon produced his money pouch. The man's hand was broader than the opening of the leather bag, so he shook the coins out onto his expansive palm.

He did not fling down the money and hurry inside as many of the rich did, anxious to be free of the smell and sight of the orphan Sparrows. Instead, Nakdimon raised each penny and placed it carefully in each small hand with a thank-you and a murmured word of blessing.

Coming last to Avel, Nakdimon held out the coin. When Avel did not reach for it, Nakdimon placed it in a pocket of the boy's robe, then laid his hand on top of Avel's head.

Avel did not shake off the touch, but neither did he respond to the prayer.

It was time to return to the quarry. Several of the Sparrows started out, calling to Avel. "Come on! Come on, Avel! Let's go."

Finally one of the others grasped him by the elbow and led him away. Avel did not see Nakdimon's sad expression as he watched the Sparrows leave.

■ ■ ■ ■

Except for a single candle in the foyer, the house was dark as Nakdimon entered.

Colorful Purim banners hung from the banister of the second floor. These were a reminder to Nakdimon that he had missed the family celebration his children had been planning for weeks. They would not understand his absence. Tomorrow he would have to face their disappointment.

He raised his eyes toward the closed doors of their bedrooms and thought of all the other Purim celebrations when Hadassah had created the most elaborate holiday parties. The house had brimmed with light and noise and squeals of laughter.

Nakdimon knew Hadassah would not approve of his placing duty to official matters above his own children.

And what good had his presence been? What had he accomplished by attending the meeting and opposing Caiaphas in the matter of the Korban funds?

Nothing.

Why had he given his word to Gamaliel that he would leave within the week for the Galil? Were the facts about Yeshua of Nazareth more important than the needs of his own children?

With a guilty sigh he tossed aside his satchel and retrieved the flickering stub of the candle. Wearily he made his way toward the stairs. He was a failure as a father and as a member of the Sanhedrin. It had been months since he and a meager handful of others had agreed with Caiaphas and his cronies about anything. The court was packed by Rome. The course was set. Anyone perceived as a threat to the high priest's ambition and power would be entrapped and discredited.

Possibly destroyed.

Since Hadassah died, he had several times considered resigning from his post. But Gamaliel kept him from it with the admonition that they must remain in the chamber as the conscience of the Sanhedrin.

And so he stayed with Gamaliel, Joseph of Arimathea, and a remnant of others. They spoke the truth, argued Torah, discussed problems, and were voted down every time.

"I'm sorry, Hadassah," he whispered.

And then he heard a stirring behind a curtain. A child's laugh. A stern warning for silence. Then a door was thrown open, and light blazed out.

"Surprise!" the voices of his six daughters cried in unison as they spilled out to greet him at the top of the stairs. Dressed in their Purim costumes, with faces painted, and silk veils flowing, they bobbed up and down with excitement.

Each of the six had some feature of their mother's. Miniature Hadassahs, all. Every beloved expression, every aspect of Hadassah's personality was implanted in the girls to one degree or another. They were cut from the same bolt of cloth. Brown hair with just a hint of gold in the sunlight. Soft brown eyes. Straight teeth. Each of them blessed with a healthy body and keen mind. Those in the marketplace often commented on how easy it was to recognize a child of Hadassah and Nakdimon ben Gurion's. All the girls resembled their mother, which was a mercy. Only the little one, the boy, had his father's features.

It was a good thing little Samuel was a boy, for he was not a pretty child: large and square. His nose already prominent. Eyes dark pools. Curly black hair. Teeth that grew in several different directions. He was the only homely one in the bunch. Thankfully, since he was a male, his looks did not matter as much.

Hannah, the oldest at twelve, was serious and businesslike. Her curly hair cascaded down her back. She looked so much like her mother had when Nakdimon first laid eyes on her.

Then there was Susanna: ten years old with wide brown eyes and coy smile. Shy with strangers but raucous and full of mischief with the family.

And Ruth, aged nine: oval face. Cheerful and excitable with a contagious laugh.

The seven-year-old twins, Sarah and Dinah, resembled their oldest sister in looks and temperament.

The youngest daughter, Leah, was a cup of sweetness. Forever bringing in little birds fallen from nests or weeping at the sight of a beggar in the street, Hadassah's heart was in her.

And then there was Samuel. A painted beard adorned his smooth cheek. He was barely eighteen months old. Hadassah had never known him beyond the life she gave him in her womb. How proud she would have been. Here was one who resembled Nakdimon at last!

"We waited . . ."

"Waited for you . . ."

"For you, Papa!"

"You didn't miss it!"

"You're to play the part of King Xerxes!"

"Here's your crown!" Leah held out a cooking pot decorated with bits of colored glass for jewels.

In the arms of his oldest sister, baby Samuel shouted above them all, "Papa! Home!"

"You see, Papa, we waited." Leah kissed Nakdimon's hand and held his palm against her cheek. "I'm playing Queen Esther. Samuel is playing Mordechai. See his painted beard? Charcoal. We couldn't have Purim without a king."

From behind the little troupe emerged Nakdimon's widowed mother, Em. Hawk-nosed and grizzled gray, she ran Nakdimon's house like a ship at sea. Discipline was everything. Except when they stood firm together against her edicts. Like tonight. Sternly she proclaimed, "They wouldn't go to bed until you came home, Nakdimon. They wouldn't eat the Purim feast Bekah cooked for them. Or perform the *megillah.* You've got a stiff-necked tribe here. They refused to have fun unless you were with them, and I wasn't about to argue tonight."

Leah tugged his sleeve. "Say a *b'rakhah,* Papa! We can't start without it! You must say a *b'rakhah* over us to begin!"

"So." He laughed with relief. "It's a blessing you're after?"

All chimed in with the request.

He raised his hands and pronounced the blessing reserved for seeing something unusually beautiful. "Blessed are You, *Adonai* our God, King of the universe, who has created such miraculous beauty for himself in his universe."

■ ■ ■ ■

On the return journey to their tomblike quarters only one of the Sparrows still had his torch lit. One light was plenty for a dozen link boys to guide on, and it preserved the other torches for later use.

The one with the flame was in the lead and kept hold of Avel for fear the unresponsive boy would otherwise lag behind and be lost.

Threading the maze of passages into the depth of the quarry, Avel knew he was nearing home. But his thoughts revolved around how Hayyim would not be there when he arrived. Hayyim would never be there again.

At the last turn into his burrow, Avel was suddenly grasped by the other wrist. Yanked loose from one grip, he was flung across the chamber by Kittim's violent tug on his arm. Narrowly missing striking his head on a projecting knob of rock, Avel wound up against a wall.

Kittim, backed by two of his older lieutenants, confronted the apprehensive younger Sparrows. "You finally return!" he said gruffly. "All of you parading across the city together, wasting torches and wasting time! Did you think I wouldn't hear about it? Did you think you were going to a Purim pageant? Link boys don't take holidays, or they're turned out!"

One of Avel's comrades protested. "But he paid us all!"

Another chimed in, "That's true! Rabbi Nakdimon hired all of us."

"And he didn't give a penny for two," a third boy nervously added. "He paid us a penny each!"

At first raising his chin doubtfully, Kittim's eyes glowed with avarice when he was finally convinced of the story's reality. "So," he said. "A good thing for you. Line up. Every second one of you, hand over his penny. Starting with you, Avel."

Thrusting his hand into the pocket of Avel's robe, Kittim raised his eyebrows and exclaimed, "What's this? Two coins?"

Shoving off hard, Avel tore free of Kittim's clutch. "You can have one, but the other was Hayyim's and I'm keeping it."

"Oh?" Kittim sneered. "You don't say what happens here. I do. And you were holding out on me earlier, eh?"

All the smaller boys were too afraid of Kittim to suggest that he had already taken a penny from Avel that day.

"Hand them over!"

"I won't," Avel replied. "I'm keeping it."

Kittim lunged.

Swinging the unlit torch, Avel struck the older boy on the side of the head. The blow did not hurt Kittim, but surprised him. "You need to be taught a lesson."

When Avel swung at him again, Kittim grabbed the torch and twisted it out of Avel's hand. With a backhand blow, Kittim knocked Avel to the ground. "Give me the pennies," he insisted.

Over the warnings of the younger link boys, Avel refused. Kittim's fist hit Avel on the chin, and Avel's skull bounced hard against the un-yielding floor. "Now!" Kittim repeated. "The pennies."

Through a haze of flashing lights and blinding pain Avel retorted, "Not Hayyim's!" and he threw one coin at Kittim's face.

Kittim's next blow smashed into Avel's cheek, then another landed on his nose and another in his stomach. Turning over, Avel covered his head as best he could, till he felt Kittim rifling his pockets.

As Kittim reached again for the remaining penny, Avel squirmed around and sunk his teeth into Kittim's arm.

The older boy cried out in pain and jerked away. Avel felt as if his head was nearly popped off his body, but the warm blood in his mouth was Kittim's.

Then the blows fell on Avel's flesh the way the hammer strikes of the quarryman had once knocked away chunks of stone.

Finally Kittim's assistants pulled him away so he would not kill the boy. "Throw him out," Avel heard as from a vast distance. "He's out, hear me? And so none of the rest of you will ever think he was right, give me all the pennies. All of them! And it's Avel's fault. Remember that!"

Dumped in the passageway, Avel lay very still until a trickle of rain crept along a seam in the rock and dripped onto his face. Only partially revived, inch by inch, he crawled toward the open air.

■ ■ ■ ■

Avel, dragging his unlit torch, retreated from the quarry. The other Sparrows did not dare raise their eyes and look at him. The cold night air stung his face, numbing the throb of his bruises. He welcomed physical pain. Welcomed the ache of battle. It somehow lessened the agony of losing Hayyim.

He gazed up at the cloudy sky and began to weep: choking, racking sobs. He told himself that his tears were because of Kittim's beating and the loss of Hayyim's penny.

These thoughts were easier than the truth. *Hayyim gone! Oh, no! Forever gone!* Losing Hayyim was harder to bear than the night his mother had shouted, *"Lo-Ahavah! Lo-Ruhamah!"*

*Ahavah!* The only one who had ever loved him was buried in a shallow grave.

*Ruhamah!* The only one who had pitied him was dead.

Avel clawed his way through the strewn rubble of the deserted stoneyard to Cripple Rock. Fifty years earlier the giant block had broken loose while being moved to the Temple building site. Tumbling down the slope, it had crushed the legs of seven masons. Amputation of their limbs was required to free them. The smashed bones of feet, calves, and thighs remained entombed beneath the discarded stone.

Each year at Passover pilgrims placed gifts of food upon this gruesome table for the lame beggars of Jerusalem to distribute.

Like a big-eyed fledgling fallen from its nest, Avel scuttled onto Cripple Rock. He turned his face heavenward in anguish.

No wings to take flight. No safe place to hide. His heart raced with fear. What would become of him? How could he live without Hayyim? How would he eat?

He covered his face with his hands and sobbed quietly for a long time. He whispered, "Hayyim! Hayyim! Why did you leave me? Hayyim! What will I do now?"

Then the weary voice of an old man croaked up at him. "You've awakened me with your chirping, Sparrow. Do you have a name, boy?"

Avel started. "I'm Avel . . . who's asking?" He brushed away his tears on his sleeve.

"Sekhel Tov, the cripple," came the calm reply.

Avel peered over the ledge at the dark ground but saw no one in the stone's shadow.

Avel challenged the old man, *"Sekhel Tov!* 'Good Understanding'? What kind of name is that for a lame man?"

The beggar countered, "First tell me how a small boy can be called Avel."

Avel spat. "What do you want?"

"To understand."

"Understand what?"

"Why a child mourns."

Avel scrambled back to the center of the block. "Kittim beat me and stole Hayyim's penny and threw me out. And today . . . this morning . . . the Roman killed Hayyim beneath his horse."

"Reason enough to wake an old man with your wailing. So where is your home, Avel?"

"In the quarry. By the charity of the seventy elders of the Jews! They give me and the other orphans the right to be here. No matter what Kittim says! I can sit on this stone if I want," Avel defended. "And I don't know any cripple named Sekhel Tov! I know all the beggars. No lame man by that name lives at the quarry! Why are you here?"

"I've come searching for legs in Jerusalem. But Sekhel Tov hasn't found so much as a crutch to lean on. And no man in Jerusalem will carry me into the Temple. They're afraid, I suppose."

"Afraid of what? Are you a leper, then?" Images of rotting flesh and dangling extremities came to mind. "No lepers are allowed at this quarry! This is where the Temple stones were cut. If you're unclean . . . go away!"

"I'm neither a leper nor a serpent that would swallow a Sparrow for supper. Though many in Jerusalem call me both."

"Go away!" Avel cried, a chill of fear coursing through him. He was certain the old man was a leper disguising himself in the dark. "I was here first!"

A low chuckle replied to the Sparrow's demand. Then, "The one who beat you and stole Hayyim's penny? The one you call Kittim. Is he in the cavern?"

"What of it?"

"If you fear anything, fear that cat and those who permit him to rule over the Sparrows. Baza is his father. Pesha is his mother. Understand me now, little bird. I'm old. Sekhel Tov has seen enough Unjust Gain and Transgressions to know. Don't go back. He'll devour everything but your beak, then use your claws to pick his teeth. He'll make his bed soft with your feathers. That's the way of things in Jerusalem nowadays. From top to bottom."

Avel shuddered at the warning and clutched his knees to his chest.

He stared at the edge of the stone, expecting Sekhel Tov to slither over the rim like a snake and swallow him whole.

But nothing happened.

Minutes ticked past. Avel heard the sound of scraping as the beggar dragged himself away, across the gravel. Avel called out, "Sekhel Tov! Old beggar! Where should I go?"

There was no reply from the old man.

Avel's teeth chattered with the cold.

# APAYIM

Throughout the Jewish provinces Herod Antipas was regarded as a fox for his cunning. But on this night of the Purim feast, while Antipas' features were wreathed with sweat and sagging from drink, it was Herodias whose face remained tack-sharp and watchful. Marcus wondered if she had particular reason to keep alert.

From the recesses of a curtained alcove came a troupe of actors made up and costumed to portray the characters in the story of Esther. The leads were introduced first. Kuza, dressed in the elegant clothes of a Persian wise man, took his bows as both narrator and Mordechai.

"And of course," Kuza explained, "it is fitting, proper, and right that the wise King Xerxes . . ." He prolonged the introduction, prodding the audience to a frenzy of cheers. "The great King Xerxes, the ruler of the far-flung Persian empire . . . will be played by our lord . . . gracious master . . . our ruler . . . generous . . . kind . . . full of the wisdom of Solomon . . . King Xerxes will be enacted by the Tetrarch of the Galil, son of Herod the Great . . . our own Herod Antipas."

The roar of approval was deafening.

Antipas, reclining comfortably on his couch directly in front of where the main action would take place, feigned resistance to the idea of participating. "Not if I have to move, Kuza."

"Oh, no, my lord! Stay where you are!"

"Where are my lines then?" Antipas asked.

Herodias, laughing, said loudly, "No script for the exalted Xerxes. Merely stay where you are and render wise judgment when the case is brought before you."

Antipas waved a jeweled hand in acceptance.

Kuza next introduced Mordechai's arch rival. Haman was portrayed by a bull-necked, heavy-jowled guard recruited from the ranks of Antipas' personal attendants. He sneered in response to the jeers of the assembly and stared coldly around the room. His triangular hat was laughed at, but he swirled his floor-length cloak around himself like a wizard about to invoke an evil spell.

It was a time before the boos and hisses subsided enough for the remaining principals to be named.

Queen Vashti was played by a thin, effeminate, long-nosed eunuch. He was homely as a horse, yet more feminine in mannerisms than most females, Marcus thought. The fellow sauntered around the high table winking and waving seductively at the men.

Last came Esther. Gliding out from behind the curtain in a shimmering gown of pale blue, Salome, the daughter of Herodias, was the perfect choice to play the beautiful young queen.

Felix raised up from where he was slumped on his couch to get a better look. Where Salome's mother was bony and pointed, the eighteen-year-old girl was slim and fetching. Where Herodias' hair was coppery, Salome's was a subdued auburn. She moved with a lithe grace that brought cries of appreciation and several ribald comments from the spectators.

Marcus leaned over and explained her identity to the gaping Felix. "So you won't say anything you'll regret later."

The remaining members of the company stepped forward, and the *megillah* began.

High comedy in its portrayal, the story of Esther unfolded in dance and mime with a chorus emphasizing the key elements in song.

Kuza began the ballad. "This is what happened in the time of King Xerxes, who ruled over one hundred and twenty provinces from India to Cush! But he could not rule over his own wife, Queen Vashti!"

The eunuch, clothed in veils and flowing silk, stepped forward. He waved toward Felix, puckered his painted lips, and blew him a kiss.

The crowd roared with pleasure as Felix leapt to his feet and bowed to the eunuch.

"Later, soldier!" the eunuch crooned.

Kuza, finding a break in the laughter, cried, "It's plain to see why King Xerxes was displeased with his queen, Vashti," Kuza went on. "She had refused his command to dance before an assembly of the king's drunken friends!"

Boos and hisses, cheers and shouts of glee followed as the play unfolded. A beautiful, voluptuous new queen was chosen.

Enter Salome. Esther. The substitute queen of King Xerxes.

Young Salome did not refuse to dance.

In the audience, possibly just Marcus detected the irony between the plot of the play and the reality of Herod's court.

Felix, who had been nearly asleep before Salome entered, was suddenly fully awake and attentive. Her long auburn hair cascaded over slender shoulders. Her complexion was smooth as cream. Lips red. Eyes wide-set and full of innocence. Salome's breasts were round and full, her waist petite and hips in pleasant proportion. She glided seductively around Herod Antipas as the story progressed.

Herodias must have been a woman of true beauty in her younger days, Marcus realized. But the hardness of life had etched itself on her face. And tonight in particular her expression was as adamant and acute as a Roman sword.

In the story of Esther, the king's wicked advisor, Haman, devised a plan to destroy the Jews of Persia, starting with the Jew Mordechai.

Esther, using her charm and beauty, uncovered the plot and convinced the king that Haman must be stopped.

It was a good enough play, Marcus thought. Not of the quality of Greek or Roman theatricals, but the tale caught his interest. How would the terrible Haman be thwarted?

By a woman's dance before King Xerxes?

Herodias' eyes glinted as she watched Salome perform. Marcus was now convinced there was a subplot to the whole evening's activity. What had Herodias devised tonight? And who was the notorious enemy she longed to destroy?

It was plain from the unyielding line of Herodias' mouth that a twist somewhere in the telling would surprise everyone. Possibly Antipas most of all.

Kuza, relishing his part as narrator, strode across the front of the hall as the story came to its climax. Now the audience was quiet as he reintroduced the character of King Xerxes.

"So!" Kuza gestured broadly to Haman, who joined Salome. They sat down together at the foot of Herod Antipas' couch. "The king and Haman went to dine with Queen Esther. As they were drinking wine on that second day, the king asked . . ." At this point Kuza bowed to Antipas. "This is where you say your lines, master."

There were chuckles as Antipas raised his cup to drink first. It was clear Herod Antipas knew the story well enough that he was undaunted by having to speak his part.

He raised the fingers of Salome to his lips and proclaimed loudly,

"Esther! My beautiful queen. Heart of my heart! Esther! What is your petition? It will be given to you! What is your request? Even up to half my kingdom! Anything you ask will be granted!"

Salome glanced triumphantly at her mother. "Anything?"

"Tell me what you crave," Herod replied.

"Should I tell King Xerxes? Or should I tell the great Herod Antipas my heart's desire?"

Herod declared loudly, "Tell us both! How can I fulfill the heart's desire of one so beautiful?"

Salome answered. "If I have found favor with you, O King! And if it pleases your majesty, this is my petition! Grant me my life! Grant me my mother's life! Grant me a return of our honor."

Was this part of the play, or were new lines being introduced?

Marcus thought he saw curiosity on the faces of the Jews in the audience.

Salome continued, "For I and my family have been slandered! We have been sold for destruction and for slaughter! If it was simply an unimportant matter I would have kept quiet, because my distress would not justify disturbing the king! But my enemy would destroy me and those I love most in the world, O great king! Grant me the head of our wicked foe. Let it be delivered on a platter before this banquet ends."

A flicker of uneasy comprehension passed through Herod Antipas' eyes. Was she acting? Or was there something more sinister about her words? Antipas continued the charade. "Who is he? Where is the man who has dared do such a thing?"

"He is near," Salome replied in a voice full of assurance. "The adversary and enemy is vile Yochanan the Baptizer."

There were a few catcalls and scattered cheers at the mention of the Baptizer. He was indeed an enemy to Salome's mother.

Herodias smiled, smug and content in the trap she had set for Antipas.

The color drained from Antipas' face. He attempted to dismiss the request as a joke. "Choose something else, Salome. The Baptizer is a vile creature, indeed, but he's in Machaerus. I've had him thrown in the deepest cell of my prison. He'll never see the light of day again."

Evidently Salome had been well rehearsed by her mother. The young woman's eyes brimmed with tears of disappointment. Her voice cracked with emotion. As the audience sat spellbound she cried, "The Baptizer's not in Machaerus! He's here in Jerusalem! Brought in this morning. He's in the dungeon of this very palace. And he waits for my famous and wise lord, Herod Antipas, to revenge the honor of my sweet and gracious mother by fulfilling your oath. Anything, you promised me. Anything. And what I ask is that you destroy the enemy of your wife . . . my enemy!"

Felix bent forward to ask Marcus, "Is this . . . part of the play?"

"No." Marcus, his gaze riveted to Antipas' face, knew it was something else. Herodias had won her battle over the preacher.

Antipas was trapped. Three hundred guests, officials and dignitaries from his kingdom, sat waiting for his reply.

Marcus had seldom seen a maneuver as smooth as this. The Baptizer, a man of the wilderness, had been penned in a cage by beasts so cunning he never had a chance.

How would the Baptizer's talmidim react when the word of this came to them? What would Yeshua do when he learned his righteous cousin had been murdered as the climax to a play?

Perhaps Yeshua would lay aside his ways of peace. Maybe now, Marcus reasoned, he would accept a crown and raise an army to take back his nation from the likes of Herod Antipas.

Antipas sipped his wine and raised his chin as if he was unafraid of the command he must issue. "Even up to half my kingdom I offered the girl." He managed to croak a laugh. "And all she wants is the filthy head of a wild-man preacher for her supper? You heard her! Well, then, I keep my villas. I keep the Galil, eh? You may have Yochanan the Baptizer, when you might have had Tiberias as your own city."

He snapped his fingers once at the burly guard who played Haman and said to the man, "So. You thought the play would end tonight with you hanging from the gallows? Did you?"

The guard stood and saluted. "What is your will, my lord?"

"It's my will that my family honor be avenged. It's my will that you go now to the dungeon and fetch the head of the Baptizer and present it to my stepdaughter. On a platter, as she requested. And to her mother. My wife. Herodias. Haven't I proven my love for her now before all of Jerusalem? This is what's done for the woman the king delights to honor!"

Cheers. The guard backed away and strode out of the hall to execute the judgment of Antipas.

Marcus was sickened. Pointless. Pointless brutality.

Felix rubbed his throat nervously. "And I was thinking of taking that pretty young thing to bed!"

"Better a viper than Salome," Marcus muttered.

"Madness," Felix added with a hint of amusement. "It's in the blood, they say. I hear this fellow's father, Herod the Great, had friends and relatives beheaded regularly. Women boiled. Babies run through. A madman."

Marcus replied sullenly, "His son takes after him, it seems."

"So we're to have an execution for the main course. This rivals any birthday banquet I've seen in Rome. These Jews compete with Germans in the novelty of their cruelty. The guests are too drunk to remember much of it. I'm feeling my wine a bit too."

Marcus and Kuza exchanged a glance of somber comprehension. Herodias knew the play. And she taught her daughter her lines. There was no stopping this. Nothing to do but go on silently, express no displeasure. Display no fear. The ruthlessness of Antipas and his woman were cause enough to stay out of their line of sight. Kuza had no choice but to continue as if this was all in a day's work.

Marcus could leave. He would be relieved to be back in the wilderness chasing bandits. At least there he knew what he was fighting against.

Kuza, pale beneath his makeup, returned center stage to finish the performance. He faltered, stammered, began again . . . "Thus ends . . . our story . . . of . . . of Queen Esther."

Antipas' mood had gone black. He ordered Kuza to go on with the play, all of it.

Kuza continued for ten minutes of narration, overcoming his own terror at being part of this event. "Mordechai recorded these things. And he sent letters to the Jews throughout the provinces of King Xerxes to celebrate annually the fourteenth and fifteenth days of Adar. He wrote to them . . . to observe the days as days of feasting and giving of presents of food to one another and gifts to the poor. . . ."

Kuza clapped his hands and the music resumed. The cloud over the audience dissipated for a time. Conversation began again. The aroma of every kind of fowl, roasted beef, lamb, and heaps of fruits and sweets was mouthwatering.

A parade of slaves circled the hall carrying heaping trays of food, brimming pitchers of wine.

And, at the last, they brought in the severed head of Yochanan the Baptizer on a silver platter.

Though no stranger to bloody deaths in battle or violent executions, Marcus felt the color drain from his face.

These people who made much of their own self-importance justi-
fied murder because of a personal slight? And slaughtered Yochanan,
whose message had been one of repentance?

If a manifestly good man . . . a prophet . . . could be destroyed at a
whim, then no one was safe. Even if a god took human form and came
to earth, powerful people obsessed with their own comfort and security
would find a way to eliminate him.

Marcus' mind reeled with these thoughts. He knew his own life was
in jeopardy because of a long-ago affront to Lucius Sejanus, now head of
the Praetorian Guard and chief advisor to Emperor Tiberius Caesar.

Though drunk, Felix was not so lost in his cups that the sight made
no impression. Leaning close to Marcus, he clasped the centurion by the
shoulder. "Tell no one what happened here tonight. And pray that
everyone's too drunk and think they had a nightmare. As for that other
business of the Jewish elders," he said, struggling against the wine to organize his concerns, "what I told you I overheard. Caiaphas wants to en-
trap the other prophet from the Galil . . . you know him . . . Neshua?"

"Yeshua of Nazareth?" Marcus suggested, then added with a shrug,
"I've . . . met him."

"They want us to do their dirty work for them," Felix declared.
"Make Rome part of their . . . but what's he done? Why do they hate
him?" The tribune's speech rambled like his thoughts. "Jealous perhaps
that all the common Jews . . . the poor folk follow after him? They hint
he may be another Judah Maccabee set on rebellion against Rome. But
we'll never get the facts from the Sanhedrin." Reaching over, he patted
Marcus' bearded face. "Don't shave," he said. "Go to the Galil. Find this
Yeshua. Observe him. Bring me a true account. Wait till we see Jerusalem
doesn't explode if this news gets out, but go within the week."

■ ■ ■ ■

The moon hovered below the eastern horizon. The rising silver glow
outlined the barren mountains of Moab from behind them.

The city was strangely quiet after the day of violence. Citizens had
gathered their wounded, their bread, and their pennies, and crawled
away home. Inside their humble dwellings they licked their wounds and
contemplated the high cost of free bread.

His own children asleep at last, Nakdimon ben Gurion stepped
alone onto his roof garden. From the parapet he could see a blaze of
lights at the Hasmonaean Palace, where Herod Antipas held his birthday

banquet. A breeze carried faint snatches of laughter and music. Then there was silence from the hall.

Behind Nakdimon the wind chimes sang a discordant song. His dear Hadassah, sweet wife, had made them from the shattered pieces of a wine jar the week before she died.

*Autumn. Just before Yom Kippur, the Day of Atonement. He remembered her there beside him, telling him where the chimes should be hung and how to do it.*

*He teased her and quoted the proverb: "Better the corner of a rooftop with peace than a wide house and a brawling woman."*

*"Admit it. You'd be lost without me." She guided his hand to her belly. The baby moved within her at his touch.*

*"Will you share the rooftop with me then, Hadassah? So many children. There'll never be peace in the house."*

*"And if I share the rooftop with you for what you have in mind, there will be even more children by Spring."*

*"I never associated the two things." He laughed as she brushed her fingertips over the shards of the wind chimes.*

*"This will always remind you." She kissed him.*

*A week later Hadassah lay cold and lifeless in their bedchamber. The wail of a newborn boy child competed with mourners keening in the courtyard. Then, as now, Nakdimon retreated here, to the rooftop.*

Tonight he brushed his fingers over the broken shards and wondered if the ache of his loneliness would ever ease. As he had done each hour since she flew away, he forced himself to think of other things. Of Uncle Gamaliel. Of the tapestry of the heavens that hung, visible to all, inside the hall of the sanctuary.

"Yes. Better. The stars. The sky. Some meaning to it all. What was it?"

He lifted his chin to study the pattern of the real heavens. A shooting star left a faint trail of fire across the panoply of night. Nakdimon traced its path as it vanished above the mountains of Judah. Late-winter sky. The constellation of Orion was still most recognizable, even though it was dropping into the west.

Orion went by many names throughout the pagan world, but the three stars of his belt and the three defining the sword that hung from it marked him as a hunter to almost every culture. The long-vanished people of Sumer thought Orion was fighting the Great Bull, just ahead of him in the sky, with upraised club and defensive shield.

Tales . . . legends . . . myths . . . prophecy?

Nakdimon shook his head. He had seldom considered the stars before today's conversation with his uncle Gamaliel. Everyone knew that the constellations glided from east to west on the same unending cycle, year after year, marking the changing seasons. Always the same.

But was a more important message hidden there?

It was the planets that flew in contrary fashion above the earth, sometimes with the backdrop of stars and sometimes counter to them. Nor did these brighter lights of heaven move at the same pace as the stars or each other; it was as if they were competing for man's attention.

Romans and Greeks believed these celestial bodies were living gods. Each was named and worshiped: Mercury. Venus. Mars. Jupiter. Saturn.

The signs of the zodiac through which the moon and planets passed were likewise the object of pagan religious dogma. Sorcerers claimed to read a man's future by interpretation of the positions of the zodiac and the planet gods. To a Jew this was akin to trying to understand the will of the Most High by reading messages in the entrails of dead animals.

At the thought of such abomination Nakdimon lowered his eyes and whispered, "Hear O Israel, the Lord our God is One Lord . . ."

Nakdimon knew that the seven-branched candlestick inside the sanctuary represented the week of creation and the seven great visible lights of heaven. Seven shining flames reminded mankind that these things were created by *Adonai* in seven days. Sun. Moon. Five planets. All that was seen and unseen. Even orbs so glowingly beautiful were not to be worshiped. But the magnificence of the Maker was to be glimpsed in His creation. "The heavens declare the glory of *Adonai*," Nakdimon said aloud.

And so what was this tapestry in the Temple sanctuary beyond the altar of sacrifice? What was this sky map that captured the position of the stars of heaven, five planets, moon, and sun together in one hour of one night during the course of a year? It was a mystery indeed.

The thought sparked a memory, a time when a real portent in the sky created a furor.

When Nakdimon was a child, people still talked about a star that appeared in the heavens. Magi came from distant lands in search of a newborn said to be king of the Jews.

Herod the Great had summoned his counselors, including Nakdimon's father, to inquire about such a thing. He was told that a message given to the prophet Micah pointed to an inconsequential village named Bethlehem.

And then the jealous, fearful king had slaughtered all the boy babies, two years and under, of that town. There would be no challenge to Herod or his chosen successor, not even if heaven ordained it.

It had been passed off at the time as another fit of the king's well-known madness. Besides, the death toll was under fifty, hardly worth mentioning compared to other massacres he had decreed.

Blood and destruction . . . and less than a year later Herod the Great was dead, foul and stinking, and eaten by worms before he was in the grave.

Could the tapestry sky point toward another such horror?

Nakdimon was certain of one thing: the map on the curtain did not mirror tonight's heavens. Nor did Caiaphas, the high priest, have anything to worry about during this season of the year, even though the turbulence of the Passover pilgrimage was approaching.

There was Orion striding across the sky and the moon pushing up in the east. No at all like the tapestry.

So what season, what strange night, did the sky map display? And why did Caiaphas fear it?

■ ■ ■ ■

Hours passed.

A gloomy mist descended to shroud Jerusalem. The darkness within Avel's heart had not lifted even a fraction.

One by one the lights of Jerusalem winked out. Distant sounds of revelry died away. He was alone in the world.

Drowsy and grieving by turns, Avel remained too apprehensive to sleep. Every noise made him jerk upright. Perched on top of Cripple Rock, Avel imagined severed legs squirming beneath his roost. From there it was no stretch to envision hands crawling toward him, long-nailed claws wriggling nearer.

The terrifying visions caused him to constantly readjust his position. The boy tried to locate the exact center of the slab, the most distance between himself and the sides that fell away into dread-filled murk.

It was the longest night of Avel's soul.

He forced himself to think about his future. As uncertain as it was, surely it must be better to regard tomorrow than to dwell on the day just past.

Sekhel Tov was right. Jerusalem overflowed with injustice. Whether because of Kittim, the Romans, or mere faceless disregard for the needy, the character of the city was horrible and deadly. Avel concluded that he would die if he remained in it one more day.

There were few alternatives, so Avel's thoughts arrived quickly at their destination. He would seek out the rebel captain, bar Abba. There was a man who took no charity and did not bow to the Romans. His life was one of being constantly pursued, and yet he had purpose.

Nor had the sicarii ever done Avel any harm. And they all had grievances against things as they were.

He would be a rebel himself, he thought. He'd find bar Abba and offer to kill Romans. He wouldn't be turned down either, not when he told his story. And if he died, at least it would be for a reason, and not by Kittim's fists. He could be as brave as any rebel.

A stone rattled in the quarry. Rolling, it clicked against others before snapping to a stop.

Avel flinched, then froze. Someone was coming. It wasn't his imagination, either.

Feeling around the top of Cripple Rock, Avel hunted for the unlit firebrand to use as a club.

Then he heard a girl's voice say too loudly, "This is it. This is the place, Emet. This is where you must stay."

There was no reply, but two sets of footsteps padded softly below and beside Avel.

"What are you doing here?" Avel demanded.

The girl shrieked. "What? Who?"

Avel could hear her spin around, trying to identify the source of the challenge. But he knew she could not locate him atop his platform.

Suddenly Avel felt encouraged. Someone else was more frightened than he! "Girls aren't allowed here," he added roughly. "You better get away while you can."

"Where are you?" the girl inquired, regaining control of her quavering voice.

For an instant the moon peeked out from the layers of cloud at Jerusalem and Avel saw the girl. About eleven, he judged. Beside her was a very small boy. The two of them also saw Avel bending over above their heads.

Then a curtain of shadows fell between them again.

"This is my brother," the girl said. "I'm bringing him here to be a Sparrow."

Avel scoffed, "He's too little! He's littler than me. Take him out of here, or he'll be dead in a week."

There was a muffled grunting sound that Avel could not understand, then the sister explained. "But there's nowhere else! We're alone, and I've sold myself as a slave . . . but they don't want Emet. They say he's a useless mouth. I can't take him with me. What else is there?"

What else indeed? "How old is he, four?"

"Nearly five . . ." Moonlight illuminated the pair again. Emet, fair-haired like Avel, fixed his gaze on Avel's mouth as if he feared what Avel would say.

"Too small! Years too small! You, Emet," Avel directed to the boy, "you don't want to stay here, do you?"

"Nuhhh," was the reply. "Nuhhhh."

"He doesn't talk," Emet's sister added. "He won't be any trouble, and he doesn't eat much. You must take him."

Avel pondered. *What will Hayyim say?* was his first thought. Then he corrected his thoughts sorrowfully, remembering that he was all alone. He was not even one of the Jerusalem Sparrows any longer.

Silence reigned. Then Avel realized the plight of tiny Emet was not much worse than Avel's own. A companion would be good. They could go to another town, set up as link boys. Avel would teach Emet like Hayyim had instructed him. When they had money saved, they could travel and seek out bar Abba.

"Can he hear?" Avel queried.

"Some," the sister said. "Reads lips very well if you go slowly. He just can't speak. He'll be no bother."

"Well," Avel said grudgingly, "all right."

The girl was suddenly brisk. "Emet," she ordered, "you must stay here."

"Nuhhh," Emet wailed, then began to cry. "Nuhhhh!"

"Hey." Avel clapped his hands together hard, and Emet turned toward him. "Stop that! Listen, I know how you feel, but it'll be all right."

When the sister spoke again, her voice came from farther off. She was backing away, unseen. "Stay here, Emet. Don't follow me."

"Come on up here," Avel suggested gently, remembering too clearly the night his own mother had deserted him. He hoped the child could not hear his sister's farewell. "You don't want to wander around the quarry. There are holes you can fall in. That's it, climb up."

Snuffling, Emet struggled up the face of Cripple Rock. He had a tiny bundle of possessions wrapped in a scarf hanging around his thin neck. "Ahgh," he moaned, calling to the girl as if trying to form the word *sister.*

There was no reply. She had vanished.

Avel put out his hand to reassure the child as panic flooded his face. Emet's arms was hot to the touch, fevered. *He's sick,* Avel thought. *Great. She's left me with a sick kid. And crying, too.*

What to do?

*Get him moving,* Avel thought Hayyim would say. *And yourself too. How long will you sit here and mourn? Get going!*

"Get up," Avel mouthed distinctly. "I'm leaving Jerusalem, and you can come too. Listen: you've got to keep up, or I'll leave you. Let's go."

Avel helped Emet down from the boulder. "Give me your bundle." Then, tying the ends of the scarf to the torch, he added, "I'll carry it for you for a while."

# VE-RAV

Wrapped in a coarse brown woolen cloak against the chill of predawn, Marcus huddled in the doorframe of the wine shop. His Roman clothes were concealed, and his beard added to the disguise.

Lightning forked downward over the mountains of Moab, illuminating Jerusalem in an eerie monochrome light. A roll of thunder followed seven seconds after. A storm was moving nearer to the Jews' Holy City. The temperature had dropped steadily through the night. Some would call the approaching tempest a portent of tribulation yet to come upon Jerusalem.

A burst of rain splattered against the pavement, then slackened and turned to a miserable drizzle. Marcus pressed himself against the locked door in an attempt to stay dry. His temples throbbed. He closed his eyes briefly, then opened them again as the clear image of the Baptizer's severed head bobbed in his imagination.

*Eyes once filled with eternal vision were empty now! The tongue that had howled righteousness and repentance from the riverbank protruded limply from his lips like the tongue of a slaughtered sheep's head in the souk! And blood, which had carried fire through his veins, dripped from the silver plate like spilled wine, staining the marble floor of the banquet hall!*

Marcus tried to shake the horror of last night's event. Why did it trouble him so? He'd seen death ten thousand times in battle. Why, then, did this one fatality make his spirits sink? Why did he feel like one of the legionaries drowning by the weight of their armor in the river at Idistaviso where the Romans, but for Marcus' courage, had almost been defeated by German tribesmen?

He waited, hoping the Baptizer's followers would come early. Instead, they were late. Since he intended to violate an order, he wanted to get it over with as quickly as possible.

Marcus had been expecting Philip and Avram an hour ago. Where were they? Had Yochanan's disciples already heard their teacher had been beheaded last night? Were they on their way out of Jerusalem, back to the relative safety of the wilderness beyond the Jordan?

Marcus peered into the leaden sky. He hoped they had the sense to run, to hide from the consuming hatred Herodias carried for the Baptizer and his talmidim.

Marcus nervously fingered two silver denarii and took them out of his pocket. Coins like these were used to cover the eyes of the dead. Marcus intended to give the coins to Philip and Avram as his contribution to the Baptizer's burial.

Marcus absently studied the Roman currency. The image of Augustus Caesar was accompanied by an inscription proclaiming the former emperor's deity. Hardly the appropriate sentiment to close the eyes of a dead Jewish prophet! Realizing the offering would be an insult, Marcus sighed and tucked the money into his purse.

Once again the clouds cracked open, tipping, pouring out rain. The streets became streams in the torrent. Moving rivulets of water washed Jerusalem clean from the spilled wine, vomit, and blood of the Purim celebration.

Heaven's tribute to the Baptizer, Marcus thought.

The world lightened to shades of blue as dawn approached behind the downpour. Two figures struggled to descend the sloping street as water licked their heels.

Not men, but children.

Ragged boys. Beggars.

The taller, no more than eight, carried a bundle tied to the end of a stick, which he slung over his shoulder. The other, Marcus guessed, was under five years old. His thin, ashen face was like a light, glowing with fever. Huddled against one another and bowed against the rain, the two moved with the weary gait of those who had no refuge from the storm.

Marcus stepped from his shelter as they neared. His appearance interrupted their progress. In unison they glanced up sharply, fearfully.

In that moment Marcus recognized Avel, the mourner who had crouched beside his dead friend in the plaza yesterday.

Avel did not recognize Marcus.

"You're out early," Marcus said to them.

"Late," said Avel. Then suspiciously, "You're a foreigner."

Marcus could see that the stick to which the bundle was tied was an unlit torch. "Are you a link boy? A Sparrow?"

"It'll be day soon. You don't need a torch. Besides, the rain would put it out."

"Where are you going?" Marcus could plainly see the smaller boy was ill. Near to collapse.

"Away." Avel spat the answer. "We only came here to get something." He picked up the largest intact piece of an amphora broken in the riot. One sweeping handle still embraced the curved throat and gaping mouth of the clay jar, but the bottom had shattered.

The boy did not explain the strange action.

Marcus challenged, "At such an hour? In such a storm?"

"What better time?"

"Your little friend here . . . or is he your brother? Is he sick?" Marcus queried.

"His name is Emet, which means Truth. I am Avel," the boy said defensively.

Marcus asked, "Tell the truth, Emet. Can you walk, boy? Are you sick?"

Emet did not answer. He looked ruefully at his rag-wrapped feet.

Avel replied for him. "He can't speak. He's dumb. Yes, he's sick. So? Staying in Jerusalem won't make him better."

"Is he deaf?" Marcus asked.

"Maybe. Mostly. But he reads lips," Avel answered.

"Where do you live, Avel?"

"I lived in the quarry. With the other Sparrows. Until now."

"Why don't you take Emet to the quarry? Let him rest out of the rain? A day or two. And then you can travel."

"Emet's too little to be a link boy. He isn't welcome in the quarry."

"Where are you headed?"

Avel answered with determined certainty. "We'll find the rebel bar Abba. Join up with him."

"You're not grown."

"I'll grow. I can be a spy. I can spy for the rebels. Tell them where the Romans are. Emet can come with me. We'll be useful to bar Abba. I've thought it all through."

"But Emet's too sick to go far."

"I can't help that. I told him if he comes with me he keeps up," Avel growled.

Emet nodded miserably.

"And how do you know bar Abba will help you?" Marcus probed.

"I'll tell him my plan. About how I'll be a spy. When I'm bigger, he'll teach me how to use a dagger."

"To what end? Who will you kill?"

"Romans," Avel declared venomously.

Marcus was glad his armor was concealed. If Avel had known who he was speaking with, the conversation would have taken a different turn. Marcus asked, "You think bar Abba can make your friend get well?"

"Bar Abba is a brave man. A true Jew. He hates the Romans. Like me," Avel said. "There's nothing else. The men who give us torches from the Temple money are all puppets for the Romans. I heard the older Sparrows talking about it. They're not Israelites anymore. The Romans own them. I won't take their charity. Not their torches. Not their straw. They're worse than Romans because they've sold us out. I'm done with them."

"Commendable." Marcus reached into the money pouch and retrieved the two silver denarii. He took Emet's frail hand in his own. He clapped the coins into the child's palm, then closed the fingers around them. This way the money would be put to better use than covering a dead man's eyes. "Two Sparrows are worth more than a penny. There, Emet. For you and Avel. Truth and Mourning are life's companions, after all. They travel in lockstep. Here's a coin each for your journey. From one soldier to another. This will buy you bread and lodging for a week or two in a stable if the rain doesn't let up. It should last you till you find what you're looking for. Take care the rebels you're seeking don't steal it from you."

Avel's eyes grew wide as he glimpsed the tip of Marcus' short sword protruding from the cloak. "You! You're one of them!" the boy cried. And then recognition and memory flooded his face. "You were there when Hayyim was killed! You asked me to fetch his family!"

Marcus nodded. "True."

Avel snatched at Emet's clenched fist. "Give the money back to him! He's a Roman! Don't take anything from him! It's a trap!"

Emet swayed against the assault but clung tenaciously to the treasure. He disagreed vigorously, refusing to give up the coins.

Avel backed up suspiciously. He crossed his arms and glared defiantly at Marcus. "All right. But you're taking them. Not me."

Emet's thin, colorless lips turned up in a slight smile. He opened his hand and stared in wonder at the gift.

Stooping to search Emet's face, Marcus remembered the child Yeshua of Nazareth had healed at the river. And Carta rising from certain death. And the others. So many wounded, broken people.

Marcus silently mouthed words he dared not speak aloud. "So fragile, aren't you, Emet? Truth. Stay alive, Emet . . . With such a name no wonder you can't speak. Emet. Find Yeshua, Emet! Yeshua . . . the Rabbi . . . in Galilee, last I knew. Emet. Live forever. Comfort Avel."

The child indicated his understanding. He smiled broadly, unafraid of Marcus.

Avel plucked at the back of Emet's tattered cloak. "What did he say? What did the Roman say to you? Idiot! You want to get us killed? Come on!" Avel hissed. "Hurry up! Hurry! We've got to get out of here! He's an officer. Men like that don't pass out silver coins to beggars and stand out in the rain unless they're going to arrest someone!"

Avel glared over his shoulder as he dragged Emet away.

Marcus could hear Avel scolding Emet as the two stumbled out of sight down the street.

As he stared up the lane in the direction taken by the two young enemies of Rome, Marcus noticed the rainy darkness had given way to a dank, gray morning. There was a heaviness in the air that settled on Marcus' shoulders like an eighty-pound pack.

The centurion had always believed in the empire. The benefits of Roman civilization were many and manifest throughout all lands bordering the Great Sea of Middle Earth. Roman engineering improved the quality of life. Roman commerce enhanced its standards. Roman military might increased security from banditry and lawlessness just as Roman authority enforced obedience.

If these advantages came at a price to the subject peoples, it was worth it.

Wasn't it?

There had never been a time since the beginning of the world like the present age. A common system of government, a common system of roads, and a common language stretched from Gaul to the Euphrates.

Rome had pushed back the darkness of barbarism at no insignificant cost to itself.

It was all worthwhile, true?

Yet somehow the planted seeds had sprouted into poisonous shoots. The world remained full of ragged little boys with no place to go.

Marcus shook his head to clear some of the confusion. Philip and Avram were very late. By now they must have heard of their master's death. If they were smart, they had left the city under cover of darkness. Marcus hoped they were on their way out of any domain under the sway of Herod Antipas or his vile and deadly queen.

He would allow them another quarter-hour to show up, and then he would give up the vigil.

Just five minutes of the allotted span remained when two cloaked and hooded figures emerged from the shadows of a nearby alleyway.

Philip and Avram flanked Marcus. "Our apologies, Centurion," Philip said gravely. "We were detained. We don't want to compound our discourtesy, but we're anxious to see him. Can we get into the prison soon?"

So they had not heard.

"There's bad news," Marcus said.

Wariness was in their manner, but hope yet gleamed in their eyes. "Tomorrow, perhaps?" Avram queried.

"He's dead," Marcus said flatly. "The Baptizer's dead." Drawing the two stunned talmidim into the shelter of the doorway, Marcus recounted the events of the previous night. "I'm sorry," he said as he concluded. "There was nothing I could do. I spoke with him yesterday. He seemed at peace. I told him you were here. That you brought his cloak. He said . . . an odd thing . . . give it to truth and mourning on the Jericho Road. That's all. And . . . that's all. There was nothing anyone could do. Only his blood could quench the fire of Herodias' hatred."

Avram growled his lip and said nothing.

Philip rubbed his hands down his rain and tear-soaked beard.

Gruffly, the way a centurion would comfort a legionary after the loss of a comrade in battle, Marcus offered, "No time for grief. Need to think of the living, meaning you. Herodias has plenty of venom left. Get out of Jerusalem, quick as you can. Don't go to the Galil or Perea. Stay out of Herod Antipas' clutches."

Philip did not respond, but Avram said vehemently, "Not without his body. We'll give him a proper burial if we die trying. Take us to him."

The level of devotion in the man's tone caused Marcus to eye him with pity. "We'll go at once."

Marcus' uniform and voice of command caused the gatekeeper of the

Hasmonaean Palace to draw back the beam without protest. The man appeared dazed, and his eyes were bloodshot. No doubt most of the guards suffered from the same excesses of Purim as the rest of the population.

"Where's the entrance to the prison?" Marcus demanded.

The guard pointed across the gardens. "Behind the building. You'll see it."

A team of drovers with four rickety oxcarts waited at the back entrance of the palace. They had been hired to haul off rubbish from the banquet. Nearby was the entrance to the palace dungeon.

Marcus indicated that Philip and Avram should wait outside and speak to no one. If Vara was within, there could be trouble.

He descended the steep, narrow stairs alone. Knocking on the thick wooden door, he identified himself. It was a long time before the peephole slid open, and the disheveled prison warden peered out at him. The man was clearly hung over.

"Where is Praetorian Vara?" Marcus asked gruffly.

At the sight of Marcus' regalia, the warden snapped to attention. "Gone, sir! Centurion, sir. Vara has returned to Caesarea! Gone last night, sir! Said he wouldn't stay one night longer in this Jewish dung hole, Jerusalem!"

"Who's in command here?"

"I . . . I am . . . Centurion."

This was good news. "Are you going to keep me waiting all morning?" Marcus impatiently slammed his fist against the door.

"Come in, sir! By all means! But Vara has gone!" The warden fumbled to let Marcus enter.

The basement prison consisted of five lightless cubicles that were barely large enough for a man to lay down in. The stink of human excrement permeated the space.

Marcus covered his nose and mouth with his hand. "You say Vara has gone?"

"Yes, sir. Left last night after the execution. Stayed to see it, then left to give Pilate the report."

Marcus adopted a businesslike tone. "Never mind. I've come for the body of the Baptizer."

"Well, sir, they were going to haul it and the head away to burn with the other rubbish. They brought the head back in a sack, you see. Saved us the trouble."

"I have my orders." Marcus clapped a denarius into the warden's greasy palm.

"As you say, sir. It's a mess in there. You know how it is with beheadings. Blood everywhere. I just opened the door this morning. Tossed the head in as it were. You never get used to it, if you know what I mean."

"Open it."

"It's not a pretty sight. No need to lock it," the warden replied. Then he made an attempt at levity. "A dead man can't run away, you see."

"Get on with it." Marcus' stomach churned as he remembered the glowing bronzed skin of the prophet and the ringing words from the center of the gentle river. And now . . . to end so terribly and be left in filth.

"As you say, Centurion." Not willing to contradict Marcus' authority, the warden bowed and took a step backwards. Turning on his heel, he opened the door of the first cell. The hinges groaned in protest.

An intense wave of aromatic burial spices mixed with myrrh overpowered the stench of the prison.

"A lamp?" Marcus asked, peering into the blackness.

The warden snatched a candle from the wooden box that served as a table. He shined the light into the den-like cubicle. With a gasp, the jailor fell back from what he saw.

The stones of the cell shone as though walls, ceiling, and floor had been freshly scrubbed.

The washed and anointed body of the Baptizer was carefully laid out on a white linen shroud. Arms were crossed over his chest. The head had been carefully rejoined to the neck by layer upon layer of linen strips. Hair and beard were combed. Eyes were closed beneath the dark brows. Lips curved in a peaceful smile.

"Who was here?" Marcus whispered in astonishment, unable to tear his eyes from the sight.

The warden was clearly terrified. "Mercy on me! Centurion! I swear, I don't know! It was like I said! They finished their sport upstairs and brought me the head in a sack. I tossed the head in with the body this morning. Bang! Slammed the cell closed and . . ."

Marcus snatched the man up by his tunic front. "Who came and did this thing? Who paid you?"

"No one! I swear it! No one got by me, Centurion! I promise I've not let a soul in or out!"

Marcus threw him back against the wall and growled, "You were drunk."

"Yes!" The warden blubbered. "Everyone was drunk! But no one came in or went out, I swear it! I saw no one!"

Marcus, his jaw set, nodded and backed away. He trembled in the presence of some unseen power. He clutched at the door frame lest his knees buckle and he fall to the ground. What was this man, this wild prophet, Yochanan the Baptizer?

Managing to bring his thoughts together, Marcus menaced the quaking warden. "Not a word of this to anyone, or I'll report you to your senior officer."

"Yes, sir! Oh no, sir!"

"I take him out of here, and as far as you're concerned he left with the rubbish. You hear me?"

"Yes, sir!" ·

"Don't touch him! Keep away from him! I'll send two fellows to carry him out. If you talk about this to anyone . . . your wife, mother, brother . . . you'll be the one rotting in this cell!"

The man raised his hands in supplication and obedience. "As you command, Centurion!"

Marcus stormed up the steps, taking them two at a time. He beckoned to Avram and Philip to come.

"Where will you bury him?" Marcus asked.

"We'll take him home. Beyond the Jordan River, into the wilderness. There is a place near where the prophet Elijah was taken up to heaven in a whirlwind." They began to explain.

Marcus held up an impatient hand to silence them. "I don't know your legends. Spare me. Is the place far?"

"Two days."

"You'll need an oxcart." He glanced toward the garbage wagons. "I'll arrange it. Go, now. Hurry. What you see will surprise you. Someone has been here ahead of us. The jailor is a blubbering mess. Say nothing to him. Get out as fast as you can."

Their eyes imploring, they did not question further as he directed them to fetch their teacher.

The scent of myrrh drifted onto the morning air, obscuring the smell of cookfires.

Marcus purchased ox and cart from the drovers, then paid them extra for silence.

Philip and Avram carried a plank bearing the shrouded body up the steps and placed it carefully in the wagon. They offered Marcus unvoiced thanks. Clearly they thought he had arranged for the Baptizer to be made ready for burial.

With a stern glance he shook his head, denying he had anything to do with it. Again he instructed them not to speak. Within minutes they were on their way.

Marcus slipped out the back gate of the palace.

■ ■ ■ ■

Avel carried the broken clay pot to the verge of the potter's field. Hundreds of amphora tops and fragments of jugs served as headstones where the poor and the homeless of Jerusalem were buried.

Where Hayyim rested now.

The ground, thick clay, was saturated with rain. Avel slogged to the place where the quarry Sparrows lay. Their graves were even more pitiful then the rest. They were marked with fractured fragments of the plainest jugs, if at all. But Avel was determined that dear Hayyim, brother of his heart, would not lie alone beneath the ground without some memorial to his brief life.

So Avel brought the shattered amphora they had hidden behind during their last great adventure together. It was a tall thing. Taller than the rest.

Hayyim would have been tall, if he had lived.

Emet followed hesitantly at Avel's heels as they approached the mound. The turned earth of Hayyim's grave was already dissolving from the torrent. Clods melting into obscurity. It was good Avel remembered the broken wine jug. Good he had not waited to fetch it and bring it to the field. Another day of bad weather and any sign that Hayyim had lived and died would be washed away.

Avel's head ached from holding back tears. But he would not let himself weep openly. He clenched his teeth and groaned with every breath.

The sun was rising.

At which end should Avel plant the headstone? Which direction had they laid Hayyim? Which was his head and which his feet? Such a thing was important, since the light would beam down through the open top of the amphora and let the face of God shine through. Avel examined the other graves and tried to guess from the jumble what was right. He could not tell.

He consoled himself that perhaps it did not matter. The sun could warm Hayyim's face or his feet.

He knelt in the mud and scraped back the earth to anchor the amphora. Emet tried to help, but Avel roared and pushed him away.

"Hayyim was mine! Don't touch it! He was mine! This is mine to give him! We hid behind it at the wine shop! The last time we were together! Get back!" The tears broke then. Avel couldn't help it. "I'm just angry!" he shouted at the deaf boy. "You hear me? I'm crying because . . ." Avel could not finish what he wanted to say.

Emet lowered his eyes and turned away from Hayyim's grave. He stood there, silent and still, like one of the gravestones of The Potter's Field.

Avel reached into his pocket and retrieved a fragment of charcoal. Yesterday morning, at this same hour, he had used it to paint a beard on Hayyim's cheeks for Purim. They had run together laughing to the celebration.

Today he scratched the letter *HAY,* for Hayyim, on the wine jug. After a while Avel got up. There was nothing more he could do. The rain would wash away the letter that stood for life. That had meant someone Avel had loved. Someone who had loved him.

The marker was taller than those of other forgotten Sparrows. Avel took satisfaction in that. Hayyim deserved . . . well? He deserved more than this, but it was something. Wasn't this, at least, something?

Avel remembered it was time to say a few words. But he could not make his voice come out.

He raised his eyes to gaze across the thousands crowded into The Potter's Field and remembered . . . God could hear his thoughts.

Avel had heard that beneath these stones of broken clay, the poor of Jerusalem slept among the prophets of old. Righteous particles of dust mixed with ordinary particles of dust. One day the Messiah would come here to Jerusalem to sort them out. He would speak each forgotten name and call the prophets and the poor, living again, from their graves.

Avel imagined such a day. Messiah would look at the tallest amphora in the Sparrow patch and be impressed. He would see that beneath it was a boy who was someone's friend.

"Remember Hayyim, God," Avel murmured at last. "He was loved. And once . . . so was I."

■ ■ ■ ■

The storm swept away toward the sea, leaving a faint streak of rainbow in its western wake.

Sun warmed the morning air, but Emet's and Avel's clothes were soaked through. They walked along the Jericho Road toward the village of Bethany until at last they neared a grove of ancient fig trees. Thick trunks, smooth and white, sent out new shoots and branches that intertwined tree with tree in an unbroken canopy. Would there be ripe fruit to eat for breakfast?

Avel was hungry, Emet ready to collapse.

"Look." Avel pointed to an enormous tree with a trunk forking in three directions to form a nest within its bole. *Plenty of room for a tribe of boys,* Avel thought. *A little dry grass to line it. Leaves as a bed.* "It's practically a house! This is a good place. We'll rest awhile there."

Emet's eyes were bright with fever. His thin face was flushed. He did not understand. Avel led Emet to the tree and boosted him up. With a signal, he ordered him to stay put. Emet did not need to be persuaded. The child nodded laboriously, curled up in the center of the nest, and closed his eyes.

Asleep so soon? Just like that? Or was he dying?

Would he ever wake up, Avel wondered? If he did wake up, he would need something to eat.

A scan of the branches showed the green figs were far from ripe. Avel set to pulling up stalks of long dry grass from the orchard floor. Here and there he found a half-rotted fruit from the last harvest. He gathered a dozen, hoping something edible might be gleaned from the brown and broken produce.

Gingerly he tested a rotten fig. A knot of worms wriggled where he bit. With a roar, he spit the muck onto the ground. Then, with some satisfaction, he splattered each of the other figs against a boulder.

A ditch beside the road was littered with fruit that had spilled from the basket of a clumsy harvester. He checked each one for worm holes. These were mostly undamaged. Past ripe, but certainly edible. Avel briefly wondered if it would be counted as theft to take them. Never mind! He scooped them into his tunic.

Then he heard the clatter of an approaching oxcart. Two men flanked the bony beast. Were they workers, sent to tend the orchard? Avel glanced down at the stolen figs. He would offer them, as a bribe.

Sad-eyed fellows, they did not speak as the cart lumbered toward Avel.

"Is this your orchard?" Avel asked when they drew nearer. "I found these. Lying there in the ditch. They'll go bad if they aren't eaten. You want one?"

"No, thanks," came the reply.

Avel wondered if they had an extra morsel of food in their cart. Maybe bread or something they would share with him. Bread and figs made a nice breakfast. "What are you carrying in there? In your wagon?"

The short, swarthy fellow of the two replied, "We're taking our rabbi home for burial."

So, no breakfast. One of the dead from yesterday's riot. It seemed there was no getting away from it. There would be many funerals around Jerusalem today.

Avel swallowed hard and stepped onto the far bank of the ditch. "Hayyim died too. My partner. Then this morning I left Jerusalem because of it. I won't go back, either. Me and Emet . . . he's about five . . . we're going to find bar Abba. Emet's sick over there. Sleeping in the tree. We're going to learn how to fight rebels."

The two travelers exchanged patient glances. "Are you hungry, boy?"

Avel lifted his chin and protectively clutched his cache of fruit.

The thin, fair-skinned man asked, "What are your names?"

Avel replied. "I am Avel Lo-Ahavah. My friend is Emet."

On hearing this, the swarthy man stopped the ox. He scratched his beard and considered Avel. Then he reached for a bundle of cloth tucked on the cart. "Avel. Emet. Mourning and Truth. To meet you on the road on such a day. Well, we haven't got any food with us. Is the one in the tree smaller than you?"

"Of course." Avel was insulted. How could anyone think Emet was bigger?

The fellow said, "You are more like a drowned rat than a rebel. "Here." He tossed the bundle into Avel's arms. "If Emet is sick, he'll need dry clothes. A cloak. Two linen shirts for you and the smaller rebel in the tree."

Avel eyed the parcel suspiciously. "Did this belong to the dead man?" He did not want to wear anything that belonged to a dead man.

"The cloak was his. His mother wove it for him. We were taking it to him before he was killed. He would want Avel and Emet to wear it, I think," said the first man.

The swarthy fellow added, "He was beloved by *Adonai*, a holy man. Yochanan the Baptizer. It is an honor to wear his mantle, boy."

The Baptizer? Everyone had heard of him! The one who had been imprisoned by Antipas! A world-famous fellow! Some said he was Elijah come back to earth. Others said he was the Messiah!

This added a new dimension to the gift. The cloak of a holy man? Everyone knew the story of Elijah and his servant Elisha. The power of the prophet's mantle. Of course Elijah was taken up to heaven in chariot and a whirlwind. This holy man was just . . . dead . . . in an oxcart going along the road to Jericho.

But what if there was power in the mantle?

Avel drew his breath in sharply at the possibilities. He wiped his nose with his finger, then chewed his lip. "There are two of us. Avel and Emet. How will we share one cloak?"

"A tribe of boys your size could make a tent of the Baptizer's cloak. He was a big, strong fellow. And kind. You will find a way." The swarthy man smiled.

The fair one clucked his tongue, and the ox plodded on.

Avel stepped across the ditch and stood in the center of the road to watch them go. He could clearly see the shroud-covered body of the Baptizer. The dead prophet had large feet.

Would some heavenly golden chariot swoop down and gather him into the bosom of Abraham?

How did he die?

And where were his talmidim taking him for burial?

So many questions Avel had stupidly neglected to ask.

After a long time the oxcart was an uninteresting dot on the horizon. Ordinary. No chariots descended.

Avel, clutching the holy man's cloak, returned to the fig tree.

# HESED

Nakdimon's departure could not be postponed any longer if he was to keep his promise to his uncle Gamaliel.

Dressed in the garb of a common tradesman, Nakdimon ben Gurion inspected his troop of children in the courtyard. Sleepy and subdued from the earliness of the hour, they peered at their father with sullen expressions.

Hannah, Susanna, Ruth, Sarah, Dinah, Leah, and tiny Samuel were still in their nightclothes. Breakfast had not been prepared. Now here they were saying good-bye when they would rather be in their beds.

The russet-colored donkey was packed with supplies for a lengthy journey. Nakdimon was dressed in the borrowed clothes of one of his servants. A sweat-darkened leather headband worked in loops and curlicues rested on his brow. What was this about?

Little Leah tugged her braids and asked through brimming tears, "But why do you have to go, Papa? And why are you wearing Eli's clothes?"

"Why indeed?" Nakdimon's mother hissed her disapproval in his ear. "Take a servant with you at least. Take Eli and his sword for protection. The hills of Judea are thick with bandits. And the Galil is worse! A dangerous place."

"It's important I blend in," Nakdimon explained. "People won't talk to me openly, honestly, unless they think I'm one of them."

"If they want a commoner to spy on this preacher, why don't they send a commoner? You! One of the wealthiest men in Judea, dressed like ordinary folk. Nakdimon ben Gurion, by your name, you're the son of a lion. But you look like a stray cat, if you don't mind my saying so. And wearing a badge of the leather guild! I wouldn't so much as speak to you in the marketplace."

"Good, Mother. Then I've achieved the proper effect. A middle-class tradesman. Yes? Taking time away from my shop to hear the Rabbi of Nazareth."

"You should be spending your time finding a wife to mother these children," she snapped.

The girls glanced up at their grandmother's comment. Clearly they, like Nakdimon, wanted no substitute for Hadassah.

It was enough of an ordeal to put up with their grandmother's overbearing behavior. She had come from her villa at the seacoast after Hadassah's death to "help out" for a few weeks. She had brought her own phalanx of servants. That had been a year and a half earlier. The old woman ran the household like a sergeant directing a troop of recruits. On top of that, she despised Nakdimon's staff and was generally irritated by the noise of young children. In addition, she hated Jerusalem and missed her friends in Joppa.

"And you're leaving Jerusalem and the management of this swarming household to me," she complained. "I spoiled you. Your father warned me. You're doing everything for him, your father said. Give the boy room to grow up, he said. I should have listened! I never came with him to Jerusalem when he was alive. And yet here I am. A slave in my old age for the sake of my only son. I'm too old for this, Nakdimon."

"Yes, Mother." His head ached with her harping.

"Get a wife," she admonished. "Let me go home to Joppa."

Did her return to Joppa depend on Nakdimon's finding a woman to take her place? It was a distasteful thought. The girls exchanged disgusted glances with one another.

Leah cried, "But you can go home, Grandmother! I don't want another mama!"

Nakdimon patted Leah's head in reassurance that a replacement mother in the ben Gurion household was not in the foreseeable future. Then he kissed each child and promised to return quickly.

A messenger from Gamaliel reached him just outside his gate and handed him a note.

*Nakdimon,*
*Use of Korban for aqueduct project cannot be prevented. Tell no one, since riots are certain when word gets out. Now more important than ever that we know about unrest in Galil.*
*Gamaliel*

■ ■ ■ ■

The recent storms had departed but done little to clear the Jerusalem atmosphere. The day promised stagnant, difficult-to-breathe air. Over Marcus' shoulder a column of smoke from the day's sacrifices propped up a colorless, overcast sky.

A week had elapsed since the execution of Yochanan. No riots had erupted. In fact, despite the number of witnesses, no one seemed entirely certain what had happened. The aftermath of the bread riot and the rumors circulating around the Holy City added to the oppressive mood. The entire place simmered; not quite ready to erupt, but nearly so.

When the pilgrims arrived for Passover, that's when it would break loose. Every warning instinct Marcus possessed based on his years in the legions told him he was correct.

After using his rank to assist Philip and Avram, Marcus had returned to the Antonia and laid aside the trappings of his centurion's uniform. Helmet, armor, and tunic were entrusted to the attendant of the officers' barracks.

The dark brown cloak Marcus wore tied beneath his chin was irritating against his beard. Bristling whiskers were bad enough, but when wool was added, the combination became miserably prickly. At least the linen tunic next to his skin was of high quality. Felix insisted Marcus travel as a wealthy merchant from a remote province of the empire. The device would explain any peculiarities in appearance or speech.

His short sword was wrapped in a spare cloak and tied behind him on the horse, along with a single change of clothing.

For the moment he was riding his favorite mount, Pavor, for the sake of speed. But when he reached the Galil he would have to stable the animal and go on foot. Beard and robe might hide the Roman's identity, but no one could fail to recognize the fiery black horse.

Reflecting on returning to the Galil made him think again about Miryam.

Being sent to observe Yeshua of Nazareth guaranteed that he would see her. What would her response be? He had not even attempted to contact her in half a year, nor had she written to him. The news of Miryam he received had been second- and third-hand reports.

Marcus remembered her famously violent temper.

Would his unannounced arrival provide such a response? Would she denounce him as a spy?

Tribune Felix knew he was asking something extraordinary by assigning Marcus to act undercover. What the commander did not realize was the personal cost to Marcus' emotions.

Marcus longed to see Miryam . . . and dreaded it.

He was eager to hear the Rabbi of Nazareth speak . . . and apprehensive lest the messianic fervor of the crowds prod Yeshua into making rashly anti-Roman statements.

What then?

He rode past the beggars huddled beside Damascus Gate. For all the excitement of last week's bread and pennies, the mendicants appeared neither better nor worse off. Blind men and cripples remained sightless and helpless. Handouts had done nothing to heal them, nor would political upheaval make them whole.

Outside the gate there was evidence of the riot: the mounded earth of recently dug graves. This was a field given over to the burial of indigents. The dusty, rubble-strewn plateau sprouted a thick crop of clay pots.

Here the graceful neck of an olive oil jug protruded from the ground. There the curved handles of a wine container survived even though the lower half of the amphora was missing. Acres of these makeshift markers were packed tight like the bodies of the dead beneath them.

Friends scratched names and dates into the earthenware monuments. Sometimes the identifying inscription was outlined with lampblack. Pathetic bouquets of flowers withered and drooped from the handles of some markers.

The names might survive one rainy season, but no more. Thereafter merely the shattered memorials would bear witness to vanished lives discarded in the place commonly called *The Potter's Field*.

Marcus spotted a familiar splintered shard. So that's what the young rebel had been up to: marking the lifeless clay of the trampled link boy.

He recalled a poem by Propertius cursing a faithless lover:

> *Let the bawd's tomb be an old broken-necked wine jar:*
> *And over it may the wild fig-tree's force thrust down.*

This was such an accursed place. Those doomed to suffer in life fared no better in death, it seemed.

Marcus nudged Pavor into a lope and left Jerusalem behind.

■ ■ ■ ■

The road chosen by Nakdimon for his journey to the Galil carried him first northeast through Jericho and then up the valley of the Jordan. It was not the most direct route, which would have been straight north from Jerusalem by way of Neapolis. But the second path crossed Samaria.

As a devout Jew, Nakdimon was loathe to enter the country of the Samaritans. He regarded the people of that territory as apostates. Although it meant prolonging his journey, he elected the more circuitous course. On foot the journey would take a week.

At Bethany, a hamlet mere miles outside Jerusalem, Nakdimon stopped for water. He watched as young women drew from the well. They giggled and whispered with one another so Nakdimon could not hear what they were saying.

Odd how uncomfortable their murmurings made him feel. Out of place, somehow, in a place he knew thoroughly. His old friend and schoolmate El'azar lived nearby in Bethany with his sister Marta. El'azar's other sister, Miryam, the young one, the pretty one, had always caused Nakdimon to stammer when she came near. She had been married off young to avoid bringing disgrace on the family. Yet, in spite of El'azar's precautions, she had eventually managed to shame herself anyway. Nadkimon bowed his head in regret. His thoughts wandered as he sipped the sweet water of the well.

In the distance a grove of almond trees bloomed.

Involuntarily his gaze followed the retreating figure of a girl of about fifteen as she carried a water jug on her shoulder. Nakdimon saw the way she glanced coyly at a young man who loitered in the doorway of his house in order to watch her pass. Her suitor's stare made her blush. The youth put a hand to his forehead in salute.

The wordless love play of the couple deluged Nakdimon with longing for Hadassah again. Thirteen years they were together, and she never tired of tantalizing him with a smile or a secret signal.

A thousand thoughts a day flew toward her, only to find the place empty where she should have been. He stared at the flowering trees and remembered. It was an ordinary day in the almond grove. She sat on the rim of the well and drew water for him to drink; insisted she fetch it herself, as if she was his servant. She held the cup to his lips and then kissed him when his mouth was moist. The workers finished pruning and left for supper. Hadassah held Nakdimon back from following. She teased him a look. He yielded easily to her. They made love in the shade of the trees and stayed long after nightfall. When they returned to the house, the servants noticed dried grass on the back of her dress. Hadassah blushed and said she had grown tired in the grove and had slept awhile. But they knew. And when it was clear she was pregnant again they counted the days back to that evening. It had all started with an ordinary cup of water.

Samuel had been conceived that night.

Samuel. Their son. Beloved by Hadassah in her womb. How delighted she had been to feel him kick. She would lie with her belly against Nakdimon's back and laugh when the baby tapped a message to them both. And what did those little feet and elbows mean to say? Life is here. Forged by the two of you; created by your joy beneath the almond tree. God was watching . . . He watches still . . .

Did Hadassah watch him as well, Nakdimon wondered?

He poured the remainder of his drink back into the well as other travelers came into the square. And then he poured the exquisitely painful memories back into the well of his recollection and forced his thoughts into the present.

There was nothing else to do.

Gathering beside the public trough was a chance assembly of travelers likewise headed north, journeying together for mutual security.

Nakdimon, in his guise as a modestly successful member of the leather guild, joined them.

The thrown-together group was an odd assortment of personalities and professions, typical of an impromptu set of traveling companions.

A portly Jewish dealer in frankincense was there, with two servants and a camel loaded with the costly, aromatic resin. Ben Gavrin, the perfume merchant, sweated profusely despite the cool air, and babbled freely that he had spent his entire savings on the cargo. He planned to resell it in Damascus for a handsome profit and officially launch his business.

His servants, hired just for the present journey, were swarthy Idumeans. Whether because of slow wits or generally bad tempers, they did not speak except to give monosyllablic replies.

A *cohen* named Aaron was also on the road. Having served his course in the Temple services, he was returning home to Capernaum. The tall, long-nosed man sized up the company. He let everyone know by upraised eyebrow and pinched nostrils that he felt socially superior.

The company also contained a young Levite. Lemuel was his name.

He proudly announced to the *cohen* that he was in the Temple maintenance administration.

Nakdimon recognized the young man, though the identification was not mutual. Lemuel was third assistant in charge of examining wood for the high altar to see that it was not wormy.

Without acknowledging Lemuel or even speaking to him, the *cohen* turned away. Thereafter Lemuel pathetically followed Aaron around, trying to engage the priest in conversation and failing every time.

And finally there was a man named Asher. He gave his profession as apprentice money changer. His clothes, though clean, were shabbier than Nakdimon expected to see on a banker. Asher was young and cheerful but vague about his reasons for going to Galilee. In fact, he acted reticent about conversing.

Perhaps he was an unsuccessful apprentice who had been let go.

There were two other odd things about Asher, Nakdimon thought. Every time Asher was upwind, there was a faint but definite wisp of rotten flesh wafting from him.

And he imitated animals. Asher passed the time on the trek making birdcalls real enough to elicit avian replies from the brush.

Nakdimon's donkey seemed to like him.

About a mile before the highway reached Herod the Great's fortress known as *Cyprus*, Asher walked up beside Nakdimon. "Came through here not long ago," he said, pointing to a dry creek bed that intersected the road. "Caravan ahead was set on by bandits outside Jericho. When he heard it, the leader of my party guided us down that wadi, there. Said it was a shortcut, safer than the main road."

"Why not tell ben Gavrin?" Nakdimon queried. "He has the most at stake."

"True," Asher agreed, then added, "but I'm the youngest here. I don't want to interfere. You're easier to talk to than the rest. Will you tell him?"

At the mention of the word *bandit*, ben Gavrin perspired even more freely. "I couldn't afford to hire more guards," he explained unnecessarily. "Yes, turn here, by all means."

And so the travelers left the main highway and entered the canyon of the older, disused Jericho Road.

■ ■ ■ ■

The tempo of the caravan diminished as the party picked its way around loaf-sized, jug-shaped rocks. Nakdimon's red donkey lifted each hoof exceptionally high to clear them. From laid-back ears to swishing tail, the animal's disapproval was silently expressed with each step.

Nakdimon's own thoughts were also restless. He was not entirely at ease with the alternate path.

The route suggested by Asher appeared secure enough, but there were no other travelers on it. Clearly the road had not been maintained for many changes of season. Washed-out ruts caused a continuous stepping down and climbing up, accompanied by much weaving around boulders. The line of march stretched. Greater gaps appeared between Aaron and Lemuel at the front, ben Gavrin's contingent in the middle, and Asher and Nakdimon at the rear.

The distance separating them did not prevent Nakdimon from overhearing the *cohen* grumble about the choice of trails. Each complaint was duplicated a second later as the Levite echoed every sentiment, together with a supplemental whine.

Ben Gavrin badgered his servants constantly about which direction to go, about exercising more care for his precious cargo, about hurrying up. Impossibly conflicting demands.

Only Asher was unaffected by the difficult road. One pace behind Nakdimon, the young man trudged silently along. His attention was fixed on the canyon walls looming ever higher and tighter as the wadi constricted. His head pivoted from side to side in a constant search pattern.

Studying the preoccupied Asher over his shoulder, Nakdimon asked, "Looking for something?"

The apprentice money changer started. Appearing flustered for the first time Asher replied with an unconvincing shrug, "A landmark . . . nothing important."

A landmark in a canyon with one way in or out? What was that comment supposed to mean?

The answer was revealed an instant later when four men rose up from behind boulders on either side of the caravan. Even more menacing: other shadowy figures lined the tops of the cliffs.

Bandits!

"That's far enough!" their leader shouted.

Ben Gavrin wailed as two of the robbers shoved aside his servants and seized the camel's rope. The hired men made no attempt to interfere.

Plunging forward to help, Nakdimon found his own donkey's halter jerked from his hands.

Asher held the lead, an insolent smile on his face. "Looks can be deceiving. You shouldn't be so trusting."

"Neither should you," Nakdimon replied. Even though he was off balance, Nakdimon swung his walking stick toward Asher's head. The backhanded blow failed to connect, but made the bandit duck. Stepping quickly closer, Nakdimon followed up the miss with an overhand blow from his fist, knocking Asher to the ground.

Then Nakdimon bounded toward the others. "Fight back!" he yelled.

The priest and the Levite, rather than jumping into the battle, backed away toward the shelter of an overhanging ledge.

Ben Gavrin's servants took to their heels, leaving the merchant wrestling with two brigands for possession of the camel.

Nakdimon was confronted by two others: the leader and a scar-faced accomplice.

A dagger flashed in the sunlight, wielded by the man whose evidence of earlier combat appeared as a puckered crease on his cheek. "Take care of him, Dan," the leader ordered. "I'll see to the priests."

Rather than wait for Dan to attack, Nakdimon charged, seeking to catch the bandit off guard. Furiously swinging his staff as a cudgel, Nakdimon made Dan give ground as the stick whistled around his ears.

When Dan lunged forward with a knife thrust, Nakdimon spun the staff downward across the robber's forearm. He heard a significant screech of pain, and the dagger clattered across some rocks.

Then someone crashed into Nakdimon from behind.

As he turned to face the new threat, a fist-sized stone hit him on the temple. His ears heard a roaring noise, as if an ocean wave were sweeping down the desert wadi, and he fell to his knees. Nakdimon's vision dimmed, and the canyon's walls contracted into a black tunnel.

Just before he passed out, he heard Dan say, "Get away, Asher! I'll finish him myself."

■ ■ ■ ■

By using the canyon road, Marcus hoped to shave an hour off his travel time. Before starting out on this journey he had consulted his campaign notes. On every duty and expedition, Marcus made a meticulous chronicle of the terrain. Water or its lack. Possible bivouac sites. Caves and ravines as possible hiding places for rebels. Such attention to detail had served him well before; he expected it to do so now.

His journal entry for the old Jericho Road indicated a rough, barely passable trail. If Marcus were leading a detachment of legionaries he would have marched them the long way round. His log added a note to the effect that it was a logical site for an ambush. Historically it had served Judah, the Hammer of the Maccabees, in such a fashion, in an attack on the forces of Antiochus Ephphanes.

It was not a place for a lone civilian, or even a small group of them, to tread carelessly.

Mounted on Pavor, Marcus believed he was equal to any attack. Still, his natural wariness urged him to disentangle his sword from the covering so its hilt was within easy reach.

The canyon was littered with rubble. The intersecting gullies were worse: steep and so choked with debris that exit through them would be nearly impossible. The serpentine twists of the wadi masked both advance and retreat. Marcus could not see more than a hundred yards in either direction. Nor did his hearing extend much further. Each abrupt curve of the canyon acted to muffle what lay beyond.

It was Pavor, his black horse, who first caught the sound. The horse's ears pricked forward as something caught his interest. Marcus reined up and listened intently. At first he could detect nothing but the sighing of the chilly wind whistling down the ravines.

Then he heard it: angry curses and cries for help.

What was he riding into? While he would not attack blindly, neither did he hesitate.

Drawing the sword, Marcus urged Pavor to advance. Shielded from view by a rockfall at the next bend in the canyon, Marcus stretched upright and peered ahead.

Bandits had waylaid a caravan. Marcus counted at least four attackers, with a dozen more watching from the canyon walls. Resistance by the victims seemed at an end.

Marcus spotted a robber standing over a fallen man. An upraised knife was in his hand. The victim on the ground stirred feebly. He was not murdered yet!

The sight galvanized Marcus into action.

At the slightest touch on Pavor's flanks the mount leapt forward. As the horse recognized his rider's urgency, he bounded over intervening boulders. Marcus was into the scene before any of the participants detected his presence.

The would-be assassin heard the galloping hooves and turned at the last second. With a panicked outcry he desperately flung up the knife hand to ward off Marcus' downward slash.

Blade to blade the short sword glanced off the dagger.

Rebounding from the force of the blow, the murderer's weapon slashed into his own cheek, splitting it open.

It was then that Marcus noticed the scar on the other cheek.

Dan, bar Abba's most expert killer!

Pavor thundered past Dan, who reeled like a drunkard.

Marcus waved his sword above his head, shouting, "To me, legionaries! Attack!" as if an entire cohort followed him into the assault. Belatedly he remembered he was not in uniform! Would the robbers still swallow the ruse?

There was too much rubble to maneuver the horse. Marcus might be terrifically outnumbered.

No chance to draw back.

The camel bolted.

"Clear out!" Marcus heard someone yell.

It was bar Abba himself!

Marcus spun Pavor in a tight circle, then spurred him toward the rebel chief.

Out of the corner of his eye Marcus sensed movement. Someone scrambled up a nearby boulder, then hurtled through the air toward him.

Marcus and his attacker plummeted from the stamping horse. They crashed into a rock wall, then wrestled for possession of Marcus' sword. Pavor snorted and pranced, sidestepping the tussling combatants.

"Asher!" bar Abba yelled. "Help Dan! Grab the donkey! I'll take the horse!"

Marcus' hands were on the blade. His foe had the hilt.

It was the point that mattered.

Each man struggled to force the tip toward the other's throat.

The sword twisted in Marcus' grasp, scoring his palms.

The assailant gave a cry of triumph. His shout changed to a startled cry as Marcus threw his weight to one side.

The tip of the sword screeched against a stone slab.

The contest for the weapon continued.

"What about the camel?" someone yelled.

"Do you want to be crucified? Leave it! Leave Jorum, too! Come on!" bar Abba commanded.

Marcus' opponent, Jorum, swiftly abandoned the fight for the sword. He drew a dagger from the breast of his tunic.

As the knife darted toward Marcus' neck, he heaved upward.

The two men rolled over, then over again.

On top once more, Jorum lifted the dagger to strike.

Marcus feinted one direction, then abruptly revolved the other. Lashing out with his elbow, he knocked Jorum's knife hand away.

The rebel could not stop his pounce. He lunged headlong . . . and impaled himself on his own weapon.

■ ■ ■ ■

Marcus heaved Jorum's dead body aside and sprang to his feet. Gripping his sword again in his bloody hand, he surveyed the battlefield for another adversary.

But the bandits had fled. The last of them disappeared around the next bend in the road . . . leading Pavor and the red donkey. The rebels on the heights above the gorge vanished, frightened away by an imaginary cohort of legionaries.

Bar Abba was clearly not ready to risk an encounter with armed Roman troops, but his excursions for supplies were getting bolder. If he, or another abler leader, managed to recruit more men, soon they would be ready to strike.

But where and how?

Marcus considered returning to Jersualem. A mounted contingent of Romans could perhaps catch the insurgents before they melted into the hills.

If he were not afoot, he could be back to Jersualem within hours and tracking bar Abba shortly after.

As Marcus stared in the direction taken by the robbers, he brooded over the loss of Pavor. He believed no Galilean peasants could manage such a high-strung animal. He hoped they would not kill him in their frustration.

Nearby, clumped together like particularly dull sheep, stood bar Abba's intended prey. A heavyset, perspiring man clung to the lead rope of a camel as if it were a lifeline. Two others were with him, exchanging shaky congratulations at their narrow escape.

None of them moved to aid the wounded figure crumpled beside the boulder.

Marcus knelt next to the victim. Blood flowed from a scalp wound, streaking the man's face. A grotesquely swollen lump on his skull distorted his features.

"Give me a hand here," Marcus called to the others.

"I can't," argued a tall, ascetic-looking one. "I'm a *cohen*. It would defile me to touch a dead man."

"He's not dead yet," Marcus protested. "Help me with him."

"No," responded the youngest bystander. "I'm Lemuel . . . a Levite. We can see the blood from here. Too much blood. He'll be dead soon. Neither of us can risk defilement."

Marcus thought what a useless religion it was that valued ritual purity more than assisting someone in need.

Stripping off his robe he cut a piece from the hem and used it as a compress on the wound. "How about you?" he inquired of the merchant. "He didn't get wounded like this while running away. Don't you owe him anything?"

Leading the camel over to the far side of the creek bed the tradesman replied, "I'll send help, but I can't stay. Not a minute. The robbers might be back! Those worthless hired men ran, leaving me alone. I'll not risk my neck . . . and my fortune . . . for someone who may be dead soon anyway. Besides, he got us into this, telling us to turn into this canyon!"

The two clergymen nodded vigorously. Then Lemuel added, "He might have been one of them! He was walking with that fellow Asher, who made off with the donkey."

"That's right!" agreed the *cohen*. "They were in it together, leading us into a trap."

"That doesn't make sense," Marcus protested.

Skirting Marcus, the Levite and the priest followed the perfume dealer back the way they had come.

"Stop!" Marcus demanded. "I'm a Roman centurion! I order you to assist me!"

"We don't see a uniform," the *cohen* replied archly.

Almost at a jog, the three cowards left the scene.

Could he chase them? Force them at sword point to help? How? Marcus knew he would not actually attack them, even if he threatened to do so. Nor was he entirely recovered from the combat himself.

"At least tell me his name," Marcus yelled after the retreating trio.

The merchant and the *cohen* were already out of sight. Over his shoulder Lemuel yelled, "Nakdimon." Then he added, "He's nobody, a leather worker." Then he too disappeared.

As the afternoon shadows lengthened, Marcus considered his options. The night would be cold. Moving the unconscious man was risky, but perhaps no more than allowing him to remain exposed to the elements.

There was no way Marcus could carry Nakdimon by himself. The fellow was built like an bull.

It became apparent no help was coming. Marcus doubted the merchant had intended to relay the call for assistance. Transporting such expensive cargo alone suggested that the proper customs duties had not been paid. He would never report anything to the authorities.

The others probably thought talking to a Roman, even to testify about a crime, would pollute them.

Nakdimon stirred, groaning. "Where? What? Oh. I didn't see it coming."

Evidently the man had the constitution of an ox as well as the size, Marcus thought. A lesser fellow would truly have been killed by such a blow to the head as he had received.

"If you lean on me, can you walk?" Marcus asked. "We need to get you to a doctor."

"Who are you?" Nakdimon asked. "Where are the others?"

Mindful of his intended disguise, Marcus supplied only his name, not his real occupation. "Never mind about the rest," he said. "Can you stand?"

"I think so," Nakdimon answered hoarsely. "Can't see well and my head is swimming, but I can walk. Take me to Bethany."

"I was going to take you to the fort at Cypress," Marcus suggested.

"Bethany . . . is as close. I have . . . friends there," Nakdimon replied. "El'azar of Bethany. Please. Take me there."

■ ■ ■ ■

Bethany was an insignificant village located on the edge of the Judean desert, on the eastern flank of the Mount of Olives. Marcus, hampered both by Nakdimon's weight and the injured man's plunges into unconsciousness, stumbled and staggered for hours.

He saw no one else on the road that night. Sensible people, knowing the way was hazardous and prowled by bandits, barricaded themselves safely indoors.

Not that they passed any doors, barricaded or otherwise.

During Nakdimon's occasional scuffles with awareness, he muttered things. Most, like garbled references to the Sanhedrin, Caiaphas, and

Yeshua of Nazareth, made no sense. What would a leather craftsman have to do with politics or religion? Probably he was repeating the last bits of caravan conversation. Despite Marcus' supposedly urgent secret mission, nearly everyone in Judea was already talking about the Rabbi from Galilee and how the high and mighty hated him.

The few comments Nakdimon mumbled that actually made sense were oft-repeated pleas not to inform his children about his injuries. "Don't tell them," he begged in a pitiable plea. "Hannah can take it. But Ruth'll be frightened. Leah's heart'll break just to hear it. Promise me you won't! Not 'til I'm better. Promise me!"

Marcus repeated the requested vow as earnestly as he could to placate the man. He wondered all the while if this Nakdimon knew how near to being killed he had come. The centurion had seen men with head injuries before. The Gauls, in particular, favored battle-axes and heavy, hammer-like clubs. Full impacts from such weapons fractured skulls like eggshells. Even glancing blows addled men's brains and caused depressed fractures that filled tight with fluid. Legionaries receiving such wounds sometimes babbled like this fellow, right till the moment their brains swelled inexorably against bone, and the pressure killed them.

And that applied to wounded men who had not been dragged miles over rough roads in damp, cold winds.

At last he reached the outskirts of Bethany.

As though summoned by Marcus' overwhelming weariness, a dimly flickering light appeared, set high in a wall up ahead.

Three minutes later Marcus propped Nakdimon against the compound's gate and pounded on the passageway door.

A sleepy, angry voice called down from the gatekeeper's window. "Who's there? What do you want? Never mind: come back at a civil hour."

Marcus hammered all the louder and yelled, "I've got an injured man here."

"So what? Go away!"

Rage building up in him, Marcus bellowed, "Where can I find the house of El'azar of Bethany?"

"Who wants to know?"

This was an unexpected and welcome bit of luck. "You mean this is his house? Open up! The wounded man's name is Nakdimon, and he said El'azar's his friend."

"Bildad!" a woman's voice shrilled from inside the ramparts. "You're waking everyone! What is it?"

Marcus waited impatiently while the night porter, Bildad, made his report to the apparent mistress of the house. Then he bellowed, "I am a Roman officer! Open this gate for a wounded man!"

This assertion did not have the desired effect. A narrow shutter opened in the portal. Through it a woman's profile could be seen, backlit by lantern light. Scattered beams fell on Marcus.

"Bandits!" the woman shrieked. "No uniform! Clear off, or I'll set the servants on you!"

"Wait!" Marcus ordered. "I'm a centurion. The man with me was attacked by bandits. He's badly hurt and asked me to bring him here."

"What is it?" inquired a male voice from behind the woman. The new questioner had an anxious tone.

"Never mind, brother," rebuked the female. "I'll handle this."

Eagerly seizing on a conjecture, Marcus called out, "Are you El'azar of Bethany? If so, Nakdimon claimed you'd help him."

"What Nakdimon?" demanded the sister suspiciously.

Marcus answered in the only fashion he knew. "Nakdimon of the leather worker's guild."

"We don't know any such!" scoffed the woman triumphantly. "A tradesman? Not likely!"

"Wait," the brother urged. "Be quiet, Marta, and let me think."

Marcus fervently agreed. He wondered how anyone could think over the woman's nagging abuse.

The gate opened sufficiently for a lantern to be thrust forward. A barefoot, curly-haired man, dressed in a short tunic, peered out as the light fell on Nakdimon's face.

"It *is* Nakdimon! Nakdimon ben Gurion! Bildad, come and help."

"Are you certain, El'azar?" Marta queried. "It could be a trick."

"Yes, yes!" El'azar replied impatiently. "Help me with him!"

El'azar, the night porter, and two other curious servants lifted Nakdimon and disappeared with him into the shadows of the compound.

Marcus also started forward, then halted when Marta planted her pear-shaped bulk squarely across his path. "And where are you going?" she challenged. Obviously, not requiring a reply, she continued, "Even if you are an officer . . . which I doubt . . . bearded, no uniform, no other soldiers anywhere about . . ." Marta contemptuously ticked off Marcus' failures to measure up. "Even if you were, you would still be a Gentile! We never allow our house to be defiled. Go away."

And she shut the gate in Marcus's astonished face.

# VE-EMET

Would Emet die without waking?

Avel, wrapped snuggly in the Baptizer's cloak, perched on a broad branch above Emet.

Curled into a tight ball, the smaller boy lay unmoving in the nest. Thin arms, spindly like twigs, covered his face.

His belly was too big, full of air, meaning it had been a long time since Emet had eaten well.

Fleas hopped arrogantly on his skin, and Emet made no move to scratch himself. This convinced Avel that Emet was dying. Only the dead could lie quiet while a troop of vicious creatures danced on an ear, bit tender flesh, or laid eggs in matted hair.

Though the afternoon was cold and the looming night promised to be colder still, fleas were reason enough for Avel not to share the Baptizer's cloak with Emet.

What could Avel do? If he spread the mantle over the dying boy, it would be infested and ruined. Emet would die anyway. And what use would it have been?

Earlier Avel had stripped off Emet's damp rags and dressed him in both of the fresh linen tunics. Emet's skin was burning hot. He moaned slightly as Avel threw his filthy, tattered clothes away, but he did not awaken. Avel hoped the clean linen would help somehow, but it was not enough. The fleas returned.

If Emet would open his eyes at least; offer some sign that he might yet survive. But there was nothing to give Avel hope. He determined he would stay near until Emet died and then he would go. It would not be honorable to let anyone that young die in a tree and go away without telling someone about it.

Emet's fragile rib cage heaved, shuddering as each breath was drawn.

The linen shirt would be a shroud.

Soon it would be over, Avel thought. Soon he would be alone in the world again.

He had seen other Sparrows die of sickness. Left to themselves in the obscure corners of the quarry, the weak ones usually expired during the night. Something about the darkness of the stone caverns called tiny, unhappy souls to fly away.

Each morning the sturdy, deaf-mute gravedigger paid by the authorities gathered the bodies. Boys and beggars and dirty straw were removed to The Potter's Field for disposal.

But here in the Bethany fig grove who would bury Emet when he died? The gravedigger was not here. There was no Potter's Field in the village.

Avel would wait until it was over and then tell someone in the village that there was a dead boy laying in the fork of a fig tree. It was only right. After that Avel would have done his duty. He would be on his way. He would go find bar Abba and carry out his plan.

Avel shuddered and stretched out on the limb like a caterpillar. He covered his head with the hem of the Baptizer's cloak to block the sight of his dying companion.

Light filtered through the threads. Avel's own breath warmed his face.

The fabric of the Baptizer's cloak was six feet wide, nine feet long, and seamless. Unusual, it had been woven on a large loom from the best wool. The pattern of alternating red, green, and tan stripes was common in Galilee. But the material was uncommon: fine and thick enough to repel moisture and keep the cold wind at bay. Avel was hungry, but the warmth of his cocoon was comforting somehow.

He closed his eyes and thought of ten days ago: Hayyim laughing as he stuffed his mouth with a fig cake stolen from the souk.

Together he and Avel had fled the shrill cries of the merchant's wife. Together they had escaped and shared lunch in the sunlight on top of Cripple Rock.

How distant that pleasant danger seemed now. Another lifetime. Their hunger had not been as sharp because they shared even that.

Exhaustion overwhelmed the ache in Avel's belly and finally in his soul. At last he slept.

■ ■ ■ ■

Hunger chewed on Avel's belly, forcing him reluctantly from sleep.

How long had it been since he had eaten bread?

It had been with Hayyim. Hayyim? Could it be? But that had been so long ago.

Avel tried to reconstruct the days and hours since Hayyim died. Where was he? The quarry? Jerusalem? No. Somewhere else.

Snug in the warmth of the cloak, he remembered everything.

The village of Bethany. The grove. The passing of the Baptizer's body. The gift of the cloak. And then the boy who had come away with him. Emet, dying. Emet, lying like an egg in the open hand of the fig tree.

Had his spirit flown away yet?

No. Avel could hear his companion's labored breathing.

Avel opened his eyes to the echo of voices.

"Is this the way, friend?"

"The village . . . up here, I think."

"Is that an inn? A caravansary?"

"The mansion of El'azar and his sister Marta. Rich but cursed by *Adonai*. A family disgrace they say. Madness in the blood. No marriages. No children. Strangers will inherit their lands one day, they say. And the camels of the caravans will rest in their gardens and drink from their fountains."

"It's early. But the lights are blazing."

"Someone's always awake. El'azar keeps a large household. Servants. They'll be baking bread by now."

"You're right. I smell it."

Avel inhaled automatically at the stranger's suggestion.

Yes! Yes! Bread! The warm, yeasty aroma wafted through the predawn air. Beautiful smell! Agonizing! Tantalizing!

Avel groaned with the wanting of hot, fresh bread. He struggled to untangle himself from the tight roll of the Baptizer's mantle, which bound his arms fast to his sides. He was trussed up like a sheep for shearing. The harder he fought, the tighter the fabric constricted. Rearing up, he lost his balance. With a yelp of surprise he plummeted from the limb and tumbled down and down toward the orchard floor. The edge of the cloak snagged a branch and unwound like a ball of yarn. Avel spilled out at the bottom. The last six feet to the ground he fell free. The shriek of rending fabric drowned his muffled cry as he hit with a thud.

The bulk of the Baptizer's cloak plummeted onto his head as he tried to suck air into his tortured lungs. Fluttering above was a shred of the holy man's once-perfect garment.

Avel's first breath was a groan. Was anything injured? Only his pride.

Only the Baptizer's mantle! He scowled at the fragment above him and fingered the jagged tear.

It served him right, didn't it? Didn't the *cohanim* of Jerusalem teach that the poor must share what they had with one another? That was the first lesson for the Sparrows in the quarry. Never be a pest while begging. No matter how hungry you might be, leave the rich to enjoy their wealth without guilt. Be grateful for what you get, and divide everything with your hungry brothers!

For the first time Avel had received one thing of value: this cloak of the dead prophet, Yochanan the Baptizer! Whole and perfect! Beautiful and clean! Yet he had not shared its warmth with Emet for fear of fleas. And this was how his selfishness was punished! The prophet had rebuked him! Thrown him out of the tree and onto his head in a heap of rotten fruit!

Avel buried his face in the soft fabric and began to mourn. Hayyim would have done the right thing. He would have shared. Hayyim always knew what to do.

"I'm sorry. Sorry. Hayyim! What should I do? Oh, what?"

Had he ever been so hungry? So miserable? For the first time he wished he was back at the stone quarry. The Sparrows would be waking up beside the fire. Someone would share a crust with him until he found another partner to link with.

Rotten figs would not keep him alive. He had to eat real food soon, or he would die as well.

It was a long time before sunup, but the sky lightened. Avel climbed back up the tree and retrieved the shred of material. Small as it was, it was plenty big enough to wrap Emet in.

Avel shinnied to where the boy lay and covered his trembling body. He pried open Emet's clenched fist and took the two silver coins the Roman soldier had given him.

"I'll go to the village, Emet. I'll buy us bread to eat. If you live, I'll take better care of you. I promise. Like Hayyim did for me. If only you'd live . . . *Adonai*. If only Emet could live . . ."

But as he prayed, Avel knew that *Adonai* of the Temple would never answer the insignificant prayer of a Jerusalem Sparrow.

Emet would not live. It was almost over. Perhaps if Avel had shared the blanket? Kept him warm last night? Probably not. But what if?

It would not be much longer, Avel knew.

And never mind the fleas. This much of Yochanan the Baptizer's mantle would be a shroud for a poor boy.

■ ■ ■ ■

Emerging from the fig grove Avel found himself on the edge of a vine-yard, properly cared for, pruned, and tidy. Beyond was a complex of barns, servants' quarters, pens, and stables.

The villa of the master stood on a low hill surrounded by straight rows of cultivation. It was easy to see why the traveler had mistaken the house of El'azar of Bethany for a caravansary. It was large enough to put up six or seven full caravans, beasts of burden, drovers, and all. Fortresslike in its construction, it was protected by walls on every side and built for defense against bandits.

A double gate twelve feet high marked the entrance for camels and cargo-laden wagons. A gate for pedestrians was beside that. Both were closed and locked from the inside. There was no latch on the exterior. Above, the light from a lantern shone from the slit window of the watch-man's quarters.

Inside, Avel knew, was a fantastic world of gardens, fountains, music, and fine food. These were luxuries reserved for the pleasure of the rich, their guests, and servants.

Outside, the temporary hovels of transient beggars were attached to the exterior of the wall like barnacles on the hull of a ship. A half-dozen shelters were cobbled together from discarded tree branches and tat-tered fragments of cloth. The dying embers of a fire smoldered outside a hut. The occupants of the shacks were sleeping, Avel guessed. There was no movement. For this, Avel was grateful.

The masters of estates commonly tolerated limited encampments of the old, the infirm, cripples, widows, and orphans outside their gates. The poor depended on the castoffs of the wealthy houses. Like parasites, their survival depended on the host. Likewise, such public display of the rich man's benevolence fulfilled the expectations of his religious con-science.

Those supplicants strong enough to work sometimes hired on as ex-tra laborers in the field at harvest. The community of the impoverished was usually protective of one another and their territory. With sticks, stones, and epithets they would drive away anyone unclean from the door of their patron.

The number of pitiful sheds indicated that the master El'azar of Bethany was cautious in his generosity. Six. It seemed extraordinary that such a fine house would not have more beggars. What if El'azar's poor fiercely protected their territory against intrusion by others? What if El'azar hated any but these beggars and whipped others from his presence? The travelers Avel overheard on the road had mentioned there was madness in the blood of this family.

Avel fingered the silver coins as he marched through the vineyard toward the house. He hoped to beg bread and receive it without paying, but that was unlikely. He was an outsider.

The smell of baking bread made him dizzy. How long until the gatekeeper opened the entrance, and the comings and goings of the day would give Avel opportunity to plead for a crust?

At that instant the first sliver of sun topped the ridge, flooding the rain-washed fields with light. As if on cue, the pedestrian gate groaned on its hinges. Moments later a pair of women servants emerged, bearing wash baskets on their heads.

But why did the supplicants not creep out to ask for bread?

Avel's knees were weak as he trudged up the hill to the villa. The breeze flapped the fabric of the lean-tos.

They were deserted.

Had El'azar evicted them all?

Avel approached the gate. Through a passageway he glimpsed the rich interior courtyard. He heard the splash of a fountain.

The gate slammed shut.

"*Shalom!*" Avel croaked. His voice trembled from hunger and fear. He glanced at the one booth where coals glowed in a shallow fire pit. Was anyone inside? A frayed strip of cloth covering the entrance shifted.

A youthful voice called out to him. "Who's there?" A boy of about ten crept out of his hovel and sat cross-legged on the ground. His eyes were marbled white and blue like a goblet in the glassblower's shop.

The blind boy wagged his head back and forth like a dog as he tried to sniff out Avel's location. He was caked with dirt. Perhaps his hair was brown. Perhaps his skin was white. But every part of him was the same color. Like dust. His eyes were the one clean-looking part of him; an idol made of clay with shining sightless eyes stuck into the mud-colored face.

"I heard your voice," the blind boy challenged. "No use pretending you're not there. Hiram the day gatekeeper slammed the door when he saw you coming. He knows a beggar when he sees one. And I know one when I hear one. And smell one. What's your name?"

"Pretty good," Avel said, taking a step toward him. "I'm Avel Lo-Ahavah. Sparrow. From Jerusalem."

"What are you doing here? No one needs a torchbearer here. Except maybe me." The sightless youth threw his head back and opened his mouth wide in a smile that showed his brown teeth. He rocked back and forth in appreciation of his own humor.

Avel squirmed uncomfortably, not knowing if he should laugh at a blind boy's joke about light.

"I . . . I'm on my way . . . somewhere."

"But why? Link boys have it pretty good, from what I hear. Carry a torch and get paid for it. A solid roof over your heads. I'd be a link boy myself if I had a torch." Another openmouthed cadaverous smile as the beggar sucked in air in an attempt at laughter.

"What's your name?" Avel tried to change the subject as a parade of images came to mind. What a sight it would be to witness this sightless creature leading pompous Pharisees into walls and ditches.

"Ha-or Tov, meaning 'Good Light.'" The blind boy laughed again. "You see why I was born to carry a torch?"

Awkward name for someone who could not see, Avel thought.

"My mother had a sense of humor," quipped Ha-or Tov. "She said I was the light of her life. She didn't mind that I was blind. I've never seen light, but it must be a happy thing. Like laughing. Warm like fire but never burning. We were very poor, but Mother laughed a lot. Father died before I was born. She said I resemble him."

"Where is she?"

Avel had a fair idea what the answer was.

Ha-or Tov countered, "Tell me first. Where is your mother, Sparrow? Avel Lo-Ahavah?"

"Somewhere . . . else. She didn't want me."

"My mother wanted me until she died. Then no one wanted me. I was a good light for her, it seems."

Avel's heart squeezed at the story. So Ha-or Tov was alone as well. Avel replied, "I heard about a man who had no eyes; he sings like a bird. Not a sparrow. A canary. He sings for a rich man in Alexandria. They dress him in silk, and he has anything he wants to eat. When the rich man goes on a journey, he takes the singer with him."

"I can't sing a note. I'm stuck here at the gate of El'azar of Bethany, I suppose. Can't pick grapes in his vineyard. I'm no use to anyone. Not even fit to be a slave." Ha-or Tov was not laughing when he finished.

"Where is everybody?" Avel peered into a hut. "Where have they gone?"

"Off. Crawling up to Galilee to hear the Teacher. The Prophet. Even some of the servants ran off. And the master's sister Miryam. The one they call the harlot? She follows after this Teacher too. The master El'azar isn't happy about it. He says the Teacher is a trickster."

Avel frowned. "She follows the Baptizer?"

"I suppose."

"He's dead. I have his cloak."

Ha-or Tov considered the news. "I suppose that means they'll be coming back soon. The master will be relieved to have his beggars and his workmen back."

"Why didn't you go?"

"I would've gone. But they left without me. Who wants to lead a blind boy clear to Galilee? I tried to go after them. For the fun of it. I've been here over two years now. Rasha, the one-footed fellow, promised to take me. He's a drunk and a swine. He led me into the fig grove and left me there. I was lost in the orchard for a day. Next morning I followed the smell of the cook fires to the edge of the vineyard. One of the vine-dressers found me crying there and led me back here to my tabernacle. I was hungry."

"So am I." Avel put a hand to his belly. "I smelled bread."

"There's room here if you want to stay and beg. We eat well enough from the scraps of Master El'azar. His sister Marta is a hard one, though. She doesn't think well of our occupation. Puts everyone to work when there's work to be done. But me? I'm worthless."

"I'm on a mission."

"What is it?"

Avel lowered his voice and glanced furtively at the gatekeeper's slit. "I'm going to join the band of bar Abba's rebels. To fight Romans. He beat them in Jerusalem. Made them take down the images of Caesar from the Antonia. He's an outlaw living in the wilderness. But he'll raise an army. He'll run them out of Jerusalem and the corrupt priests with them. I want to help."

Big mouth smile. A braying laugh. Head wagging. Nose pointed sky-ward. Arms flapping in approval. "Well done, Avel! I wish I could go."

The image of the riot in Jerusalem leapt into Avel's mind. Bar Abba had a fellow bandit at the gate pretending to be blind.

Would bar Abba not welcome a real blind beggar into his band? How much more useful would an authentically sightless fellow be sitting at the gate and acting as a spy?

Avel expressed this idea to Ha-or Tov.

"Would you take me with you then?" Ha-or Tov exclaimed, jumping to his feet and reaching to embrace the air with his thin brown arms. "I can do it! My hearing is excellent! I can smell a leper a mile away. A Samaritan. Or a Roman. I can be useful! Let's go right now!"

Avel explained, "I have to stay awhile longer. My friend is dying in the orchard. He's in a tree. His name is Emet. I left him wrapped in part of the Baptizer's cloak. He's dying, and I can't leave him until he flies away. I promised. And I need bread to eat, or I'll die too."

"Yes. First you should eat, then we'll go together to the orchard. We'll wait together for your friend to die." He groped for Avel's arm. Finding it, he grasped it hard with both hands. "Lead me to the small gate."

Avel complied. The stumbling, hesitant walk of the blind boy made Avel wish he had not rashly offered to conduct him all the way to bar Abba's camp.

Ha-or Tov thumped hard on the wood door with his fist and bellowed, "Hiram! Hiram! Open up! It's me! It's Ha-or Tov! Did you forget my breakfast?"

It took a few repetitions before the gate flew back. A frail old man squinted at Ha-or Tov. Cataracts covered his eyes. He seemed not to see Avel. He called, "Good lad. Still alone, are you? Or have the fools come back?"

Hiram cupped his hand around his ear. Certainly he was hard of hearing. Perhaps he was mostly blind too.

Ha-or Tov shouted his reply cheerfully. "Just me and some friends, Hiram. We're off to fight Romans. A large sack of bread this morning, if you please. We'll be gone awhile."

"Well, then. Fight Romans? Good lad. Good lad. You'll need supplies, eh?" Hiram chuckled. Leaving the door ajar, he shuffled away.

Ha-or Tov remarked, "Hiram couldn't go to the Galil either. His mind is unraveling, they say. Sometimes he thinks I'm his master as a boy. Be patient. He'll be back."

The two boys flanked the doorway. Avel saw the fountain in the center of the courtyard. He observed as a tall, elegantly dressed man walked past and stared pensively down into the water. Presently the man was joined by a harried-looking woman. Frumpy and agitated, she exclaimed over the incompetence of the kitchen staff since the cook had run off to hear the Teacher of Nazareth!

Were these two Master El'azar and his sister Marta? They did not look as if they were in the grip of madness.

Hiram approached El'azar and Marta but acted unaware of their presence.

They greeted him, then fell silent as he walked on.

"You see what I mean, brother? This is the sort left to run the house and guard the gate?" Marta resumed her angry tirade against the substitute cook and the average age of the servants who remained.

The whole world, it seemed, had run after Yeshua of Nazareth! And what about Miryam? What were they going to do about Miryam, she wanted to know?

Oblivious, Hiram the gatekeeper carried the bulging bag. He did not raise his eyes as he brought it to the gate. "Here it is then." He gave it to Avel.

Did he believe that Avel was Ha-or Tov? And that Ha-or Tov was a young El'azar? "Enough for a day of fierce warfare, boy." Hiram smiled toothlessly. "Share with the sparrows, why don't you? Enjoy yourself."

The gate slammed.

The sack contained three fresh, warm loaves.

■ ■ ■ ■

As they left El'azar's house behind Avel recited to Ha-or Tov the details of how he came to Bethany.

The riot. Hayyim's death. Kittim's cruelty. The warning of the old man at Cripple Rock. Emet's arrival. The cloak of Yochanan the Baptizer.

Now they had only to wait for Emet to die. Nothing else held Avel back from his avowed purpose.

Sensing the presence of death ahead, Avel and Ha-or Tov entered the orchard.

It was cold. The warmth of the sun barely penetrated the canopy of broad leaves and intertwined branches.

A chorus of birds chirped in the artificial twilight.

"He's just ahead," Avel whispered. "In the crook of the oldest tree."

Avel saw a glint of color from the Baptizer's robe. With disgust he noted that it had fallen into Emet's nest. Thus onto Emet. There would be fleas to contend with after all.

Ha-or Tov lapsed into silence as they neared the enormous fig tree where Emet lay. Avel rubbed his eyes and peered into the dappled green gloom.

Placing Ha-or Tov's hand on the trunk, Avel instructed the blind boy to hold the satchel of bread and stay put.

Avel climbed up, expecting to find Emet. Instead there was just the largest piece of the rumpled mantle in the nest. The body had vanished. Likewise, the tiny square of cloth that had covered Emet was gone.

Had Emet convulsed in death and fallen from the tree? Avel bent over to look. The orchard floor was littered with leaves and rotten fruit but no dead boy.

Had a passing angel spotted the holy man's cloak and swooped down to gather Emet into Abraham's bosom without customary burial? A whirlwind? Chariots of fire?

"Emet," Avel cried in alarm. "Have you flown away?"

The braying laughter of Ha-or Tov replied and then, "Your friend is here! He's here! Come down, Avel. He's here with me."

Avel cried out with surprise and alarm as he peered down to see Emet, his scrap of cloak covering his head, grinning up at him.

Was he a ghost?

No. Emet opened the bag of bread, looked in, and rubbed his stomach.

Spirits were never hungry. His color was good. Eyes clear and bright. He seemed fully recovered.

"You're alive?"

In reply, Emet tore off a crust and crammed it greedily into his mouth.

"Where were you?" Avel queried, sliding down.

With a sweep of his hand Emet signed that he had been searching throughout the orchard. And that he was hungry. Also, he was pleased to have such a fine garment to wear. Lastly he pulled a diminutive feathered thing from his tunic pocket.

He had found a fledgling sparrow on the orchard floor. It had fallen from its nest. Emet had hurried down to retrieve it but could not find its house. It quivered in the cup of Emet's hand. Covered with down, it opened its mouth wide in hunger.

Emet rolled a fragment of bread into a seed-sized ball and poked it down the chick's throat. And then again. It ate greedily and was revived instantly. It begged for more.

"It'll die," Avel pronounced. "Baby birds can't live when they fall."

With a frown, Emet held the fragile creature close against him protectively. The gesture said, *Well if I lived, why can't a bird?*

Ha-or Tov said, "I heard of one that lived. Not a canary. A sparrow. A boy found it and carried it everywhere. Shared his food with it. It grew up and he turned it loose. It lived for many years in the Temple at Jerusalem. It's good luck if you find a fledgling sparrow and it lives, they say."

"Is it bad luck if it dies?" Avel asked suspiciously.

"No. It's just dead."

Avel remarked, "They never live."

"But Emet lived." Ha-or Tov let Emet guide his finger over the fuzzy head of the tiny bird. "I say let him keep it. It'll be our mascot. We *are* Sparrows, aren't we?"

Technically Avel was the lone one qualified to call himself a Sparrow, but he liked the idea of it.

The three shared breakfast with the sparrow, dividing one loaf among them with a knife old Hiram had placed in the sack.

Emet cradled the baby bird in a fold of the fine fabric of the cloak. The bird thrived and ruffled its feathers cheerfully with each morsel of bread Emet fed it.

Ha-or Tov joked about what a fine spy the bird would make for bar Abba.

Avel chewed in silence, staring at the creature. Thinking, thinking, wondering what had changed to heal Emet? He scanned Emet's complexion for a sign of flea bites. The creatures had vanished. Was it the cloak of the holy man? Had the Baptizer somehow driven off the army of fleas? Perhaps there was enchantment on the cloak?

After breakfast Avel brought Ha-or Tov and Emet to the shallows of the river where livestock drank. The three stripped and bathed in the frigid water. Like holy men did when they took a vow, Avel explained.

Ha-or Tov's skin was white. His hair was orange and curly down to his shoulders. He appeared quite different without the thick layer of mud.

With the bread knife, Avel divided Yochanan's mantle further, cutting away head coverings and boy-sized cloaks for each of them to wear.

Red, green, tan; red, tan, red; tan, green, red.

They matched.

Like a uniform.

Or like a righteous shield! Would the angels passing by recognize the fabric of the Baptizer's cloak and stoop to lend protection to the Sparrows?

They were soldiers in an army now. They made a vow to fight for Israel's redemption.

The baby sparrow riding high on Emet's shoulder would be the symbol of their platoon.

# NOZER

They called the sparrow *Yediyd,* "Beloved Friend."

Sometimes Yediyd rode on Emet's shoulder, sometimes on Avel's arm. But since Ha-or Tov always slept propped upright, Yediyd always nested at night within the tangle of Ha-or Tov's red locks.

As the company of sparrows journeyed in search of bar Abba's camp, Emet's coins supplied them with food.

Every time they encountered a traveler, Avel studied his face and dress.

Ha-or Tov sniffed the air suspiciously, rejecting two they met as Samaritans and another as "Some kind of foreigner."

Finally Emet consulted Yediyd. If the sparrow remained relaxed, then all was well. But if the bird became agitated, chirping and hopping, then the boys said nothing and went on their way without speaking to the stranger.

Each time their consultation resulted in a favorable conclusion, Avel would approach the man and ask for any information regarding the rebel leader's whereabouts.

Surprisingly, this approach actually worked.

The common people of the land . . . the *am ha aretz* . . . did not despise a troupe of beggar boys. This was because the *am ha aretz* knew what it was to be looked down upon.

The Sadducees and the rest of the Temple faction believed themselves descended from aristocracy. Consequently everyone else was beneath their station.

The Pharisees likewise spurned the *am ha aretz,* but for a different reason. They concluded that the people of the land did not follow stringent enough guidelines about ritual purity. They suspected commoners did not adequately keep the myriad of Pharisee additions to the Torah. The *am ha aretz* were, therefore, mostly likely defiled.

The common folk in turn envied Sadducee affluence and scorned Pharisee legalism.

The *am ha aretz* were not all ready to pick up swords and follow bar Abba, but neither were they prepared to turn him over to the Romans. As far as the common folk were concerned, Roman rule mainly existed to maintain the status quo, keeping the powerful in power and the wealthy in riches.

If only Messiah would come! Then all would be put in order as it should be. The last would be first and the first last. The *am ha aretz*, who remembered that Mosaic tradition taught the dignity of all work, also recalled what they had heard in synagogue:

> *Say to those with fearful hearts, "Be strong, do not fear;*
> *Your God will come, he will come with vengeance;*
> *With divine retribution he will come to save you."*
> *Then will the eyes of the blind be opened and the ears of the deaf*
>    *unstopped.*
> *Then the lame will leap like a deer, and the mute tongue shout for joy.*

So anyone approved of by Avel's judgment, Ha-or Tov's nose, and Emet's sparrow spoke to the boys with respect. Many times they furnished clues as to where bar Abba had last been seen, what waterhole his band had used, what direction he was headed.

Any suspicion on the part of those being interrogated was eliminated by the youthful age of the company, Ha-or Tov's manifest blindness . . . and the bird hopping about on Emet's shoulder.

■ ■ ■ ■

Nakdimon heard quiet murmurs from far away, distant conversations in a fog. Astonished whispers. Conjecture about why one of the rulers of Israel was in the company of a foreigner. How had he come to be on such a dangerous road? Where was he going, and why?

Easily explained if Nakdimon had felt like talking. But he did not. His head throbbed with every heartbeat. Drifting in a twilight sleep he imagined he replied to El'azar's and Marta's concerns and then told them to please shut up.

Silence.

Visions entered the room where Nakdimon lay.

*Hadassah stood at his bedside. Cool fingers stroked his forehead.*

"Nakdimon," she soothed. "Nakdimon?"

"Yes. Yes. It hurts. Where have you been?" he asked. She had been gone so long. What had taken her so long to come to him? Hadn't he ached for her every day and every night? Did it take his getting knocked on the head to make her come home?

"Nakdimon? Where were you going, Nakdimon?"

"To find . . . Yeshua of Nazareth."

"Everyone is looking for him."

He could not comprehend her words. He asked Hadassah like a petulant child, "Where have you been, Hadassah? I was looking for you."

El'azar and Marta interrupted his conversation with Hadassah. Rude and oblivious, they talked to one another as though Hadassah was not there.

"He thinks I'm her, poor thing."

El'azar clucked his tongue in pity. "It may be awhile before we get the facts. That was a Samaritan he was with, I think. You should have got the facts before you ordered him away, Marta. It's been two days now. What if Nakdimon ben Gurion doesn't come round? What will we tell the council?"

Hadassah stooped close to Nakdimon's ear and murmured, "What happened?"

Nakdimon tried to speak, but his lips would not move. He groaned the words inside his head.

Surely Hadassah could hear what he was thinking. In life she had known his thoughts. In death she would be even better at it, wouldn't she?

"Did you see it coming, Hadassah? Your leaving me and the children alone to struggle on without you, I mean? Did you know ahead? Or did you get up and walk into the light without remembering I couldn't follow? And if you knew, why didn't you tell me?"

"I am born again, Nakdimon."

"But do you live again?"

"Differently."

"With me? No. I don't understand. I don't understand, Hadassah!"

"The light. The light. Walk toward the light, and everything will be clear."

"I want to see you! Only you! How can I live on without you?"

"You're badly hurt."

"Hurt? Badly? I've been dying inside ever since you left us. Hurt? The word doesn't even touch what I feel without you here! If it wasn't for the *children . . . Oh, Hadassah! The children! They need you so! They try. Carry on, you know. But none of us understands the why of it. How long this life feels without you. The girls acting parts they learned from you. Each a different role. None of them complete. The baby never even knew you. He looks like me. The girls . . . some piece of you! I look at them and sometimes can hardly bear it. All trying to be like you. All listening for you to tell them how but not hearing. They need you to see them. Like the Spring needed you to admire it. Stars are there . . . but what are they when you're not with me to gaze at them?"*

El'azar broke into the vision unexpectedly and asked, "Nakdimon ben Gurion. Should I send word? Your family?"

*Hadassah stepped back, receded from his sight.*

Nakdimon heard his own voice moaning, "Noooooooooo! Not yet . . ."

"You see, Marta. Something's up. He was traveling on official business. In disguise, no doubt."

Marta's voice replied crisply, "On his way to Galilee with the rest of the world. It's too much. Too much, I say. What's it coming to?"

"Rebellion," El'azar replied grimly. "Revolt. Surely it's coming. And that trickster is using Miryam to help finance it."

Marta gasped, "Our own flesh and blood. She'll bring this house down with her. We'll be judged because she followed after him."

What were they babbling about? And why? Couldn't they see Hadassah had come from a far place to speak with him?

Nakdimon mustered all his strength to shout, "Shut up!"

Marta and El'azar fell silent. But where had Hadassah gone? Had she left?

*"Come back, Hadassah! Don't let go so easily! Oh, my love!"*

She did not reply.

Empty wind roared his ears.

■ ■ ■ ■

It took the Sparrow company only days to locate the rebel encampment that Governor Pilate or High Priest Caiaphas would have paid a thousand denarii to discover. The last and key bit of information came from an actual member of bar Abba's band, one Judas by name.

He went by the surname *Iscariot* and pretended it meant he came from the village of Kerioth. But it really referred to his alliance with the assassins: Judas the Sicarius.

The Sparrows met Judas beside a dry water hole in one of the myriad of branching canyons in the Judean wilderness. Footsore, out of the bread provided by Hiram, and desperately thirsty, Avel tried to cheer the other two by coaxing Yediyd to chirp. By turning the bread sack inside out Avel located a few meager crumbs. With Yediyd perched on his finger, Avel waved a fragment of crust in front of the bird's beak. "Now," he urged. "Say please."

Obligingly the sparrow peeped.

"Very clever," applauded a voice.

Yediyd dropped the crumb and hopped agitatedly up and down. The bird jumped back to Emet and huddled next to his chest. The mute boy tucked him away out of sight inside his robe.

"Avel," Ha-or Tov said, "I . . ."

The newcomer appeared unexpectedly from behind a boulder, as if he had been listening before revealing himself. "Nothing in the pool?" he complained good-naturedly. "And I was counting on a good wash to take away the stink of travel. Would you care to share my water?"

After introductions Judas produced a skin bag and allowed the Sparrows, including Yediyd, to drink their fill. He was a pleasant-looking fellow, of middle height and weight. His light-brown hair, though powdered gray with road dust, was tied back neatly at the nape of his neck. He had quick, darting eyes. Even when he spoke to one of the boys he observed each of the others in turn.

His voice was soothing, like oil on scraped skin.

"I have heard," Judas said as the water skin went around the second time, "of young men about your age who are searching for bar Abba, the patriot. You haven't seen them, have you?"

This was different. Always before it was Avel who initiated the questioning.

"It's us," Avel confirmed. "We want to fight Romans. I know Jerusalem like the back of my hand. Ha-or Tov and Emet can be spies . . . real beggars instead of pretend ones like Asher."

Judas' gaze snapped back to Avel. "You know Asher?" he repeated. "Clever boy. But tell me. Why do you want to kill Romans?"

Avel described again the death of Hayyim, concluding with, "And besides, if the Romans were gone there'd be more justice for everyone, including beggars . . . wouldn't there?"

"Justice? Yes, and freedom too," Judas agreed warmly. "But do you know that bar Abba's men take a blood oath? Death before betrayal is the motto."

Avel lifted his chin and spoke for the group. "Where else can we go? No one else wants us. If bar Abba takes us in, we'll swear any oath he names."

"Good lad," Judas applauded. Lifting both arms high overhead, he placed his palms together, then with deliberation lowered them in front of his chest. "Now it's safe to enter."

The gesture was a signal to a guard posted high on a chimney of rock looming over the wadi.

Judas showed them the constricted entry to a walkway behind a heap of fallen stones. Without someone to reveal it, the opening would have been unguessable from more than two or three feet away. After ten or twelve twisting paces, the channel broadened into a passage, through what appeared to be unbroken, unscaleable sandstone walls. It was big enough to drive a camel through and opened to a secret oasis at the far end.

■ ■ ■ ■

Surrounded by barren rock walls that offered no clue to what lay concealed within them, the enclosed canyon was large enough to accommodate half a thousand insurgents. About a hundred men appeared to be presently in residence, either living in caves honeycombing the slopes or camped beside a pond in the center.

As far as Avel was concerned it was an adventure story made real: David before he was king, hiding from Saul in these very hills. Caves, hidden passageways, an army of patriots. It was a boy's dream come true.

That was Avel's first impression.

But bar Abba's camp was in an uproar. When Avel and the rest emerged from the concealed access, a violent argument was going on. Half the rebels believed that Roman legionaries were about to descend on them at any instant. The others retorted that the secret base was more secure than anywhere else; besides, where was the proof that any troops were coming?

"What proof indeed?" Judas asserted, approaching bar Abba. "I have walked from Jericho, and there is no sign of unusual activity there or at Fort Cypress. I think you ran from shadows."

"Jorum was not killed by a shadow," bar Abba blustered. "It was a Roman centurion."

Judas shrugged. "Someone killed him. I saw the body . . . and the vultures. And I also saw something you did not." Judas tossed a leather pouch to bar Abba. "Lost by someone in the caravan you attacked," he said. "Open it."

The bickering stopped, and a crowd of onlookers gathered.

Untying the leather strings that secured the purse, bar Abba extracted the message given by Gamaliel to Nakdimon. When he had read it he thumped it against his palm. "This is it!" he exulted. "This will rouse Judea from its complacency! Proof that the high priest and the Roman governor are conspiring to defile the Temple and steal the Korban money. And here are the names of two of the key conspirators. With this news thousands will join us!"

"And disappear again at the first battle," Judas added cynically. "I've said before, we must give them more than just something to fight against. We must have something to fight for . . . a king!"

"Yes," bar Abba mused, "but will he agree?"

Who was this mysterious "he"? Avel wondered. Avel knew about King Herod the Great. Were they talking about one of his offspring? But the *am ha aretz* had never acknowledged the Idumean Herod as the true king of Israel.

And why would anyone not want to be a king?

Coming out of his own reverie, bar Abba appeared to finally notice the Sparrows. "What's this? Part of your disguise?"

"We want to fight Romans," Avel asserted boldly.

A round of laughter erupted in the rebel camp, making Avel thrust out his jaw defiantly. His gesture produced another louder set of guffaws. "We can spy, we can steal, we can go where you would be arrested if so much as your nose showed. You need us!"

"He's not wrong," Judas said in their defense. "Blind, mute, and begging? How menacing are they? Or how dangerous is any group traveling with them? Besides, I didn't bring them; they found you on their own. Such resourcefulness should be rewarded, not laughed at."

"But what are they wearing?" bar Abba queried, pointing at the identical striped caftans. "Are they runaway slaves from a rich Levite?"

"This is our uniform," Avel asserted.

Emet and Ha-or Tov nodded vigorously.

"A beggar's army!" someone shouted and the laughter rolled again.

"It's the robe of a holy man, Yochanan the Baptizer," Avel added with eight-year-old dignity.

Judas stared at Avel. "How?" he demanded. "Where did you get it?"

"His talmidim gave it to me as they were taking his body away to bury," Avel declared.

The mocking laughter was replaced with an angry murmur. "Can it be?" bar Abba queried.

Stepping closer to the rebel chief, Judas retorted, "If true, then it's the key. If Herod Antipas has murdered Yeshua's cousin, then Yeshua must agree to become the leader . . . he must! He can't hear of it from me, of course, but I must return to the Galil at once."

"It's time for me to see him too," bar Abba insisted. "And as soon as I have this black demon horse broken to ride, I'll offer him my service as his military commander."

Turning to the Sparrows, bar Abba said, "With this information, you have earned the right to join us." He smiled. "I even have a company commander suited to your age. Kittim," bar Abba called, "here are your new recruits."

■ ■ ■ ■

All broad smiles and fawning agreement to bar Abba's face, Kittim grabbed Avel and Ha-or Tov by the scruffs of their necks as soon as the meeting dispersed. "Avel!" Kittim said as if delighted at the renewed acquaintance.

Then he thumped their heads together with a sharp crack.

He tried to rap his knuckles on Emet's skull, but the mute boy ducked aside.

"Someone informed the Temple authorities that I was over the age limit," Kittim hissed in Avel's face. "And someone said I was extorting money from the Sparrows. Can you think who that might have been?"

Avel shrugged. As much as he hated Kittim it had never occurred to him to go to the authorities. Why would they take the word of a Sparrow about anything?

"But I was going to join bar Abba anyway," Kittim insisted.

Avel disbelieved that idea totally. The money-loving bully Kittim was afraid of the lash and fearful he might have to work for his bread. Living in the desert as a rebel must have been a last resort.

Avel wisely kept his conclusions to himself, but did speak up for himself and his companions. "You may be in charge of us, like in the quarry," he asserted, "but bar Abba himself wants us for the trip to the Galil. Don't forget that."

"See you jump when I say hop," retorted Kittim with a scowl. "And show me proper respect, too. It's a long way to the Galil, and the nights are dark. Now hand over any coins you have!" Pocketing the remaining pennies of Emet's money, Kittim stalked off, muttering more chilling threats.

Avel, Ha-or Tov, and Emet huddled closely together. "These are the heroic freedom fighters we came to join?" Ha-or Tov queried dryly. His nose wrinkled toward the direction taken by Kittim's departure.

"They aren't all like Kittim," Avel argued. "Bar Abba is a real patriot. Judas, too. You heard what he said about loyalty and betrayal. We'll do our part, and they'll soon know what a momzer Kittim is. Only," he added emphatically to Emet, "keep Yediyd out of sight when Kittim's around, agreed?"

Emet nodded vigorously, cupping his hands protectively over the lump on his chest that was their beloved friend.

■ ■ ■ ■

Nakdimon awakened from his long sleep with a sob. He opened his eyes, remembering everything. But he was sure of nothing. What was real and what a dream?

The dull ache of certainty pressed against his heart: Hadassah no longer needed him.

She had weaned herself from this world and from his love like a child weaned from its mother's breast. She had smiled gently down at him, no longer comprehending his agony. She had seen sights that made her speak to him like a mother speaks to a child in the midst of a night-mare. *"There, there now. It'll be all right. You'll find the light and under-stand. . . ."*

He had accused her, upbraided her for leaving them.

In turn she did not acknowledge his sorrow but spoke of being born again. Putting away the world, she had also laid aside his worries. They were not hers any longer. She did not wish his wishes. Nor fear the fu-ture. Nor cherish anxiety. Nor rage against injustice. There was true joy and freedom in her eyes. Hadassah had thrown off the chains that bound the living.

Then she had vanished without giving him answers to the mysteries he pondered. As though sorrow was simply a white stone marker along the highway that he must pass or lose his way. As though he could not make the journey through life without pausing from time to time at milestones of grief; to gather strength or courage or new understanding.

And then walk on to the next stone and the next and the next to the end of the road. . . .

How he ached for the journey to be done.

But she did not pity him. *"Walk toward the light!"*

Which light?

How he longed for her pity! Needed it.

But she could not hear him. An eternal song had drowned out his cries as his heart shattered on the white stone of her dying.

■ ■ ■ ■

In all bar Abba's camp, only Asher seemed kindly disposed to the trio of boys.

Asher, who smelled worse than an old rubbish heap, was a strange fellow. He had once been a Sparrow himself in the Jerusalem quarry, he told them. When he grew a beard, he had been run off. For a time he made a living as a porter, hauling animal carcasses from the Temple to sell in the shambles of the meat market. After a year of being cheated, he had slain his cheating employer, using a leg of mutton to bash in his head.

He had been on the run ever since.

But he was not a bad sort, Avel mused. Avel knew this because Asher hated Kittim. Kittim feared him. And Asher liked Yediyd the bird. He told the boys Yediyd was a good-luck charm.

Emet plucked the bird from inside his robe and put him on the lip of the stone trough. Yediyd fluffed his feathers, then cocked his head to the side as Asher whistled at him.

Low cheeps and chirps were followed by a soft trill.

Then the unexpected happened.

Yediyd, having shown no previous sign of readiness, attempted to fly to Asher's outstretched hand. Asher caught him mid-fall and lifted him to his filthy lips for a kiss. "Not yet, little friend. Soon."

Avel remarked, "He likes you."

Asher nodded, stroking the top of the bird's head and crooning to him. "Animals do," he said. Inherent in that was the fact that people seldom did. He made chirping noises at the little bird. Yediyd did not mind the stink of him.

It was good, Avel thought, to have at least one human in the whole rabble who liked Sparrows.

# CHESED

elow the caves of the rebels was an oasis. A spring of water bubbling out of the rock nourished a ring of date palms. Around a shallow pool the ground was marshy. There was grass enough for a flock of sheep, or a couple cows. At the moment, however, there was just one animal present, and he was not grazing peacefully.

Far from it.

From their perch on a rock ledge Avel described the scene in the oasis to Ha-or Tov. "The rider's up. He's got a big handful of mane in one hand and the reins in another. He's ready. The groom let go. . . . Oh!"

The exclamation coincided with a loud thump and a cry of pain.

It was also accompanied by the echo of laughter from the onlookers. "What?" demanded the blind boy. "What?"

"He's off already," explained Avel. "The instant the helper let go the horse jumped straight up! He twisted in midair, and the rider flew off . . . like that." Avel clapped his hands together to demonstrate the suddenness of the parting. "He landed on his back in the mud."

The rider needed help standing. Three men grabbed the trailing lead rope, the reins, and the halter. They fought the horse to a standstill.

Ha-or Tov's mouth spread in an expansive grin. He rocked from side to side with merriment.

Emet, seated on a boulder, chuckled loudly. His own cheeks stuffed with bread, he offered another crumb to Yediyd the bird, perched on his shoulder.

This was the fourth failed attempt by bar Abba's band to conquer the Roman mount. Despite the corral improvised from the trunks of fallen palms and a string of riders, no one stayed aboard more than a minute.

Avel knew bar Abba wanted the animal for himself. The rebel commander's vision included leading an army into battle while mounted on the flashy black horse.

While it was an image worthy of someone trying to be the heir of Judah Maccabee, Avel did not believe it would happen. The beast was too wild, too dangerous.

Nor did Avel join wholeheartedly in the laughter as rider after rider got thrown. This was the horse of a Roman. Though it was a different color, a different animal entirely, its viciousness reminded him of the one that had caused the death of Hayyim. Violent, brutal Romans all had matching ferocious mounts, it seemed.

Kittim watched from the opposite side of the clearing. He swaggered forward, tapping his thumb against his chest. *Watch me,* his manner said. *I'll show you how it's done.*

Avel was unclear who to root for. As much as he hated Romans and wanted revenge for Hayyim, he was torn. Arrogant, bullying Kittim or the black horse?

A tough choice.

From the circle of skeptical grooms Kittim summoned the biggest one. He said something to the man, who acknowledged the request and laid hold of the halter.

With a rush, Kittim scrambled up.

Ears laid back, the black horse craned its neck around and bared its teeth. Together horse, rider, and groom circled furiously in the grass at the edge of the pond.

"What's happening?" Ha-or Tov asked.

"So far the creature hates Kittim the most," Avel explained. "Everyone else, he dumped. Kittim, he's trying to bite! Smart horse."

This observation made Emet laugh again. As the boy's shoulders bounced cheerfully, Yediyd flapped his stubby wings to keep his balance. Apologetically, Emet reached up and the sparrow hopped into his hand. Emet cradled Yediyd in a fold of his striped robe.

The groom finally regained control. With one hand he gripped the halter to keep the horse's snapping jaws away from his face. With the other he twisted the black's ear into a corkscrew.

The groom next clamped his teeth onto the tip of the animal's ear.

When Avel described this to Ha-or Tov the blind boy quipped, "I wonder how he would like it if the horse did that to him?"

More gales of laughter.

Kittim compressed his knees firmly. He drew reins and mane into a compact double handful. Kittim nodded. The groom released the horse's ear.

Docilely the black mount took two steps, then another two.

Avel sat up and leaned forward. It couldn't be this easy! Kittim was already insufferable! He couldn't win so easily!

Avel discovered he was definitely rooting for the horse.

One circuit of the palm trees.

Still no response from the animal. Nothing except a dispassionate, deliberate pacing.

Another turn around the pool of water.

Avel grudgingly relayed the scene to Ha-or Tov. "Kittim has won."

Even bar Abba, on the stump of a palm tree at the head of the clearing, showed signs of approval.

Then a bolt of black lightning detonated in the oasis.

With a ferocious toss of his neck, the horse demonstrated it was premature to call him subdued. Bucking and kicking, the animal plunged around the circuit of the clearing. Every bounce jolted Kittim skyward. He shrieked and wailed in terror.

"He's . . . ," Avel began.

"Don't bother," Ha-or Tov replied. "I think I see it!"

The horse planted his front feet and kicked his hind legs. He spun sideways, then reared as if he would climb the sheer rock wall. Next he ran straight toward Avel and the other Sparrows.

Avel, frightened that he would be trampled like Hayyim, threw himself sideways into a crevice.

At the last second the horse reversed his direction. His flying hooves struck sparks from the rocks below Avel's head as he pivoted.

Then the black galloped directly at bar Abba, with Kittim screeching all the while. His bowed neck tucked under his body, the animal kicked upward as if he would deliberately roll over on top of Kittim.

But Kittim was no longer there.

The last thrust had unseated him. Kittim flew through the intervening space. His limbs flapping in all directions, Kittim struck bar Abba crossways in the back. The two men sprawled on the ground.

This time it took six rebels to corral the beast.

"Kill him," bar Abba said with disgust as he dragged himself to his feet. "We'll eat him."

Kittim, limping, echoed the words. He added with a snarl, "Let me do it."

Ha-or Tov turned downcast at the words. "I won't eat," he said to Avel. "It isn't right."

Emet shook his head fiercely. He clamped his hands protectively around the little bird. He did not approve of killing the horse either.

Avel was torn. Kill the horse of a Roman? Why not? There were no Romans nearby for Avel to kill, but why not start with the horse?

All the while he was inwardly pleased to see Kittim humbled. Avel regretted that Kittim would once again strike something unable to defend itself.

Kittim advanced toward the animal, dagger in hand.

When he was still twenty paces away, the black horse charged. Dragging the six handlers after him as if they were inconsequential, the black horse acted as if he could not wait to take Kittim's head off.

Kittim dropped the knife and fled.

A lunge to one side dislodged three of the grooms. Lashing hooves and three kicks removed the other three.

Vaulting over the stump on which bar Abba had lately stood, the horse knocked aside two more rebels who could not get out of the way fast enough. Then he dashed off down the trail out of the canyon.

The ease of his escape made Avel wonder if the horse had been toying with them all along. If an animal could best the rebels so handily, how would they fare against Roman soldiers?

Avel shelved the thought as soon as he could. A more immediate concern presented itself. Avel knew how dangerous it was for the weak and defenseless when Kittim's pride was injured.

He resolved not to let the shadow of a smile cross his face in Kittim's presence. He warned Emet and Ha-or Tov about it also.

■ ■ ■ ■

Mile by weary mile, Marcus retraced his steps. It came to him strongly that no Galilean peasant could control Pavor. He visualized following the retreating rebels by a string of dumped and crippled riders.

At the least he could locate the outlaw band by following the horse. Perhaps Pavor's tracks would lead him to their lair.

Another white mile marker gleamed in the morning light. The Roman insistence on orderliness measured his progress even when the rolling hills stretched in an endless procession of sameness.

Marcus' thoughts turned to the wounded man. Whoever Nakdimon the leather worker was, it was clear he loved his family. Despite Nakdimon's wandering wits, the injury had not damaged his heart. Marcus counted seven names spoken with tenderness and concern: his children, without a doubt.

The fellow's longing for his loved ones had an interesting effect on Marcus. Who would he call for if he lay dying? And who, in the whole world, would care if he no longer lived?

At thirty-two years of age, Marcus doubted he would ever have children of his own, a son to carry on the clan of Longinus.

But no. It was more than that ... *A child to watch for his coming home. To run out to meet him and call him Daddy. And ride upon his shoulder through a glen. Or stand beside him on a riverbank and skip stones on the water. And lay awake until he came in to tell a story of battle and triumph. A kiss good night. Another in the morning ...*

No. Such joys were not destined for a centurion of Rome.

Despite the Imperial cults that deified emperors and set them among the heavens, Marcus did not believe in immortality. A man lived after death only in the memories of others and in the children he sired.

Otherwise lives were like candles blown out by the hot breath of the Khamseen wind.

Weren't they?

Some Jews believed otherwise, Marcus knew. The Pharisees held that there was life beyond life. Reunions there with vanished loved ones.

There had been another name spoken by Nakdimon: *Hadassah.* This had been murmured with such reverence and pangs of desire that Marcus wished he knew more. Was she Nakdimon's wife? A lost love? Clearly Nakdimon, in his unguarded comments, did not feel entirely whole without her and missed her terribly.

Marcus envied the man his love for one woman.

And with that thought came an overwhelming ache within his own heart. Though desire for Miryam suffused Marcus' dreams, how often he denied he loved her. Turned away from it. Buried yearning with duty and endless tasks. But here it was. Loneliness shouted to his soul: *There are in this life partings as final and terrible as the grave!*

How he missed Miryam! How he regretted the death of their child. Oh, what might have been! He saw it clearly. A baby. A child. A youth who resembled Marcus. A man grown to become friend, as well as son!

And what had Miryam lost? As much as Marcus and yet ...

After receiving the forgiveness offered by Yeshua, something extraordinary had happened: Miryam had forgiven herself. Her life had been altered. It was as if she had died and come back to life. Somehow reborn in the same body but with a pristine spirit. A soul washed so clean that the joy of it shone on her face.

Marcus did not doubt that Yeshua was a healer of illness and injury. The centurion had himself witnessed the miraculous restoration of his servant, Carta.

But what else was Yeshua?

How do you define someone who mends broken hearts and wounded souls?

Marcus needed to see Miryam, to view again the changed life, to question her about it. Perhaps she could help him understand.

Besides understanding, he wanted to see her again, because . . . he missed her with the kind of hunger he heard in Nakdimon's voice.

Highway to turnoff to serpentine ravine, Marcus covered the same ground as before, both in his mind and on this road.

Approaching with caution, Marcus returned to the scene of the ambush. While remaining concealed from view, he heard the sounds of scraping in the dirt. Carefully he peered over a boulder.

It was Pavor, trailing a broken lead rope, pawing the sand near the spot where he'd been stolen.

■ ■ ■ ■

The next day Judas Iscariot prepared to leave the rebel camp. He would arrive in Galilee before the others. "I'll return to Yeshua," he explained. "I'll test the sentiment of the crowds too. Meet me six days from today on the hill to the north of Capernaum . . . the abandoned oil press . . . just after sunset."

"I know the spot," bar Abba said. "And will you tell him at once that the Baptizer's dead? If Yeshua's the leader that you claim, perhaps he'll be ready to strike."

Judas demurred. "It'll have to be handled carefully," he replied. "Yeshua doesn't yet understand what can be achieved. When I saw him last he spoke of 'loving your enemies.'"

Dan snorted and barked a derisive laugh. "I do love Romans," he asserted. "Dead. I'd promise to love every one of them that way too."

Avel agreed with that sentiment.

Dan continued, "This is a waste of time. A king? He's a wandering Rabbi who talks nonsense. The Romans will understand nothing but a

Jewish army ready to fight. A legion of our own. Five thousand men with swords and spears."

"Wait till you see the crowds that follow him," Judas replied. "And keep your mouths shut." To bar Abba, he added, "Remember what I said: we must give the people a king to follow, a king to fight for . . . we need *him*."

■ ■ ■ ■

"He wept all night and called for his wife again and again." The words of Marta in the corridor awakened Nakdimon.

"Poor fellow," El'azar said. "I wonder, should we fetch his family? His children?"

Nakdimon struggled to sit up. "No!" he shouted. His head ached. His stomach churned. "I'm up! I'm awake! Don't worry them!"

El'azar peered cautiously into the room. Marta crowded past her brother.

"He's alive," Marta said with astonishment.

Nakdimon scowled at them. "So it would seem."

"We weren't sure you would make it." Marta was matter-of-fact.

Nakdimon touched his bandaged head. "It'll take more than one stone to kill me."

"Yes." El'azar sniffed with satisfaction and grinned as he came to the bedside. "That's what I said when I saw you. I told Marta it would take more than one stone to kill such a bull as Nakdimon ben Gurion. Didn't I say that, Marta?"

The sister eyed her brother doubtfully. If they had placed a bet on the outcome, Nakdimon was sure that Marta had lost money.

Regaining her composure she queried, "Can you eat?" Then to her brother, "I'll get him something. I've had oxtail soup simmering since that Samaritan brought him here. It's a wonder he didn't finish him off. Swine. All of them." She bustled off.

"Samaritan?" Nakdimon could not remember who had brought him to the house of El'azar and Marta. Only that someone had driven off his attackers. Bound his wounds. The others had fled, but one man stayed with him for a time and helped him back to Bethany.

El'azar sat beside him and stared at his bandaged head. "You're lucky, you know, Nakdimon. How did this happen?"

"I was traveling to the Galil. There were several of us. We didn't see it coming."

"To the Galil?" El'azar probed.

"Partly official business and partly curiosity, I admit."

"To see the Rabbi, then? The Galilean?"

"To observe. Ask questions of those he's met. The ones who claim they've been healed."

"Our sister follows after him." El'azar's mouth twitched. He glanced out the window, unable to meet Nakdimon's gaze at the admission. "You remember Miryam."

Nakdimon did remember. A beautiful and wild creature. "She was young when your mother . . . died."

"It affected her. Badly. She's always been seeking for something. Chasing after someone. Some man. It's no secret what this family has endured because of her behavior. I'm going to fetch her back here."

Nakdimon considered how much El'azar must love Miryam to bring her into his own home after her shameful life. "You're a good brother."

"Yes. What else can I do? She's squandering her estate at the command of this Yeshua. She's sold half her lands and peopled her villa with beggars. Outcasts. Turned her servants to the task of caring for the homeless while she sits at this Galilean's feet and laps up every word he speaks."

"Beggars?"

"Homeless. Children. Widows turned off their farms and the like. She feeds them from her own purse. The place is like a common inn of the lowest sort. They file in through the open gates to eat. Soup kettles steam in her courtyard. I intend to bring her back and lock her away before she wastes her fortune. It's my duty as next-of-kin."

"This isn't the Miryam I remember." Nakdimon wondered at the change. Had Miryam lost her mind? Or was this a sign she had turned her life around?

"No. She's not like Marta. Sensible Marta."

"Everyone is running after Yeshua," Nakdimon commented.

Marta entered, carrying a tray with soup and unleavened bread. She joined the conversation midsentence. "The hills are full of rebels these days. There was a time when we never locked the gates at night. Never thought of it. There was order in those days. But these days, the whole country's gone mad. Searching under every rock for a Messiah. For a prophet to set them and Jerusalem free from Rome."

"You think this Yeshua is somehow allied with the rebel bands then?" El'azar asked his sister.

"There are whispers of it. I wouldn't be surprised. And when it comes out, and he and his followers are arrested, I'll be hauled up before the authorities because of Miryam unless we do something about her soon."

Nakdimon gingerly tasted the broth. The hot, salty liquid soothed his stomach. He had been sent to listen and observe. But the conversation between El'azar and his sister took on the bitter edge of gossip and foolish speculation. Nakdimon thought that if Hadassah had been there she would not have liked Marta, the sister of El'azar of Bethany. She was a woman who stuffed her mind with useless things; and eventually they found a way out of her mouth.

"I've heard that Joanna, the wife of Herod Antipas' steward, is a follower," El'azar interjected.

Marta prattled on, "Then Kuza should look to his own household if he intends to continue overseeing the house of Herod Antipas. This Yeshua will bring disaster on us if we're not careful. Half my servants have run off to hear him. If he put swords in their hands . . . well, there are more of them than there are us." She sat forward in her chair. Her eyes were wide, as if imagining hordes of former cooks, gardeners, and house servants breaking down the gates of El'azar's estate to ravage and pillage the family fortune.

Nakdimon drained the bowl. "Good soup," he remarked dryly.

Marta did not respond, as if she did not hear the compliment. Her face shone ecstatically, apparently thinking about all the excitement of possible rape and murder. "It's happened before, hasn't it?" Marta finally said, putting a hand to her throat.

"Not here in Judea," El'azar comforted his sister.

Nakdimon felt much better. "Soon. Two more days, I think . . ."

"What's that?" Marta started as if Nakdimon had predicted that tomorrow her enemies would come crawling through the windows.

Nakdimon smiled as he considered how Hadassah would have reacted to this sad spinster's hysteria. "I meant the soup. It's the soup. I feel better. Yes. A couple days. Then I'll be ready to travel. I need to see this Yeshua with my own eyes. What is it that makes a young widow sell off her estates to care for clouds of beggars?"

"She's a madwoman!" Marta pounced. Her voice was shrill and full of disdain. "That's the only explanation there is!"

"We'll go together," El'azar replied quietly. Did Marta's outburst embarrass him? Or had he become accustomed to it after the many years with her running the house and his life?

Marta declared forcefully, "I'm going too. I won't stay here alone. To be murdered in my bed. No use trying to talk me out of it. I want to see this rebel miracle worker before Rome comes to its senses and crucifies him."

Nakdimon abandoned any thought of arriving in the Galil unrecognized.

# LA-ALAFIM

Two days' ride and Marcus reached the northern end of the Jordan River valley. As he left the territory of the Decapolis, the ten Greek cities planted by Alexander the Great, and entered the Jewish Galil, a plan formed in his mind. Before returning to Capernaum, where he had last seen Yeshua and where he expected to again find the Teacher, he would first ride to Magdala. Miryam already kept the chest containing Marcus' few valued possessions. Certainly he could leave Pavor in her care as well. That way he would appear on foot and in civilian dress when he joined the crowds around the Rabbi.

In moments of candor, Marcus admitted to himself that this strategy fulfilled an even more basic desire: he wanted to see Miryam. Brusquely he set this thought aside by reducing its emotional significance. Miryam would be a good source of news about the mood of the Galil. She would know the whereabouts of Yeshua. She could also bring Marcus up to date on how Carta was doing.

That was it. Purely practical. It had nothing to do with the ache inside his chest when he thought of her. His motives did not include the half-fearful yearning to catch a glimpse of her and read on her face how she felt about Marcus Longinus.

Not at all.

The solder who had withstood the barbarian onslaught at Idistaviso was nervous. The Roman legionary who received the crown of heroism for saving an entire army was apprehensive about seeing a woman.

It was shortly after dawn when Marcus rode into the sleepy lakeside settlement of Magdala. Faint trails of cookfire smoke traced the awakening life of the settlement. No one was abroad on the highway. It was a strategic choice, this time of day, Marcus told himself. Drop off the horse. Transmute the last brass of Roman-ness into common clay.

It had nothing to do with seeing Miryam in the morning, her hair unbound, her skin lit with sunrise. Or with catching her by surprise and thereby having an advantage.

Not at all.

The gates to Miryam's villa were closed. Marcus knocked.

From within the confines of the courtyard Marcus heard stirring and what sounded like the cry of an infant. An animal, no doubt, that peculiar human mewing. Then footsteps pattered purposefully toward the entry and the door was thrown back by Tavita, Miryam's elderly and cantankerous servant. "Yes?" the old woman demanded. "It's early to be . . . Master Marcus, is that you?"

The warmth of welcome in the tone caught Marcus entirely off guard. From the way Tavita flung wide her arms, for a moment Marcus thought she would hug him. Extraordinary thought. Very unlike the grouchy woman he remembered. "It is so good to see you," she chattered. "I almost didn't recognize you with your beard. But it looks good on you. Very distinguished. Makes you appear Jewish," she added with a laugh.

Peering over the top of her head, Marcus found more to mystify him than merely this cheerful soul inhabiting Tavita's body. The courtyard was certainly Miryam's, but not as last seen by him. Tables ringed the arcades. Soup kettles . . . big ones . . . stood between potted palms. And overhead, dipping and swaying in the breeze off the lake? Silks? Military ensigns?

Laundry.

The sky over Miryam's villa was festooned with the battle array of wash day: tunics, robes, and linen.

It *was* an infant whose plaintive bleating Marcus had heard. From the rooms off the courtyard and from the alcoves around the fountain he heard the noises of many people waking up. Children inquiring about breakfast, and mothers offering sleep-muted responses.

"What's happened here?"

Tavita beamed with pride. "Isn't it wonderful? Women with nowhere else to go. Girls with infants. Pregnant girls rejected by their families. We have just thirty-five here at present. . . ."

"Thirty-five!"

"But you should see it at noon when the soup is ready and the rest line up for a meal. What a commotion. A regular tower of Bavel!"

At the balcony encircling the courtyard a woman appeared. Cradling babies in both arms, she called out with good-natured impatience,

"Tavita? Where are those diapers? I've got two very soggy bottoms here."
Marcus recognized her as Yeshua's mother. "Where has Carta run off to?"

Marcus smiled. So Carta was nearby.

"I'll be right there, Mistress Mary. I'll get them myself." Turning to
Marcus again, Tavita reported, "That boy! Run off, no doubt! Hates anything to do with diapers! But oh," Tavita babbled on, "the mistress isn't
here. She's in Capernaum . . . or perhaps it's Bethsaida today . . . with
the Master."

"Master? Yeshua?"

"Of course. Who else would it be?" Finally, *there* was a flash of the familiar, sharp-tongued Tavita. "Joanna is with her too, of course, and her
boy, Boaz."

So the craving and trepidation about facing Miryam again was
wasted. Postponed. Relief and frustration flooded Marcus in mingled
proportions. Like a reward delayed and a punishment deferred and so
still to be confronted, neither sentiment was satisfactory.

Clearing his throat, Marcus tried to be businesslike. "Doesn't matter,
really," he insisted. "I came because I need a place to stable Pavor. Would
your mistress mind if I took him to the north pasture?"

"Not through the courtyard!" Tavita scolded with a sweep of her
arm that encompassed stewing pots and clean laundry. "Around the outside wall to the garden gate. Now, I've got to go."

Leading Pavor beside the whitewashed stone fence encircling
Miryam's estate, Marcus remembered other visits here. Standing on Pavor's back to leap the wall in the dead of night. Miryam's reputation to
consider. Miryam's anger. Even surrounded by servants, her former
aloneness and isolation. Marcus marveled at what he had just seen. This
was no side of Miryam he'd even suspected, let alone glimpsed. What
had happened?

The garden gate opened as Marcus reached it. A tall, slender youth,
shoulders broadening and red beard beginning to sprout, appeared.
Dressed as a Galilean peasant, Carta's appearance was so different that
Marcus stared. A foot taller the boy was, at least!

The stare was returned and then, making a quicker recovery than
Marcus, Carta launched himself at his master's neck. The embrace both
flattered and embarrassed Marcus. A year earlier it would have angered
him.

Perhaps the changes were not entirely on one side.

"Master!" Carta said with excitement. "Tavita said someone needed me. I thought she meant someone wanted me to carry firewood or fetch wash water. But it's you. I'm so glad to see you." The boy drew back, but his gaze never left Marcus' face.

"And I thought you were staying with Joanna in Capernaum."

"True," Carta agreed. "I was. But I'm needed here. I'm the man around this place, you see. Did you know women can't properly reeve a pulley or hang a door straight from its hinge? Anyway, Joanna and Mistress Miryam asked me to help out." Then a bit apologetically he added, "They said you wouldn't mind. Was that right?"

"No . . . yes, I mean. I don't mind. But what has happened? What is this? Even Tavita is . . . different."

"It's Yeshua," Carta explained matter-of-factly. "He changes everyone. No one ever spoke or acted as he does. He heals people . . . lepers and the blind."

The memory of Carta's own battered body after Vara's brutality flashed through Marcus' mind. Carta personally knew a great deal about Yeshua's healing touch, if he only remembered.

Marcus was thankful the boy did not.

"But listening to his words makes a difference, too. Everyone is going to him," Carta resumed. "*Am ha aretz* in the thousands. People from Jerusalem. Foreigners from Tyre and Sidon. Old, young, rich . . . not as many of those . . . but all the poor. Crippled beggars. An army of followers. A whole army!"

In tones of reverent awe Carta had uttered the word Marcus dreaded to hear. Carta saw with the eyes of wonder and spoke from a heart full of esteem.

But it was not political reality. It was not the sentiments of either the Roman or the Jewish rulers. Fear and suspicion dominated their thinking. Not joy and certainly not admiration.

*An army? Is Yeshua a threat? Is he a danger to Roman sovereignty and the peaceful collection of taxes? Will he dislodge Caiaphas and the council from religious leadership? Could Yeshua displace Herod Antipas in the succession to the throne of Israel?*

"So he's a lot like what the Jews expect of a messiah, eh?" Marcus asked casually.

Carta lurched back abruptly. He studied Marcus's beard and dress. "You're still a centurion," he stated bluntly. "When I saw . . . I thought . . . but you're on duty, aren't you? You want to leave Pavor here because you're in disguise? You're spying?"

Marcus recognized with an odd rush that this was the first time distrust sprang from his being out of uniform instead of in one. "In a way," he admitted. "But listen," he said firmly. "I'm still me." *Was this a positive or a negative thing to say?* "I'm here to see for myself. I'm here because Tribune Felix trusts me to give an honest account. You can trust me too. Do you know where Yeshua is?"

It was as if a shade had been drawn over Carta's exuberance. The cork had been replaced in the bottle. Politely, but without warmth, he suggested, "On the east shore. You'll know by following the . . . you'll know."

■ ■ ■ ■

It was not yet dawn. The morning star shone radiantly just above the horizon beyond the rebel camp.

"Get up!" Kittim kicked Avel hard in the back, rolling him toward the fire pit.

With a startled cry, Avel scrambled away from the hot embers.

Kittim, bar Abba, and Dan towered over the three Sparrows.

Dan laughed and hefted Ha-or Tov by his red hair. The blind boy flailed helplessly in the brigand's grip.

Emet started awake by the ruckus. He curled into a ball, protecting Yediyd from Kittim's blows.

"Get up! Lazy idiot! Get up! We'll make a little use of your worthless life!"

Bar Abba made no attempt to stop Kittim's abuse of the mute child. Avel, fearing Kittim would kill Emet or crush tiny Yediyd, turned with a roar and threw himself against Kittim's legs.

Only then did Kittim turn his fury away from Emet. Snatching up a firebrand he came after Avel.

With a blow across the face, bar Abba sent Kittim sprawling. "Enough!" shouted the rebel chief. "They're no use to me dead!"

"They're no use to anybody alive," Kittim grumbled, rubbing his cheek.

Bar Abba scowled. "That's for me to say." He clenched his fist and held it threateningly beneath Kittim's chin. "And I say these three useless mouths are the sort who flock to Yeshua. Blind. Mute. So, hear me, you! These three are the perfect cover for us. If they die by your hand, you die. Got that?"

Kittim nodded sullenly and picked himself up from the dust. Avel saw hatred flash in his eyes. Kittim might not kill them, but he would certainly make their lives miserable along the way.

In Avel's opinion, the little band of rebels assembled for the journey to the Galil looked singularly unimpressive. Dressed in ragged, dirty garments, the adults appeared completely unheroic.

Avel knew the purpose of the mission was to approach this Rabbi named Yeshua about being king of the Jews. He also knew that to get there undetected by the authorities this disguise was necessary.

Dan, Kittim, and Asher were clad as beggars, as was bar Abba. All of them, including the rebel chief, were afoot, a fact no one mentioned aloud.

Besides the discomfort of wearing tattered castoffs, Kittim was further vexed by his crutch. Bar Abba had decreed that the young man's costume would be improved if he traveled as a cripple: with halting steps, a turned-in foot, and much halting on a forked sycamore branch.

Kittim hated it almost as much as he hated being nursemaid to the boys.

Ordinarily Avel would have approved anything that made Kittim unhappy, but in this case he agreed the crutch was a bad idea. It extended Kittim's reach and increased the force of his blows.

At sunup it was time for bar Abba's contingent to head out of the secret base.

Ha-or Tov whispered to Avel, "Are we really going to meet a king?" He had posed this question a score of times already.

Kittim's crutch whacked Ha-or Tov on the shoulder. "Nobody asked you," he said. "You three are along to fool the soldiers and nothing else, got it? You do exactly what I say and you may live to get back here with your skins. And don't think I don't know you're up to something. I've seen you acting guilty. It's only a matter of time before I know what it is."

Kittim's ranting was interrupted by a loud whistle from the lookout posted overhead. The canyon was clear; the travelers could leave undetected.

"Remember," Avel hissed to Ha-or Tov. "Whoever is carrying Yediyd, the other two stay between him and Kittim."

Nodding forcefully, the Good Light took his station beside the Mourner. Cradling the tiny feathered body of Beloved Friend in the folds of his robe, Truth exited the passageway well ahead of Kittim and his crutch.

■ ■ ■ ■

It was nearly noon when Nakdimon, El'azar, and Marta, surrounded by eight servants, entered the town of Magdala.

Marta took the lead. Her demeanor warlike, she marched along the road toward her sister's villa with an unerring sense of purpose. Her mouth was turned down in a disapproving scowl. She had never liked Galilee, she informed her brother and Nakdimon. Especially not the town of Magdala. She would be glad when they completed this nasty business and got back home to Bethany.

El'azar had been cowed to silence through most of the journey by his sister's constant vehemence. He said wearily, "It won't be long. Miryam's estate is around that bend of the road."

Nakdimon raised his eyes to follow El'azar's gesture. A cluster of *am ha aretz* blocked the turning ahead. They were shabbily clothed women with swarms of ragged children at their skirts. No men among them.

Suspicious of the trio of obviously well-to-do travelers and their coterie of servants, the crowd lapsed into silence and parted at their approach.

Marta held a perfumed kerchief to her nose as they passed through.

She exclaimed loudly as they entered the street of Miryam's house, "But what *are they* all doing *here!*"

The gates of the villa of Miryam of Magdala were thrown wide. A long queue packed the lane.

At least three hundred indigents inched ever forward. Unlike the handful of beggars waiting at the gates of a wealthy house for a handout, these moved through the portals! Could it be? They entered the confines of the inner courtyard itself!

"You see!" Marta wheeled on El'azar. "It's true! Everything we've heard about her! It's true!"

The brother did not reply. His lips were pressed together sternly as he observed the lavish waste of Miryam's wealth on the poor.

*Yes,* El'azar's demeanor seemed to say, *Miryam has finally lost her mind.*

Nakdimon hung back. He was cognizant that a family confrontation lay ahead.

El'azar's servants likewise remained outside the gates.

Nakdimon asked a dirt-caked, tattered child with a crutch and a begging bowl, "What's happening here?"

The lame boy hesitated, unsure if Nakdimon was addressing him.

Nakdimon repeated the question gruffly. "Yes. You. What is this about? Is this the house of the harlot of Magdala?"

"I wouldn't know anything about that, sir. This is the house of a *zadiyk!* A righteous woman, sir. Zadiyk Miryam Magdalen they call her! Unwanted women and children of the Galil are given shelter here. It's a lovely place. We can eat on the lawns. Sit in the garden or by the water. As if it is our place."

"But isn't that Miryam called the harlot?"

"I wouldn't know whose house it used to be. Maybe a harlot owned it once. But now it's the house of a *zadiyk!* I only heard of it last week. So I came and they gave me bread and soup to eat each day at this time."

"By whose authority?" Nakdimon was impatient.

El'azar and Marta pushed through and disappeared into the courtyard of their sister's house.

"I wouldn't know that, sir."

"Who buys the food for this enterprise?"

"Only the Zadiyk herself at first. And today others give to the cause as well. Miryam is one of the talmidim of the Teacher of Nazareth, they say. But I've never seen her."

"Does she live here?" Nakdimon fixed his gaze on the entrance to the house. Clearly something incredible had happened in the life of the whore of Magdala. But was it manifest insanity as El'azar and Marta believed? Had Miryam been bewitched? Or something else?

"They say she's gone to Capernaum with the Teacher now. While she's away, this place is run by an old woman who was once the Zadiyk's slave. Set free by the Zadiyk. Tavita is the slave's name. A pleasant old woman, she is. Also Yeshua's follower. She gave me extra to eat because she said I am too thin."

"Do you sleep here?"

"No, sir. I'm nearly eleven. The ones they take in to sleep in the rooms are castaways. Women as have babes in arms but no husbands. If they aren't sick, the castaways cook the soup and bake the bread and do the washing and the like. They care for one another and feed those of us who eat supper each day. The women come from all over. As far as from Jerusalem to Zadiyk Miryam's house some of them . . . with babes in arms. Others come for shelter. Many need help birthing. They come because their families will not have bastard children in respectable houses, if you know what I mean, sir."

"Is this not a respectable house?" Nakdimon queried.

"I suppose not, sir, not by your light. Not by the light of your kind. Those who have never known trouble. But the house of Zadiyk Miryam Magdalen is a merciful house. And for those who have nowhere else to turn, sir, mercy is the one light that shines for us."

Nakdimon drew himself up and considered this in silent anticipation. He would like to speak with Miryam. Hear the why of all this before he judged her sanity. He wished Hadassah was there with him to see it. He sensed somehow Hadassah would have approved of this kind of madness.

After a short time Marta and El'azar emerged and paddled against the flow of the crowd back toward Nakdimon. Puzzled and uneasy, their servants followed.

Marta led the troop out of the packed lane and into the open. Her expression was one of furious disapproval. El'azar appeared simply confused.

"Well!" The word was a declaration of war. "So she's off in Capernaum with that . . . that . . . that! And left everything in the care of the old witch Tavita! And we, her own flesh and blood, may not even stay in the house because every bed and space is taken by whores and bastard children! Nor may we even taste the food because it is promised to others!"

El'azar snapped, "Please. Marta."

"Not that I would put that food to my lips anyway! I would sooner starve than . . ."

El'azar rubbed his head. "Please! Marta! Give me a minute to take this in."

"A minute to take it in?" she raged. "What is left to take in? Or should I say who? Miryam has *taken in* every unmarried, pregnant harlot in Judea and Galilee! Her own guilt has pushed her over the edge! We'll follow her to Capernaum, won't we? Confront her with the facts? Shut down this absurd . . ."

And the tirade continued.

How obvious it was that Marta hated her younger sister, Nakdimon thought. How brimming with anger she was. And El'azar was her mute accomplice. Did he have no voice of his own? He spoke the words she ordered him to speak. Embraced her ideas as though they were his. Followed her. As the eldest sibling, she steered his ship by the rudder of her bitterness.

Nakdimon was tempted to leave these two to tend their family business, but somehow the change in the Harlot of Magdala intrigued him.

Marta formed her plan. "Our cousin Ya'ir is leader of the synagogue in Capernaum. We'll stay at his house. Explain what's happened to him. He'll sign the papers committing Miryam to us. El'azar, as her brother, you have the legal right to take control of management of her estate. Before she gives everything away. It's your duty, El'azar."

El'azar nodded. Yes. Right. Duty.

A permanent frown creased his forehead, El'azar hung back with Nakdimon as they set out for Capernaum.

■ ■ ■ ■

At early evening on the sixth day of their journey, bar Abba led the rebels to a plateau overlooking the Sea of Galilee. There, at the planned rendezvous point beside a gethsemane, an oil press, a spring bubbled out of the rock. There they would wait for Judas.

Below Avel and about a mile away Bethsaida occupied a peninsula jutting into the lake. As sunlight faded, he traced the rising slope from the town up to the sheltered hollow of their camp.

Now used for grazing sheep, the limestone ridges had once supported olive orchards. An abandoned olive mill, its top stone missing the wooden handle, was partly overgrown.

Avel heard Kittim's approach in time to duck under the swing of the crutch. The stick whistled past Avel's ear. "We didn't bring you here to gawk at the sights!" Kittim said. "You and the others fix supper."

Since Emet was too scrawny to help and Ha-or Tov was blind, camp duties landed mostly on Avel. But the fare was so meager, there was little for Avel to do. Preparing the meal meant merely warming stale loaves by a fire and distributing the last of the dried fish. Water from the spring was the beverage.

With Asher posted on a higher knoll as a lookout, bar Abba, Dan, and Kittim rolled themselves in their cloaks to sleep.

Avel and the Sparrows did the same on the far side of the oil press. Their backs leaning against the circular base, the three snuggled close to each other, with Emet in the middle.

Avel studied the purpling west and the darkening of the green grass and the red anemones that sprouted around his feet. The same funnel of sky that swallowed the sunlight was relentlessly draining the color from the world. Avel wanted to comment on this to the others, but could not imagine how to explain it to Ha-or Tov. Instead he said, "Maybe tomorrow we'll go down to the lake."

"And maybe meet the king?" Ha-or Tov wondered aloud.

Emet tapped Avel on the shoulder and gestured toward the tiny bulge of Yediyd. Was it safe, his sign inquired, to bring their friend out for a while?

Throughout the journey north the three friends kept Yediyd's existence a carefully guarded secret. On occasion this resulted in fits of feigned coughing to cover the bird's chirps, but so far they had succeeded.

With nothing but snores coming from the opposite side of the camp, Avel signaled his agreement. Soon the sparrow was happily hopping up and down Emet's arm. Yediyd pecked at crumbs scattered on the Baptizer's cloak and dipped up water cupped in Emet's palm.

The moon was overhead. It stood directly beneath the mouth of the constellation known as *Aryeh*, "the lion." "They say," Avel mused, "that the sign of the lion means something important."

The symbol of the tribe of Judah was a lion. The expected future king of the Jews was spoken of as *The Lion of the tribe of Judah*. Avel wondered if Rabbi Yeshua was that *Aryeh*. Then, remembering Ha-or Tov, he explained, "Those stars make a lion." Stopping in consternation he said, "Stars are. . . ."

"I know what stars are," Ha-or Tov corrected. "My mother explained them. I know what a lion is too. I felt a dead one, once. Shaggy head and fierce claws. Go on. The stars make a shape?"

Avel's view of the lion in the sky was unexpectedly blocked by a form that loomed up out of the darkness.

Kittim.

"We're on short rations, and you feed our bread to a bird?" he hissed. Lunging, he made a grab for Yediyd. "Then I'll eat *him*."

Before Kittim's fingers closed around the sparrow Avel hit him in the throat with his forearm. The blow had no real force behind it, but it made Kittim miss. He fell across the three friends.

Making hoarse, incoherent cries, Emet struggled to escape and protect Yediyd at the same time. Ha-or Tov from one side and Avel from the other rained blows on Kittim's head and neck.

Kittim grabbed a rock, aiming at Emet. Avel seized the upraised arm. "Run!" he said to Emet.

Emet wriggled free and jumped to his feet. Kittim swung the stone toward Avel. The clout glanced off Avel's nose.

With Ha-or Tov hanging around his neck, Kittim launched another strike.

Then the rock stopped in midair, and Kittim was dragged backwards. "I told you we needed them alive," bar Abba thundered. Kittim continued to squirm. "You we can do without. Stop this!"

"*Shalom*," hailed Judas from outside the circle of the gethsemane. "Or is peace too much to hope for from this rabble?"

Calling for a torch to be lit, bar Abba sent Kittim off to join Asher, promising to deal with him later. "Have you found Yeshua?" he asked Judas.

A sly smile crept across Judas' face. "Him and the thousands that are following him . . . already hailing him as king! Tomorrow, at Capernaum, you'll see for yourself!"

■ ■ ■ ■

Bar Abba's rebuke of Kittim did nothing to reassure Avel. To the contrary, the boy was convinced Kittim meant to kill him and the little bird at the first opportunity.

Avel never slept the rest of the night. Every time his eyelids drooped, he pictured Kittim sneaking up in the darkness. The image jerked him awake once more. He scrutinized every shadow, every clump of brush, certain Kittim was already watching for the opportunity to strike.

When the moon sank in the west, Avel became even more apprehensive, detecting a stealthy footstep in each sigh of the wind. The warble of a nightbird brought him up with a rush, standing defensively in front of Emet.

Emet and Ha-or Tov slept soundly. Emet, being deaf, heard nothing alarming. But Avel could not imagine how Ha-or Tov managed to snore away in the midst of terror. Unless he was so tired he had no choice. Avel earnestly wished one of them would rouse to keep him company, but neither did.

It was a long night.

When the first change from black to gray occurred, Avel gave a sigh of relief. Moments later bar Abba roused the camp, ordering them to get ready to move out at once.

Each time Avel glanced around, Kittim was watching him. Though Kittim kept his distance, the malevolent stare reinforced Avel's sense of danger.

"Yeshua intends to speak in the synagogue today," Judas Iscariot explained. "Get there early, or you'll never be close enough to hear. I must leave now and rejoin him."

By the time the file of rebels descended the hillside, the trails were already lined with hordes of travelers converging on Capernaum. From the oil press it was about a four-mile walk to the synagogue.

Because of Ha-or Tov's real disability and Kittim's assumed one, their progress was awkward. Bar Abba visibly chafed with the delay. Avel overheard him hiss at Kittim, "Hobble faster! Act like you're eager!"

Despite bar Abba's prompting and the fact that it was early in the morning, the square in front of the synagogue was thronged with onlookers. Yeshua had not arrived, and yet the space inside the building's main hall was jammed.

It was Avel who seized the opportunity. "We can get into the women's gallery," he said. Without awaiting bar Abba's permission, he led Emet and Ha-or Tov up the stairs where none of the men could follow.

In contrast to the sanctuary, the gallery was barely half full. Since women had the child-care and household responsibilities, it was not as easy for them to get away early in the day. No one objected to the arrival of the Sparrows, and they soon found a corner to themselves. There between a pair of high-backed benches Avel discussed his concerns.

"Kittim is going to kill Yediyd," he asserted flatly. "Probably kill us too, but he'll kill the bird first if we don't get away."

"But how can we?" Ha-or Tov objected. "Where'll we go?"

"I don't know," Avel admitted. "But this isn't like I expected. Hiding in canyons, sneaking into towns, stealing food. And taking orders from Kittim? I could've stayed in Jerusalem if I wanted a daily beating! Besides, if everybody wants this other man to be king, why are we following bar Abba? Why don't we go to Yeshua ourselves? We could be *his* spies."

"What makes you think Reb Yeshua wants spies?" piped a girl's voice from the front row. Above the seat back a thicket of blond curls rose into view, followed by the bluest eyes Avel had ever seen. "And do you mean the rebel bar Abba? And who's Yediyd that someone wants to kill?"

"Don't you know it's wrong to snoop?" Ha-or Tov scolded.

"I was here first," protested the girl. "And I have a right. My father's Ya'ir, one of the elders here. Besides, you weren't whispering. I can't help it if I heard."

"Even so," Ha-or Tov scolded.

But Avel was immersed in the pool of her eyes. "It's all right," he said quickly. "I'm Avel." He introduced the other boys. "What's your name?"

"Deborah. Who's Yediyd?"

The gallery filled with women and other children.

Emet glanced at Avel for permission and received a nod. He withdrew the tiny sparrow from his robe and held it shyly for Deborah to inspect.

"You brought a bird to synagogue?" she asked.

"Yediyd goes everywhere with us," Avel asserted. "We're the Sparrow company . . . that is, we were."

"I see," Deborah returned. "But you don't know where to go next."

Avel concurred with a shrug.

"Deborah?" a woman's voice called from the stairs. "Are you already here?"

"Yes, Mother," Deborah replied. Then she put her finger to her lips and murmured to Avel, "We'll talk more later."

■ ■ ■ ■

Nakdimon, El'azar, and Marta reached the village of Capernaum. Uncertain about the location of their cousin Ya'ir's house, they went straight to the synagogue where he served.

Though the town was an unimpressive place, Capernaum's house of worship was a bright, new building overlooking the placid waters of the Sea of Galilee. Tiers of scaffolding climbed the north wall, where construction continued to enlarge the main hall. Marble columns supported a roof over an open porch where services could be held if it was too warm indoors.

Throngs of people overflowed the synagogue, spilling out into the street.

How many were outside, Nakdimon wondered, trying to get in? A thousand?

Standing tiptoe at the fringe of the multitude, Marta arched an eyebrow and commented with pride to Nakdimon, "Our cousin Ya'ir is cantor of this synagogue. He's got a lovely singing voice. Always did. I used to say he would do important things, even though his branch of the family is quite poor."

The implication was, of course, that the evident success of this congregation was due to the outstanding vocal prowess of Marta's relative.

*With a song, Ya'ir had hewn the pillars and carried them on his back*

*from the hills. He alone had set them in place. Because of his abilities as can-
tor, the entire population of the Galil wanted to worship here. Clever fellow,
this cousin. And because Marta had once noticed as a child that Ya'ir could
sing, she took upon herself a vast amount of credit in his achievement.*

All this was in her expression even though she had not seen Ya'ir or
been to Capernaum in years.

El'azar, as though he read Nakdimon's mind, gestured with embarrassment and said quietly, "He's second cousin to our father. Not a close
relative. And we don't know that Ya'ir is still cantor, Sister."

Her expression darkened. "No doubt, if he's not, he headed up the
building committee. Ya'ir always was an intelligent, industrious fellow."

An hour remained before services would begin.

El'azar asked a plump, red-bearded fellow standing near, "We're
looking for Ya'ir. Our cousin. He was cantor here last we heard."

They were greeted with a laugh. "That's me. I'm Ya'ir. Cantor. And
you? Cousin? Is it El'azar? You've grown a beard. Is that Marta? Little
Marta? Thin little Marta? Fifteen years! I've gained a few pounds myself
along the way." He embraced her. She blanched at his reference to her
weight but carried on.

Well, Nakdimon observed, so it had indeed been a very long time
since they had seen one another.

El'azar introduced Nakdimon as a good friend and an official from
Jerusalem. He did not mention the Sanhedrin, though Marta would
have touted Nakdimon's impressive connection if she had not been
sternly warned to keep silent about it.

The pleasantries of their conversation were brief. Nakdimon inquired about the vast number of people who had come for the service.

"The Rabbi of Nazareth is back," Ya'ir explained excitedly. "He and
his talmidim have been traveling. Teaching and healing throughout the
Galil and across the lake. He stays here in Capernaum sometimes at the
house of one of his talmidim who was a fisherman. But as you can
see . . . We overflow our banks when he comes among us." He laughed
delightedly.

Marta nudged El'azar. At her prompting El'azar blurted, "We've
come about our sister, Miryam . . ."

"Oh! Of course! Certainly. I should've guessed. She's in the women's
gallery with my wife and daughter and the others. They're all there.
Joanna, Shoshana, and the women who work with the poor at the house
in Magdala."

Marta blinked up at her cousin. "You know about it?" Her demeanor indicated that she was not pleased by his cheerful attitude.

"Of course. Wonderful. Wonderful."

Marta blustered, "You've seen?"

"Everyone knows. Even among the Gentiles there are supporters of the work. It's because of Yeshua. A true prophet is among us."

Marta grimaced. "Whatever you say," she commented archly. Her attitude conveyed a challenge. How could Ya'ir, a respectable leader of the synagogue, be pleased by the presence of Yeshua of Nazareth? How could the leaders permit such a circus in their own congregation?

But Nakdimon was intrigued.

Within the cold, austere exterior of a once-deserted synagogue, the stony ground of men's hearts was being softened, healed, transformed.

A known harlot had thrown open the gates of her lonely house to those in need. By her own hand and with her own wealth she provided for those who could not provide for themselves.

And at Miryam's side in this humble mitzvah was Mary, the mother of Yeshua. And with them? The wealthy wives of Herod Antipas' court manned soup kettles and washed laundry and kept dry the bottoms of babies whom no one else wanted. Were there ever such unlikely alliances?

Where Yeshua walked among the rubbish heaps of human misery, gardens bloomed.

Nakdimon had a good view over the heads of the mass into the dusky interior of the synagogue.

Was that Yeshua coming to the *bema?*

Tall and slender. Prayer shawl covering his head.

Strong, yes. Broad shouldered. Like a man accustomed to bearing beams of wood in a carpenter's shop.

Dark hair framed his face. Eyes wide set, brown, and gentle. Teeth white as milk. Mouth turned up at one corner in tender acknowledgment of all who fastened their eyes upon his face.

He bent down to kiss the open scroll.

A hush fell over the multitude.

How could Nakdimon convey to Gamaliel back in Jerusalem the enchantment in that tiny fishing village as Yeshua opened his mouth to read?

His lips moved.

The *am ha aretz* leaned toward him; souls eagerly reaching for the word. From this distance none could hear more than a murmur.

But yes! Those near . . . the lucky ones . . . they would come out later and repeat every word that proceeded from his mouth!

And now . . . ah, look!

*Look!*

Yeshua raised his eyes and smiled at someone in the gallery.

Yes. Yeshua smiled.

At . . . *one!*

Nakdimon wished he knew who it was.

And why Yeshua had at that instant gazed only into that one face. Singled out that one soul.

Ya'ir whispered to Nakdimon and El'azar, "You must hear him for yourselves. Come with me . . . through the door of the *cohanim*."

# NOSEI

For several days Marcus had traveled the Galil in disguise. He had listened to the teacher several times, but never yet crossed paths with Miryam. Marcus was eager to hear Yeshua speak again. Today's audience in the Capernaum synagogue was the largest yet.

And perhaps Miryam would show up.

Yeshua stood before them, waiting patiently for the conversation of the congregation to cease.

Dust motes danced in the beams of light entering the high east windows. Shuffling feet, the undertone of voices, the rising temperature in the already overcrowded space . . . the air of the Capernaum synagogue simmered with expectation.

Marcus found a place at the side of the sanctuary where the curve of a heart-shaped pillar provided an island of solitude amid the sea of jostling men. The pedestal of the column also gave him a view over the top of the other spectators.

The cloak of his hood was flipped over his head, and his beard was fully formed. The Roman passed easily for a Jew lately arrived from a distant part of Judea to hear the Teacher.

Marcus was apprehensive of what he would hear. Many used the word *Prophet* when they spoke of Yeshua. Others called him *Elijah,* as they had Yochanan the Baptizer. Some mentioned the long dead Jewish seer Jeremiah, or other names unfamiliar to Marcus.

And many used the title Marcus once applied to him: *King.*

And not merely King of the Jews. Tetrach, Ethnarch, any of a hundred largely ceremonial local honors. The Romans would gladly promote whoever offered them the best chance of peaceful collaboration. Titles like those carried no real authority apart from that dispensed by Rome. Herod Antipas could be discarded without a backward glance.

But this buzz of political speculation went much further: could Yeshua be the king of a restored and liberated Israel? A nation free of Rome altogether?

Marcus studied the room. There had to be a thousand men jammed into its confines. That many more again clustered around the doors and windows. The gallery was packed with women and children.

The scene had the makings of a revolution.

Once the Emperor Tiberius had been affronted by a fishmonger who had the audacity to offer a mackerel to the "Son of God." Tiberius had the man pinioned on the ground and his face scrubbed raw with the offending fish.

What would Tiberius think was adequate punishment for someone who so insulted his dignity as to seek to replace him as ruler?

Then without introduction Yeshua of Nazareth addressed the crowd. "*Shalom*," he greeted them. "Peace be with you all." The murmuring died, except for a persistent, exuberant chirping.

Marcus, like the rest, sought the source of the piping trills. It seemed to be coming from the gallery. There, hopping on the fist of a boy, was a sparrow. Warbling, it bounced as if cheering.

"I see you there, Yediyd, beloved friend," Yeshua said, acknowledging the bird's greeting. His smile broadened. The throng laughed, relaxing at the sound of his pleasant voice and his gentle manner.

The centurion recognized the boy holding the sparrow. So Emet, the mute child, had indeed located Yeshua. And beside him stood Avel the Mourner. Would Avel find comfort here? Would he lose the fierceness in his young soul?

Marcus thought it could happen, for at that instant, glowing with the light of inner peace, he saw the face of Miryam: radiant Miryam, watching from behind the boys. Miryam was the living earnest money of real change. If her life could be transformed, then no one was without hope.

Marcus felt the tension leave his shoulders and neck. Surely it would be all right. This was Yeshua the Healer. Yeshua, who pardoned sin and made it possible for crippled souls to pardon themselves.

Another disturbance interrupted the proceedings. The hazzan cried out for the crowd to part. Three men, obviously important, were escorted through the press to a seat of honor at the front. To Marcus' surprise, he recognized them.

It was no shock to see Ya'ir. Marcus had grown to know and respect the amiable synagogue official during the time when they worked together on the building's refurbishment.

But the two fellows with Ya'ir were Nakdimon, whom Marcus had last seen gravely wounded, and El'azar of Bethany.

Snapping his head around, Marcus again examined Miryam's face as she gazed down at her brother. Her features drooped with the pain of unresolved grief. Though changed herself, she obviously had not yet been reconciled with her family.

"*Shalom,*" Yeshua repeated to the late arrivals.

Ya'ir beamed back at the rabbi. Nakdimon appeared keenly attentive. El'azar scowled.

With the chirping of the sparrow as introduction to the teaching, Yeshua began.

"Listen." Yeshua raised a hand to call attention to the chirping bird on the hand of the boy. "Today's lesson is brought to us by . . . a sparrow. Yes?" More chuckles. "What's that? You can't understand what he's saying to you? Ah. Well. Not understanding the language of our teachers can be a problem." Yeshua nodded. "So, I'll tell you what he said . . . Don't worry about your life, what you'll eat or drink; or about your body, what you'll wear. Isn't life more important than food, and the body more important than clothes? Look at the birds. . . ."

Yeshua waved toward the sparrow in the gallery, and the crowd laughed again.

"They neither plant nor harvest, nor do they gather food into barns; yet your heavenly Father feeds them. Two sparrows are bought for a penny. But not one falls who isn't seen by your heavenly father. Are you worth as much as they are? Eh? Can any of you . . . by worrying . . . add a single hour to his life?"

Yeshua paused there to let that thought sink in, then he resumed, "And why be anxious about clothes? Think about the fields of wildflowers and how they grow."

Marcus knew that the whole audience pictured the Galilean hillsides draped in scarlet, golden, and royal purple.

"They don't work at the loom or spin thread. Yet I tell you that not even Solomon in all his glory was clothed as beautifully as one of these. If that's how *Adonai* clothes grass in the field, which is here today and gone tomorrow, thrown in an oven, won't he much more clothe you? What little trust you have! So don't be anxious, asking, 'What'll we eat?'

or 'What'll we drink?' or 'What'll we wear?' For it's the pagans who set their hearts on these things. Your heavenly Father knows you need them. But seek first the kingdom of *Adonai* and his righteousness and all these things will be given to you as well."

There! Marcus recognized the concept he had feared. Yeshua's enemies could make much of the fact that he spoke of a kingdom! And yet the notion of a kingdom of heaven, a kingdom of righteousness, did not sound threatening to Rome.

But it did sound revolutionary just the same. Clearly others were uneasy with what they heard. El'azar squirmed on the front bench as though bursting to offer a comment.

"Remember," Yeshua added, "not everyone who says to me, 'Lord, Lord,' will enter the kingdom of heaven, but those who act on what my Father in heaven has commanded in Torah."

Apparently unable to contain himself any longer, El'azar stood up. "Rabbi," he asked in a confrontational tone, "what should *I* do to obtain eternal life?"

"What's written in Torah?" Yeshua replied. "How do you read it?"

El'azar answered haughtily, quoting the books of Deuteronomy and Leviticus. "'You are to love *Adonai* your God with all your heart, with all your soul, with all your strength, and with all your understanding,' and 'your neighbor as yourself.'" He concluded with an uplifted chin, like an arrogant schoolboy challenging his instructor. His attitude registered superiority: *everyone knows that.*

"That's the right answer," Yeshua replied. "*Do* this and you will have life."

Marcus grinned and others chuckled aloud. Yeshua suggested that knowing the correct answer and acting as God required were two different things.

His face flushed with embarrassment, El'azar shot back, "And who *is* my neighbor?"

In reply Yeshua raised his finger and captured his audience with a look. He strode across the front of the platform and stooped to address Nakdimon directly. "A man was going down from Yerushalayim to Yericho, when he was attacked by robbers."

Marcus saw Nakdimon suddenly sit up straighter. Yeshua nodded, rose, walked to the other side, and continued.

"So. These bandits stripped him naked and beat him up, then went off, leaving him half dead. By coincidence a *cohen* was going down that road; but when the cohen saw him, he passed by on the other side. Too busy maybe? On his way to Jerusalem to pray maybe?" The crowd loved it. They nudged one another and winked as haughty religious officials in the auditorium squirmed and reddened. Yeshua continued, "And likewise a Levite who reached the place and saw him also passed by on the other side. But!"

There was a delay as Yeshua selected the next word. During the silence his gaze sought Marcus' face and their eyes met.

*He knows,* Marcus thought. *Somehow, he knows.*

"A man from Shomron," Yeshua resumed, naming the territory of the despised Samaritans, "oh, yes! A fellow from Shomron . . . who was traveling came upon our injured friend; and when he saw him, he was moved with compassion. This Samaritan went up to him, put oil and wine on his wounds, and bandaged them. Then the Samaritan set him on his own donkey, brought him to an inn, and took care of him! The next day, the Samaritan took out two silver coins, gave them to the innkeeper. . . ."

Marcus, remembering the coins he gave to Emet, shot a glance toward the gallery. Was there anything hidden from Yeshua?

"The Samaritan said, 'Look after him,'" Yeshua continued, adopting a thick Samaritan accent as he played out the role, "'and if you spend more than this, I'll pay you back when I return.'" Yeshua ended the story with a shrug and a shake of his head. He walked to the platform and stood directly in front of El'azar, his accuser. "Well?" Yeshua challenged, "of these three, which one seems to you to have become the 'neighbor' of the man who fell among robbers?"

In a chastened voice, El'azar replied after a long beat, "The one who showed mercy toward him."

Yeshua spread his hands as if to pluck the answer from midair like a bird in flight. He inclined his head and nodded. "Well spoken . . . friend. Now, you go and do as he did."

Marcus understood the test. El'azar had not offered his home to receive a wounded man until he knew Nakdimon's identity. Even then it was because Nakdimon was apparently someone influential; El'azar and his sister would never have opened their gates to Nakdimon the leather worker.

"Come on, Rabbi," someone in the crowd shouted. "Give us a sign! Prove yourself to us!"

Marcus reflected that there were always those for whom extraordinary ways of *thinking* were not enough; they must have entertainment. This was no request flowing out of need; no aching longing for a healing touch. *Dazzle us with your power,* the spectator dared. *Show us what you can do.*

Yeshua was not remotely tempted. "When it's evening," he responded, "you say, 'Fair weather ahead,' because the sky is red; and in the morning you say, 'Storm today!' because the sky is red and overcast. You know how to read the appearance of the sky, but you can't read the signs of the times! A wicked and adulterous generation is asking for a sign? It will certainly not be given a sign—except for this . . . the sign of Jonah!"

What did that mean? Marcus, not familiar with Jewish lore, did not comprehend the rebuke. But the faces of those around him exhibited the same confusion.

Yeshua sighed as if weary. "A sign." He closed his eyes briefly before speaking again. "Once . . . there was a rich man who used to dress in the most expensive clothing. He spent his life in magnificent luxury. At his gate had been laid a beggar named . . . El'azar."

Though Marcus saw El'azar's shoulders stiffen, Yeshua was not looking directly at the man, but up at the gallery again. And El'azar, Miryam's brother, was certainly no beggar, but a wealthy man.

Yeshua went on. "So. Poor El'azar, he was covered with sores." A groan of disgust went up from the crowd.

"He would have been glad to eat the scraps that fell from the rich man's table; but instead the dogs would come and lick his sores. In time the beggar died and was carried away by the angels to Avraham's side. And the rich man? Well, he also died. And he was also buried. But he was led away to Sheol. In Sheol, where he was in torment, the rich man looked up and saw Avraham far away with El'azar at his side. He called out, 'Father Avraham, take pity on me! Please! Just send El'azar . . . only to dip the tip of his finger in water to cool my tongue, because I'm in agony in this fire!' "

Where was this story leading, Marcus wondered? Was it about the evils of wealth? About being uncharitable? About God rewarding the righteous and punishing the wicked? What?

Yeshua resumed, "However, Avraham said, 'Son, remember that when you were alive, you got the good things while he got the bad; but now he gets his consolation here, while you are the one in agony. Yet that isn't all: between you and us a deep rift has been established, so that those who would like to pass from here to you cannot, nor can anyone cross over from there to us.' "

How was the crowd taking this? Marcus knew that if any Sadducees were present they would sneer in derision. Their beliefs held no place for an afterlife, good or bad.

But Yeshua was telling this story as one recounts a family tale. Not as a parable with a moral at the end, but as something he had actually witnessed.

Yeshua paused, then went on, acting out the parts. "The rich man answered, 'Then I beg you to send El'azar to my father's house, where I have five brothers, to warn them, so they may be spared having to come to this place of torment too.' But Avraham said, 'They have Moshe, Torah, and the Prophets; they should listen to them.' However, the rich man said, 'No, Father Avraham, they need more! The writings of Torah are not enough! The prophets are not enough! But if someone from the dead goes to them, they'll repent!'"

Marcus could see the audience agreed with the sentiment of the dead man. Heads bobbed. Was this to be a ghost story? It was a good one.

Yeshua took the tale in a different direction. His voice rose in climax as he portrayed Father Avraham. "Something to think about, yes? But . . . Avraham shouted across the gulf to this fellow . . . 'IF THEY DON'T BELIEVE WHAT IS WRITTEN BY MOSHE IN THE TORAH . . . IF THEY DON'T BELIEVE THE PROPHETS?'" Yeshua boomed out the questions across the chasm of understanding.

The echo died. Yeshua lowered his voice once again to speak to those present in the room. There was a tinge of sadness in his tone. "If they don't believe what is written? Then they won't be convinced . . . will they? Even if someone . . . even if El'azar . . . or another . . . rises from the dead!'"

Thus ended the lesson.

Yeshua took a step back and bowed his head. The stunned multitude, including Marcus, had not even realized he was finished speaking.

What *would* convince men to change their lives, Marcus wondered? Was Yeshua saying that the gulf between righteousness and selfishness was too wide to be bridged?

What could the story mean? And what truth was written in the sacred Jewish scrolls that could direct a man to eternal life? What was Yeshua saying about someone coming back from the dead to tell them?

With his own eyes Marcus had witnessed four miraculous cures performed by Yeshua. Five, when he counted Miryam's transformation.

Roman level-headedness prompted him to describe them as "wondrous and unexplained events," but Marcus' own mind allowed no escape into rationalization. He believed Yeshua indeed possessed great power. But Marcus could not comprehend what it meant to him personally.

The child at the riverbank. The paralytic at the house of Joanna and Kuza. Then Kuza's son, Boaz. Carta. And suicidal Miryam. All had faced definite, seemingly inescapable sentences of death.

The toddler was born with a life-ending condition.

The paralyzed man had to be carried to Yeshua by his friends.

Boaz was poisoned by a ruptured belly.

Carta's snapped neck left him with mere hours to live.

Miryam's mental imbalance drove her toward ending her own existence.

Yet all had been brought back from the brink to vigorous life.

But dead was dead. Once that Rubicon was crossed, no one returned. Marcus had witnessed the flame of life wink out too many times to doubt its finality.

Yeshua seemed to lay the question of resurrection at the door of possibility. Was he saying it could be achieved? Did he mean that even with such a miracle men would still not believe?

Just a parable. Only a story, Marcus thought, as he studied the tall, lean man before them.

But who was this enigmatic Yeshua? A carpenter from Nazareth? Then where did his incredible power come from?

That was the question Marcus had been sent by Felix and Imperial Rome to probe and answer.

Marcus was compelled to learn the full truth for himself. Not because he was ordered to do so. Not for Rome. Nor for Miryam's love. But because he had come face to face with someone who grasped true wisdom! This knower of secrets; this Yeshua of Nazareth; reached into people's hearts and changed everything!

The hazzan approached the platform on which Yeshua still stood in prayer.

"Rabbi," the hazzan whispered hoarsely, loudly enough for Marcus to hear. "I'm sorry to disturb you, but I have a message. Your mother and your brothers are outside and would like to see you. They can't get through the crowd but say they must speak with you. A family matter."

So, Marcus thought, the Rabbi's kinfolk had come to take him to safety. Perhaps Carta had told her Yeshua was being watched by a Roman centurion? No. That would be no real surprise. Something more serious. A family matter. If Mary, the mother of Yeshua, had come to Capernaum from Magdala, leaving her foundlings and outcasts behind, it could mean just one thing: she was afraid for her son and rightly so. Perhaps she had come to warn Yeshua to flee the territory controlled by Herod Antipas. It was madness to stay in Galilee. Antipas might easily have Yeshua arrested and killed as well.

Good, Marcus thought. Yes. Yeshua should go. He would be safer in the territory of Philip, across the lake.

Lifting his head, Yeshua offered his thanks to the messenger and prepared to depart. Then he paused mid-stride and studied the gallery. He smiled again. His warmth swept across the whole auditorium. He left them with this question: "Who are my mother and my brothers?" he asked. "They are you . . . yes . . . you . . . everyone who hears my message and acts on it."

With that, he slipped out the building through the back door.

■ ■ ■ ■

There was an excited buzz as the women's gallery emptied after Yeshua's departure from the synagogue. Avel heard many comment that Yeshua must be a prophet. Like Isaiah, some said. Elijah, maybe.

But why did he mention Jonah?

Jonah was no one's favorite prophet; he hadn't even wanted the job. And when he finally preached repentance it was to those pagan Syrians. It would have turned out better if they had not repented and *Adonai* destroyed them!

And the same went for the Samaritans! Prophets were always saying shocking things, but the idea that one of those apostate half-breeds might be more righteous than a *cohen* or a Levite? Amazing notion!

If Yeshua was trying to shock his listeners into paying attention, he had succeeded, Avel thought.

Deborah lingered behind. Going straight to Emet, she put her face next to Yediyd and said, "You! Little bird! You were brilliant! I had no idea you knew so much. And here you chirped a whole sermon! Well done!"

Yediyd preened and bowed in Emet's open hand, so Avel knew Deborah was approved.

Even so, when she lifted an upraised palm toward the sparrow, Avel expected the bird to flee from the stranger.

Still more, he expected Emet to draw back in alarm.

But Emet extended his fist, and Yediyd hopped instantly onto Deborah's hand.

Avel described what had happened to Ha-or Tov. The blind boy was impressed with Deborah's winning way.

"Who are you with?" Deborah asked when the boys made no move to head for the stairs. "Won't they be waiting for you?"

This was an unpleasant reminder of their circumstances. During the discourse of Yeshua, Avel had decided he was indeed through with bar Abba and the rebels and most especially with Kittim. He didn't even need to poll the group; he was certain they agreed.

"We're with nobody," Avel responded carefully. "Just us."

"Are you servants?" Deborah inquired, fingering the sleeve material of Avel's robe. "This is very nicely made. My mother is teaching me to weave. We're weaving a robe for Reb Yeshua. You didn't steal it, did you?"

"No," Avel replied. "It was a gift."

"But where are you staying? Do you have food to eat? Would you like to come to my house? My father would be glad to give you food."

Avel considered how to answer this. The silence was finally broken by Ha-or Tov. "Go on," the blind boy urged. "Tell her the truth."

"We came here with bar Abba," Avel admitted.

"The zealot?" Deborah grinned with excitement. "Is he going to kill someone? Here today? In Capernaum? In the synagogue?"

Avel explained. "He's around somewhere. He wants to make Yeshua king. We came all the way from Judea for bar Abba to meet Yeshua."

"But Reb Yeshua would never be king of thieves and assassins," Deborah asserted.

Avel thought about Asher and Dan, and particularly about Kittim. He was sure Deborah was right. He tried to explain but fell short. "It's only that . . ."

"What?"

"We took an oath. All about loyalty . . ."

"Don't forget the part about dying if we betray them," Ha-or Tov chipped in. "If we go out, they'll make us go back with them."

"Kittim . . . he's the worst . . . he's going to kill us anyway," Avel concluded.

Deborah studied the ceiling, then declared staunchly, "You can hide in our barn."

Avel brightened. Here was hope. "If you tell anybody . . . Your family could get hurt. We'll wait until dark and then leave."

Deborah shook her head. "Don't they know you're in here? What's to stop them from coming after you?"

Avel's face fell.

Deborah's blue eyes flashed, as if pleased with the adventure. "So! You need my help. I'll hide you in the synagogue where they can't find you," she reassured them. "After sunset I'll lead you to our barn." She addressed the bird somberly. "But you! Yediyd! Remarkable bird . . . you'll have to keep quiet."

■ ■ ■ ■

The Teacher, his mother, brothers, and talmidim would be long gone by the time Marcus got out of the synagogue.

But it was not Yeshua who made Marcus impatient to leave.

Marcus, made desperate at the sight of Miryam in the gallery, struggled to get out before her; to be there, nonchalant, at the foot of the stairs when she came down. Caught in the slowly moving human current pouring from the synagogue, Marcus traveled with one eye on her. Miryam had not spotted him in the crush. She seemed to be in no hurry to end the pleasant conversation with the women and children around her. And so she lingered, nodding, laughing, embracing little ones who sidled up to tug shyly on her skirt.

Once she cast an anxious, hopeful look at her brother, El'azar, who merely raised his hand in acknowledgment that yes, he had come to Capernaum about her. Marcus saw her smile briefly falter. Then she squared her shoulders and greeted a young blond girl brightly.

It was like seeing a different Miryam than the tortured beauty he had known. As if she had somehow been born again, to be what she had been intended to be all along. Yes, she had been breathtaking as a courtesan, living as a moral outcast. But virtue had added yet another dimension to her beauty. Indefinable.

A different kind of love possessed her now. Not the love of one man. Not love of herself. No. Her eyes seemed to gather in everyone around her, welcoming, caring. Her expression was, Marcus thought with astonishment, like that he had seen on the face of Yeshua.

A pang of envy shot through him.

Love was not everything, was it? Not bread nor wine. Not shelter in a storm. Nor a good night's sleep after a long journey. Love was not the blade of a fine sword. Nor a war horse to carry a man into battle.

Love could not stitch a wound. Or set a broken leg. Or pull a drowning man from the sea. And yet . . . Marcus knew how near Miryam had been to death, all for lack of love.

Marcus stared openly at her face. Beaming. Vibrant. Interested in whatever that woman who clutched her hand was saying. Yes, exquisite in beauty. No denying it. Love had transformed her.

He had desired her. He had hated her. Yet he had longed to lose himself in her passion. He had been jealous of all other suitors . . . would have killed for her. But he had not truly loved her until he saw her sitting at the feet of Yeshua.

Loved by Yeshua . . . in a way Marcus could not comprehend . . . her life had begun all over again.

What would she say when she saw Marcus after so much time had passed? The path they walked together was grown over with scrub oak and briars as though it was never there.

But Marcus saw her, there in the gallery, and he remembered how her fingers played on his back and her lips moved against his ear as she whispered to him. He had taken the memory of her away with him, as a man will. And now he brought it back with him again.

He sighed as she turned away and exited the synagogue. She would be outside before him. There could be no accidental meeting. He would have to call out to her. Call her back. And when she turned to him, would she remember? No. He was certain that the memory of their nights together was his alone. If he spoke of it to her, she would look at him curiously and say he had dreamed it. His dream. Not hers. All that was finished. As though it never happened.

He burst into the sunlight and scanned the retreating forms in the crowd for her.

Where was she?

Had she already gone back to Magdala?

Was she off to the home of a friend for supper?

And then Marcus spotted a familiar face fifty yards away.

Bar Abba! Here!

The rebel leader was on the fringe of the thousands. He, also, appeared to be searching for someone. He vanished and appeared again, an apparition, beckoning Marcus to duty, drawing him away from his pursuit of Miryam.

Marcus pivoted toward the brigand and instinctively grasped the hilt of his sword beneath his cloak.

Love was not everything, was it?

There would be blood spilt before the sun went down. This time bar Abba had strayed into Marcus' reach. He would not get away.

Suddenly Marcus heard a voice call out to him.

Her voice.

"Marcus! Marcus Longinus!"

Love was not everything, was it?

He could pretend he had not heard. Keep going. Smash through the human wall that separated him from his quarry. And then?

"Marcus! Turn around! It's me! Miryam!"

He stopped. Glanced away from bar Abba. When he looked back, the outlaw had vanished.

Marcus frowned and pressed his lips tightly together. He waited until her hand grasped his sleeve.

And then he turned toward her. Her deep brown eyes, glowing with pleasure, gazed happily up at him. He blinked at her stupidly, saying nothing. He wanted to kiss her, pull her into his arms and carry her away.

"You've come back," she said, as though she had been expecting him.

"Yes." He could not look at her. So striking. The memory played again and again in his mind.

"Your beard. Like one of us."

"I've been . . . The desert, you know. On patrol."

"I didn't know."

"Yes."

"Any success?"

He wanted to ask her what she meant. He had been entirely unsuccessful at forgetting her.

"No."

"Well, then . . ."

"No success at all, I'm afraid."

She nodded uncomfortably at his awkwardness. "Carta is well. At my house."

Here was a subject he could talk about which did not ring of summer nights with moonlight glowing on her skin.

"Carta! Yes! I saw him!"

"At my house?"

"At your house. Yes. Quite a generous use you've made of the place. Very . . . nice . . . Miryam."

"Filled with the sound of babies . . ."

Marcus stared down at his feet. Their baby would have been over a year old. The house would have echoed with the cheerful voices of their own children if he had not been so stupid. Selfish and blind. So she had found a way to make up for the loss of one child with the lives of others. But they were not their babies. They were not their babies together. What might have been squeezed at his heart and made it more difficult to talk.

"Well . . . yes . . . then. I hope Carta has been a help to you."

"He has. He is. A good boy."

Marcus said gruffly, "He's nearly a man. Don't make a kitchen maid out of him."

She laughed. "That sounded like something he said last week. You know, it's amazing how often his mannerisms, even his tone of voice reminds me of . . ." Her words faded away as Marcus lifted his eyes to hold her in his gaze.

"Who does he remind you of?" Marcus asked.

"You."

"I didn't think you would remember . . . me . . . much."

"Every day."

"Yes." He exhaled loudly. The crowd had broken up. He raised his chin slightly toward the lakeshore. "Can you walk with me a bit? I mean . . . will it raise eyebrows to be seen with me?"

"And if it does?"

"Well . . ."

"You are my . . . dear . . . brother. Marcus? I owe you so much. It was you who brought me to Yeshua. All along you knew. Before I knew what I was longing for. Come along then." She struck out toward the lake and, with a smile over her shoulder, invited him to follow her.

# AVON

The inside of the Torah scroll cupboard was hot and cramped for three boys and a sparrow. It was still so new that it was free of dust, and the aroma of its cedar construction was intense.

The hiding place was actually in a separate compartment beneath the Ark, and Deborah assured Avel they were committing no disrespect or blasphemy. "Our building has so many closets that this one isn't needed yet," she explained. "Besides, since the door opens on the side of the Ark and not at the front, not many people know it's here. I found it because I watched it get installed, but not even my father remembers it. I'll come back after dark."

That seemed like several days ago by Avel's reckoning, even though he could see through the cracks around the door panel it was still full light. When he, Ha-or Tov, and Emet first entered the cubicle it was fun, exciting. The cedar odor was exotic, like incense.

Now it was just overpowering, no longer merely a smell. Avel was certain he could feel cedar branches creeping down his throat and into his eyes.

And the cupboard was no longer a mysterious, secret haven. It was merely a confined space barely big enough to sit in. Avel was stiff, hungry, and getting cranky.

"Scoot over," he muttered to Emet, nudging the smaller boy with his elbow.

"Nuh!" Emet responded. He thumped his own elbow on the side to show he was already up against the wall. Yediyd, sleepy with the darkness, perched on Emet's shoulder with his head under his wing.

"Be quiet," Ha-or Tov cautioned. "You want to give us away?"

"To who?" Avel scoffed. He did lower his voice to add, "How long do you think bar Abba will hang around for the likes of us? Don't you think he's got his own worries? There were Roman soldiers here today, you know. Will he wait for someone to say, 'Look, there's bar Abba, the famous rebel! Let's go tell a soldier and get the reward'?"

"Deborah," Ha-or Tov said archly, "told us to wait. She looked out the gallery window and said she saw a skinny fellow with a thin beard watching the stairs. It had to be Kittim."

Avel suppressed a shiver and responded stoutly, "So what? He won't wait forever either. You want to do everything Deborah says because she touched your hair and said what a pretty red color it was."

Instinctively Ha-or Tov raised his hand to his curly auburn locks. "Maybe," the blind boy agreed.

Avel disliked the dreamy tone. Jealousy flared. "You don't know anything! I'm getting out of here!" Avel announced. "Even if we don't go outside the synagogue till dark, why do we have to stay cooped up in here? We can. . . ."

"Shh!" Ha-or Tov hissed.

"Don't shush me!" Avel responded.

"Shh!" Ha-or Tov repeated, clamping his hand over Avel's mouth. With his lips next to Avel's ear, the blind boy murmured, "I heard something."

Avel stiffened. He signed to Emet to keep still.

Straining his hearing, Avel picked up the sound of Ha-or Tov's breathing and the beat of his own heart, but nothing else. "I don't. . . ."

The floor up in the gallery creaked.

Rivalry instantly forgotten, Avel and the others pressed closer together, as far back from the cupboard door as they could squeeze. "They have to be here somewhere," Avel heard Kittim say. "I could see both doors and the outside stairs, and they didn't come out."

"Then we'll find them," replied a voice Avel recognized as belonging to Judas Iscariot.

Of course! Bar Abba could not spend time walking openly in Capernaum, but a disciple of Yeshua could. And no one would recognize Kittim. If questioned, Judas could claim that the Teacher had left something in the synagogue.

"They aren't up here," Kittim announced. "I searched under all the benches."

Avel shuddered. The space beneath the gallery benches had been his first choice for a hiding place before Deborah showed them the cupboard.

Footsteps clicked down the interior flight of stairs and padded across the floor of the sanctuary.

Avel held his breath.

"I'll check the classroom," he heard Kittim state. Avel sighed with relief. The Torah school study hall was a room build off the rear of the sanctuary while the Ark was at the front.

But where was Judas?

Footsteps crossed the hall toward *bema*, then stopped abruptly.

Had Judas heard something? Had the hammering in Avel's chest given them away?

Emet raised his eyebrows questioningly at Avel.

With clenched jaw, Avel gave the tiniest shake of his head he could manage. He was afraid his teeth would chatter and betray their whereabouts.

Betray! And betrayal meant death.

Yediyd roused and fluffed out his feathers, then settled them again with a shake.

The tiny flurry sounded to Avel's tightly strung senses like a giant windstorm howling in from the desert. What if Yediyd peeped for water or food?

Where were the pursuers? Was Judas right outside the cupboard?

With a clatter that made Avel jump, a cupboard door was flung open. Avel's head bumped the back wall of the closet at the same instant the panel banged against its frame.

It was the door to the Torah scroll cupboard at the front of the closet . . . no more than six feet away and just over their heads. Had Avel's jolt been noticed? Was their shelter about to be unmasked?

Avel could feel a scream bottled up in his throat. He was so sure they were about to be discovered that he wanted to get it over with. Perhaps they could tell Judas about recognizing the Roman centurion in the crowd and hiding in fear of him.

Footsteps rounded their side of the cupboard. Closer. Three feet away at most.

Avel knew he'd scream when the door was opened. Why not go out now and take their chances?

In his memory he saw again the gesture Judas had made: a cut throat for a betrayed oath.

He stayed frozen.

From the rear of the hall Avel heard Kittim ask, "Have you found something?"

"No," Judas called back.

Would he add that there was one more place to search: this door around the side of the *bema?*

Judas was near enough that his voice reverberated inside the cupboard. It made Avel feel trapped, surrounded.

A instant later Avel's hunched shoulders slumped with relief when Judas added, "They slipped past you in the crowd. You've been watching an empty building, and we're wasting time. Let's go."

*Yes!* Avel silently urged. *Go! There's no one here!*

"I know they're here," Kittim vowed. "They have to be."

"So? Who let them get up to the gallery in the first place?"

*That's it,* Avel silently cheered. *Kittim had let them slip away. They were long gone. Time for Kittim to report back to bar Abba.*

"Let's go," Judas said again.

Two sets of footsteps retreated.

■ ■ ■ ■

From the beach, the retreating sails of three fishermen's boats stood out against the line of gray storm clouds gathering on the far shore.

The wind was up. A slight stirring only, but portent of greater force to come. Marcus could see the froth of the waves tipped by the approaching gale.

Yeshua was in one of those boats, Marcus knew.

Miryam, perched on the belly of an upturned skiff, observed, "A storm's brewing."

"Where's he going?" Marcus asked.

She did not answer him. Perhaps she did not know. "Sometimes he just leaves."

"Where?" Marcus hoped to follow him.

"I think it's maybe all the people. Everyone needing so much. It's unending . . . all the needs, I mean. He goes away to the mountains. To be alone beneath his stars. He harvests the quiet. Gathers peace into himself and remembers how it was. Knows how it will be again. He rests from us awhile. Weeps quietly by himself, I think, so he can stand among us without weeping. Then he can gaze into faces longing for his answers and not break into a million pieces and tear the universe apart with the grief of it. He loves us all. Every one of us. And oh! Love is such a heavy burden to carry sometimes."

Marcus knew about that. The loneliness of loving. The agony of it. And Marcus had loved only one. Only Miryam.

What must it be like to love the whole suffering world?

Marcus gazed out at the darkening sky. The little fishing boats beneath the clouds. Sails like seabirds gliding on the wind.

He crossed his arms and remembered everything that had passed between him and Miryam. It came to him how much of her decline had been a result of his anger and selfishness.

She was waiting patiently for him to explain. At last he made a clumsy attempt. "I never stopped thinking of you. Six months in the burning desert. I never stopped thinking of you. Not one day passed without a thought of you."

She waited for him to go on. And then she said, "I'm happy now, Marcus."

"No thanks to me."

"That's not it. Please. It wasn't you."

"Then what?"

"It was . . . me. Bitter. Angry. Loaded with self-pity. Holding on to everything. An illusion of what I thought my life ought to be. And blaming everyone else . . . everyone else . . . because I wasn't happy."

He forced himself to look into her eyes. "I need to ask . . ."

"You don't need to say it, Marcus."

"But I do. I have to hear my own voice speak words I've been too proud and foolish to say."

"All right, then."

"Miryam? I . . . Would you . . . forgive . . . me?"

"With all my heart. Long ago." She was smiling. Her radiant face beamed joy and love.

A sense of relief washed over him. Tears brimmed. He cleared his throat uncomfortably and glanced away. So much he wanted to say. But this was not the time. She had called him *brother*. If he told her how he felt, would she not suspect his contrition had an ulterior motive?

He said simply, "You are . . . someone else."

"As are you. Though I think you don't know yet how changed you are, Marcus."

"Not who I'd like to be," he confessed.

"Nor am I. But I've got time to make amends, I hope. He says, you know, we're on a journey together. Carry one another's burdens, he says. He took one look at me and laughed at my extra baggage! He told me, Lay down the sack of stones, Miryam. They aren't jewels. Just rocks. Even a tiny stone in your shoe can make you lame. Empty your arms and your pockets and your shoes and your rucksack of useless weight. What purpose does it serve? Empty your heart of self-pity and blame. Open your eyes, he said! Look! There's a hungry child calling by the roadside who needs you to carry him home and care for him. Now! He'll die if you don't. You can't fill your arms with love and haul a load of stones too! Be my hands. My heart. Be love in action to those in need."

Marcus nodded, admiring her willingness. "And you opened your home."

"A small thing. I'm more blessed by it than anyone. He loves children, Marcus. Little ones best of all. So . . . I laid down every useless burden at his feet. And I'm free now. I asked him once how I could ever thank him. And he told me that anyone who does a *mitzvah* for a little child does it for him." She shrugged. "Yeshua needs . . . nothing . . . There is no thing I could offer him that could begin to thank him for his mercy to me. Instead, I offer what I have to the babies. And all the time I see Yeshua in their faces. You see?"

Marcus did see. But for a minute he could not reply. So this was what the revolution was about! Children were the kingdom; love was the power; and self-sacrifice was the glory of Yeshua of Nazareth!

Marcus shielded his eyes and strained to see the fishing boats. "Such philosophy could turn the world upside down."

"I do hope so. I think it will, Marcus. But there is much to do and few who are willing."

Behind them the snap of a twig underfoot announced the arrival of El'azar.

"I should have known you would be someplace with a man," El'azar observed with disdain. He exhaled loudly. "Some things never change, do they, Miryam?"

She remained seated and smiled sadly at her brother. "No. I suppose some things do not change. . . . *Shalom,* El'azar. This is my friend. . . ."

"We've met." Marcus nodded curtly in perfunctory greeting.

El'azar's eyes narrowed with suspicion. "So, you are a follower of this Yeshua as well? That explains the Samaritan of his parable."

"I am a Roman." Marcus corrected him stiffly, without regretting the end of his disguise. He did not like Miryam's brother.

"One is as bad as another." El'azar raised his chin, defying Marcus to argue. "I must confess I wondered where the preacher got his tale of bandits and good Samaritans. You must have shared your little adventure with him. Even dogs can wag the tail and be docile. Nakdimon ben Gurion was fortunate you came along. But I don't let one good deed cloud my judgment of you, Roman." He directed his conversation to Miryam. "If you can tear yourself away from your . . . *friend*, Marta and I have come a long way to speak with you. We are staying at cousin Ya'ir's house with Nakdimon ben Gurion, whom you know is a member of the Sanhedrin. He's also here for our cause and . . . other things. You can't keep him waiting."

"As you say, brother," Miryam replied, expression amused.

She slid from her perch and raised her hand in farewell to Marcus.

Her brother grasped her elbow hard and said nothing more as he led her away.

■ ■ ■ ■

From where he stood beside the entry, Nakdimon noted two elements of color in the confined, otherwise drab front room of Ya'ir's home. The brightest light in the space was Deborah. Where did the girl get that flaxen mane and those shimmering azure eyes? Ya'ir was ruddy and his wife, Elizabeth, dark, but Deborah was undeniably their child in all other features. Her mother's easy smile. Her father's ready wit. She was a talker, this girl. Engaging and intelligent. Named after Deborah, the prophetess of Judges, she honored her namesake in looks and personality.

The other splash of brightness relieving the smoky tan of the interior was the weaving in progress on the loom occupying one entire wall. On it, half finished, was wool fabric, distinctively striped in striking shades of red, tan, and blue.

"Deborah," the girl's mother said crisply, "these matters don't concern you. Either go up to your room or outside until we finish."

Deborah responded eagerly, "Outside, please."

"Don't go far," Ya'ir cautioned.

"I'll play in the barn," the girl replied. She paused beside Miryam, pecked her on the cheek in encouragement, then hurried through the door as if anxious to get out of earshot.

It was a compact act of kindness toward a woman very much outnumbered this evening.

Nakdimon approved of Deborah. Open and transparent. A child, yet on the verge of budding into womanhood, she was near the same age as his daughter Hannah. The two would be great friends, he thought, if they should ever meet.

He did not blame the girl for being eager to leave. In fact, he wished he could escape.

As the lone outsider attending this family conference he felt out of place and forced to pass judgment in a matter he did not wish to meddle in. Worse, there were many arrows of ill-will flying about; he was certain some would strike him.

On one side of the table sat the Bethany contingent: brother and sister, El'azar and Marta. Marta had adopted the seat nearest the cheery fire, but only after she had rearranged the position of the few sticks of furniture to suit her. Despite having gotten her way in every issue, from the salting of the barley soup to correcting Deborah's grammar, Marta's lips continued to be drawn down at the corners. A hard and bitter spinster, Marta doled out smiles when it suited her purpose. Nakdimon had yet to glimpse a shred of genuine kindness in her actions.

Beside her, El'azar appeared gruff and anxious to get the present trouble resolved. His face registered the expectation that his concerns would immediately be settled in his favor. He gave emphatic nods every time Marta expressed an opinion.

Opposite them sat Ya'ir and Elizabeth. Ya'ir mainly looked puzzled. Thus far he was not out of sorts, but the crease in his forehead had deepened visibly, and his usual smile was absent.

Elizabeth, who was Miryam's friend, stared daggers at Marta. She was plainly not happy at having her home invaded. Since Marta and El'azar were kin to her husband, and wealthy kin at that, she could not express what she was thinking. Nakdimon read the hostility on her face and in the stiffness of her posture.

The one person in the room who seemed to be bearing up best was, surprisingly, the object of the discussion.

Miryam sat on a low stool in the far corner, beside the loom. Modest in dress and behavior, she appeared neither belligerent nor frightened, but immensely sad. In sharp contrast to her sister Marta, she was also extremely beautiful, Nakdimon noticed. Her thick dark hair shone in the lamp light. Her body was nicely proportioned and her poise pronounced . . . not in the least like the outrageous, depraved outcast described repeatedly by Marta.

"The property was my husband's," Miryam stated again calmly. "As we have no heir and he no surviving close kinsmen, there's no reason I can't do with it as I see fit. If I choose to open my home to the homeless and the unwanted, how can it be anyone's business?"

"There," Marta hissed, her eyes darting from Nakdimon's face to Ya'ir's and back. "You see? She admits it."

"Of course she admits it," Ya'ir returned, a hint of exasperation creeping into his tone. "This is a secret? Everyone in the Galil knows of the charity of Miryam of Magdala. Her penance, they say, for her former sins."

"She has sold orchards and given the money to this itinerant Preacher," El'azar objected. "She's either crazy or bewitched. Anyone can see that. No one sane takes in soiled women and their sinfully conceived offspring."

Miryam's mission of caring for unwed mothers and unwanted babies was something Nakdimon's dear Hadassah would have approved of. In fact, Hadassah had often spoken about her desire to do more for the destitute. She would have given away much more than required had Nakdimon not put limits on her charity. Truly Hadassah would have admired Miryam's courage.

Nakdimon knew his presence at the gathering was meant to lend weight to El'azar's assertion that Miryam needed her brother to act as her guardian. El'azar and Marta expected Ya'ir, as a local authority, to commit her to their care. Since Nakdimon had arrived with them, he was expected to support their side.

As a member of the Sanhedrin, Nakdimon's opinion would not be opposed.

"Clearly the notorious life she led damaged her wits," Marta asserted. "She was so beyond the bounds of decent society that she's now incapable of making reasonable choices."

Miryam asked softly, "You preferred me to remain . . . what I was?"

Marta squirmed uncomfortably at the reminder of what Miryam of Magdala had been.

Lifting his gaze from the bantering, Nakdimon studied Miryam. Of those in the room, she seemed the least crazy, or at least the most composed. Was the ability to face such a storm of hostility without flinching another symptom of madness?

Despite what Nakdimon had heard of Miryam's wanton former life, she acted totally changed. Not simply turned away from sin, but having started completely over.

How was that possible?

She was strikingly attractive, Nakdimon cautioned himself. She always had been, even when he had known her as a young girl in Bethany, but now even more so. If she was under an evil influence, perhaps she was capable of enormous deceit. He would have to be cautious lest his judgment be clouded by her beauty or demeanor.

Ya'ir argued, "Many people, including other women of independent means, support Yeshua. Many have obeyed his commands to give generously to the poor."

"And you and the elders of the synagogue do nothing to arrest such a charlatan?" El'azar demanded. "Can't you see he's preying on silly, weak-willed women?"

Miryam Magdalen did not act or sound either weak-willed or silly. It was said she had once been a businesswoman of extraordinary ability. Even now her accounts showed she ran the charity sensibly, using profits from orchards and livestock to feed, clothe, and house the poor.

To offer that observation would be throwing grease on a fire, Nakdimon thought.

But it was time for Nakdimon to speak. Elizabeth, who had said little, showed readiness to leap over the table and strangle Marta. Goodwill had deteriorated when Ya'ir's true feelings on the matter were revealed.

Clearing his throat to gain a measure of attention, Nakdimon said, "I was sent here with that exact question in mind: is Yeshua of Nazareth a righteous man or a wicked one? Does he encourage righteousness or disregard for Torah?"

"A deceiver. A liar," Marta argued, rising from the bench. "We saw his tricks at a wedding in Cana last year. . . ."

She sat down abruptly at an authoritative wave of Nakdimon's hand. "I'm not finished," he sternly warned. "I haven't had time or opportunity to complete my investigation. It may be the luxury of some"—he stared pointedly at El'azar—"to be able to rush to conclusions. But in my position I can't afford to. For the sake of *Hashem,* I am brought here as a judge in other grave issues concerning our people and our nation. This matter is merely part of the bigger picture. Yeshua seems also to bring division in families . . . but I won't make any judgment hastily. I think the best thing to do is conclude for the moment until I gather more facts."

Marta struggled between flaring at him and trying to win his support by her upright correctness.

Cajolery won. "Quite right," she said, simpering. "A Dani'el! A righteous judge! A Dani'el come to judgment."

■ ■ ■ ■

In the purple of twilight, Capernaum appeared deserted. Doors and shutters were closed against the wind. After Yeshua left the town, the people returned to their own villages and homes. Everyone had run for shelter as the storm closed in. Marcus regretted again the loss of his own Capernaum home.

Where had bar Abba run to, Marcus wondered, as he scanned the doorways of the houses. The rebel had taken a great risk to come here. Why had he done it?

Was bar Abba, chief of the Zealots, hoping to make a king of Yeshua? A messiah to redeem his nation from political tyranny and religious corruption?

Had he come to confront Yeshua? To challenge him to rally an army behind him? To take Jerusalem by storm at the Passover celebration two weeks from now?

Passing the home of Simon the Pharisee, Marcus recalled clearly what Yeshua had said to him the night Marcus knelt and offered Yeshua the *corona obsidionalis* as a sign of profound respect:

*"Marcus, I saw you at Idistaviso. There is no greater love than for a man to lay down his life for his friends . . . but my battle is not yet done. I have another crown waiting for me in Jerusalem. And I promise you this, Marcus Longinus; you will be at my feet when I wear it . . . and then you will understand."*

Since that night Marcus had tried to sort out the meaning of Yeshua's words a thousand times. Always his explanation had come up empty. With the appearance of bar Abba on the fringes of the crowd, Marcus began to piece together the possibility that Yeshua was indeed going to declare himself king in Jerusalem.

It could not end well. Not for the kindly Rabbi. Nor for any who followed him.

Rome would be waiting with swords drawn and lances raised to pierce him through. Yeshua had specifically said that Marcus would be at his feet when he fought his battle and wore his crown. Did he mean that he intended all along to defeat the Roman forces occupying Jerusalem? That Marcus would be among those opposing him? Laying down his life because of Yeshua?

It had not seemed so at the time. But now?

Any rebellion was sure to be unmercifully crushed. Marcus did not doubt that Caiaphas, Pilate, and Herod Antipas had their own spies in Capernaum today. They would be drawing the same conclusions as Marcus.

*"Yes, my lord,"* they would say, *"there is a revolt in the works in Galilee. Always Galilee. That's where it starts and then the blood will flow through Pilate's aqueduct in Jerusalem!"*

Perhaps bar Abba had spotted one of the agents. Or he had caught sight of Marcus and vanished the instant Marcus looked away. In that case bar Abba would be many miles off by now. The question was, had he followed after Yeshua with an offer to make him king? Were the two plowing the field of Israel in tandem all along? One planting seeds of hope and redemption while the other harvested growing dissatisfaction with Rome and the religious leaders?

It began to rain as Marcus passed the synagogue.

With Ya'ir he once had labored over the redesign of the structure. He had loaned his soldiers to the task of roofing and rebuilding. It felt like a very long time ago.

He knew a way in and a place where he could sleep through the night out of the weather.

He approached the back entrance to the structure. To his surprise it was open. Hesitating, he backed into the shadows of a tree trunk as four children emerged.

"This way. You'll be safe in our barn. I've left your supper for you in a sack. Why should he hunt for you in the barn of the cantor?"

So Ya'ir's daughter, Deborah, was up to something. She had three ragged boys in tow. Avel. Emet. And another. A blind boy who turned his face up to the rain and opened his wide mouth as if he was thirsty. Who or what were they hiding from?

Avel, clutching the hand of the blind boy, said, "Bar Abba will kill us if he finds us."

So! They had completed their quest and stumbled into bar Abba's camp! No doubt they knew enough to sink the rebel chief.

Deborah locked the door and replaced the key beneath a stone.

Marcus let them go, hissing and sputtering all the way. He knew where he would find them tomorrow. Nothing to be done about bar Abba tonight. Exhaustion drew Marcus on. Retrieving the key, he unlatched the door and slipped in.

It was dark and soothing inside. His footsteps echoed hollowly in the stillness. With a sigh, he wrapped his cloak around him, lay down beside the *bema* and was soon fast asleep.

# VA-FESHA

The first rumble of thunder rolled down from the Golan and splashed into the Sea of Galilee. Breakers smashed against the shore of Capernaum. Trees bowed before the howling gale.

The three boys and the sparrow were safe and warm among the sheep pens and the chickens roosting in Deborah's barn.

Ha-or Tov, Good Light that he was, said he could not see the lightning but heard the battle going on in heaven. The noise was the clash of swords as good angels and bad angels fought for men's souls. Or so his mother had always told him. A fierce fight it was, too.

Emet could not hear the thunder but saw the forked fire strike the surface of the water. He cupped his hands around Yediyd to shield the little bird from the terror of the sight. Emet sat hunched in the doorway and shook his head as though he saw a desperate struggle on board the boats that had carried Yeshua and his followers toward the far shore.

Avel covered his legs with straw and rested against the wall to watch as lances of light were flung down from the clouds to pierce the raging waters again and again. He thought that maybe come morning the rabbi Yeshua would be drowned and his men with him. There had not been time enough for them to cross the lake. The wind howled like the keening of ten thousand voices. Rain sluiced down on the rooftop and dripped from the eaves.

Deborah joined them as the angry voices of her elders punctuated the violence of the storm.

Even inside the barn the hostility coming from the house was plain to Avel.

Deborah was also angry; her fists were clenched. "I wish they'd go home," she said. "I wish my cousins would leave. Not Miryam," she clarified. "The other two."

"They don't like her much." Ha-or Tov sat with his ear cocked to catch the diatribe. "But they don't like anybody. I know them both from Bethany."

"They say Cousin Miryam's crazy. But she's nice to me and everyone else. Mama likes her. But Cousin Marta is hateful. Bossy and hateful. Papa says they want to steal Miryam's property before she gives it all away. She's a widow, but the other two never married."

"Who'd want them?" Ha-or Tov posed.

It was difficult for the older three children to restrain the volume of their laughter.

Emet climbed with Yediyd into the loft to sleep. Dust specks drifted down. Deborah brushed Ha-or Tov's shoulder and picked a strand of straw from his head. "Your hair is the color of saffron strands," she said in admiration. "If you like, I'll braid it for you." She pulled a comb from her pocket and began to work on his reddish locks.

"My mother used to brush my hair." Ha-or Tov stared skyward with his sightless eyes, as if remembering what it was like to be loved.

Avel's mother had never brushed his hair.

*"Lo-Ahavah!" She had grasped Avel by his mane and beat him bloody with a leather strap. "Lo-Ammi!"*

When Deborah was not looking, Avel scrunched his tight curls to see if they could be braided. Not possible.

"Good bread," he said loudly, waving half a loaf. "Your mother is a fine cook."

"Ha-or Tov . . . the 'Good Light,'" Deborah mused out loud. "Such a funny name for someone who is . . ."

"Stone blind." Ha-or Tov finished her sentence.

Deborah stopped fussing with Ha-or Tov's hair and blurted, "Yeshua heals people. Cripples, lepers, deaf ones like Emet. And blind folks, too. I know one. A blind beggar used to sit outside the synagogue and last week Yeshua made him see."

Ha-or Tov said, "The Rabbi did that?"

"Can't do it," Avel threw in. "Not the Rabbi. Not us. We can't even go near him. Can't even tell him where we are."

"Why not?" Deborah asked.

Avel snapped, "Bar Abba!"

"So?" Ha-or Tov and Deborah said in unison.

"Ha-or Tov, did you forget . . ." Avel caught himself before mentioning Judas by name. "One of Yeshua's talmidim belongs to bar Abba's band?"

"Oh," Ha-or Tov said regretfully.

"Who?" Deborah inquired. "I'll tell my father. I'm sure Yeshua doesn't know it."

"No," Avel corrected hastily. "You can't tell anyone. He'll kill us and maybe you too. Promise?"

Deborah agreed reluctantly. "But it's not right. Everyone who wants to see Yeshua should get to."

"We don't want to see him if it gets us killed. Better to stay blind and stay alive. Right, Ha-or Tov?" Avel asked.

The blind boy's shoulders had narrowed appreciably, and he was hunched over with his head turned to the side. Disappointment had sapped his desire for conversation. He didn't respond.

Beside the pen where two nanny goats rested was a smaller enclosure containing a single ewe and her lamb. The lamb butted his mother in the flank, but she nudged him away.

When Avel stuck his fingers between the railings the lamb latched on to them and pretended to suckle. "He likes me," Avel remarked. "What's his name?"

"Doesn't have one," Deborah corrected. "Just lamb. For Passover. Papa says not to name him. There's grain in that pot by the back wall. Would you feed the animals for me, Avel?"

"Of course," Avel vowed stoutly. "You leaving?"

"I don't feel well," Deborah said. "The fighting . . . and the thunder . . . gave me a headache. I'm going to bed. And Avel? I want you to know . . . I think you have a heart like a lion. Bringing them all this way. So." She shrugged and kissed him on the forehead. "Good night, Avel, dear lion cub."

■ ■ ■ ■

The number of visitors taxed the capacity of Ya'ir's home. In order to accommodate all the guests, the two bedrooms were converted into men's and women's dormitories. Elizabeth, Marta, and Miryam slept upstairs in the cubicle with Deborah.

The men were downstairs in what was usually Ya'ir and Elizabeth's room. Nakdimon, as the guest of honor, was given the bed. El'azar and Ya'ir made do on the floor atop blanket-bundled heaps of rushes.

Even though everyone had a space, Nakdimon wondered if anyone slept. The wind, which had been rising since late afternoon, swelled into a gale after sunset. Close on the departure of the day, clouds swept to blot out the stars.

Cold air from the elevations of Mount Hermon met moist air slotting in from the Great Sea by way of the Acco Gap and the Valley of Jezreel. Directly over the Sea of Galilee, these relatively benign breezes collided headlong with the drier and hotter Khamseen gusts.

The result was one of the spectacular storms for which the lake was famous.

Nakdimon first heard the thunder far off, grumbling in the heights of Golan like the children of Israel complaining in the wilderness.

Wide awake, Nakdimon reviewed what he had heard Yeshua speak in synagogue. Loving your neighbor sounded fine as long as your neighbor was lovable, but Yeshua suggested . . . no, *expected* . . . that love of neighbor went beyond that, even beyond charity.

God demanded that we love the unlovely, the Teacher proclaimed.

What's more, Yeshua turned the audience on its head by making the Samaritan the hero.

Nor could Nakdimon argue with the conclusion, since he had been the one rescued by a foreigner.

How did Yeshua know what had happened? Of the thousands gathered around to listen, only Nakdimon and El'azar knew the reality, and neither of them had spoken of it to Yeshua.

Of course Ya'ir had heard the account. Could he have shared the tale with the Rabbi? That would explain things.

But while the parable was offered in response to El'azar's challenge, Nakdimon personally felt its impact.

Nakdimon would have died in that canyon if he had not been rescued by the unknown benefactor. Clearly he owed a debt to whoever had saved his life; that man had been a true neighbor.

Before long the disturbance in the heavens changed to drumming. It sounded as though a herd of wild creatures stampeded around the bowl of the Galil.

Flashes of lightning, glimpsed at first as threadlike flickers in the distance, lit the night. As they drew closer, Nakdimon saw each jagged streak fork and divide and split many times. They grew in intensity and frequency until the air had the metallic tang of a coppersmith's shop.

What about the second story Yeshua told? A dead, uncharitable rich man, a beggar, and Father Abraham . . .

Because of the choice of names, it was impossible for Nakdimon not to picture El'azar of Bethany as his namesake in the tale. Yet El'azar as a beggar outside a rich man's gate? El'azar dead? And what did Yeshua mean that even if someone came back from the dead, people still would not believe? Was anyone so hardheaded that they could not be convinced by a message delivered in such a form?

But that was impossible anyway. Since the age of the prophets, no one was brought back from the dead. No one had that sort of power anymore.

There was a lull in the storm. The wind subsided. The lightning retreated. Nakdimon's eyes drooped. Perhaps sleep would come at last.

Then, unaccountably, the hairs on his neck prickled as if anticipating danger. Nakdimon's beard tingled, like no sense of peril he'd ever experienced.

A gigantic thunder clap detonated directly above Capernaum. Simultaneously a silver-white sheet of lightning ripped apart the darkness. The sawtoothed blade of its passage left a brilliant imprint on Nakdimon's closed eyelids.

The house rumbled and shook. Out in the front room a pair of oil lamps tossed from the mantle shattered on the floor. The bed jumped, as if the house had been struck by an earthquake. From outside came a rending crash as the lightning bolt exploded in the crown of a nearby oak tree, splitting it in two.

And then an instant stillness followed the explosion. Nakdimon, fully awake again, listened and heard nothing. Nothing. Not a breath of wind, not the sound of distant thunder moving away. Nothing.

The storm's fury had not subsided; it had dissolved.

From overhead, Nakdimon heard the pat of footsteps and a bump as someone, unfamiliar with the house, collided with an object in the dark. Low voices murmured words he could not understand. There was the sound of something being shaken, the rustle of bedclothes.

Had someone been injured by the gale? Had lightning actually struck the house?

The voices grew in number. More people were awake. The tone of what he could hear took on an edge of fear. He recognized Elizabeth calling the name of her daughter, Deborah.

Then a flurry of footsteps pounded down the stairs, "Ya'ir!" Elizabeth burst out. "Something's wrong with Deborah! She's burning with fever, and I can't rouse her!"

■ ■ ■ ■

Marcus was awake throughout the storm, but after the final, climactic blast, the tempest's unexplained departure allowed him to sleep deeply.

Another crash in the light of predawn woke him: the clatter of the synagogue's front door being thrown back. A jumble of men crowded through the entry.

Marcus laid hold of his sword. Had someone reported his presence in the sanctuary? Was this a gang of rebels coming to attack him? Marcus knew his thinking was sleep-muddled. Recognizing Ya'ir's voice in the group, he relaxed and listened.

"Thank you, my friends," he hard Ya'ir say. "For coming out so early. I wouldn't ask if it wasn't an emergency. Deborah is very sick . . . so sick! . . . I'm afraid she'll die!" The man's throat, gripped by emotion, barely allowed the last words to escape.

"Are we a minyan then?" El'azar asked. "Six, seven, Nakdimon is eight . . . yes, ten."

Nakdimon prayed the eighth blessing of the *Amidah,* "Blessed are you, O *Adonai,* King of the Universe, who heals the sick of his people Israel."

After a chorus of *"Omaines,"* Ya'ir prayed the words of Psalm 139. *"Adonai,* you have probed me and you know me . . . You fashioned my inmost being, you knit me together in my mother's womb. . . ." Then he broke down, unable to keep a formal tone in the midst of his anguish. "And Deborah! You know she is our only child, the light of my life! Don't take her from us!"

Feeling he must speak, Marcus raised up. The men in the circle facing him jumped back in alarm as if he was a spirit. "Ya'ir," he said. "Friend! It's Marcus Longinus. I'm sorry to startle you, but . . . you know what happened when Carta was hurt. You went with the others to Yeshua on my behalf . . ."

El'azar growled accusingly, "A foreigner! And saying exactly what you'd expect from one who defiles our synagogue! You and that fraud should both clear out!"

"Wait," Ya'ir said, staring at Marcus. "This man loves our people and blessed our synagogue . . . helped us rebuild it . . ."

The other members of the congregation buzzed with the recognition of Marcus.

"I took shelter here from the storm," Marcus apologized. "No disrespect. But Ya'ir . . . Deborah's sick? Where's Yeshua? Fetch him, fast as you can."

"He's gone," Ya'ir said dismally. "Sailed off before the gale hit. Who knows where he is? He might even be drowned."

■ ■ ■ ■

Miryam was so sure of everything. Once again Marcus noted her transformation. Into someone he had never known. Beautiful, yes, she had always been that. But now another kind of beauty radiated from within her. She was at peace.

She gazed confidently at the lake and said three times to Marcus and Ya'ir, "He'll come back. He'll be here."

She had reason to hope. After all, Ya'ir was her cousin. Deborah was his single child. Let her brother, El'azar, and sister, Marta, stay behind at the house and sit the death watch beside Deborah's bed!

Miryam, instead, had gone in search of Yeshua!

But hours passed and Yeshua did not come back.

The two men, Jew and Roman, sat silently beside her on the hill overlooking the calm surface of the Sea of Galilee. Clouds above the eastern shore reflected in the water. Yellow daisies were in bloom. Broad swaths of gold carpeted the distant land. Blue lupines cast the mountains of Golan in a rich purple hue.

It was the third hour of the morning. Ya'ir had not spoken since before dawn when people began to arrive in ones and twos at the lake shore.

Would Yeshua come today, they wanted to know?

Two thousand or more watched for the return of the fishing boats. Were these people desperate? Did each one have a request? A petition? A sickness to be healed? An inner thirst only Yeshua's words could quench?

Human longing cluttered the beach like debris washed up by last night's storm. When Yeshua came . . . if he came . . . he would not be able to walk without tripping over need. So many. Such a multitude, all of whom would reach out to him at once, call his name with one resounding cry. How could he touch them all? Answer every request?

Perhaps it was this realization that made Ya'ir raise his head and study the featureless surface of the lake. "Even if he comes," Ya'ir said at last, "how will he hear me with all these others calling to him?"

Miryam replied, "Your name is Ya'ir, *Fear God*. Fear God then and stand in awe of what He can do."

"I fear."

"Believe! Can you doubt after what we've seen?"

"Not if he was here. But he's not. No sign of his coming back. I should go," Ya'ir replied. "What if Deborah calls for me and I'm not there? Maybe it's already too late . . . and if . . . if . . . if it's too late? Elizabeth will need me. Poor Elizabeth."

Miryam answered, "Ya'ir. Don't be afraid."

"I can't help it, Miryam. Good cousin. My whole life is tangled in hers. There's no net for me to draw in hope if she doesn't live. If she goes under, I go too. I'll tell him that when he comes. Yes. Yes. I'll tell him straight out. He'll understand, won't he? I'll make a bargain. My life instead of hers. I don't care for my own life. But her? I've never stopped dreaming for her since I first held her in my arms. Twelve years. Only twelve! How short her life turned out to be, compared to what I dreamed! I never minded that we only had one baby. Elizabeth pined over not having more. But I always said Deborah was more to me than a whole tribe of sons and daughters."

Ya'ir lowered his head, pressing his brow against his knees and hiding his face. He made no sound, but Marcus knew the man was weeping.

Miryam patted his shoulder. "Rest awhile, cousin," she comforted the grieving father. "I'll wake you when I see a sail." She returned her gaze to search the waters for any sign of a boat on the horizon.

Ya'ir slept in the grass. Sleep was, Marcus thought, the one mercy for such suffering.

An hour passed.

No breeze. The sea had been becalmed since the storm died abruptly the night before. There would be no sail unfurled, Marcus knew. If Yeshua and his talmidim returned to the Capernaum shore today, they would come with difficulty, rowing, sweating under their own power.

As if to contradict his thoughts, the heads of daisies bowed down at his feet and bobbed up again. A fresh breeze sprang from the east.

Miryam smiled serenely. Confident.

Now. Yes. Now. A faint red square against the line of blue water. Another and another close behind. Three vessels with red sails billowed in the wind.

Yeshua! Coming back!

And at last every doubt was removed from Marcus' mind about Miryam. What had happened? What miracle had made her someone new? What had she learned sitting at the feet of Yeshua of Nazareth that made her so fearless?

She inclined her face slightly, the way she used to when she wanted him to kiss her.

And yes, he wanted to kiss her. But he did not.

Her dark eyes sparkled.. "I know what you're thinking," she said. She placed her hand on his to silence him. "It's not about me anymore, Marcus. The view from my window is vast. I can't say, 'That's me,' anymore when I look in a mirror. I look up at the stars and say, 'This is. This is his. He made it. And he made me too.'"

"I don't understand." He leaned toward her, wanting to put his cheek against hers and inhale the sweetness of her skin.

"Look at the sails. There. You see? He fills them with the breath of his will. I am . . . in awe of it, really. He comes to us in a rickety little boat . . . across waters so wide . . . so deep . . . so we'll know we aren't alone. He's coming. To us, Marcus. To Ya'ir and Carta and Deborah and all the others he's touched. He's here to redeem Israel—one soul at a time, I think. He's the one we've been waiting for. And from this hour the world will never be the same."

■ ■ ■ ■

"Avel? You want bread?" Ha-or Tov tore his chunk in half and extended it toward his friend. "Avel?" It was a generous offer. There was no way to know when the next meal might come . . . or from where.

Avel saw the gesture and heard the words but just shook his head. For the moment he had forgotten that Ha-or Tov was blind, just as he had forgotten that Emet was deaf. He was no longer worried that they had nowhere to go except this barn, nor any way to get food if Deborah died.

Deborah could not die! She must not!

Avel thought of nothing else. The refrain of his protest played over and over in his head, eliminating other concerns.

There had been few people in Avel's life who cared about him. After Hayyim's death Avel wanted to die too.

Then Emet came along and Ha-or Tov and tiny Yediyd, beloved friends every one. Avel had not died. Having them with him was more important to living than having something to eat, he thought. There were other ways to starve to death besides having an empty belly.

They were friends, true enough, but they depended on him, not the other way around. Deborah was one of a handful of people in Avel's life to offer him kindness.

Avel wanted to pray, to ask *Adonai Elohim* to spare Deborah's life, but did not know how.

He had been to the Temple and watched trembling petitioners present their sacrifices. But this corner of the Galil was far from Jerusalem and he had no lamb to offer, nor a *cohen* to do the slaughter.

Avel had seen Pharisees praying on the street corners. With uplifted arms and bellowing voices, they thanked the Almighty for every blessing, virtually demanding His attention.

Was that how it was done?

Did the Almighty only listen if you shouted at Him with high-flown phrases?

Did He only heed those wearing richly embroidered robes?

Did Adonai only hear if you came to Him armored with phylacteries proclaiming your righteousness?

Avel was poor, miserable, and far from righteous, and he knew it.

"Please," he whispered to the cobwebs in the rafters. "Have mercy on her. And please don't refuse because it's me who's asking. Lots of people love her and don't want her to die."

No sooner had the request come from his lips than it was denied.

With the suddenness of the lightning bolt that shattered the oak, the fabric of the day was ripped apart by a drawn-out shriek.

Avel jumped to his feet and ran toward the door.

Ha-or Tov heard him and guessed his intent. "Stop! Avel! You can't go out there! You don't know where bar Abba is, where Kittim is! Stop!"

The screech from the house was joined by a woman wailing and then another. "Deborah! Deborah!"

Leaning against the closed door. Avel cried out through gritted teeth, "No!" He put his fists over his ears and pounded the sides of his head as if he could make it stop; force the sounds of grief back out of his hearing.

But when he stopped the keening continued and then increased in volume. Avel clambered out the door and scrambled up into the branches of the sycamore tree. Her window was there, as she had told him. He shinnied out along the limb and peered in just in time to see everything come to an end.

Deborah's mother knelt beside her, pleading for her not to leave.

No use. No use, Avel knew. No use praying for things to be different.

No use begging the dead not to go. There was no angel, no *Adonai* in the rafters of the barn to hear his plea. All of it was a sham! The Levites, *co-hanim*, scribes, and Pharisees! A joke! Their offerings and sacrifices? A waste! Their prayer shawls and broad leather bands holding the phylacteries to forearms and foreheads to announce their piety? Simply costumes for actors. They performed for a deserted theater.

Avel stared through the window as Deborah's soul wrenched free from her body. She had been so beautiful, so bright, so filled with joy. Now this. Suddenly he knew there was no *Adonai* to hear the desperate please of mortals.

There was only . . . mourning. And that Avel knew well.

And so, Deborah, daughter of Ya'ir, convulsed upon her bed and died.

The wail of her mother pierced the morning air. The woman threw herself across her daughter as if to keep Deborah's soul from flying away.

Futile hope.

Perched on the limb of the sycamore tree, Avel could see clearly through the bedroom window as the color drained from Deborah's face. The tip of her nose grew ashen. Then forehead, chin, cheeks, ears; all became a translucent gray. Blond hair, damp with perspiration, clung to her cheek. Her blue eyes, wide and fixed, stared vacantly past Avel at the sky.

So this is what death did to beauty.

Avel mourned.

"Avel? What's happened?" Ha-or Tov, on the branch beneath Avel, raised his blind eyes skyward.

Avel, taking it in, could not reply.

"What's wrong?" Ha-or Tov queried impatiently.

"She's dead." Avel managed to choke the words out.

Emet, not comprehending, held the bird to his cheek and grinned.

And then a woman ran shrieking from the house, fell to the ground, and flung dust into the air. Neighbors who had come to wait began to keen.

Little Emet, startled by the violent emotions of the women, watched them for a long moment and then blinked back tears of understanding. He looked questioningly at Avel.

Could it be? The beautiful girl who had protected them from Kittim, fed them, cared for them, had flown away?

Avel jerked his head once in acknowledgment and drew his index finger across his neck, giving Emet the sign for death.

■ ■ ■ ■

At first warning of the girl's imminent death, Nakdimon had stepped out of the courtyard of Ya'ir's house and into the street, lest he be defiled. As a *cohen,* a descendant of the priestly tribe of Levi, Nakdimon was forbidden to come in contact with the dead. This involved not necessarily physical contact but being under the same roof with a corpse. Under open sky a *cohen* could not approach a grave nearer than six feet unless the deceased was a close family member.

Physically Nakdimon distanced himself from the tragedy.

For the sake of compassion, however, he forced himself to consider what he would feel if he lost Hannah, his twelve-year-old daughter. Even with seven children, none could take the place of another. Each life was precious and irreplaceable in his love. What then, he wondered, would Ya'ir feel at the loss of his only child? What would he say to Yeshua of Nazareth when word came it was too late for a miracle?

The loss of one that young, her parent's one hope, was a tragedy beyond comprehension!

A peaceful death following a long life blessed with health and vitality was not a calamity.

Nakdimon knew well the saying of Solomon, "A good name is better than precious oil; and the day of death than the day of one's birth . . ."

As a Pharisee, Nakdimon believed that for a Jew this life was simply a corridor leading to another world. There was a homeland to come, *olam haba,* where a man would be judged. His soul would continue to flourish.

But the younger and more precious the individual, the more painful the loss to the living. At twelve years of age, Deborah had not yet tasted life.

There could be no loss as great as this.

The untimely death of this only child destroyed the hope of future joy from the house of Ya'ir.

With these thoughts, Nakdimon sprinkled his head with dust. He sank down in the shade of a large tree to mourn. He called forth grief with the thought of his dear wife, Hadassah. Remembering the day of her dying, tears came easily to him. He raised his face toward heaven and groaned as the wails of women punctuated the morning air of Capernaum.

Word of the tragedy spread like a wildfire. Soon the lanes leading to the modest house were crammed with people.

There were many dear friends who flocked to the house of Ya'ir that day. People who loved Ya'ir, Elizabeth, and young Deborah. After all, the girl had been part of their lives for twelve years. Such a tragedy was unbelievable; paralyzing in its enormity!

Thankfully, Marta of Bethany, as nearest kinswoman, took charge of arrangements.

The villagers pondered the awesome ways of *Adonai*. Many remarked it was no coincidence Marta and her brother El'azar arrived in Capernaum in time to lend a hand.

Funerals and the seven days of *Shiva* that followed were expensive affairs.

The linen shroud and burial spices cost six months' wages. Abundant food and lodging would have to be provided for those who came from distant places.

Musicians and professional mourners began to appear immediately. They would expect payment.

Everyone knew Ya'ir and Elizabeth were poor. Ya'ir often remarked that their sole treasure on this earth was Deborah.

How could he provide the kind of funeral she deserved?

But here was Marta, who did not know the girl enough to truly feel sorrow. Marta the practical, calmly rising from the confusion of the community's grief to organize everything and everyone properly.

First, she declared, Ya'ir must be fetched back from chasing after impossible miracles. False hopes had come crashing down around their ears. Not even the bones of the prophet Elisha could bring Deborah back, Marta said fiercely.

Nakdimon was rousted from his mourning and instructed that he and El'azar must go immediately to find Ya'ir and notify him that his little girl had died. There would be no magical healing on this day, Marta snapped. Ya'ir was to come home instantly.

Grief-stricken friends were admitted to the home. Practiced keeners and flute players were arranged outside in a display of carefully orchestrated anguish.

The body must be washed, anointed, and dressed for burial with *kibud ha-met*, the honor due even to a lifeless human being. Marta would see to that herself. She would personally prepare the child for burial with the help of a small group of other women.

A tomb would have to be purchased. Within twenty-four hours interment was required to take place.

Marta assured El'azar and Nakdimon that by the time Ya'ir returned home from his fool's errand Deborah's body would be prepared. The tomb would be ready.

"And," she told her brother, in a conspiratorial whisper loud enough for Nakdimon and several bystanders to hear, "We are first kin to this poor family. This poor, dear child. Ya'ir could never give her the sort of funeral she deserves. It's our duty, El'azar. We'll cover the cost of everything from our own purse. It's the least we can do."

# VA-HATA'AH

T he three boats were lost in the sun. Blinding. Painful to look at. Yet Marcus could not tear his eyes away. Was Yeshua on board, he wondered? Or had Miryam simply caught sight of a trio of vessels fishing on the lake and foolishly wished the Teacher was coming?

Others in the crowd began to stir and stand and point.

"Is it him?"

"Is the Rabbi in the boat?"

A cloud passed over the light. The silver glare vanished. Three dark red sails appeared. Swelled with wind, they pushed the battered craft in a direct line toward the shore. An audible sigh of excitement rippled through the masses.

Miryam gently shook Ya'ir awake. The man sat up with a start. "What news? Deborah? No! Is she gone?" he cried. His unhappy dreams pursued him into consciousness.

"It's Yeshua," Miryam assured him. "See there. The center boat. That's him standing before the mast."

The wine-colored fabric of the sails behind him, Yeshua extended his arms, as if to embrace those waiting on the bank. He was glad to see them. Glad to be home, it seemed to Marcus.

What would Marcus tell Felix about all this? Yeshua came to his people not like a king, but like a much-loved brother.

And his family welcomed him with a roar.

Ya'ir's eyes widened with hope. One glimpse of Yeshua in the vessel and Ya'ir clambered to his feet.

Running, stumbling, he pushed his way through the crowd.

Too many people! Too many bodies between him and Yeshua! How would he reach him with his petition?

Miryam grasped Marcus' hand and followed after, stopping at the edge of softly lapping waves as Ya'ir plunged ahead into the lake.

Wading in waist deep beyond the crowd, he cupped his hands and shouted, "Please! Rabbi! Oh, Yeshua! My little girl! It's Deborah! You know her, Rabbi! Please! Over here! Put to shore here!"

Yeshua stepped to the bow and turned his gaze on Ya'ir.

Miryam squeezed Marcus' hand. "Look! He sees him!"

Yes. From among the shouts of hundreds Yeshua had heard the frantic cries of the cantor of the Capernaum synagogue. Yeshua nodded once and spoke a command to the helmsman. He pointed at Ya'ir. The boat changed course.

Expectant silence fell over the multitude. The craft scudded over the surface. Ya'ir lowered his arms in exhaustion as tears of relief ran down his cheeks. The sounds of flapping sails and waves against the bow were punctuated by his sobs.

The vessel came abreast of Ya'ir. Marcus watched with astonishment as Yeshua leapt from the prow into the lake. He linked arms with Ya'ir and the two waded ashore as Yeshua's talmidim pulled the three boats onto the sand.

Ya'ir sank to the ground at the water's edge and pleaded with Yeshua. "My little girl is dying, Rabbi! Please! Come with me! Put your hands on her so she'll be healed! So she'll live!"

Yeshua took him by the hand and lifted him up. Dark eyes searched his face.

What peace was in that look.

What assurance that somehow all would be well!

Memories flooded Marcus as he watched Yeshua.

The day Carta lay dying Marcus had thrown himself at the Rabbi's feet and implored him to save the boy's life. Yeshua had gazed into his eyes with the same calm assurance. Carta had been healed.

And then again, that terrible morning when Miryam cowered on the pavement of Jerusalem's temple before the scribes and Pharisees. Confronted with truth about their own guilt, her accusers turned away in shame. *"He who is without sin among you . . ."*

Yeshua was the only one with the right to condemn her and yet he had said simply. *"Neither do I condemn you. Your sins are forgiven. Go and sin no more. . . ."* With mercy he had healed her broken soul. Changed her life forever.

And now, here was Ya'ir. A good man, an ordinary man, whose only child lay dying. Was it too much for Yeshua to go to the girl and touch her? To make her whole again?

Yeshua replied with a smile. "Ya'ir? Good friend. Don't be afraid. Come on. We'll go to your house together."

At once the mass of supplicants went wild. They began to push one another, fighting to get near Yeshua.

Yeshua's twelve talmidim protected him and Ya'ir. Shi'mon, large and coarse-featured, pushed men and women away. John, also strong and gruff, scowled at those who attempted to rush in. Judas took the lead in the right-hand column. He, alone of the group, carried a sword, Marcus noted. Mattityahu, once a tax collector and now among the talmidim, guarded the left flank. The rest were human shields against the onslaught of desperation. They were, thought Marcus, like royal bodyguards, attempting to open a path for Yeshua and Ya'ir. It was not surprising that Yeshua had chosen such strong young men to be his followers. If one day he was indeed king and Israel was his kingdom, surely these twelve would be there to protect him night and day.

But the mass of people was too much even for them. Clawing hands reached for Yeshua between the gaps. Tugging at his clothing, shoving rolled scrolls of petition toward him, they pressed in. Progress was made by inches. Ya'ir's face took on a desperate, panicked expression. Would they arrive too late to do Deborah any good?

Marcus placed Miryam squarely behind him. "Stay close to me," he shouted. "Don't let go!" She grasped him around the middle and they crept forward. They managed to keep abreast of the Teacher by Marcus' strength and determination.

So many desperate people! And each one wanted something. Every mouth shouting out a plea, a petition! Beggars mingled with housewives and wealthy merchants. Here and there Marcus spotted the rich livery of the religious rulers who had come to spy from Jerusalem. What report would they give to Herod Antipas? To the high priest, Caiaphas? To the Sanhedrin? To Governor Pilate?

Would their testimony be like the deposition Marcus intended to make to Felix? *"Yeshua teaches mercy and kindness to the poor. He heals the sick. I don't know how, but he does. He preaches about doing good to others. He says his kingdom is not of this world. But in heaven. What harm can such gentle teaching be to Rome?"*

No. Marcus anticipated that accounts of Yeshua's effect on the common folk would terrify Herod Antipas, infuriate Caiaphas and the Sanhedrin, irritate Pilate, and perhaps require action from Rome. And then it would be time for brutal men like Praetorian Vara to step in.

Perhaps, in the end, all of Yeshua's talmidim would carry swords. This rabble would never be able to stand up to the might of Imperial Rome, Marcus knew. If Yeshua was made the leader of a political rebellion, the authorities would make certain he was the first to die.

But not today. No. Today Yeshua was going to the home of Ya'ir. To visit a sick little girl. Today there was no thought of revolt. Of death. Only life.

"We're going too slowly," Miryam said in exasperation.

It could not be helped.

Then, suddenly, Yeshua stopped. He held up his arms and turned around. One flash of his eyes, and the mob grew silent and stepped away from him. The twelve turned outward in a protective circle, glowering at the multitude. Somewhere at the back of the crowd a baby cried.

Yeshua asked, "Who touched me?"

Shi'mon glared at his leader in astonishment. "What do you mean, Rabbi? Who touched you? Look at all these people. Everyone is touching you. And you want to know who touched you?"

"Someone touched me," Yeshua insisted.

Ya'ir, frantic, said. "Teacher, can we go on now?"

Yeshua persisted. "Someone touched me. I felt power go out from me." He earnestly searched the faces of those around him. At first everyone denied it, including those Marcus had seen touch him. "Tell me." At last Yeshua leveled his gaze on a thin, pale woman of about forty.

At his word she burst into tears and fell to the ground. "I'm sorry, Rabbi! I came behind you. I knew if I could touch the fringe of your cloak I'd be healed. I didn't think you would know! Twelve years I have been bleeding. . . ."

Miryam whispered, "Oh, no! Marcus! Such an illness means she's unclean. Outcast. She can never go to synagogue. Not allowed to touch anyone. Since she's come in contact with Yeshua, the law says he's unclean for twenty-four hours. See how everyone moves back from her. That's why she was afraid to come openly to him. He can't go to Deborah now."

It was one way of breaking up the crowd, Marcus noted, as men and women scrambled back from the scene.

The woman continued, "Sir, I had nowhere else to go."

Beads of sweat popped out on Ya'ir's face. He mopped his brow. "We have no one else to turn to. . . ."

"The doctors took my money and I still got worse!" the woman explained. "When I had nothing left, they said I was incurable. Twelve years I've been dying. . . ."

Ya'ir covered his face in frustration. "Twelve years of life . . . that's all Deborah had. She hasn't yet tasted life."

The woman cried, "Twelve years of darkness . . ."

Ya'ir murmured, "Twelve years of light coming to an end."

"Twelve years without hope!"

Ya'ir's worry tumbled out. "She's been my one hope. For me and her mother."

"No future . . . ," the woman begged.

"We have no future but our little girl's life . . . ," Ya'ir pleaded.

"I had nothing left to lose," the woman cried.

"I have everything to lose," Ya'ir whispered.

"And then I touched your cloak." The woman sat in the dust. "I knew at once . . . I'm well!"

Satisfied, Yeshua took her hand with no show of reluctance and lifted her to her feet. "Daughter, your faith has healed you. Return to your life in *shalom*."

But it was too late for Deborah.

Marcus spotted the grim faces of El'azar and Nakdimon pressing through the mob. The two men entered the circle. There was an instant of unspoken comprehension. El'azar, as kinsman, took Ya'ir by the shoulder.

Miryam said softly, "Oh. Blessed *Adonai*. No. It can't be."

But it was so. Written on the faces of the messengers was Deborah's death.

Ya'ir shook his head in vigorous denial before the words were expressed.

El'azar said, "Come home, Ya'ir. Don't bother the Rabbi any longer. She's dead."

Yeshua stepped between El'azar and Ya'ir. Placing a hand on Ya'ir's trembling arm, Yeshua told him, "Ya'ir. Live up to your name: Fear *Adonai*, but nothing else. Stand in awe. Stop *being* afraid. Just believe, and your daughter will be healed."

There was a moment when Marcus saw fear and faith struggle for the heart of Ya'ir. The cantor put his hand to his chest, as though the pain was too great to bear. He stared hard at Marcus. Questioning. Memory of Carta's healing passed between the two men.

*Believe! What have you got to lose?*

Marcus nodded.

With that, Yeshua commanded the crowd to disperse.

There had been enough excitement for the day, Marcus thought. And now great hopes were ending in sorrow.

Yeshua chose three of his talmidim, Shi'mon, Ya'acov, and John, to go with him and Ya'ir to the house.

Eyes to the ground, El'azar, Nakdimon, Marcus, Miryam, and a handful of others trailed along after.

■ ■ ■ ■

Emet, huddled into a ball hunched against a post, held Yediyd cupped in his hand. Over and over the boy stroked the sparrow's head with one finger.

Did Emet fully comprehend what had happened, Avel wondered? Emet could not hear the violent cries of grief.

Lucky Emet.

Hayyim's funeral had been so silent, so without any display of emotion. *He's dead and that's that.* There had been nothing like this noisy demonstration. Was grief more real or felt more deeply if it was loud?

To the discordant howling was added another note: the squealing of flutes. In a minor key the pipes added a further layer of melancholy certainty to the anguish.

Ha-or Tov buried his face in his arms and rocked back and forth. The braid Deborah had woven in his red hair had come loose. "I wish it would stop," he moaned. "I wish they'd go away."

Instead the clamor grew as word of the girl's death drew more and more mourners to the small house.

How long had it been since El'azar and Nakdimon had gone to find her father? It came to Avel that maybe they would have to carry Ya'ir back home on a stretcher. The man would not live long now that Deborah was gone. Grief would carry him away.

Avel pitied Deborah's mother, too. He thought of Elizabeth and Deborah singing as they wove the red, tan, and blue fabric. Just to see them laughing and talking had made him happy, almost as though he had a sister, a mother, and father. He had let himself imagine he was part of a real family.

Who could take Deborah's place at the loom? Who would finish Yeshua's cloak?

The din of hysteria increased outside in the yard.

Over it Avel heard someone yell, "Look! It's Yeshua! He's with Ya'ir!"

What good could his arrival do? Would he say comforting words to Deborah's parents? Tell them Deborah had gone to a better place?

"I'm going to see," Avel announced. This time Ha-or Tov did not try to stop him.

Into the loft and out into the branches of the sycamore.

From his perch Avel saw both Deborah's window and the front of the house, with all the commotion, flute players, and yowling mourners veiled in black.

Inside the bedroom there was calm, deliberate motion. Avel saw figures circulating purposefully. Deborah's mother. Marta, weeping profusely. A few others beating their breasts slowly and raising their tear-streaked faces in agony.

And Deborah. As white as the dress she wore. Oblivious to all of it.

The contrast hit Avel strangely. Dead was indeed dead. The dead required certain services. Yammering cries did not bring them back; they merely punctuated the sequence of time. The keening made a statement: an empty spot now existed that could never be refilled. Perhaps the shouts reminded the living that they were alive, even though they might wish to follow after the dead.

From the direction of the lakeshore Avel saw figures approaching. Yeshua, striding purposefully, holding the elbow of Deborah's father.

Beside them were a pair of men. Avel recognized them as Deborah's relative, El'azar of Bethany, and Nakdimon ben Gurion from Jerusalem. Next were a trio of Yeshua's talmidim. They were not happy to be following Yeshua to this place of grief.

Further back a man and a woman approached together. Avel recognized the man as the Roman who had given him and Emet two silver coins the morning they left Jerusalem. What was he doing here?

Yeshua passed through the crowd of professional mourners. At the sight of such a celebrity the actors threw themselves more boisterously into their roles.

The Rabbi's jaw was set. Anger simmered in his brooding eyes. When he spoke, his voice was controlled, but it was plain he did not like the display. "Why are you howling?"

At his fierce glare of disapproval some among the mourners backed away. He held each person in his gaze. The pipes groaned to uncomfortable silence. At last only one hysterical woman foamed at the mouth and writhed on the ground.

She was extremely good at mourning, Avel thought.

Yeshua towered over her. "Enough."

She stopped mid-cry and sat up. "But sir," the woman protested, "we've already been paid. Marta of Bethany . . ."

Yeshua said, "The child isn't dead. She's sleeping."

Deborah's father's face displayed confusion. Yeshua's three talmidim exchanged uneasy glances.

The Roman touched the fingers of the woman he walked with and bowed his head.

Avel stared through the window at Deborah.

White. Unmoving. Dead.

No. This was not sleep.

Avel saw the women inside the bedroom turn and face the front of the house, wondering why such utter silence had fallen.

And then it began. A jeer from the back of the crowd outside.

"What? What did he say? Sleeping?"

A twittering of mocking laughter followed.

The excellent mourner rose to her knees and threw a handful of dust at Yeshua. She spat. "You defile the dead! You mock the family! Sleeping! Sleeping, he says!"

Others began to heckle Yeshua.

One of his talmidim wiped his mouth with the back of his hand and peered around in embarrassment.

"She's . . . what?"

"Sleeping!"

The exclamation of disbelief was repeated over and over by the troupe.

The laughter grew more ugly with scorn.

With a voice almost inaudible Yeshua commanded, "Leave this house!" Surprisingly his words echoed back from the lake like distant thunder.

The paid mourners gazed fearfully at Ya'ir. Deborah's father bit his lip and nodded once.

Silenced by Yeshua's word, the lamenters backed away from the entry.

Yeshua watched them go. He stood to one side as the dwelling cleared of people. Then he uttered a couple of words to his companions and entered the home with Ya'ir and his three talmidim.

Nakdimon, El'azar, the Roman, and the woman remained outside.

Yeshua disappeared momentarily from Avel's view, then reappeared in Deborah's bedroom.

Yes. Yes. His eyes brimmed with compassion as he glimpsed the dead body of the girl.

Ya'ir flung back his head in anguish as he saw his daughter dead. He clung to his wife.

Deborah's mother, drained, sagged into his arms.

Yeshua turned to them. Gently he touched the cheek of the girl's mother in reassurance. He put a hand on Ya'ir's shoulder. The gesture called for him to have courage. Yeshua said something meant for the ears of the parents. Avel thought he heard Yeshua say "asleep" and "believe."

Marta bustled to him. Her eyes flashed with resentment. Indignant, she challenged Yeshua.

Yeshua ignored her ranting. His gaze was riveted on Deborah. He waved Marta away, as though she was a persistent fly. The largest of the three talmidim grasped Marta by the shoulder and escorted her away. With a little nudge, he pushed her out and closed the door in her face.

And then they stood alone in the room with death.

Yeshua stepped between Deborah and her parents.

Leaning over the girl, he tenderly searched her ashen face. He smoothed back a lock of her hair from her brow. He smiled softly, like a father smiles at his slumbering child. Then, glancing up for an instant, he looked out the window, directly into Avel's face. Dark eyes, deep and soothing, were like a comforting hand on Avel's cheek. Yeshua did not disapprove that one mourner remained. He understood why Avel had climbed the tree to say good-bye to her. Nor did he give away Avel's presence to the rest.

But what did he mean? Asleep? Avel had seen Deborah gasp her last breath. He had watched her limbs shudder as her soul tore itself free from her body!

Yeshua turned toward the bed. Even though touching a dead body would defile him, he reached out toward Deborah's colorless hand lying atop the cover. He cradled limp fingers in his strong, callused palm.

And then, bending close to her ear, he spoke to her.

What did he say? Just a whisper! So quiet. Avel could not hear his voice. Did he say good-bye? What? What?

Ya'ir choked out a sob and stepped toward his child . . . hoping.

Avel shivered.

Deborah did not move.

Elizabeth buried her face in her hands and wept.

Too late. Too late.

The three talmidim shifted uneasily and turned away.

Deborah did not breathe.

Avel shook his head sadly.

White. Still and white. No color on her cheek.

Yeshua hovered over her, his eyes waiting for a sign. His full lips curved slightly in a smile.

A breath?

The fluttering of an eyelash?

What was it? Avel cried out as Deborah's arm unfolded and reached upward toward the ceiling. She spread her fingers, stretching, as though she had been asleep a long time.

Opening her eyes, she said after a lengthy moment, "*Shalom*, Lord."

Yeshua nodded once, satisfied. Not surprised. "*Shalom*, Deborah."

Avel heard them speak! Both of them! He rocked forward, lost his balance, and almost fell from the limb.

The girl yawned.

Her mother gasped and slumped into Ya'ir's arms.

Deborah did not appear alarmed at the presence of the strangers in her room. She got up. Swung her legs over the side of the bed. Stood and walked toward the window.

Though Avel felt like cheering, he saw that all the adults in the room were openmouthed with astonishment.

Save one: Yeshua.

Eyes bright, amused, face radiant, Deborah leaned against the sill and grinned at Avel. She raised her eyebrows questioningly. What was he doing in the tree? Spying through the window?

He blinked at her stupidly and began to creep away before he was seen.

Sleeping? No.

Dead? Yes.

Alive again? How?

Had Yeshua not said, even if someone returned from the dead, no one would believe?

Yeshua was right! No one would believe this!

Avel scrambled down the tree and back into the barn. Trembling all over, not trusting what he had witnessed with his own eyes, Avel huddled between Ha-or Tov and Emet and the little sparrow.

They were fast asleep. The bird made a nest in Ha-or Tov's tangled locks.

Asleep. Yes. There was a difference. Yes. Avel knew the difference. Only a fool could not tell the difference.

# VE-NAKEH

Had there ever been such a meal prepared for one young girl?
Her father bellowed exuberantly, "'Feed her,' he said to Elizabeth and me! As plain as that. Like she was coming home from a journey! 'Feed her!'" Ya'ir laughed as he turned the meat on the spit. "'Go fix her something to eat!'"

Neighbors came; first at the shouts of jubilation from the little house. Strangers came when they heard the news that something extraordinary had happened in the house of Ya'ir, the cantor of Capernaum.

A flock of chickens was put on the grill. Then the lamb reserved for Passover was butchered. Then a second lamb was butchered. The air was permeated with the aroma of roasting meat and tangy wood smoke. Everyone brought food for everyone else. So much to eat. So much to think about. Hungry eyes could not get their fill of staring at the girl who worked at her mother's side ladling out supper. Such a feast!

Look!

There she is!

Look, look at her!

There was music. Dancing!

Wine flowed abundantly!

But Yeshua was not here to share in the meal. He had slipped away before anyone realized.

The yard was crowded with people who wanted to see for themselves that *she* was alive!

And the question was: but had she actually been dead?

Miryam Magdalen, former courtesan, joined the neighbors who had come to help in the celebration. She plucked chickens as though she was born a servant. But she would not speak about what had just happened.

Then there was Miryam's spinster sister, Marta of Bethany. Humbled and chastised, tearful from the unspoken rebuke of Yeshua's incredible deed, she replied with quavering voice, "Yes! Yes, she was! I washed the body myself. Oh! Don't ask me more! No! Don't ask! I don't know! Something happened! Yes! He did! Don't ask me! I can't think about it! I can't! Terrifying! No more! I can't!"

Their younger brother, El'azar, pale and wide-eyed by the event, stood amidst the guests with his food untouched. He could not eat. His mouth was half-open, expression glazed. His bitter skepticism about the Teacher had been irrevocably shattered. *Could it be true*, his demeanor seemed to ask? *Well, yes . . . obviously. It was true, wasn't it? A wondrous power was at work in Yeshua.* To the probing of others El'azar replied quietly, distractedly, "No. I didn't see it . . . I was outside . . . he told everyone to stop wailing . . . Yes. Yes. Drove everyone out but her mother and father. Also three of his talmidim. No . . . mere minutes . . . No . . . I didn't hear what he said to her. And then he left. Said to us . . . to me . . . to all of us . . . no one should talk about this and he . . . just left."

Marcus, outside the familiarity of the gathering, observed everything from the stone wall of the sheep pen. Miryam carried a heaping plate to him. They had not spoken more than a few words in hours.

She seemed . . . what? Was there a way to describe Miryam Magdalen that afternoon? He tried on a host of adjectives and could say only that she was not surprised by the joy. Not surprised by the miracle. Perhaps no one else would have believed that a day begun with such wrenching grief could culminate in celebration. But Miryam believed. She was at peace with it, as if it was a natural and expected part of being near Yeshua.

Marcus finished eating and licked his fingers. A tribe of half-naked children played tag under the almond tree. He envied them the shade. The sun was high. The day was hot.

Marcus broached the subject with Miryam at last. "'Don't tell anyone about this,' he said."

Miryam brushed back a lock of her hair. "You understand why."

"Impossible." Marcus tore off bread and threw it to the remaining fowl. One rooster and two hens. They rushed in to snatch it up. "Did he think they could possibly keep this quiet?"

Miryam did not reply. She would obey Yeshua's impossible command and keep her mouth shut.

Don't speak about this? Had Marcus heard Yeshua's instruction clearly? Not talk about someone brought back to life? How could the child's father and mother not talk about it? Did Yeshua think the neighbors wouldn't notice?

Here was the result of his command to secrecy! A feast! A celebration!

The residents of Capernaum would break if they couldn't replay the day and the moment over and over again, each time asking: did it really happen that way?

Once again Marcus was struck by how different Yeshua of Nazareth was from anyone he had ever encountered. Unlike the gods and demigods of Greek and Roman mythology, there was no desire for fame in him. No striving. No hunger for public acclaim or wealth. Indeed, here was the stuff from which legends were born and stars were named and worshiped!

Yet Yeshua was no mythic deity! The miracles were real, not the product of human fantasy. He was flesh and blood. By every appearance he was an ordinary man.

But no one had the power to restore life unless . . . unless what?

Marcus thought he understood Yeshua's request for silence in this matter. If Herod Antipas, Caiaphas, and the rest were already disturbed by Yeshua's teaching . . . if they were apprehensive about his popularity . . . what would they do if it was said Yeshua could raise the dead?

The tetrarch's thoughts would leap to one recently murdered: Yeshua's cousin, Yochanan the Baptizer. If Yeshua did indeed have power even over death, what hope did Herod Antipas have to stand against him?

To this thought Marcus added another: if Yeshua had the authority to call back the human soul to its earthly habitation, could he not also conquer kings and kingdoms? Topple empires? Bring mighty armies down to the dust with one word?

Marcus quaked inside with cold terror at what had transpired inside that ordinary little house. He longed to understand. His mind shouted questions at him that he could never answer on his own.

Months before, Marcus had acknowledged the Teacher as someone extraordinary, someone who transcended earthly experience.

But who was he? What was he?

One did not approach such incredible force lightly. To approach Caesar without invitation could mean instant death. Ceasar believed himself to be divinity in human form. And no one had ever held a banquet honoring the ruler of Rome for raising a dead child back to life! Tiberius and his predecessors rose to their positions because they were skilled at ending human life. Their enemies were promptly dispatched.

Yeshua, on the other hand, spoke of life. Abundant life. God's love nourishing the human heart with peace and joy.

Unlike the kings and rulers of the world, Yeshua was approachable. He welcomed people to himself. How many times had Marcus seen him cradle a child in his arms? His kindness drew the hurting and needy to him like a bright light in the darkness.

And what darkness there was in the world! How in need of light was the human heart!

Like the experienced soldier he was, Marcus knew he must gather more information. Scout the territory. Talk to someone close to the truth.

Marcus exhaled loudly. "Miryam? You've followed him for six months . . ."

Laying a finger on his lips, she urged him to silence. "No. Not me. Don't ask me. I follow from my heart. I see what he does. I'm amazed by what he can do. But I don't ask how. Or why. I just believe him and . . . I'm happy. You need answers to satisfy your head." She indicated Nakdimon. "There's the place to start."

Marcus followed her gaze to Nakdimon, who stood soberly apart from the celebration and simply watched. "Him?"

"He's on the same quest. Nakdimon ben Gurion, an elder of my people. A fair man, from what I know. Nephew and student of Gamaliel. Not here to challenge or oppose. Maybe to learn? Like you, but for different reasons. Ask him."

Marcus did not need to seek out Nakdimon. A minute later Nakdimon and Miryam's brother, El'azar, approached Marcus and Miryam.

"*Shalom,*" Nakdimon addressed Marcus without hesitation. "El'azar tells me you are the Samaritan of Yeshua's parable. And the fellow who saved my life?"

Marcus replied, "Roman. But . . . yes . . . we've met. I thought you were a leather worker."

Nakdimon countered, "Would you have helped me if you'd known the truth?"

"Truth. A rare commodity these days."

"That's why we're here, isn't it?" Nakdimon asked. "To seek it?"

"To find it," Marcus replied.

Nakdimon addressed Miryam. "You know Yeshua. There are two others besides your brother and me who have come looking for the Teacher. They have important news for him, they say." He jerked his thumb toward two men Marcus recognized as the followers of Yochanan the Baptizer. Philip and Avram stood in animated conversation with Ya'ir.

El'azar blurted, "Miryam! I need to . . . I must have a word with Yeshua!"

Between Miryam and her brother there had been an awkward silence, as though he could not bear to look at her. And she had no way to break through his reserve until now.

"I know of a place . . . he goes there sometimes," Miryam volunteered. "Tonight then?"

■ ■ ■ ■

It was late afternoon. Ha-or Tov and Emet were asleep.

It had been an eventful couple of days. Escaping from bar Abba and Kittim, hiding in the barn, Deborah dying, but somehow alive again.

Boats on the lake in last night's storm were not tossed around as much as Avel's emotions. Fear, grief, astonishment, relief: too much.

Too much.

Avel could not take it all in, and he was exhausted.

There would be no difficulty sleeping, now that things were quiet around Ya'ir's household. The constant stream of wide-eyed visitors anxious to get a glimpse of Deborah had finally slowed to a trickle.

All day Avel had hoped Deborah would sneak away to the barn. But she had not come. How could she? Every eye followed her wherever she went.

At sunset Avel ventured out of the barn.

*Give her something to eat,* Yeshua had said. That commonplace utterance rapidly circulated around Capernaum and spread beyond the little town into the countryside.

Consequently, everyone who came to Ya'ir's home brought food as an acknowledgment of the miracle. It was as if by responding to Yeshua's instruction, everyone in the community could share in the blessing.

Avel wondered how many of the dishes had been prepared for the bereaved family before the news of her restoration to life. Did Deborah realize she was participating in a supper that everyone expected would be after her funeral?

So many clay cook pots arrived that there was no room for them around Ya'ir's hearth. The extra donations were placed on a low shelf around the side of the house from the front door.

Avel slipped out and returned with a kettle of stew, a bundle of dried fish, and an armload of bread.

But food and emotion had done their work. Rest was a requirement. Avel had volunteered to keep watch, but his eyelids were drooping. Besides, the presence of the boys in the barn remained unsuspected.

Bar Abba and his band were certainly far away. Whomever they might threaten, it no longer affected the Sparrow company.

Avel knew sleep was overtaking him, but he let it come. He drifted off thinking about what Deborah suggested about Yeshua.

Yeshua could heal Ha-or Tov's eyes; could make Emet hear and speak!

Could Yeshua also do something about the lonely ache in Avel's chest?

A man who could raise the dead was capable of anything! Anything! How Avel longed to serve him as a way to thank him for Deborah. Avel brooded on it. To receive a proper acknowledgment, Yeshua would have to go to Jerusalem. Maybe soon. Especially with Passover near. Maybe bar Abba's plan would come true. Yeshua would lead them as king and general! He would stand up and denounce the leaders for their misuse of the Korban funds. There would be a holy war! If the Roman army killed rebel soldiers, Yeshua would raise them to life again! All except Kittim. Against such a force the Romans would not have a chance!

And as for Yeshua? Maybe when he came to Jerusalem he would need a guide to the city. A torch to lead him through the night. Perhaps he would give Avel that duty. Link boy to a king!

If only there was a way around the presence of Judas.

Tomorrow.

Avel would consider the problem properly tomorrow.

He dozed off.

■ ■ ■ ■

Something poked Avel in the ribs, interrupting his dreamless sleep. Must have rolled over on the handle of a rake. Grimacing in his sleep, he pushed it away.

It poked him again, harder. Avel moved his hand just in time to prevent a sandaled foot from kicking his side a third time.

"Get up!" Kittim hissed. "And keep quiet. Dan has a knife on your blind friend's neck. It doesn't matter to me, but don't try to run or he's dead. Let's go."

Ha-or Tov, suspended from Dan's hand by his hair, worked his mouth in horror. Marbled eyes gaped wide at nothing. Little Emet, protecting Yediyd, cowered beside a feed trough.

Kittim's savage eyes turned on Emet and the bird. He sucked his teeth, sneered, and sauntered toward the mute child.

Emet, covering the sparrow with his hand, crouched lower.

"Leave him alone!" Avel sprang to his feet in an attempt to draw Kittim's wrath from Emet.

But this time Kittim's malevolence would not be diverted. He spat on Emet, then snatched him up by the scruff of his neck. Laughing, Kittim shook him like a rag doll. Yediyd tumbled loose from Emet's protection and fell, cheeping, to the floor of the barn.

Avel scrambled to retrieve the bird but Kittim stopped him with a hard blow to the stomach. Hitting a post, Avel fought to breathe.

"What's this?" Kittim held Emet facedown, almost within reach of Yediyd. The tiny bird flapped uselessly. "Looks like we've shaken loose a cockroach. A cockroach with feathers!" Kittim nudged the quaking sparrow with his toe. "Yediyd you named him? This is your beloved friend?" He laughed again, then said to Avel, "Hey, Avel . . . remember what the horse did to your friend? To Hayyim?" He snorted and whinnied. He raised his foot over Yediyd. . . .

"NO!" Avel managed to shout. He attempted to thrust himself against Kittim's legs.

Too late! Too late! Kittim struck full force, crushing Yediyd's frail body.

■ ■ ■ ■

Wildflowers decorated the late evening hills. Orange poppies and pools of bobbing blues. Avel turned his head to watch as boys played with wooden swords behind little houses along the way. He envied them their mothers who shouted their names and called them into supper from pretend wars.

Their feet carried them home along familiar paths. Maybe they hated the plainness of their lives. They resented fathers telling them to feed the livestock. Sisters who made them carry in the wash. Mothers who required they bathe on Friday afternoon for Sabbath.

Yes. Avel envied them their plain lives. Envied them nights camping on the roof of their father's house when they talked longingly about adventures.

They didn't know how lucky they were.

Did it matter anymore what path Avel walked? Where it led? Who he was with? Did anyone care?

The weight of hopelessness settled on his heart. Ha-or Tov, still blind, stumbled along at the point of Kittman's blade. The blood of tiny Yediyd was on Kittim's shoe.

Just a bird. Only a sparrow. Yediyd.

But hadn't Yeshua seen him? Hadn't Yeshua laughed with pleasure at Yediyd's chirping in the synagogue? Hadn't he called him "Beloved Friend"? Hadn't he taught the whole world something important about little birds and poor boys and God's love that day? That God sees when a sparrow falls?

Yet Yediyd was crushed. Broken bones and feathers in disarray. Abandoned in Deborah's barn to be dragged away and eaten by a cat.

Such was the inevitable result of loving.

Emet's downcast face reflected his misery. The mute child clutched at his heart where he had carried Yediyd on their pilgrimage.

Avel took the blame for everything. He was certain this grief was his fault. He had gone searching for freedom. Ready to fight Romans for it if he could. Instead he was a captive of assassins and devils who took delight in the feel of crunching bones beneath their feet.

He had failed his friends. Ha-or Tov still could not see the flowers blooming over there. Emet could not hear the voices of mothers calling sons to come home for supper.

And as for Avel himself? Each tantalizing glimmer of hope he glimpsed made the darkness that much darker.

They passed the white milestones marking the distance from Jerusalem. Was he better off here than when he perched on Cripple Rock in the quarry yard and shivered in the rain? Was he less afraid than when old Sekhel Tov had crawled beneath the rim of the stone and asked him how a boy could be named Mourner?

Maybe now Avel could give the old man a better answer.

He thought the reason was his mother at first. Then Hayyim. After that it was everything else. Ha-or Tov's shining red hair that he would never see. The chirping of Yediyd, which Emet never heard. And then Yediyd beneath Kittim's foot. Everything connected. Each day heartache came in a different disguise.

Avel knew why his name must always remain Avel lo-Ahavah. It was just the way of things. What could a Jerusalem Sparrow expect? He had been stupid to think he could find . . . whatever it was he thought he longed for.

Avel's heart had cracked, and his last hopes spilled out. He was the Mourner because . . .

His mother. Hayyim. Yediyd. All the wide lonely world.

Joy was just grief waiting to grow up.

# VE-AHAVTA

It was an odd assortment of five men who followed Miryam through the darkness and up the grassy slope into a canyon heading north from Capernaum.

El'azar of Bethany, former skeptic and enemy of Yeshua, was first at the heels of his sister. Contrite and seeking guidance from the Teacher, he had spoken little since the events of the morning.

Behind him came Nakdimon. As a Pharisee and member of the Sanhedrin, his journey to speak with Yeshua was no longer hostile, yet there were still questions to be answered.

Third and fourth in line were Philip and Avram, talmidim of Yochanan the Baptizer. They carried with them dreadful news and a warning of personal danger.

Guarding the rear was Marcus Longinus. His sword was drawn against the possibility of attack. But by whom? Possibly bar Abba's faction, seeking to take Yeshua by force and make him king of the rebellion? By the soldiers of Herod Antipas? Or a troop of Praetorian guard under Vara's command?

The night was rank with danger. By his demonstration of power and mercy to the family of an obscure synagogue official in Capernaum, Yeshua had raised the stakes of the political game.

Yeshua often withdrew to a quiet place. The hidden glade to which Miryam directed their steps was one the Teacher sometimes used.

The night was dark; the moon not yet risen. The heavens were lit with a myriad of stars.

Nakdimon studied the constellations. Aryeh, the lion, had clawed his way farther west than on his last observation, but this sky was still unlike the one depicted on the Temple's curtain. Nakdimon thought about the promised messiah as the Lion of Judah, but could make no connection between kindly Yeshua and a kingly rampant lion.

The toe of his sandal caught on the projecting root of a venerable olive tree. Nakdimon grabbed a branch to steady himself. Best pay attention to the path and leave off stargazing for another time.

He murmured a word of warning to those who came up the trail behind him.

Nakdimon considered the change in Miryam's brother. Witnessing Deborah's death and restoration to life had made an enormous difference in El'azar. He was not the same arrogant, opinionated, grasping individual who had come to the Galil with Nakdimon.

Nakdimon fully understood the alteration. He, too, had moved from suspicion to ambiguity and on to the belief that Yeshua possessed extraordinary abilities.

Who was Yeshua? What gave him the right to speak as he did? Where did his power come from?

Many men appeared in Israel, claiming to be anointed by the Almighty. Some raised armies of followers whom they led to destruction. Not one of them caused any lasting transformation of men or governments.

Famous teachers existed in Israel: profound thinkers, able to explain Torah and unravel knotty problems in the Law. Nakdimon's uncle Gamaliel was accounted one of the best of these expositors.

But Yeshua was not like any of them either. He had never been formally educated, yet his public speeches reflected wisdom.

Expert scribes, when discussing points of Torah, always carefully presented their interpretations of Scripture like two sides of a coin. *"So-and-so thinks this . . . on the other hand . . . the meaning could be something entirely opposite."*

Yeshua delivered his views as correct and indisputable. He cited Moses, the prophets, and the Almighty as his corroborating authorities. Never hedging answers, he was totally unintimidated when challenged. Nakdimon had never heard any teacher so skilled at quoting Scripture accurately and in its entirety.

The time had come for Nakdimon to confront him face-to-face. But how did one approach a man who could make death relinquish its grip? Where could Nakdimon begin?

In its capacity as the high court of Israel, the Sanhedrin could summon people, compel them to give testimony or explain their actions. Many of the council's members adopted such tones of authority as their own.

But one who could breathe life back into a heap of clay would not be impressed with Nakdimon's credentials.

Nakdimon wondered if Yeshua would speak to him at all. Miryam reported that everyone who approached Yeshua with a true desire to learn was treated kindly, but Nakdimon had doubts about his own reception. After all, other Pharisees were the most outspoken critics of Yeshua as a fraud and a troublemaker. Moreover, Yeshua would see this nocturnal visit for what it truly was: an attempt to keep others from knowing about his interest. If the mob got wind of it, rumors would fly over the country that a member of the Sanhedrin was one of the Rabbi's talmidim.

The orange glow of a campfire winked through the branches from up the slope.

The six travelers were confronted by two burly Galileans whom Nakdimon recognized as the fishermen Shi'mon and John. The men stood in a posture of defense until they saw Miryam; then they relaxed. Miryam explained why they had come, then asked if the master was asleep.

"He never sleeps," Shi'mon growled. Then consternation flooded his face and he grinned sheepishly at John. "Except on boats in storms." Shi'mon shook his shaggy head as if to clear it of a disturbing vision. "He's beyond the camp, beside a big rock there." The fisherman pointed.

Marcus Longinus remained outside the encampment, Nakdimon noticed. So the "good Samaritan" of Yeshua's parable continued to watch out for those who actively hated him. Of everyone there tonight Marcus was, Nakdimon thought, the most unusual performer in this long drama of Israel.

"We'll wait for you," Miryam suggested to Nakdimon. It was a matter of respect for his office that placed Nakdimon at the front of those who had come to see Yeshua.

Miriam and the others warmed themselves by the fire. The undertone of their conversation followed Nakdimon into the shadows.

Nakdimon entered a clearing overhung with the interlaced branches of two oaks.

Yeshua rose at Nakdimon's approach. "*Shalom*," he said. "I'm glad you've come." Somehow Nakdimon did not doubt that the rabbi had known he was coming. Yeshua indicated a patch of ground and invited Nakdimon to sit with him.

Nakdimon sank down against the boulder. Inhaling deeply the sharp aromas of sage and wood smoke, he launched in without preamble. "You know who I am. And why I've come."

Yeshua did not reply. Nakdimon felt the Teacher's gaze upon him, somehow sorting out what was true and what was pretense. No point in dancing around why he had come. Nakdimon might as well speak bluntly.

"Rabbi . . . we know it's from *Adonai Elohim* that you've come as a Teacher. No one can perform the miracles we see you do unless God is with him."

Seconds slid by before Yeshua's reply. "I'll tell you the truth, Nakdimon . . . No one can see the kingdom of God unless he's born again."

In this way Yeshua took the focus off his miracles and put it on the truth of what was in the hearts of mankind. He set the tone of their conversation. It was to be within the dialogue of Teacher to pupil. Question. Argument. Rebuttal. Logic. Debate. How Nakdimon enjoyed such encounters with other scholars!

From the glint in Yeshua's eye, Nakdimon surmised he too enjoyed this method of discourse. Yeshua had honored him by adopting this form of conversation.

And so it began. Lesson one. Nakdimon dared not answer without thought. He considered the statement for a long time.

*Unless a person is born again, he can't see the kingdom of God.*

Deborah, daughter of Ya'ir, had been reborn in a way. One who was dead and brought back into this world was as newborn as a tiny baby because she had a life ahead of her. A second chance to live. Did Yeshua mean you had to die to be reborn? Or was he speaking of a second chance to live?

*Born again?* Nakdimon recalled a feverish dream, one in which Hadassah had said much the same thing.

At last, not comprehending Yeshua's opening words, Nakdimon asked, "How *can* a grown man be born again? Can he go back into his mother's womb and be born a second time?"

Yeshua welcomed the question. "Unless a person is born from the water and from the *Ruach HaKodesh* . . . the Spirit of God . . . he can't enter the kingdom of God. What's born of flesh is flesh; what's born of the spirit is spirit."

Silence.

Then the branches of the old oaks stirred and creaked above their heads. Leaves tapped against leaves in a rushing sound. The old trees seemed somehow alive as they swayed and danced above the meeting. Yeshua smiled, as if knowing Nakdimon's thoughts. "The wind blows wherever it pleases. You hear its sound, but you don't know where it comes from or where it's going. That's how it is with everyone who's been born of the spirit."

Nakdimon understood that Yeshua had made a play on words. Wind and spirit were the same term, *ruach*.

One could watch the wind rustling the leaves of the oaks without actually seeing the wind. The wind was bigger than the tree, just as God's spirit was bigger than a man. The tree did not make the wind. Nor could it hold onto the wind. The wind blew where it pleased, touching every variety of tree from the tall cedars of far distant forests to the olive trees that grew in the hills around Jerusalem. Could Yeshua mean that *Ruach HaKodesh* could stir the hearts of non-Jews?

When the wind came it made the tree dance and rejoice, no matter where it grew or what kind of tree it was. Perhaps in the same way, one could know with a certainty that he had been touched, stirred, and transformed by the *Ruach HaKodesh* . . . the Breath of God.

"How does this happen?" Nakdimon probed, wanting to know more about the workings of heaven.

Now Yeshua's tone grew more serious. "You're an elder of Israel and a scholar of Torah and don't understand? I tell you the truth: we speak what we know. We give evidence of what we've seen. But people don't accept our testimony. I've spoken to you of common, earthly things and you don't believe. How will you believe if I tell you about heavenly things? No one has gone up into heaven . . . except the one who came down from heaven: the Son of Man."

Nakdimon struggled to credit what he had just heard. Leaping to his mind was a passage about the promised messiah from the prophet Dani'el:

*In my vision at night I looked, and there before me was one like a son of man, coming with the clouds of heaven. He approached the Ancient of Days and was led into his presence. He was given authority, glory and sovereign power; all peoples, nations and men of every language worshipped him. His dominion is an everlasting dominion that will not pass away, and his kingdom is one that will never be destroyed.*

By connecting himself with Dani'el's prophecy, Yeshua identified himself as the Holy One of Israel . . . the Messiah! Openly claiming to have come from heaven to earth, he gave testimony to what no man had seen; that he understood from where the spirit came; how it moved and changed the human heart.

Yeshua went on. "Look to the writings of Moses. He wrote about me. Just as Moses lifted up the serpent in the desert, so must the Son of Man be lifted up. Then everyone who trusts in him will have eternal life."

Was he saying the events of ancient days described in Torah were somehow a picture of what was to come when the Messiah appeared to redeem Israel?

Nakdimon's heart was pounding. He tried to analyze what he had heard. Yes. The story in the scroll of Numbers. When the forefathers of Israel had been wandering in the wilderness, they grumbled and complained and accused God of misleading them. The Almighty then sent poisonous snakes into the camp. Those bitten could only avoid death by looking at the brass model of a snake hanging from a pole in the center of the camp. It was as if by obeying such foolish-sounding instructions the punishment was transferred back to the image of the serpent on the pole.

And the Son of Man, the Messiah, was to be "lifted up" to become such a picture of divine punishment? And those who looked at him and believed were somehow saved?

Yeshua appeared to understand Nakdimon's confusion and anxiety for he said kindly, "Here's how to make sense of it: God so loves the world . . . so loves you . . . that He gave His one and only son so that whoever believes in Him won't die, but have eternal life. God didn't send His son into the world to condemn it, but to save the world through him. Whoever believes isn't condemned. But whoever doesn't believe stands condemned already, because he hasn't believed in the name of God's one and only son."

The words of Yeshua resounded in Nakdimon's ears, echoing like ten thousand voices singing from the hillsides and the wadi. Who in history had ever expressed such a thought? That the omnipotent God, Ancient of Days, Lord of all creation, took a special interest in the individual lives of those He created! That He loved mankind so deeply that He sent His son to offer them a new life, a second chance to *live*. . . .

Was Yeshua the messenger? Was he The One? Every word and every deed seemed to prove he was!

*God loves the world.*

*He loves you.*

*He gave His only son for you.*
*Believe in The Name!*
*Yeshua* means "Salvation"!

There was a roaring in Nakdimon's ears like the sound of rushing water, like the blast of a storm surging through the treetops.

A meteor blazed across the sky.

Pointing up toward the glowing streak, Yeshua added, "The court of Israel has come to question me through you. Then here's the verdict: light has come into the world. But people love darkness rather than light because their deeds are evil." His eyes shone as he spoke. "Every person who does evil hates the light. He won't come into the light for fear his deeds will be exposed. But whoever lives by the truth not only comes into the light . . . he seeks the light . . . runs to the light, so everyone will plainly see that what good he's done has been done through God."

"Through . . . God." Nakdimon muttered the words of the *b'rakhah* "Blessed are you, O *Adonai*, Knower of Secrets!"

"Yes." Yeshua smiled.

Was Yeshua saying he was the light? That he came from heaven to live out the truth of how humankind was meant to live? Yes. Of course. Everything Nakdimon had witnessed proved that Yeshua was the fulfillment of the law of love.

*Who is my neighbor . . .*

The challenge had been given.

And Yeshua had declared publicly:

*It is not enough to look pious!*
*Not enough to know the rules and pretend to be holy.*
*Everyone is your neighbor!*
*What will you do with my light? My truth?*
*Forgive those who wrong you!*
*Love your enemy!*

*Next time you pass someone in need and do nothing, how will you justify your apathy in the light and truth of what God requires of you?*

*Next time you destroy someone's life with gossip remember the truth you have turned from!*

*When you tear down your loved ones with anger and wound them with cruel words, remember the light you have rejected by your actions!*

How fiercely hypocrites and liars despised that message!

Nakdimon knew well that evil men feared Yeshua above all because his teaching illuminated the hatred and falseness of their lives, the hypocrisy of their teaching. He knew those same men would attempt to destroy him.

Yeshua had stood up on the Temple Mount and publicly proclaimed he was "the light of the world."

Recognize Yeshua as the light of the world?

Acknowledge him as the son of the Most High? The Messiah? The Holy One of Israel predicted by the prophets?

*Teshuvah!* "Return to the Lord!" Turn away from sins, ask forgiveness, make restitution to those you've wronged and begin life anew?

These were the teachings of Yeshua. Was that what it meant to believe in him and be born again?

Could it be that Nakdimon now was in the presence of the One whom generations had been yearning to see? Was Yeshua of Nazareth the Messiah? The fulfillment of everything written in the *Tanakh*?

Nakdimon considered the prophecy in Dani'el. Another Passover and the years predicted would be complete. Dani'el had said after this the Anointed One would be cut off!

If Yeshua was the Messiah, what did that mean? The one capable of explaining the riddle was Yeshua.

But he had no more to say about such matters.

Yeshua stood. The wind caressed Nakdimon's face.

Thus ended the lesson. Another pupil waited in the shadows to speak to him. There was El'azar, warming himself by the fire.

Nakdimon rose and Yeshua put a hand on his shoulder. "You'll see her again," he said. "In *olam haba* . . . the world to come."

An arrow of longing went straight through Nakdimon's heart. How had Yeshua known his grief and the question that plagued him every day? Nakdimon grasped Yeshua's hands as a passage from the book of Job leapt into his mind. He whispered in gratitude, "My ears had heard of you but now my eyes have seen you!"

It was clear Yeshua knew the Scripture. "You say this because I said, 'You'll see her again'?" he queried. "Nakdimon ben Gurion, you'll see greater things than that. And don't fret because you can't yet acknowledge me openly. A time will come when you'll be my witness in ways you cannot imagine."

The conference was finished. El'azar stepped past Nakdimon and into the presence of the Teacher. Scant minutes passed before the rich young man emerged from the shadows. His face was a mask of sorrow.

He stumbled toward his once-rejected sister, took her hand, and led her toward the edge of the camp. His urgent entreaty drifted in fragments to Nakdimon's ears. *"Miryam! . . . Sister! You've . . . done what he asked . . . rightly. Sell everything and give . . . he said . . . And I? . . . I can't . . . such a coward. Forgive me, Miryam! . . . didn't undertand . . . can't give up everything . . . not like you! Will you come home with me and Marta awhile? Come with us to Bethany? So much to learn. . . ."*

Lastly Philip and Avram, the talmidim of Yochanan the Baptizer, entered the glade. When, finally, they returned to the warmth of the fire, Yeshua was not with them. They waited, but he did not emerge.

Philip stretched his hands to the blaze. After a time he said with resignation, "We've told him everything now. His cousin Yochanan was executed by Herod Antipas. We buried Yochanan ourselves in the land of Elijah. You are his talmidim . . . if you love him, get him out of here tonight! Leave the Galil."

Avram added, "Convince him. Take him out of the territory ruled by Antipas if you want him to live. Go to the territory ruled by Antipas' brother. He may be safe there."

Nakdimon got up. It was time to speak the truth. The danger was not only from Herod Antipas. "Tell Yeshua also . . . Judea isn't safe. Jerusalem is full of plotters who fear him. And hate him. And Galilee is thick with rebels who would use him for their own goals. Yes. These two men are right. Take your master far away for a while or he'll be arrested and murdered like his cousin. And you who follow him will die with him."

■ ■ ■ ■

Afraid to falter or cry out for fear that Kittim's knife would plunge into Ha-or Tov's neck, Avel stumbled through the darkness. It was nearing dawn when they arrived back at the abandoned gethsemane.

Beside the stone oil press Kittim shoved Avel to the ground. "I found them," he announced to bar Abba, Asher, and Dan. "Can I kill them now?"

Death was the price of betrayal. Death could come at any moment, and Yeshua was not nearby to bring them back. They would be dumped in a cave and that would be the end.

"Shut up!" bar Abba said with a scowl. "It's your fault they were lost in the first place. But what about it?" he addressed Avel. "Why shouldn't I let him slit your throats?"

Plucking up his courage Avel said, "It's true we're afraid of Kittim. He wants us dead." He glanced over at where frail Emet, shaking with exhaustion from the forced march, stunned with grief, knelt on the ground. Ha-or Tov wept without tears; his wide mouth was open and gasping.

Avel pleaded, "We did what you said . . . about getting close to Yeshua. Were you inside the synagogue with him? We were. We heard him. And there's more . . . we went with the daughter of the cantor. She got real sick. Yeshua called her soul back to her body! And I saw it happen."

"Gibberish!" Kittim took a menacing step toward Avel.

"What do you mean?" bar Abba demanded. "You mean healed? Was she sick?"

Avel shook his head. "Not just sick . . . dead."

Kittim cuffed the back of Avel's head. "He's making up stories to save his neck."

"It's true," Avel vowed. "If you weren't camped way out here you'd already know. She was dead and he brought her back to life!"

The focus in the rebel camp was no longer on the boys. Asher spoke up. "If this is true . . . even if it isn't, so long as people believe it . . . he'll be king! You saw the crowds: two thousand people . . . maybe more!"

Bar Abba said thoughtfully, "But it has to happen soon. Things are already in motion for Passover."

What about Passover? Avel wondered. What plan had been hatched by bar Abba?

"We must get Yeshua to Jerusalem and proclaim him king!" bar Abba continued. "News of the misuse of the Korban funds is spreading. Timed properly, the whole country will have reason to ignite, and Yeshua is someone they'll listen to."

"And," Dan growled, "since the priests and the Sanhedrin all hate this man already, the mob will slaughter them too."

"Not that we'll leave that to chance," bar Abba corrected. "I've already made the list."

What list? Avel silently questioned. Aloud he said, "I don't think Yeshua wants to be king."

Bar Abba snorted. "Then we'll make him. Where is he?"

When Avel didn't reply, Kittim raised his hand to strike. Bar Abba warned Kittim off. "You're the one who failed, not them. This is valuable information. These boys are of good use to us." He spat at Kittim's feet and cursed him. "From now on, you keep away from them. You spill a drop of their blood and you answer to me! Got that?" Then he shoved Avel toward Asher. "Asher, you take charge. Now, where's Yeshua?"

"I don't know," Avel insisted. "But he won't be hard to find. I heard people talking last evening . . . everybody wants to see the man who can make dead people live again!"

■ ■ ■ ■

The lane outside Miryam's home was deserted the evening following the visit to Yeshua's retreat. Marcus had come to retrieve his horse and then ride on to Caesarea Maritima.

The aroma of star jasmine hung in the air. This time of year it bloomed in fragrant clumps outside her balcony. The sweet scent brought a thousand memories to mind as Marcus knocked on the gate. Images of her in his arms, turbulent and troubled as the sea in a tempest, rose and fell and rose again with a dull roar.

Did she, being someone new, remember how the moonlight danced on the warm water as they swam one summer night? A chorus of ten thousand crickets had sung, and he had whispered the poetry of Propertius against her ear.

> "Your house is blest—if only you have a true friend.
> I will be true: then hasten, girl, to my bed!"

Did she let him come to her in her dreams? Or was dreaming no longer part of her existence?

Lapping the shore of emotion, longing for her washed over him and then receded.

He knocked again. There was a horse to fetch. A journey to make. A report to be given.

The homely, wrinkled face of Tavita appeared as the square peephole in the door snapped open. Sour turned to sweet at the sight of him. She slammed the bolt open and threw back the door. A single lamp flickered inside.

She put a finger to her lips in warning as she greeted him softly. "Ah, bless me! Centurion Marcus! You've come back. Welcome! Welcome! We're caught up on the day. Babies and mothers fed. All asleep except Miryam and a dozen or so of us workers here at the house. Joanna. Aquilla. Carta. They're in the garden resting after a most blessed day! A healthy baby boy arrived this afternoon. And on top of that Miryam's catching us up on the news from Capernaum! And what news! What wonders! Eh?"

"Yes. Wonders," Marcus agreed, aware he must keep his voice low for the sake of new babies and sleeping mothers. He glanced up at the banners of laundry strung like signal flags above the open courtyard.

A baby cried. Women's laughter echoed from the open door leading to the balcony and the garden.

"Come along! Have you eaten?"

"I have. Yes. Thank you. I can't stay. I came for Pavor. I'm expected in Caesarea and . . ."

Miryam entered. "Marcus?"

Tavita declared, "Well, I'll fix you a meal to take along on your journey." She shuffled off, leaving Marcus alone as Miryam hurried to his side.

Miryam treated him like an old friend dropped in for a visit. Or worse, like a relative. She grasped his hands in hers and tugged him toward the balcony. "You've come to collect Pavor? He's gotten fat on my pasture, I'm afraid. Come on out. Say hello to . . ."

He drew back, hating the fact that she could talk to him as if they had never loved one another. "No time. Sorry." His tone was too curt. He did not mean to be short with her. But she had entered his reality grinning and gushing like a sister welcoming a long-lost brother. And at the very instant he had remembered lifting her from the water and making love on the beach.

She did not let go of his hand but stood silently before him. "Marcus?" She uttered his name with such pity. So she knew what he felt. She explained, "I'm going home to Bethany. To be with my brother and sister for Passover. Yeshua and his twelve are coming too. I . . . don't know . . . if you can imagine what it means to me. My family. My brother, El'azar. Marta, my sister. The great Teacher with us. There are still things between Marta and me. Things to talk about. To work out. But Marcus, for the first time in my life . . . I have a family. Can you understand?"

Yes. He did understand. Resentment pushed at him. "No room for . . . what did El'azar call me? A Samaritan?"

"Oh no!" She squeezed his fingers. "He doesn't feel that way anymore! I tell you, Marcus, everything . . . everyone . . . is changing! The world is turned upside down! What I was trying to say . . . I mean . . . El'azar told me before he and Marta left for Bethany . . . he wanted me to invite you to share *seder* with us! At our house. If you would like to come? You would be most welcome."

Taken by surprise by this reversal, Marcus simply blinked down at her. What would she say if he took her in his arms? Kissed her the way he longed to kiss her? Would she slap his face? Order him out? Withdraw the invitation to share a meal with her family and the Teacher?

Marcus stepped back from her and bowed his head curtly. "I am honored. Yes. I am. Thank you. But you must know, Miryam. You and your brother should be aware . . . Jerusalem is a boiling cauldron of politics and revolution. The authorities expect it to spill over during Passover. Now that news about the Baptizer's death is out. And Korban funds are openly being used for Pilate's aqueduct. The common folk are ripe for revolt. We're all sure to be on high alert. I don't know if I can get away."

Was that a flicker of disappointment in her eyes? "Well, then." Her tone was subdued, accepting. "You'll let me . . . us . . . know?"

"I'll send word. And, listen, stay out of Jerusalem during Passover week. There's danger. If Yeshua enters the city and the Temple grounds, I believe it will end in violence. Innocent people could get in the way. There are factions willing to tear down the whole world for the sake of their own ambition. Tell him my concerns, will you?"

"I will," she replied earnestly. "Thank you."

He did not let his gaze meet hers. He felt her eyes searching his face for a sign of what he was feeling.

He dared not reveal his heart to her. The gulf between them had been wide before. Now perhaps it would be wider still. Were they soon to be made unwilling enemies?

He took his leave. Slipping into the pasture, he called Pavor to him with a whistle.

# LE-RE'AKHA

Avel liked Asher, even though he smelled bad. Though strange in many ways, and the only rebel who treated the Sparrows kindly, Asher was absolutely devoted to bar Abba. He was determined to carry out the rebel chief's commands, especially the one putting him in charge of the Sparrow company. He was an unsleeping, impossible-to-elude jailor but also a resolute protector. He did not allow Kittim to bully the boys.

Yet Avel still felt Kittim's eyes on him. In the early morning back on the knoll above Bethsaida, when Asher walked outside the camp, Kittim approached. "Just wait." Kittim lifted the sole of his shoe and slammed it down in a reminder of what he had done to Yediyd. "You're already dead . . . only you don't know it yet."

Emet, witnessing what was happening, led Ha-or Tov to the other side of the olive press.

As Avel shrank away from the expected beating, there was a menacing growl from the matted thicket of bee plant and wild dill on the hillside. The brush trembled. Something was about to attack.

Kittim gasped and leapt away.

Asher lunged, growling, from the undergrowth.

"Sheol, Asher," Kittim said nervously. "You scared me! I thought you were a wild dog!"

Asher's response was to snarl again, moving his head from side-to-side as if selecting which of Kittm's legs to bite first.

Kittim hastily backed away. "I was just . . ." Excuses and lies were of no avail. He swore at Asher.

Asher circled him with a stiff-legged sidle.

Kittim lowered his head and raised his fists warily. Still Asher advanced, circling menacingly. "I'm going," Kittim said, stretching out placating palms. And he did leave, backing away without losing eye contact until fifteen yards separated them. Turning, he strolled back toward Dan.

Just that quickly Asher's role as bloodthirsty carnivore passed and a grin crept across his face. Plopping down on the rim of the oil press beside Avel he said, "He won't bother you." He sniffed. "I smell something . . . dead."

Avel had been smelling the stench of a dead thing for two days. He had assumed it was Asher. But even when Asher was not near, the smell followed them.

Asher crooked a finger at Emet, calling him over. "What have you got in there, boy?" He plucked at Emet's robe. Emet protected his belly the way he used to do when he carried Yediyd around. "Come on. What're you hiding?" He grasped Emet and pulled on a string around Emet's neck. Out of the cloak he withdrew the body of Yediyd! "The . . . bird! He's got a dead bird round his neck!" Asher exclaimed. "Some sort of good-luck charm? Well, boy, no one will come within a mile of you until this thing dries up." At that, Asher strode away.

Ha-or Tov covered his nose and began to weep. Avel covered his face and began to cry at the pitiful sight of their little friend. Nothing but feathers and pulp where life had been.

The grief was renewed.

There was no convincing Emet that Yediyd was past help. That he must be buried. Emet would not give him up. No matter how bad the smell.

■ ■ ■ ■

Later that day rebels summoned from their desert lair arrived at the meeting point in Galilee. Bar Abba's message called for two hundred men and fully that many arrived in fives and tens to gather in the hollow of the gethsemane.

Bar Abba stood on a flat rock up the slope. "You know why I've sent for you! It's time." His voice boomed and echoed on the hills. "Time to give the people a leader they will follow. I've seen him! And heard him. I know how eagerly the people follow him around. Yeshua of Nazareth is the one! I hear he won't agree to be crowned, but how can he refuse if an entire crowd demands it?" The rebel captain explained his plan. "Wherever Yeshua teaches, we'll join the mob! Spread yourselves throughout, in groups of no more than three together. At my signal you will shout 'Yeshua for our king!' Then when the people have joined you begin the chant, 'On to Yerushalayim!' Make it sound as if the whole assembly agrees and soon enough they will. We'll leave here with a thousand men and a king to sit on the throne in Jerusalem, even if we have to force him!"

Avel noted bar Abba's rousing speech without emotion. How pointless it seemed. Bar Abba did not understand that Yeshua of Nazareth could flatten him with a wave of his finger. With a wish and a bat of an eyelash Yeshua could send down fire to consume the rebel chief. Such was the power of Yeshua, Avel knew. Ha-or Tov and Emet believed it too.

And yet sometimes Avel doubted. When he saw the contorted body of little Yediyd, he doubted.

Emet cradled the stinking carcass. The odor permeated his clothes. He still would not give up Yediyd for burial. Avel thought he understood why, so he quit trying to get Yediyd away from him. Emet wept bitterly when Avel signaled the hour was coming when they must bury their little friend.

"What about Deborah?" Ha-or Tov asked.

Avel thought about her. What had happened. "Yes. Just think. If something this tiny smells so bad, I'm glad Yeshua didn't wait long!" Avel replied.

Ha-or Tov's sense of smell was especially keen. The rank odor had even been enough to make Asher comment. And in the whole world no living human stank like Asher.

But Avel's and Ha-or Tov's sense of hope began to grow. They had a chance, didn't they?

"We're going to see Yeshua," Ha-or Tov said. "Maybe to . . . see . . . you know? And Emet to speak and hear. But before I ask him about getting eyes, there's Yediyd . . . why not?"

"Yes," Avel agreed. "Why not?" but he thought of Hayyim moldering beneath a shard of broken pottery in Jerusalem and he knew why not.

■ ■ ■ ■

Marcus reined up beside a public fountain a half mile outside the limits of Caesarea. For the last hour of his journey to the seacoast he had ridden beside the aqueduct that delivered water to that basin on its way to supplying the port city.

While Pavor drank his fill, Marcus plunged his hands into the jet from the mouth of the carved lion head and scrubbed his face and hair. The temperature of the water was cold, bracing. Forty years before, the ambition of King Herod the Great and Roman engineering skill had combined to bring the precious fluid ten miles from its source on Mount Carmel.

There was an object lesson in that mixture. What could resist ruthless ambition mixed with military and technological superiority? The farther from the rustic, backward Galil Marcus traveled, the more he questioned the wider application of Yeshua's teaching. Given the might of Rome and the tempo of Imperial life, how could Yeshua possibly be a threat? Perhaps a more realistic question was: would anyone outside the Galil bother to listen?

This last pause in Marcus' journey was important for him to organize his thoughts before meeting Governor Pilate. The water from the canal was also a pointed reminder of the complexity of Judean politics.

How could anyone object to abundant fresh water? And yet that was precisely at issue with the Jerusalem project.

And the aqueduct was merely one of the thorny problems Governor Pilate faced. Marcus reminded himself that he need only make his report, keeping to the facts. Pilate and others had the burden of acting on them, not Marcus.

He mounted and rode on, entering by the north gate beside the colossal amphitheater, scene of gladiatorial contests. The shining new city was bustling. The road was jammed with merchants and the harbor packed with commercial shipping. Marcus saw a vessel capable of transporting three hundred tons of cargo. Hoisting main and foresails it made toward the open sea. Its capacious shape, the high, gilded prow and the gilt-covered figure of the goddess Fortune at its masthead made the Galilean fishing boats miniscule mud ducks to this giant swan.

Minutes later Marcus arrived at the governor's villa. Because of his dress and beard, Pilate's guards, newly recruited from Cyprus, showed doubt when Marcus announced his identity. He was grateful Dio Felix was available to vouch for him.

"Do I have time to bathe and shave before meeting the governor?" Marcus asked the immaculately uniformed tribune.

"Sorry," Felix replied. "Pilate's already chafing to get your report. He's heard conflicting things from other sources. In fact I had to convince him to wait for your account before acting."

"And doing what?"

Felix raised his eyebrows but lowered his voice. "Vara wants to send troops to the Galil. He's almost convinced Pilate. But here's the governor."

Pilate eyed Marcus' sweat-stained tunic but said nothing. With a curt greeting, he summoned the two officers into his chambers. Marcus was relieved that this time they did not descend into the musty subterranean interrogation vault. It was much more pleasant to remain where the sea breeze mingled with the scent of orange blossoms outside the windows . . . more agreeable and much less ominous.

"I'm glad you've returned at last, Centurion," Pilate remarked. "I was beginning to wonder if you'd gone native altogether."

This witticism was not merely an observation on his appearance. Marcus was certain Praetorian Vara missed no opportunity to remind the governor that Miryam had been Marcus' *Jewish* mistress.

"I'm prepared to make a full report," Marcus suggested.

Pilate waved a hand of approval; it was almost a shrug. The governor's attitude suggested his mind was already made up.

"I've studied both the man, Yeshua of Nazareth, and his teachings," Marcus stated. "There's no sedition in his messages. He speaks of love and kindness, repentance and righteousness. He has never once advocated any treason or violence."

"Oh?" Pilate said skeptically. The single syllable conveyed utter disbelief. "Isn't this the same man who disrupted commerce on the Temple Mount two years ago? Wasn't that the same Passover of the Jerusalem rebellion when the standards of Rome on the Antonia were made into a religious object lesson? Weren't my nostrils blasted with the stench of protestors in my very own courtyard?" Pilate shook his finger toward the plaza.

"Excellency," Marcus corrected, "the man Yeshua of Nazareth was not among those who appeared here. He speaks no treason."

"Doesn't he call himself king?"

"He speaks of the kingdom of God and the kingdom of heaven . . . surely not a threat." There was much Marcus would not say about the miracles of Yeshua.

Pilate said coldly, "I have only met one god in the flesh: Augustus Caesar. And that makes Emperor Tiberius the son of a god, doesn't it? Does this Yeshua suggest he is of higher birth than the emperor?"

This line of reasoning came dangerously near to *maiestas*, the capital crime of attacking the dignity of Rome or her rulers.

Hastily Marcus chose a different tack. "Even if Yeshua were talking of an earthly kingdom, surely he would be a better ruler than Herod Antipas."

"Yes. Antipas, the son of Herod the Great Butcher, as he is called." Pilate stared at Marcus. "Are you suggesting this country preacher might cooperate with us if we installed him in place of Antipas?"

Marcus was trapped. Fearing for Yeshua's life, he said nothing.

Pilate stopped scowling. "Antipas *is* a thorn in my side," he said, sipping his wine thoughtfully. "Always writing critical letters to the emperor, trying to get me recalled. And that after he caused the Purim bread riots in Jerusalem . . . which I'm convinced he did on purpose to make me look bad! I hear he thinks this Yeshua of Nazareth is Yochanan the Baptizer returned from the dead!"

Marcus interjected, "You can easily see the family resemblance. In their smiles and facial features. Strong. Lithe. Hair and eyes as dark as night."

Pilate smiled with pleasure. "Two baptizers! What lovely dreams that must give the pig! We should make this Yeshua a friend of Rome to irritate Antipas!" He stared into his cup. "But still . . . it's been reported to me that known rebels . . . even the notorious bar Abba . . . have been seen in Yeshua's company."

"But not among his followers," Marcus pointed out.

"But you admit you've seen rebels around him? Zealots?"

Marcus knew he'd never get away with lying now, so he merely nodded.

"Men like bar Abba don't care that," Pilate snapped his fingers, "for repentance and righteousness. They're up to something. But what? And is this Yeshua part of it?"

For the fist time in the meeting Felix spoke. "Why not let me return to the Galil with the centurion? One more observation should clear this up. Then we'll know if we're facing trouble on two fronts or just in Jerusalem during the Passover holiday."

"On hearing news of the Baptizer's death, Yeshua withdrew from the public."

"Do you know where he is?" Pilate queried.

"No one seems certain. Bethsaida perhaps. Korizan."

"Can you find him?" Felix asked.

"If he will be found," Marcus replied, feeling he had unintentionally made a dangerous situation even more so for Yeshua.

"Go," Pilate ordered. "At the moment Jerusalem is not your concern. In fact plans are already in place to deal with any trouble there. You may leave, but return within the week."

On exiting Pilate's office, Felix and Marcus encountered Praetorian Vara. The black-uniformed Vara, sporting a recently sprouted beard, smirked at Marcus. His sneer indicated he had not forgotten Miryam or Carta. Or that he took Marcus' threat to kill him as an inevitable invitation to one-on-one combat.

Marcus would welcome that hour.

Emerging into the sunlight, Marcus breathed deeply.

"So." Felix grinned. "Still have plans for Vara's sudden demise, do you?" Felix took Marcus' arm. "He hates you with equal fervor. And for now he has Pilate's ear. Be careful, my friend."

"What about Jerusalem?" Marcus brushed past Felix's warning.

"It's the aqueduct, of course," Felix explained. "Korban money. The Sanhedrin sees the benefit. The common folk are screaming about it. The governor expects protests over it during the Jewish holiday. As for his plans to counter them. . . ." Felix spread his hands. "Praetorian Vara has been in charge of those."

■ ■ ■ ■

Some days later word came to the rebel camp that Yeshua had received news of his cousin Yochanan's death. As a result he had withdrawn for a time to be alone, it was said. Judas left a message for bar Abba in the usual place, but even he could not indicate where the Teacher was going . . . Yeshua had not said.

Yeshua and his closest associates had simply gotten into a boat and sailed off: destination unknown, length of stay unknown.

Avel knew Yeshua's disappearance could not have happened at a worse time for bar Abba's plans. There were barely enough days left to compel Yeshua to accept the kingship and then return to Jerusalem for the critical proclamation and uprising.

Of almost as much concern to the rebel commander was the presence of two hundred of his followers. Mixed with a mob around Yeshua they would be invisible. But as a unit keeping to themselves, such a troupe could not both remain together and unremarked by the authorities. "Scatter!" bar Abba told them. "Find him! Bring me word."

Feeding the rebels was the other mounting problem. There were so many pilgrims wanting to hear Yeshua that the Galil . . . never before a significant destination for outsiders . . . was already running low on provisions. The matter was further complicated by bar Abba's prohibition against theft. Not only did he want to avoid the unwelcome attention of the Roman garrison at Tiberias, he also feared alienating the very *am ha aretz* expected to rally to his cause.

They sold Nakdimon's red donkey and used the little money it brought to buy measly, expensively priced loaves of barley bread. Thereafter the Sparrow company became the pack mules. Avel was pressed into service carrying waterskins; Ha-or Tov carried a sack of bread. Emet, stinking, trailed mutely along behind Asher.

On the third day of searching they received a rumor that Yeshua had been spotted on the northeast shore of the lake. Accordingly bar Abba abandoned the base near Capernaum and led a tramp over the peninsula on which Bethsaida was located.

Once again the gossip proved false. Yeshua had not been seen in Bethsaida, not for some time.

The days drawing near to Passover were getting warmer, the trails dustier. Stops for water grew more frequent.

The next day, as soon as bar Abba decreed a halt for him to consider where to try next, everyone called out to Avel for a drink. Tension, frustration, and hunger combined to make the rebels grumpy. "Hurry up, boy," one insisted, even though Avel would have had to yank the skin bottle away from the present user to move any faster.

"Me next," argued another.

A fight broke out.

Avoiding flying fists, Avel failed to notice that he had come within reach of Kittim. Kittim's out-thrust foot hooked his ankle, and Avel tumbled over a jagged rock. The waterskin cushioned his fall but burst on the sharp edge of the boulder.

Cuffs and curses rained on Avel while Kittim looked on smugly.

"Stop this! Stop it at once!" bar Abba ordered.

Asher lifted Avel to his feet and sent him over to rejoin Emet and Ha-or Tov.

"It's a waste," argued Dan. "Playing children's games chasing the hills, going hungry . . . and for what? What difference can one rabbi make? We should be in Jerusalem, getting ready to cut throats! I say we leave now!"

"And I say *I* give the orders here," bar Abba snapped.

"Maybe that needs to change too," Dan retorted.

Avel could feel the blood heat in the air.

Then Asher crowed like a rooster. A warning someone was coming.

"Yeshua's there," the scout called, panting from his run. He pointed toward the south. "His boat was sighted coming toward shore an hour ago. He may already have landed. Thousands are flocking to him!"

"Hurry!" bar Abba commanded. "So we don't lose him again." Then to Dan he asked, "Are you with us? Taking my orders?"

"Yes," Dan returned. "For now."

# KAMOKHA

Avel had never seen so many people together in one place. Beneath the Golan, between the lakeshore and the looming ridge, the unnamed valley was packed. Thousands had come to see and hear the man who could raise the dead.

Avel thought entire villages must be deserted. He pictured vacant houses, unoccupied shops, abandoned orchards and fields. All the Galil, it seemed, was crammed into this narrow space.

Verdant hillsides previously highlighted in reds and blues by wildflowers now bloomed with robes, headscarves, and sashes. Thickets of crimson, bundles of indigo, masses of amber formed a gigantic patchwork. Family groups, distinguished by the handiwork of each clan's loom, produced gaudy clusters resembling banks of flowers grown enormous in size.

Bar Abba's two hundred were lost in the crowd, random drops in a surging ocean. The rebels no longer worried they would stand out too much, that they would be detected by Roman soldiers or spies. Now bar Abba's concern was that his men were too few to make any difference. Even two hundred voices would have no impact on twenty-five thousand sets of ears!

Avel's hopes and fears grew in proportion to the size of the throng. He knew they could slip away from their keepers. There was no way to track three boys in this swarm.

At the same time he worried about getting close enough to Yeshua to make his requests known.

One other thing nagged Avel's thoughts. The last time he had been in this sort of setting had been in Jerusalem, the day Hayyim died. Hayyim had been young, strong, clever, quick . . . and none of those qualities were enough to keep him alive.

Avel gazed at his friends: blind, small, helpless in most ways.

He shuddered and pressed forward.

■ ■ ■ ■

Marcus and Felix stood on a knoll overlooking the natural amphitheater in the hills. Despite the remoteness of the site—it was not near either Capernaum or Bethsaida, but about equidistant from both—the hollow was blanketed with a living carpet of the needy.

"Near to twenty-five thousand," Felix commented. "Close to five thousand men and the rest women and children. A sizable number for one man, especially in a rustic setting like the Galil."

Felix's comments worried Marcus. To call the gathering "sizable" was a masterpiece of understatement. It was an *enormous* crowd. More than Marcus had seen collected in one place to hear Yeshua speak. More people were gathered here in this wilderness than the population of any Judean city except for Jerusalem and Caesarea.

Would the Roman officer perceive Yeshua's popularity as dangerous? Could such a perception be avoided?

Yeshua's extended teaching in that place reminded Marcus of a classroom: an end-of-term summation given before examination time. In parable after parable, Yeshua reviewed the significant points of his message.

*What's the kingdom of God like? It's like a mustard seed, which a man took and planted in his garden. It grew and became a tree, and the birds of the air perched in its branches.*

The seed of Yeshua's words and deeds had been planted. The tree was now in full leaf in Galilee. The birds perched in its branches.

Felix remarked, "You say this man has no formal education, no training? Yet he sounds like academics I heard in Athens. All of them claim their version of truth is universal."

Marcus was torn in his emotions. If Felix equated Yeshua with the other prating, self-aggrandizing philosophers, then Rome's political response would be a shrug of the official shoulders.

There was safety for Yeshua in that.

But Marcus wanted Felix to listen with his *heart*.

Yeshua continued,

*"A man was preparing a great banquet for his friends. At the time of the banquet he sent his servant to tell those who had been invited, 'Come on. Everything's ready.' But they all made excuses . . .*

"*Then the owner of the house became angry and ordered his servant:* '*Go out into the streets and alleys in the town. Bring in the poor, the crippled, the blind and the lame.*' '*Sir,*' *the servant said,* '*what you ordered has been done, but there's still room.*' *Then the master told his servant,* '*Go out to the roads and country lanes and make them come in, so my house will be full. I tell you, not one of those men who were invited will get a taste of my banquet.*'"

"Now *there's* something everyone here can relate to," Felix quipped. "Food!" And then, "But if he invites the blind and the lame, no one important will want to eat with him. Radical. But not dangerous . . . except to the religious leaders."

Marcus was grateful for the tone of Felix's conclusion. The tribune would convey to Pilate that Yeshua was no threat to Rome. That much was a reprieve.

Then Nakdimon ben Gurion joined the two Romans. "*Shalom,* Marcus."

It was clear from Felix's expression that he recognized Nakdimon as a member of the Sanhedrin. "We were just talking about your friends. So what does the ruling council think of this man's dinner plans?"

Nakdimon's expression was pained. "Yeshua suggests he is the one offering the feast and that the time to come to him has arrived. He's saying something is going to happen soon."

Suddenly Marcus was sorry Nakdimon had appeared and opened his mouth. What if Felix reinterpreted the parable to mean an uprising, a rebellion? What if Yeshua's preaching was meant to rouse an army of beggars to throw out the established rulers? One could take his words that way.

"With respect," Felix responded, "the problem with philosophers is that they're seldom practical. Take today for example: we're a long way from inns or shelters or markets, and it's already late afternoon. As far as I can see, there's been no provision for caring for this mob. They applaud his words now. But let them walk five miles on an empty stomach and find everything already sold when they arrive . . . that's another story. They won't be as eager to hear him next time. Empty belly always overrules eager mind, eh, Marcus?"

Marcus breathed another sigh of relief. Marcus had also counted five thousand males in the crowd. That number of men of military age was equal to a whole legion of soldiers . . . almost exactly. It was, in fact, more than the total number of troopers in service to Rome in all of Judea and the Galil. For the sake of Yeshua's well-being, it was crucial Felix see no hint of organization.

"I've seen enough," Felix concluded. "I can make my report to Governor Pilate with a clear conscience. Yeshua of Nazareth may attract large crowds, but he says nothing seditious, no one has tried to proclaim him king, and"—Felix added with a wink—"the stomach of the audience is about to meet its backbone. Words alone will not satisfy much longer . . . and never will. Can't feed an army on parables. Come along. Let's follow our own advice and get back to town while there's still food to be had."

■ ■ ■ ■

Blocked! Every way Avel turned he met a solid wall of people. There seemed to be no route to Yeshua, no way to reach him. With Ha-or Tov grasping Avel's shoulder and Emet holding a strap of the blind boy's backpack, the trio could inch forward.

Yeshua had finished his latest story. Perhaps he was through for the day. This was not working out as bar Abba planned, Avel knew. There had been no moment of high drama when a cry to make Yeshua king would fit.

There was no food in the valley. It was as if the onlookers had finally awakened to the fact they were hungry. It distracted them and made them grumpy.

Avel overheard families discussing where they would go to find something to eat. How far to a meal was it? The gathering would shortly be breaking up. Perhaps the handful of stale, gritty barley loaves and measly parcel of dried fish in Ha-or Tov's pack was the last provision among the thousands.

Even though he was hungry himself, Avel would wait to produce the meager supply.

He remembered what happened in Jerusalem. People trampled for a loaf of bread!

Frustrated and tired, Avel was ready to give up. It was Emet who propelled him one last time toward Yeshua.

Emet, desolate and miserable, attracted unpleasant attention. "You, boy," a woman scolded. "Move farther off. Don't you ever bathe? Are you deaf? Move!"

Avel's temper flared. Yeshua should do something for Emet, *must* do something. And Ha-or Tov. Grabbing the smaller boy with one arm and Ha-or Tov by the other, he dragged them on.

Danger or not, nothing was going to happen unless he got to Yeshua. Perhaps there would never be another chance. Even if nothing came of it, he had to try. He would warn Yeshua that bar Abba was near by. Perhaps the information would be worth something—Ha-or Tov's eyes? Emet's ears?

Snaking through knots of people, Avel got close enough to hear a circle of Yeshua's talmidim discussing the food situation. "Send them away, Master," one of the Teacher's followers said.

"You give them something," was the reply.

A tall, curly-haired man who appeared familiar to Avel spoke up. "Eight months' wages wouldn't give each one of them one mouthful."

It was one of Yochanan's followers whom Avel had met outside Bethany . . . He was the one who had given him the cloak of the Baptizer! Avel had a flash of hope. If he could reach that man and be recognized! He looked down at the red, green, and tan striped robe. It might be remembered.

Halting Ha-or Tov with a palm on his chest, Avel said, "Give me the pack!"

"What?"

"Wait here! Give me our food!" Placing Ha-or Tov's hand in Emet's, Avel lunged with the bundle.

If the robe was his identification, then the food might buy his admission.

"I have food to share," he called. "Not much, but you can have it!"

Yeshua's talmidim frowned at the interruption, but a big man with a kind face stepped near. "What have you got?" he asked.

Avel told him.

"Wait here," came the instruction.

Did Avel's desperation show in his face? His blood was rushing in his ears. So near to Yeshua, and yet a cluster of Galileans formed a human barricade around him.

Avel heard the man explain: "Master! There's a boy here with five small barley loaves and two fish. It won't go far."

Success! Now he would see Yeshua! Avel caught Yochanan's follower eyeing the striped robe curiously.

Avel inched forward until he was almost at Yeshua's side.

His heart beat faster. He thought of Emet, Ha-or Tov . . . and Yediyd.

And then a darkly handsome, smiling figure stepped between Avel and the circle of disciples.

Judas bent down in front of Avel and stared the boy in the face. "Thank you." His eyes narrowed in unspoken threat. "Let me help with that."

Judas! How had Avel forgotten Judas? Avel handed over the pouch and backed up a step. "Run along now." Judas lowered his voice. "Remember what we spoke of before."

Avel didn't need to be reminded. The knives were real. The threat was real.

The disappointment was overwhelming.

It was the end of every hope. Crushed with his failure, Avel stumbled back toward Ha-or Tov, even as he heard Yeshua's talmidim calling out for everyone to "Sit down! Sit down! Groups of fifty and one hundred."

When Avel reached his friends he grasped each by the hand again. "Come on," he said bitterly.

"What's happened?" Ha-or Tov asked.

"Nothing," Avel replied. "I'm sorry. Nothing. I gave them our food."

"What are you, crazy?" Ha-or Tov challenged.

"Yes," Avel admitted.

Behind them, in plain sight of the hill, Yeshua held up a pathetic barley loaf. He raised his voice in a *b'rakhah*. "Blessed are you, O Lord, king of the universe, who gives us bread from the earth."

Avel could tell from the weary looks of the spectators that they were being polite. Of course their expressions agreed that giving thanks to the Almighty was the proper, pious thing to do. But really! The insignificant lump of barley loaf in Yeshua's hands was barely visible farther back than three rows of famished onlookers. Was Yeshua going to eat in front of them? Would he feed his close friends while everyone else looked on?

Stomachs rumbled all around Avel, as if the whole mob were one gigantic hungry animal. The crowd's appetite motivated it to get this scene over with and get out of there.

And Avel had handed over his friends' food and achieved nothing! Where would they go? How would they live?

Why?

He grabbed Ha-or Tov and Emet by the hands and turned to go.

Suddenly a thicket of raised hands barred Avel's progress: some pointing, some waving in amazement, some lifted toward heaven.

An awed whisper swept over the throng, rapidly growing louder. As Avel turned, someone thrust a half loaf of warm barley bread into his hands.

Where had it come from? It surely wasn't the stale crust he had just delivered. This was fresh, fragrant with newly baked goodness.

Ha-or Tov sniffed the air appreciatively. "I smell bread. . . ."

Avel divided the loaf with Emet and Ha-or Tov. No sooner had he taken a bite than his hands were filled with a slab of smoked fish. Not dry, dusty shards of last year's catch such as Avel had relinquished, but generous, nourishing chunks!

Yeshua's hands were never idle. Continuously breaking and passing, everyone received food: bountiful, satisfying food, and yet the supply was not exhausted. Hot, fresh barley loaves! Delicious fish!

Yeshua had thanked the Almighty for giving them bread and fish to eat, and twenty-five thousand people were devouring the result of the blessing!

And the morsel Yeshua had blessed came from the meager supply of Avel, Emet, and Ha-or Tov! The food of Yeshua's banquet multiplied on and on! No matter how many were here, there was more than enough! If he could provide food for thousands, then Yeshua could make Ha-or Tov see! He could make Emet hear and speak!

It must be! They had not come so far, endured so much, to be overlooked. Avel had to get close enough to be seen and heard.

Was there no way around Judas? No way to get close to Yeshua? "Rabbi!" Avel called. "Please! We . . . It's us! Emet can't call you! Listen to me! Ha-or Tov can't find his way, so I brought him! Help us! Over here! Yeshua!"

■ ■ ■ ■

Halfway to where Pavor was staked, a growing clamor from the throng drew the Romans' attention.

Felix queried, "I was hoping he'd perform. Did I miss it?"

Marcus wondered that also, but the response of the audience did not suggest it. Instead of crowding around closer to the Teacher, they were sitting down . . . and still an astonished din rose.

"He's distributing bread," Nakdimon observed. "Breaking a loaf in half and handing it to his talmidim."

"Does he want to start a riot?" Felix questioned. "He can't possibly have enough to feed these people. It'll be Antipas and Jerusalem over again. He'll be attacked as soon as they figure out there's not enough to . . ."

The words *go around* died on his lips.

Marcus knew Felix saw the same thing as he and drew the same baffled conclusion: the bread in Yeshua's hands was never exhausted. Though no one handed him additional loaves, he always had another to break and pass, break and pass. Yeshua's methodical precision suggested there was no need to grab for a morsel . . . wait your turn, and you would be fed. Unlike the chaos caused by Tetrarch Herod Antipas in the Jerusalem bread riots, this was both orderly and adequate. Yeshua's manner said, *No hurry, there's plenty for all.*

The multitudes systematically plumped down on the hillside in proper groups to facilitate the distribution. By fifties and hundreds they formed neat units . . . identical in number and manner to Roman cohorts.

Turning to watch Felix's reaction, Marcus found the tribune staring at him. "How many times on campaign have you ordered your men to fall out for meals?" Felix asked. "And every time the tesserarius shouts the same thing: 'Cohorts of fifty! Sit down to receive rations!'" His eyes wide Felix demanded, "Haven't you? Is it a trick? A delusion?"

"His banquet for the beggars," Nakdimon said. "It's proof. Our prophet Moses fed the people in their wandering with bread from heaven, and Yeshua is doing the same. There was always enough! A miracle from the pages of Torah!"

*A miracle,* Marcus thought bitterly. But incredibly alarming to Rome. Coarse bread and dried fish: typical provisions for an army on the march! As he reviewed it, the implications grew greater and darker.

Here was a man who could attract a legion of men to follow him, provision them from nothing . . . nothing! And bring them back to life if they were killed in battle!

Such a leader was invincible.

If Yeshua showed the least ambition to lead a rebellion, he would have to be stopped by Rome . . . if stopping him was even possible! Thank goodness Yeshua was a Teacher, a Healer, a man without political ambition.

Then the clamor started on the far side of the bowl-shaped valley.

"Yeshua for our king! On to Yerushalayim!"

The shouts of hundreds came across to Marcus' ears, but a massed bellow of thousands of throats propelled it back again: "Yeshua king of Israel! King Yeshua and Israel!"

"Crown him! Crown him!"

The hillsides reverberated with the outcry until the very rocks and trees seemed to cry out the same: "Yeshua of Nazareth must be king!"

Marcus glanced at Felix. The tribune's jaw was clenched, his expression stony. "To the horses," he ordered. "And then to Caesarea. Governor Pilate will have to be warned at once."

"Yeshua will never agree to be made king," Marcus protested. "He didn't want this."

Coldly Felix said, "Are you one of his disciples, Centurion? I order you back to Caesarea with me. Now! At once!"

Reluctantly Marcus took Pavor by the reins to go. Would Pilate send a legion to crush Yeshua and his followers because of . . . bread? Perhaps Marcus could defuse the fear he sensed in Felix. Quickly he said, "If Yeshua refuses to go to Jerusalem, won't that mean something?"

Felix, clearly shaken by what he had witnessed, did not fully agree. Yet didn't it stand to reason that anyone wanting to rebel against Rome would have to have support in the capital city? If Yeshua remained in the Galil, perhaps he was no threat. It would certainly demonstrate absence of ambition . . . or fear of the consequences.

"Urge Yeshua to stay away from Jerusalem," Marcus said hastily to Nakdimon. "Maybe this incident will die here without official response. Otherwise he and many others will certainly die by the hand of Rome there!"

Nakdimon did not reply, perhaps unable to speak in the face of such irrefutable evidence of Yeshua's power and authority.

The centurion clasped hands with Nakdimon. Then Marcus mounted Pavor and galloped after Felix toward Caesarea.

■ ■ ■ ■

Avel's plea for attention was buried by an avalanche of clamoring shouts.

"Yeshua for our king!" was the cry.

Avel spotted Asher standing in dazed confusion. There had been no signal. This was not the planned, prearranged excitement envisioned by bar Abba. Yet the hillside swarmed with enthusiastically gesturing supporters of the same idea.

"Make Yeshua king!"

If there had been no riot during the allocation of the food, there was the real danger of one now. Thousands were on their feet, ready to make Yeshua ruler by acclamation. Bread like manna in the wilderness! Never hungry again!

Sweep aside the rulers who lined their pockets by the blood of the poor!

Bring in the one who supplied provisions free for the asking!

Could he do the same with oil? With wine?

Of course he could!

Yeshua for king!

"Now's our chance!" Avel shouted, seizing hold of Emet and Ha-or Tov and reversing direction once more. "While everything is crazy. We'll duck around Judas and go to Yeshua."

But where was the Teacher? He had disappeared behind a wall of jostling supporters. Was he being swamped by adoration? Trampled by zealous fervor?

Avel's despairing thoughts threatened to overwhelm him. To be this close and yet not to reach Yeshua? How could it be?

Avel linked his arms through Emet's and Ha-or Tov's. They must not be separated or the blind and the mute would be crushed to death like Hayyim.

Avel heard the brawniest of Yeshua's talmidim bellow, "Where's the Master?"

"I don't know," another replied. "He was here and then he just wasn't!"

"Back to the boats!" someone yelled. "Quickly!"

Yeshua gone? Avel had missed him again? The Sparrow company forced to accompany bar Abba back to Jerusalem?

*No!*

"Avel? Avel?" Ha-or Tov sounded panicked, near tears.

"I'm here," Avel reassured him. "We're escaping. Now! Everyone is milling around. Into the hills. Let's go!"

*Protect Emet and Ha-or Tov. Survive the crush of the crowd. Escape from Kittim finally and completely. Find a place of rest and safety.* All these things swirled through Avel's thoughts.

Yet even as the trio of friends ducked in and out of the surging crowd, Avel's spirit bowed beneath utter disappointment. It didn't matter if Yeshua was king, or if the Romans came and there was more killing.

Either way Yeshua would never again have time for a Jerusalem Sparrow.

The last, best chance for Avel, Emet, and Ha-or Tov had been lost; wasted because Avel had been afraid. He had hesitated, and now all hope was extinguished.

The last crumbs of miraculous bread turned bitter in his mouth.

# ANI-ADONAI

Night fell. The trio of boys huddled together beneath a stone ledge in a wadi. The thousands of pilgrims had gone back to their homes. Bar Abba and his band were doubtless marching on to Jerusalem for Passover.

Avel, Ha-or Tov, and Emet had no safe place to go. One fragment of Yeshua's miraculous barley loaf remained in Avel's pocket. How long would that last?

A day begun with hope ended in despair for the Mourner, the Good Light, and Truth.

Beloved Friend lay rigid and stinking on Emet's lap. Tears dripped from the boy's eyes onto the feathered remains of the tiny bird.

A breeze sprang up and rattled the branches of the sagebrush behind them. Avel shuddered. His heart pounded with terror as images of Kittim, with the curved blade of his drawn dagger, reared up in his imagination. How he hated the darkness! How badly all his dreams had ended.

Ha-or Tov, being blind, did not mind the pitch-black night. But the stench of death troubled him. He said miserably, "Well? Do you think Emet will let us bury poor Yediyd now?"

Emet was racked with sobs. He cradled Yediyd and moaned pitifully.

Avel, knowing all about mourning, said, "He's got to cry awhile. Then he'll sleep. Then maybe he'll let go." Avel felt like his heart would crack. He rested his cheek against his hand and stared down at the form of the sparrow. Avel murmured, "He was almost big enough to fly."

Ha-or Tov buried his face against his knees and began to weep. "I want to go home! I'm tired of fighting Romans! I'm tired of this adventure! I want to go home!"

"Yes. *Home.*" Avel said the word aloud. But where was home? And what was it to them? Did Ha-or Tov mean home to Bethany? To a hovel at the rich man's gate? A bit of beggared bread each day?

"I want my mother!" Ha-or Tov wept. "Mother! I want to go home!"

Well, then. So that was what he meant by home.

Impossible wish.

Ha-or Tov wanted to be loved again. Just as Avel had spent his life wanting to be loved. And Emet, too.

Love.

More than sight.

More than hearing.

More than bread or a roof overhead or a bed of fresh straw.

More than breathing. More than life even.

But Avel knew such a dream could never come true for the likes of them.

After a while, Emet cried himself to sleep. It was a mercy. He lay curled on the dirt with Yediyd cradled in the crook of his arm.

Avel gingerly lifted up the body of Yediyd and held it in his palm. Then, like his companions, he raised his face to the star-frosted sky and began to mourn for what had never been and never could be.

Tomorrow they would lay their hopes to rest.

Tomorrow they would bury their beloved friend. They would lay the last bit of bread beside him, a gift for the journey. Avel would say something about the little bird flying now in heaven. They would cry and cover him with dirt. And they would find lovely stones to mark the grave with. Maybe Ha-or Tov would sing a song.

After that, still blind, deaf, and mourning, they would go . . . somewhere. But where could they go that bar Abba and Kittim would not find them and slit their throats? Not Jerusalem. And they could not stay in Galilee. They dared not go back to Deborah's barn in Capernaum.

Avel held the sparrow in his cupped hands. "I'm sorry, Yediyd." His eyes rained tears. His nose dripped. He couldn't smell Yediyd anymore.

Ha-or Tov stopped calling for his mother. His sobbing fell to a low snuffling, accented by an occasional shudder. This was a sign that soon the Good Light would soon fall asleep.

Terrible night. Lonely night.

Avel wiped away his tears and gazed up at the vast night sky. What right had he to imagine that God would care about anything so insignificant as a sparrow? Or about three Sparrows and a little bird?

So much for hope!

So much for . . .

*"What was that?"* Ha-or Tov hissed.

Fear was the only safe emotion. It warned you when something was out there in the dark. When you should be quiet . . . When you should hunker down behind the bush. When you should warn Ha-or Tov to shut up!

Avel stopped crying. "Shut up!" he warned Ha-or Tov. They clung to one another and to Yediyd and crouched low behind the sagebrush.

Ha-or Tov cocked his head and said in a barely audible whisper, "Someone!"

The sound of sliding sand and shale announced that someone was walking up the wadi toward them!

Ha-or Tov trembled all over. Did he recognize the rhythm of the step? The scent of the man? Was it Kittim?

Had Kittim followed the scent of death up the wash to find them?

Cautiously, Avel peered through the brush. Yes. A man. Dark beneath his hooded robe. Features indistinct. He paused on the path and raised his nose to sniff the wind.

Avel tasted fear like iron on his tongue. Blood rushed in his ears until he could hear nothing but his heart beating the message, *Be still! Be still! Be still!*

Then Emet, somehow sensing danger, awakened with a startled cry. In garbled protest he searched for the body of Yediyd and wailed when he did not find it.

The head of the searcher turned toward the trio. They were found!

Ha-or Tov clutched at Avel's sleeve. "It's him! He's come for us!" To Avel's horror the blind boy leapt to his feet.

Had he lost his mind? Had stark terror pushed him over the edge? Did he want to die?

Yes.

Well, yes.

Perhaps he did.

What was the use?

Avel stood up beside him.

Emet, seeing that Avel held Yediyd, joined them.

Fearless, shoulder to shoulder, the three watched in silent acceptance as their pursuer strode toward them.

Thirty paces away the man paused and glanced around him. He stooped and retrieved a club of wood. He intended to beat them to death.

Avel resisted the urge to run. He would not leave his friends to meet their fate alone.

And then more branches were scooped up.

"What's he doing?" Ha-or Tov asked.

"Gathering wood," Avel replied in astonishment.

Perhaps the stranger was not Kittim after all.

Loading his arms with sticks the traveler thrust his chin forward to hold the highest piece in place. He carried his bundle to a clearing and arranged it. His back was to them.

"He's building a campfire," Avel related.

"Does he know we're here?" Ha-or Tov squeaked.

"Maybe he's deaf. Like Emet."

"And blind? Like me?" Ha-or Tov remarked dryly.

Of course the traveler knew they were observing his labors from just up the ravine. He ignored them.

In seconds a spark was fanned into flame, flooding the gully with shadow and light. The boys huddled in darkness just beyond the perimeter.

Ha-or Tov sniffed the pleasant aroma of rising smoke. "Will he have food, you think?"

Emet smiled and cocked his head slightly, as if he was listening.

Avel gazed down at little Yediyd. He slipped the bird into his pocket.

A quarter of an hour passed without acknowledgment. Certainly the solitary figure must be aware that three boys crouched hungry in the shadows beyond his camp. He grilled a meal of fish on the coals and set loaves to warm on stones near the fire. The flames sputtered. The scent was tantalizing.

Avel studied the broad shoulders of the traveler. Something familiar . . . what was it? His cloak? Where had Avel seen it before?

The man poked the embers with a long branch, stirring coals. He rested his chin on his hand and gazed into the flame.

Emet crept forward, nearer to the light. Grinning dumbly, he sat on a stone.

Ha-or Tov inhaled the aroma of sizzling fish and licked his lips like a dog waiting for scraps.

Avel's belly growled. Hunger gnawed at his insides.

What was it about the cloak? Red, tan, and blue. The homespun robe of a Galilean, yet unlike any other.

Emet laughed aloud and got up. His expression was bright with joy in the firelight.

"What?" Ha-or Tov queried.

And then it came to Avel. The fabric of the traveler's cloak. It had been on the loom at Deborah's house in Capernaum.

The traveler rose to turn the fish. And for the first time Avel caught a glimpse of his face. Amused by his unseen audience.

"Yeshua!" Avel breathed the name in wonder.

Yeshua turned toward the trio. "I was wondering how long it would take." He swept his hand toward the meal, inviting them. "Hungry?"

Avel dragged Ha-or Tov into the circle of light and down the slippery slope toward the camp. Suddenly shy in the gaze of Yeshua, Emet held back, waited, and followed them to the fireside.

Ha-or Tov babbled all the way, "What? What? What? Where are we going?"

"To see Yeshua! Ha-or Tov! To see him." Avel crowed triumphantly. "To talk to him! Emet! To talk to him!"

He called to Yeshua, "We've been looking for you! Trying to find you! Emet can't hear! Ha-or Tov is blind!"

Yeshua laughed. "Truth. Good Light. Mourner. I was searching for you."

Avel began to run to him, stumbling, dragging Ha-or Tov. Emet skipped along behind him.

Yeshua's face was radiant with pleasure as they charged into his camp. Opening his arms, he gathered them in as though this were a family reunion. He knelt and embraced them, holding them as if they were his own children come home after a long journey. As Avel had seen fathers embrace returning sons.

All three at first.

Avel began to cry. His tears dampened the fabric of the cloak Deborah had made.

"My sons," Yeshua whispered. Avel burrowed his face against Yeshua's chest and heard the great heart beating. He felt the breath of Yeshua on his hair.

And then. One at a time.

Ha-or Tov first.

The blind boy's red hair glistened in the light. Yeshua cupped Ha-or Tov's upturned face in his hands and studied the white and blue marbled eyes.

What would it be like? Avel wondered. To see for the first time?

Could Yeshua do it? Make Ha-or Tov see? Create a vision where there had never been so much as a glimmer of light?

Yeshua's face was mere inches from Ha-or Tov's. Eye to eye, he was. Then, with a touch of his forefinger on Ha-or Tov's lids, he said, "Blessed are you, *Adonai*, Lord of the Universe, who has allowed us to live to see this hour . . ." And then, "All right, now."

Ha-or Tov opened his eyes. Blinked. Raised his hands to his face in awe.

"Tell me what you see." Yeshua smiled into his beaming face.

"I see . . . the Good Light! Yeshua! Salvation! You!"

Yeshua kissed his forehead. With a thumb he wiped away a tear from Ha-or Tov's cheek. The boy, seeing, stared at the fire, at the sizzling fish. Everything! Everything! Everything! It was all miraculous! To see what he had only heard and smelled and guessed at. His own hands! His fingernails! His toes! Staring at the fabric of the Baptizer's robe, he traced the line of color with his finger. He turned to Avel. "Avel?" Then Emet. "Emet?"

"Yes!" Avel cried joyfully. "Yes! We're us!"

Yes. It was Emet's turn.

"What about you, Emet?" Yeshua grasped the deaf-mute child by his frail arms and gathered him to himself. "Truth must have ears to hear and a voice to speak in such a world as this."

With a confident wink, Yeshua brushed Emet's tousled locks back. Then he covered Emet's ears with his hands. Closing his eyes, Yeshua sang softly, "Blessed are you, oh *Adonai,* who has given us a song of truth. . . ." He lowered his hands. "You must sing the song with me, Emet . . . Say your name."

Emet's mouth worked like a rusty hinge. Finally he croaked the answer, "Truth."

Avel and Ha-or Tov gasped.

Yeshua nodded. "And what do you hear?"

"Your voice," Emet answered. Yeshua and Emet gazed at one another for one last long silence. Understanding seemed to pass between them. Truth finally had a voice.

Emet threw his arms around Yeshua's neck. Yeshua did not let go of him as he motioned for Avel.

Avel pointed to himself in question. What could Yeshua do for him? He could see. He could hear and speak. He was not lame. Not sick. Had no broken body parts.

"Avel?" Yeshua called him to his side. "In the quarry I asked you how a boy came to be called by your name. Avel lo-Ahavah?"

When had Yeshua spoken to him, Avel wondered? "You have been to the quarry?"

"Yes. I know the names of the Sparrows."

"Then you know . . . my beloved friend Hayyim gave me the name *Mourner* when my mother left me there. When she called me lo-Ahavah. Not loved."

"And Hayyim? Where is he, Avel?"

"Dead. Buried beneath a shard of pottery. No one remembers Hayyim but me. And so I'm Avel lo-Ahavah." At this confession of heartache, Avel's lip trembled.

"Ah." Yeshua nodded, frowned, and holding Emet, he asked, "What's in your pocket, Avel?" He extended his left hand, palm up.

Well, here it was. Inevitable. The stink of Yediyd had become noticeable. Avel reached in and retrieved the dead sparrow. He placed the body in Yeshua's hand.

Emet released his grip on Yeshua's neck to stare at their dead little friend. Ha-or Tov crowded in to see.

Yeshua tugged Avel around until he stood directly in front of him. Then he covered the sparrow with his right hand. Yeshua's eyes. Warm. Deep. Kind. They reached into Avel's soul. Yeshua said to him, "Blessed are those who mourn. For they will be comforted." Then he asked Avel, "Do you believe this, Mourner? Can a fractured heart be whole?"

So this was the broken thing in Avel. Yeshua saw it. Found it. Understood it . . . it was Avel's heart all along.

Sorrow. Despair. Loneliness. A longing for love. Were these wounds harder to heal than eyes that had never seen the light? Ears that had never heard the truth? A voice forever mute?

Avel was not sure. He could not answer. He was not loved. Could Yeshua fix that? Hayyim, whose very name meant "life," had died. Could Yeshua raise him? Men like Kittim were always around to bully and beat those weaker than they. To kill even small joys . . . like Yediyd! *Beloved Friend!*

Yeshua said, "Avel, even when one sparrow falls your father knows . . . and cares."

Yeshua did not demand an answer from Avel. He held up his cupped hands and breathed into them, making a low, sustained whistling sound. Then he held his hands beneath Avel's nose.

The scent of lavender rose in the night.

With that, the Teacher took away his right hand, revealing the feathered body of Yediyd in the nest of Yeshua's palm. He seemed to be sleeping. Eyes closed. No longer contorted in death.

"Avel," Yeshua said, "tell me what you see?"

"Yediyd. My Beloved Friend. Sleeping."

And then, with a squeak, Yediyd opened his eyes and blinked up at the cluster of faces.

Yeshua asked, "Avel? Tell me what you see."

Emotion choked Avel. He bit his lip, barely able to speak. "I see . . . Hayyim . . . Life!"

The sparrow shook his feathers and climbed onto Yeshua's thumb.

"Yes." Yeshua grinned. "Can you let him go now? He was never meant to stay with you. He has another life waiting. He's not afraid to fly. Do you love him enough to let him go?"

Avel glanced at Emet and Ha-or Tov. They nodded in unison. Avel answered, "Yes. Yes! Let him go . . ."

Yeshua let each boy kiss Yediyd farewell on his little head.

Yeshua stood then and stretched to his full height. He gazed toward the stars and raised both arms as though reaching into heaven. A soft flutter of wings followed as Yediyd flew away.

Avel whispered, "*Shalom,* Yediyd. Hayyim. Beloved friend . . ." And suddenly, Avel was overwhelmed with a sense of peace. As though the peace he had wished for Yediyd had somehow come back to flood his own heart.

For a time Yeshua stared up at the sky, as if he could see Yediyd flying for a great distance.

Silence.

At last he looked down at Avel. Laying a hand on the boy's head, Yeshua said, "Blessed are you who mourn. You will be comforted." And then, "Two sparrows for a penny. You are worth much more than that. I came to you tonight to tell you that the Lord loves you much more than all the birds of the air. Do you believe me?"

Avel nodded. Yes. How could he doubt it? This whole time he had been searching for Yeshua. And Yeshua had his eye on him all along.

Yeshua patted his cheek. "From tonight I give you a new name. You'll no longer be Avel lo-Ahavah. But you will be called Friend to the brokenhearted. Son of Yeshua . . . Haver bar Yeshua."

They ate the supper Yeshua had cooked for them. He taught Emet how to sing and named the stars for Ha-or Tov as the constellations slid across the sky.

And as for Haver bar Yeshua? The boy leaned his head against Yeshua's arm as he told them stories far into the night.

Haver, comforted at last, drifted off to sleep to the sound of his father's voice.

# EPILOGUE

"... We had heard about him with our ears, but now our eyes have seen him in the flesh and we know and tell of his love for all mankind. I, once called the Mourner, speak what I know. . . . Blessed are you who mourn, for you shall be comforted. . . . And thus ends the testimony of Haver bar Yeshua."

Moshe Sachar's voice echoed in the deep recesses of the holy mountain as he spoke the final words of the scroll.

There came a sound like the stirring of wind in the branches of a tree. The scent of lavender and a faint aroma of wood smoke hung in the air.

Moshe picked up the sparrow feather and twirled it between his thumb and forefinger. *Yes! He sees even the sparrows when they fall. . . .*

Moshe replaced the feather on the square of red, green, and tan homespun fabric, all that remained of Avel's robe. Tracing the vine leaf pattern on the neck of the amphora, Moshe remembered Hayyim's broken gravestone in the Potter's Field. That memorial had long since crumbled to dust.

It was this story, written and sealed upon the very heart of God, which contained the true memorial to Hayyim. *To Life!*

Though Jerusalem's Sparrows had fallen long ago, they lived still because Yeshua, the One they were seeking, had come to find them.

*Truth,*
*The Good Light,*
*Beloved Friend,*
*And, finally, the child who had been called the Mourner*
*At last were comforted.*

Alfie lay on his back on the floor, smiling up at the starry universe depicted on the ceiling of the chamber.

His hands were beneath his head, as though he was sprawled on a grassy hillside in Galilee.

He sighed at last and said, "I saw the stars moving, Moshe, when he was here. See? Yes. He was here. With us. And there is Yediyd, his sparrow . . . flying still."

Moshe involuntarily glanced up at the painted sky. For an instant he thought he glimpsed the shadow of a bird, soaring high.

Was it true? Had the map of heaven changed a bit in the telling of this story? Indeed, there seemed to be more swirling galaxies than he had seen before. And all the stars somehow shone brighter.

■ ■ ■ ■

*Adonai, Adonai El rahum ve-hanun erekh apayim ve-rav hesed ve-emet: Nozer chesed la-alafim nosei avon va-fesha ve-hata'ah ve-nakeh.*

Exodus 34:5–6

*Ve-ahavta le-re'akha kamokha ani Adonai.*
Leviticus 19:18

# GLOSSARY

Adonai—Lord

aliyah—pilgrimage

bema—pulpit of a synagogue

B'resheet—book of Genesis

centurion—Roman officer commanding a century

century—company of 100 Roman soldiers

cohen (pl. cohanim)—priest

cohen hagadol—high priest

cohort—Roman military unit containing about 500 men

corona obsidionalis—Roman battlefield wreath awarded for exceptional heroism

denarius (pl. denarii)—standard Roman coin, made of silver

Ha'Elyon—the Most High

haftarah—a scripture portion

HaMashiach—the Messiah

Hoshana Rabbah—lit. "the great hosanna"; the last day of the feast of Succoth

kaddish—synagogue prayer that begins, "Magnified and sanctified be His Great Name . . ."

karkom—crocus bulbs whose flowers produce the spice saffron

khamseen—hot desert wind

maiestas—crime of defaming the Roman emperor or state

mikveh—ritual bath

Pesach—Passover

pilum—type of javelin

Praetorians—elite unit of Roman soldiers, designed to be the emperor's bodyguards

Primus Pilus—lit. First Javelin; the leading centurion of a cohort

rebbe—rabbi or teacher

Rosh Hashanah—New Year, the beginning of the ten Days of Awe

Ruach HaKodesh—the Holy Spirit

seder—Passover service including a ceremonial dinner

shammash—synagogue attendant

Shema—central tenet of Judaism: "Hear, O Israel, the Lord our God is one Lord."

sicarius (pl. sicarii)—assassin

Succoth—Feast of Tabernacles, the fall harvest festival

talmidim—followers

Tanakh—Holy Scripture

tesserarius—guard sergeant

Torah—Jewish sacred scripture; corresponds to the first five books of the Christian Bible

Yom Kippur—Day of Atonement